The Case of the Singer and the Showgirl

Lisa Hall is the #1 bestselling author of six psychological thrillers, including *Between You and Me*, *The Perfect Couple* and *The Woman in the Woods*. Lisa lives in a small village in Kent, surrounded by her towering TBR pile, a rather large brood of children, dogs, chickens and ponies, and her long-suffering husband.

Also by Lisa Hall

The Hotel Hollywood Mysteries

LISA HALL

THE CASE OF THE SINGER AND THE SHOWGIRL

hera

First published in the United Kingdom in 2024 by

Hera Books
Unit 9 (Canelo), 5th Floor
Cargo Works, 1-2 Hatfields
London SE1 9PG
United Kingdom

A CIP catalogue record for this book is available from the British Library.

Print ISBN 978 1 80436 659 2
Ebook ISBN 978 1 80436 658 5

Look for more great books at www.herabooks.com

Printed and bound in Great Britain by Clays Ltd, Elcograf S.p.A.

1

To my lovely dad

Chapter One

'This is my favourite part.' I turn my tear-stained face towards Eric as Scarlett O'Hara watches Rhett Butler walk away from her, out into the fog without giving a damn. 'It's so *sad*, she's finally realised what she wants—'

'She's a brat,' Eric tuts, and hands me a tissue with a grin. The pathetic artificial Christmas tree I bought from Walmart for fifteen dollars twinkles away behind him, giving his hair a multicoloured glow. 'Pull yourself together, Lil, you know she's a brat.'

I sniffle into the tissue, not quite sure why I find this scene so brutal. Scarlett *is* a brat – every old movie fan knows that – but even so, something about it hits hard. 'Want to watch something else? We can do something less... emotional? *Gaslight?* Or we can even bring it into this century and do *World War Z*. I could do zombies for you, seeing as you've just done over three and a half hours of the American Civil War for me.'

It's a rare rainy Sunday evening in Los Angeles, and after a week on my feet cleaning the bedrooms of the Beverly Hills Hotel, there is no more perfect way to spend the evening than sobbing in front of old movies with a pint of ice cream, if you ask me.

Eric, my best (and only) friend in LA, disagrees.

'No can do.' He gets to his feet, placing his ice cream spoon on the coffee table. 'I have to get going.'

Sitting up, I blow my nose and grin at him. 'Where are you off to? Are you taking Saffron out?' I already know the answer – Eric and Saffron have been joined at the hip since they first swiped right on each other's Tinder profiles eight months ago. If he's not working, surfing, or here at my apartment, he's with Saffron.

'Uh… yeah.' He gives me a sheepish grin. 'Actually, I am. I'm going to ask her something really important.'

The words are unexpected, and I feel a temporary lull in the wind in my sails, but I force my grin wider. 'Well, tell her I said hi. Hang on. *Wait*. What are you going to ask her?' Something that feels a lot like anxiety starts to squirm in my belly.

Eric shuffles, suddenly uncharacteristically shy. 'I was thinking… you know how I feel about her, right? She's the best thing that ever happened to me… so I was thinking that I might ask her to move in. To my apartment. With me.'

'Oh. *Wow*.' This is huge. The majority of men in Hollywood (especially the ones I seem to stumble across) appear to suffer from an extreme phobia of commitment – any hint of wanting to settle down and they sprint for the hills. I don't know Saffron that well; I've met her a few times, but it always feels a little awkward, in a way I'm sure it wouldn't if Eric's best friend was a man instead of me – Lily Jones, twenty-five-year-old displaced Londoner with a penchant for boba tea and classic Hollywood movies. After matching online, Eric met Saffron for the first time after he played the Viper Room with his band. They'd arranged to meet for drinks there after his set, and she'd snuck in early to watch him play (I'm guessing it would have been a perfect way to suss him out and make a break for it if she decided he wasn't for her – smart girl). I hadn't been there that night – usually I would have been, but I was working an extra waitressing shift at the Saddle Ranch Chop House on Sunset, a cowboy-style restaurant known for its giant candyfloss cocktail, if you can believe it. Tips are always better on a Saturday night. Eric had come over the next day, raving about this cool girl he'd met – *she looks like Lana Del Rey, Lil* – the first one who had properly turned his head in the whole time I'd known him.

'I knew I should have come to the gig. I could have vetted her,' I had teased him, as he blushed and I had batted away the dishonourable – and if I'm brutally honest, *selfish* – thought that this was something serious – this girl could change our entire dynamic.

'Ha. No way.' Eric had shaken his head. 'You're a terrible wingman. You always dazzle them with your British accent and then they only want to speak to you instead of me.'

Now, I say, 'I mean *wow*, Eric. This is huge. Do you think she'll say yes?'

Eric is pulling on his battered leather jacket, smoothing his unruly dark blond hair in the mirror. He turns back to face me, a faint shadow of concern flitting briefly across his features as he takes in my tear-stained cheeks, the slowly melting pint of Ben and Jerry's on the table, alongside a takeaway cup containing the dregs of a brown-sugar boba tea. 'I hope so.' He gives me a nervous grin. 'Will you be OK if I go? You're not going to spend the whole evening crying over old movies, are you?'

'What?' I follow his gaze. 'Don't be daft, of course I'll be OK. This is a *moment*, Eric. My little buddy is all grown up.' I get to my feet and standing in front of him I tweak his hair, so it falls perfectly across his forehead. 'Go on.' Turning him by the shoulders I march him the three steps to the front door and open it. 'Go and ask Saffron to move into your apartment – she'd be a fool to turn you down.' I wink. 'And don't do anything I wouldn't do.'

The apartment is quiet once Eric leaves, the only sound the rain that splatters sporadically against the windows, making me feel a little homesick, as the Christmas tree lights flash red, blue, green on repeat. I have been living in Los Angeles – West Hollywood to be exact – for a little over two years, and while there have been times that I've felt at home here – sometimes more than others – when the weather is like this it makes me miss London. I miss the crunch of autumn leaves underfoot, the slap of a frosty morning across my cheeks. The feel of a steaming hot chai in a Starbucks mug against cold fingers doesn't hit the same when it rarely seems to get below twenty degrees outside.

Shifting my weight on the sagging, second-hand couch, I feel a twinge of dissatisfaction tug at my bones as I swap tea for a glass of wine and dig my spoon back into the ice cream tub, even though I already feel a little sick. I'm glad Eric has a girlfriend. Really, I am. I mean, it's probably going to totally change *everything* if Saffron agrees to move in with him… I get the impression she's not going to want a third wheel from South London with a perpetual whiff of misery and loneliness around her hanging out with them all the time.

'I'm *thrilled* for you both,' I whisper under my breath, trying the words on for size. Eric's been my best friend ever since I first arrived here. We work together, we spend most of our free time together. There will never be anything romantic between us – that would be too weird given how I spent my time in the past trying to deal with my raging attraction to his great-grandfather – but even so, I feel off-centre. I've felt this way for the last eighteen months, ever since I cleaned the Paul Williams Suite for the first (and last) time at the Beverly Hills Hotel.

'Pull yourself together Lil,' I mutter, echoing Eric's words from earlier. I am *living my dream*, I tell myself, I wanted to live in Hollywood and here I am. OK, I didn't dream of being a housekeeper in a hotel, even if it is one of the most famous hotels in the world, nor did I dream of taking a second job as a waitress just to make ends meet, but even so, I should be grateful for what I have. I take a large mouthful of wine, noticing that *Ocean's Eleven*, the original (and best, in my opinion) version starring Frank Sinatra, is about to start on the TV. It was one of my mum's favourite movies, and the sight of Frank, Dean Martin and Sammy Davis Jr is familiar and comforting. Lord knows, I could do with a bit of comfort right now, as I have the feeling everything is about to change.

–

I jerk awake sometime later, my neck cricked where I have slumped down on the couch, my mouth sour with old wine. It's dark outside, the only light in the room the blue glow from the television screen and the repetitive flash of the Christmas tree lights. My phone buzzes, a text lighting up the screen. Reaching forward, I lift the phone, smiling as Eric's name shows on the screen.

> She said yes!!!! Don't wait up!! Catch up tomorrow before our shift starts ☺

It's actually happening. Eric and Saffron are going to live together. I find I really am pleased for him, even though the flicker of loneliness that I've felt almost constantly since my mother died licks at my skin, familiar and not particularly welcome.

I text him an aubergine emoji, grinning to myself, but as my eyes wander to the still flickering television screen, my smile freezes in place. If I had been watching Netflix, it would have been OK, the app would have booted me out hours ago. But *Ocean's Eleven* was playing on Turner Classic Movies, and I'd fallen asleep in front of it. Now, a familiar scene from a different movie plays out.

A gleaming white Cadillac comes into shot, its tyres screaming over the loose dirt and gravel, as a blonde woman grips the wheel. The impossibly handsome dark-haired man beside her gestures, throwing his hands wide.

'Oh phooey,' the woman says, her eyes fixed on the windshield ahead. 'I know when you're lying, and this is one of those times.'

'Please, Sofia,' the man implores, 'you need to slow down!'

Suddenly chilled, I reach for the TV remote. I know how this scene plays out, despite never being able to watch *Goodtime Gal* from start to finish. The scene ended very differently the first time it was shot, and it's the memory of this that makes me head to the fridge for a fresh bottle of wine. Twisting off the cap, I pour another glass and watch as the movie cuts to another scene, where Honey Black and Billy Walters kiss passionately, Billy bending Honey back in his arms.

I take a huge gulp of Sauvignon, letting tears fill my eyes as I stab at the remote to mute the television, not quite able to bring myself to turn it off completely. Seeing Honey on screen for the first time since I came back to my own time is like seeing an ex that you've never quite got over, especially as I wasn't expecting it. The sight of her is like a punch to the gut, and with it comes the *what if*? What if I had stayed in 1949? Could I have made things work, or would I have imploded the world as I now know it?

Earlier, that final scene with Scarlett O'Hara begging Rhett to reconsider leaving her hit me hard, and it's only now, a couple of glasses of wine in, that I'm realising why. At the end of the movie, Scarlett has realised that she isn't living the life she wants, and she knows that only she can do something about it. *That's me*, I think. It doesn't matter how much I tell myself I'm living my dream, no matter how much I love spending time with Eric, I don't feel as if I belong here, especially now that Eric has found his soulmate online. It always feels as though something is missing.

Online. The thought tickles the back of my mind, the way it has on and off ever since I returned to my own time. I've tried so hard to live in the moment since I came back, pushing away thoughts of the people who meant so much to me back in 1949, too terrified to give into the urge to google their names. Even the idea of it usually makes me go cold, the fear of finding out something horrible killing the thought before it begins to fully formulate, but tonight, half drunk and desperately miserable, I reach for the laptop.

Honey Black. Celebrated movie star and the first person I met after I smacked my head on the side of the bath in the Paul Williams Suite at the Beverly Hills Hotel, and found myself in 1949. Since I already know that Honey went on to be a huge star her name is a safe bet. My fingers fly over the keyboard and it's a matter of seconds before her face fills the screen. A gasp escapes my lips as I lean forward, greedily running my eyes over the Wikipedia page. I know it's not entirely accurate, but even so my gaze goes to her bio on the right-hand side of the screen. *Born 26 June 1928. Spouse: Magnus Michel m. 1946 Div. 1949, Joseph Faulks m. 1949.*

My heart lifts, and I top up my wine as I read on. *Married high school sweetheart Joe Faulks in 1949... remained married until his death in 2014... currently resides in a nursing home in Sonoma County, California. Patron of the Honey Black Foundation in support of victims of domestic violence.* I click the link to Honey's charity, and it opens on an auction page. Holding my breath, I scroll the auction list, letting out a squeak when I see the dress Honey wore in *Goodtime Gal.* I can still see it in my mind, hanging forlornly on a hanger when I visited the set with Jessica Parks after shooting had finished for the day. The next item makes my heart stop dead in my chest. It's a long-sleeved, pale blue satin dress, with a V neckline and tiny buttons dotting a line from the neckline down to mid-thigh. Also pictured beneath the dress is a pair of rose gold sparkly heels. *This is my outfit. The outfit I wore to Honey's twenty-first birthday party.* An auction note beside the photo reads, 'Outfit from the vault of Honey Black's wardrobe. Believed to have been loaned and worn by an unknown friend.' Beside the note is a black and white photograph from a newspaper. It shows Honey in the garden of the Beverly Hills Hotel on the night of the party, while I stand with my back to the camera, clearly wearing the dress. The bidding for the outfit – *my outfit!* – starts at a cool ten thousand dollars.

I stop reading then, blinking hard. Honey is still alive, and she kept my dress and shoes for all this time. She's old – really old – but still here. Should I go and visit her? Or will that be one glitch too many for the matrix? Swiping at my salt-stained cheeks, I smile and turn back to the laptop. Maybe I shouldn't have been so afraid after all. My mind flies to Louis, but still, I can't quite get my fingers to type his name.

Instead, I type in *Evelyn King*. The Evelyn I knew was sour, sarcastic, and more than a little possessive over Louis, long after he stopped being her boyfriend. She had her heart set 100 per cent on marriage, babies, and a white picket fence, and she would do whatever it took to make it happen. Now, as I wait for the search results to load, a bubble of apprehension pops in my belly. Despite Louis Jardine being Evelyn's boyfriend, there had been an unavoidable spark between us, and I don't think I imagined the last words he said to me before I slipped beneath the water in the bathtub of the Paul Williams Suite and returned to my own time. Even so, as a page of Evelyn Kings appears on my screen, there is still a smidge of worry in my veins that maybe I heard wrong.

I scroll through results for Evelyn King, American singer, and Evelyn King, British politician, until – on the verge of giving up completely – I see my Evelyn's features smiling out from a grainy black and white photo. Gulping the warm Sauvignon in my glass, I pull a face, and then with one deep breath, I click. Almost immediately, I wish I hadn't.

It's a newspaper article, in the *LA Times*. At first glance I think it must be some sort of wedding or engagement announcement, as the words 'husband' and 'marriage' leap off the page. A huge splashy spread in a prominent newspaper is exactly the kind of thing Evelyn would want to announce any upcoming nuptials, even though she wasn't from a family that was particularly prominent, but as I read, my spine liquifies and an icy chill cloaks my shoulders.

MELROSE HILL WOMAN FOUND SLAIN

Police were called yesterday evening to a home in Melrose Hill where the badly beaten body of a woman was discovered. The victim has been identified as the wife of a local businessman. Evelyn Castillo, née King, was a beautiful young lady who had recently moved to Melrose Hill from West Hollywood with her husband, and the pair have been described by neighbors as having a 'perfect marriage'. The brutal savagery was discovered by the deceased's mother following a desperate call for help, but despite her frantic dash across town, Mrs King was unable to save her daughter, instead finding her broken body in the bedroom of her daughter's new home. Despite rumors of a perfect marriage, evidence at the bloody scene suggests that the young woman's husband of eighteen months, Mr Jackie Castillo, is most likely responsible for this unbelievable act of violence and police are keen to talk to him. This heinous crime has sent a shockwave through the community, and despite the police urging the public not to panic, residents are advised to keep their doors locked. If you encounter the suspect, please do not approach him as he is considered a dangerous individual – please call the Los Angeles Police Department via the operator.

I close my eyes, wishing I hadn't read it, but I can't help myself from returning to the page like some rubbernecker at the scene of an accident, the lure of the terrible too strong to resist as I reread the article, the words *"brutal savagery"* making me wince.

Feeling strangely numb, I sit back after rereading for a third time, my mouth sour with the taste of old wine, my stomach roiling with too much ice cream and an unexplained feeling of… what? Fear? Regret? Ashamed as I am to admit it, there is the tiniest hint of relief that it wasn't Louis's name that followed Evelyn's – relief that he never married her, coupled with relief that his name didn't appear in the article in connection with her death. I didn't like Evelyn, but I never would have wanted anything like this to happen to her.

I scroll up to the date on the blurry newspaper article: *22 December 1953.* Reaching for my phone, I tap the screen, the date and time illuminating. Today is 6 December. A little over two weeks before the anniversary of Evelyn's death. The tips of my fingers tingle, and my stomach gives a familiar lurch. *I couldn't, could I?* I glance again at Evelyn's face, her pout that I know, despite the photo being black and white, is a deep glossy red. Her blonde hair, so carefully styled around her shoulders. She's a bitch, but I don't hate her so much that I feel I can ignore what I just read. I neck the remains of my wine and slam the lid of the laptop closed.

I have to go back. Suddenly sober as a judge, I sit up, pressing my hands over my face before flipping the lid of the laptop open again. I've never allowed myself to even think about the possibility of going back, although some nights I dream I am there, dancing at the Palomino, sipping on a (disgustingly strong) cocktail. I've always been afraid that if I tried to go back without good reason, it simply wouldn't happen and then I'd have to accept the idea that there was no possible way I could ever see the people I loved there ever again. I don't think my heart could take it, knowing for sure that I would never see Louis again – and all the time I don't try, there's always that hope.

But *what if?* What if it wasn't a fluke the first time? What if I've just been given my reason to return? What if I could go back and save Evelyn?

Chapter Two

Getting to my feet, I begin to pace, my veins buzzing with something more than sugar and wine. Now I've let the idea unfold, I can think of nothing else. My gaze goes to Evelyn's face, still lighting up the laptop screen. *I could save her*, I think. I could. *But what about Eric?* His face looms in my mind's eye and I come to an abrupt halt by the single window of my apartment. The first time I went back, it wasn't intentional. I slipped and hit my head on the side of the bath, with no idea that I was about to wake up seventy years in the past – I didn't have time to think about Eric, or any other consequences. But this time… if it's intentional, can I really leave behind the one person I have here in Los Angeles? What if I can't get back a second time?

Standing at the window, I look out at present-day Hollywood. The rain has stopped and the sidewalks glitter with puddles that reflect the streetlamps and the thin strands of Christmas lights that glow in the windows of the apartment building across the street. As cars crawl by despite the late hour, a homeless man huddles in the doorway of a chicken shop, trying to keep warm, and a group of men stagger past, drunk and obnoxious, not caring about the people they might be keeping awake. Litter erupts from an overflowing bin, cigarette butts and used napkins welded to the damp sidewalk. This is the side of Hollywood that the tourists don't see, the streets away from the lights of Sunset Boulevard, from the star-stamped pavements of Hollywood Boulevard.

In a few short hours I'll have to be dressed and ready for another long shift at the Beverly Hills Hotel, cleaning and scrubbing until my hands are sore, then I'll have an hour – maybe ninety minutes max – before I have to be showered and changed for my regular Monday night shift at the Saddle Ranch. Cleaning and waitressing, on repeat. While I still dream of working in the movies, it's hard to land a role when your references are from 1949. I glance again towards the laptop, towards Evelyn's wide smile. Eric is moving in with Saffron, and that means he's starting a whole new life that I won't be a part of. He might miss me for a while if I wasn't around, but it wouldn't be long before he and Saffron got married, had a family together. Pushing away the idea that perhaps it's been me holding him back until now, I close the laptop, and channel my inner Scarlett. *I'll think about it tomorrow.*

Only tomorrow, I'm not just going to think about it. I'm actually going to *do* something about it.

–

As I stand in the California sunshine a few hours later, waiting for the best vintage store on Hollywood Boulevard to open, butterflies swarm in my stomach and my eyes are gritty from lack of sleep. But as I had locked my apartment door earlier this morning, I'd felt nothing but a sense of freedom, instead of the lump in my throat I was expecting.

Rifling through the racks, I pull out a Fifties evening dress, in a delicious blue brocade fabric, a knock-off version of the dress Donna Reed wore to the 1953

Oscars. It's not an ideal style, given that it is an off-the-shoulder floor-length evening gown, with a nipped in waist, complete with pale pink sash, but when the only other dress in my size in that section is a silky Hawaiian muumuu, I can't afford to be picky. This time, I want to blend in, to seem as if I really do belong there, and an evening gown in Fifties Hollywood is surely less conspicuous than ripped jeans and my old Pearl Jam T-shirt. It's with shaky hands that I hand over my credit card – with a quick prayer that it doesn't get declined – before I hurry over to the hotel, the skeleton key that I brought back with me from 1949, alongside some old coins, burning a hole in my pocket.

As I approach the Beverly Hills in its quiet, residential setting I let out a long, slow breath. Immaculate hedges hide the hotel from prying eyes, and as I walk along the winding path to the entrance I soak up the atmosphere, the sensation of luxury that oozes from every part of the building, from the red carpet that stretches out from the hotel entrance to the high-end cars parked in the lot by the valet. In stark contrast to the traffic-jammed Sunset Boulevard, the only sounds are the birds that flit overhead, and the rustle of the palm trees that line the street. It feels like another world and I don't think I'll ever get bored of it.

'Lily! Where have you been? I thought we were going to catch up before our shift?' Eric appears as I hurry towards the staff entrance at the side of the hotel, and my heart sinks. It would have been so much easier to do this without seeing him first.

'Sorry, I was just—' I stop, not sure how to go on.

'Shopping?' Eric says, glancing down at the bag in my hands containing the new dress. 'Last night was great, by the way. I mean… it went well. *Really* well. Which you would know if you'd read the text I sent you this morning.'

'Eric, I'm sorry.' This is harder than I thought. 'I do want to hear about you and Saffron, but I just…' I blink, suddenly tearful. 'I have to head to the laundry and deal with this for a guest and I'm already late.' I hold up the bag, praying he doesn't ask to see inside. 'Listen, how about I do the suites today, so you can get away early? You take the bungalows.' Everyone prefers the bungalows.

'Really? Is it my birthday or something?'

'You'd be disappointed with that gift if it was. Yes, really.' I pause, swallowing down the lump in my throat.

'But you hate doing the suites, even more than I do, ever since… well, ever since that time you cleaned the Paul Williams Suite for me.' Eric peers closely at me. 'Lily… is this to do with me and Saffron moving in together? Because it won't change anything, I promise. She likes you—'

'It's nothing to do with that,' I say gently. Saffron may like me, but everything will change. 'I'm so thrilled for you, I swear. You deserve to be happy, and you and Saffron are perfect together.'

'You're not upset?'

'No, of course not.' I blink hard, shielding my eyes as if there is a glare from the sun. 'I think it's brilliant news. I should probably get going if I'm going to do the suites.'

'Catch up with you later?'

'Uh, sure. OK.' I nod, looking away, pretending to fumble in my pocket for my keys.

'My apartment, tonight? Around seven?'

'Yeah.' The word comes out faint, wheezy on the early morning air. 'See you then.'

'Lil? Are you sure you're OK? About me and Saffron?'

I force myself to meet his eyes, and smile. 'Yes, I'm sure. Why wouldn't I be?' Moving closer I reach out and squeeze his hand. 'You're my best friend, you know that? I'm happy for you. And I want to hear all about it. I'm just… late. See you tonight.'

Eric nods, and then heads back into the depths of the hotel, ready to start his shift. I watch him go, suddenly unsure if I am making the right decision. *It might not even work.* The words are a whisper, and I hurry away from them, into the hotel.

–

At reception, I paste on a smile and pray that I don't look like the horrible liar I am as Lyle, the receptionist, wishes me a good morning.

'Lyle, I'm not sure if you know, but there's a situation in the Paul Williams Suite.'

'What?' Lyle frowns, beginning to tap away on his computer screen. 'No one stayed in that suite last night. How can there be a situation?'

I raise my hand gesturing for him to stop his urgent tapping. 'It's the… air conditioning. It's… errr… it's leaked. All over the carpet. Horrible mess. Big stains.'

'Leaked?' Lyle frowns.

'Leaked.' I nod gravely. 'Don't worry though – I've called an engineer out, and I'm going to go directly to the suite now and clean the stains. It'll be right as rain, but it's probably best that you don't book the suite out until tomorrow at the earliest. You don't want guests breathing in damp spores. *Asthma*, you know?' I have no idea how long it's going to take me to try and replicate the time-slip process, given that I'm not even sure if it'll work, but if Lyle can just keep the suite free until tomorrow there should be plenty of time to figure things out.

Lyle adjusts his state-required face mask at the word 'asthma'. 'Tomorrow...?' He can't seem to stop repeating what I'm saying and my mouth feels horribly dry. 'Lily, why are you telling me this? Where is maintenance? They should be dealing with it.'

I flap a hand, aware as my palm flies through the air that it is sweaty and damp. 'They were so busy, I called it in myself.' I lean in, my voice barely above a whisper behind my own face mask. 'You know how it is. Since the pandemic we all need to look out for each other.'

Lyle gives a wide-eyed nod and I would high-five him, but social distancing and all that. Instead I just say, 'You'll make sure no one books into the suite until tomorrow? You're a gem.'

I make my way down the corridor, imagining I can feel Lyle's eyes boring into my lying back, my palms only drying once I reach the Paul Williams Suite. Standing outside, something unsettling washes over me. It's a mix of nostalgia, fear, excitement and buried underneath, a little bit of doubt. Doubt as to whether I can do this, doubt as to whether I should even be trying.

I haven't stepped foot inside the Paul Williams Suite for eighteen months, and now my hands shake and the soles of my feet itch, as if warning me against stepping inside. I hesitate for just a moment, teetering on the edge of chickening out, but then I think of Evelyn, and how even though I don't like her, she doesn't deserve what is going to happen to her. If I can pull this off and find my way back to 1953, then I will be the only person who knows what is going to happen to Evelyn – and I will be the only person who can stop it from happening. It's the same situation I found myself in a year and a half ago when I was the only person who knew Honey Black would be murdered. Things worked out then, so...

I take a deep breath. *It stands to reason that I will be able to save Evelyn.* Squaring my shoulders, I smooth down the soft, worn cotton of my uniform and give a sharp rap on the door. According to the hotel's booking system, the suite is empty, but you never know. After a few seconds, I dig out the housekeeping key and wheel my cleaning trolley inside.

Everything is the same. I don't know why I was half expecting it all to have changed, but everything is just as it was before, when I found myself cleaning the suite for the first time as a favour to Eric. The décor, famously kept the same since the well-known architect Paul Williams designed the suite in 1948, is still just as luxurious as I remember it. Heavy pale green drapes hang at the doors out on to the patio and the air smells of jasmine and honeysuckle, wafting in from the plants that sit on the private patio. The thick cream carpet almost bounces under my feet as I make my way across the suite, bypassing the bar stocked with champagne, shining flutes alongside it, past the piano where Honey would always leave her script. Averting my eyes from the light camel chaise longue with its pile of mauve and teal cushions, I hurry into the bathroom.

The huge bathroom is the epitome of luxury. Timelessly elegant dual basins line the back wall in a warm shade of creamy marble, while two wall lamps on either side of the mirror ensure perfect lighting. Fresh white gardenias decorate the vanity area, giving off a heady floral scent that adds to the luxury. The bathtub shines, surrounded by the same immaculate marble, and I feel a wave of nausea as I look down into the perfect white enamel, fear whipping up a cyclone in my stomach.

Just do it, Lily. I turn on the bath taps and water thunders out like a waterfall, my heart rate increasing to match the rush of liquid against the tub. Raising my eyes to the mirror, I run my tongue over dry lips. My dark curls are – for once – tamed, perfect spirals, without a hint of frizz, but despite the exquisite lighting and the smile I'm trying on to reassure myself this isn't a crazy idea, my face is pale, and my eyes are haunted by dark circles from lack of sleep. In short, I look as terrified as I feel.

I pull out the printed newspaper article on Evelyn and run my eyes over it one more time. The last time I did this – which was a total accident, by the way – I was thinking about Honey Black as I fell, so I force myself to reread the article, my eyes skipping over the words and imprinting Evelyn's picture on the back of my eyelids, before I tuck the article into the sash around the waist of the vintage dress, along with the old skeleton key and the coins, and pull my uniform over my head. *What if it doesn't work?* Panic flutters its wings inside me and I take a deep breath as I drop my uniform to the floor. *What if it* does *work? What if I change things in the worst possible way?* It's a chance I have to take. I couldn't live with myself, knowing what happened to Evelyn and knowing that I didn't make any attempt to stop it. Even if I fail, even if it all goes horribly wrong, at least I will have tried to help her.

The tub is nearly full and the bathroom is cloudy with steam. Last time, my travel to the past was purely accidental, and I had worried as I replicated the moment – the bath, the running tap, the water closing over my head – that my return wouldn't be so simple. Now, I just have to hope that recreating the same environment will take me back there. In my underwear, I take one last look in the mirror before I step into the water. It's slightly too hot, stinging my ankles as I stand there, but it doesn't stop the goosebumps that erupt all over my body. Breathing in, I lower myself into the water as steam mists the mirror over completely, rendering me a fuzzy, pink blob. With one last check that the vintage dress sits on the end of the bath, I close my eyes, summon up Evelyn's face and sink beneath the water.

—

My lungs strain for air, my chest beginning to ache and, grasping the cold enamel of the bath, I pull myself into a sitting position. The bath water is still hot, but I am cold to my core, my hair hanging in limp curls around my face as my teeth chatter. I close my eyes, feeling sick and dizzy, before they fly open again. *Did it work?* The vintage dress still sits neatly folded on the edge of the bath; a vase of flowers still sits by the sink. Everything looks the same. Cautiously, I lever myself out of the tub, yanking the plug out and sending the water gurgling into the drain before reaching for the thick fluffy towel on the rail. Shivering as the cold air meets my damp skin, I wrap it around myself, immediately beginning to feel better and once completely dry, I pull the vintage evening dress over my head. It's a little rumpled and a bit snug across the chest, but the moment I smooth the material over my thighs, I feel a change come over me. I feel different.

It's not just the dress. As I catch sight of myself in the mirror over the sink it's as if I myself am a vintage piece, albeit with damp curls that could do with some serum. I slide my hands down the fabric of the dress and tie the sash tightly around my waist, checking to make sure the skeleton key and coins, alongside the folded article on Evelyn, are still tucked safely into the fabric. My phone lies on the bathroom floor and I hesitate for a moment before picking it up and jabbing at the screen. It stays blank, and my heart skips a beat. Last time, my phone was dead the entire time I was in the past. *Did I charge it last night?* I don't remember – the wine and the shock of reading about Evelyn's murder meant I had drifted to bed in a fog of confusion, worry and a smidge of anticipation.

I tuck the phone behind the thick, heavy fabric of the sash too, feeling the case press reassuringly against my belly, and then slowly, I move to the bathroom door, relief washing over me as I peer out into an empty suite. *Thank God.* The idea of having to explain my presence to a guest is more than my throbbing head can take – it was difficult enough last time. Moving silently across the carpet I slip out of the suite into the corridor, a tickle of anticipation running along my spine and bringing goosebumps to my bare arms. I'm not sure if I'm imagining it but the corridor feels brighter, fresher, the carpet not quite so worn with thousands of footsteps, the banana leaf wallpaper clean and vibrant, and I feel a surge of excitement as I hurry towards the lobby.

Hope ripples through me as I near the end of the corridor. *Louis, Louis, Louis.* His name beats insistently in my brain, drumming a tattoo on repeat. *Did he miss me? Will he even remember me?* My mouth is suddenly dry as I reach the lobby and the doors to the Polo Lounge face me.

I step out, pausing for just a moment. Two women pass by, one of them giving me a smile as she runs her eyes over my outfit. She wears a white T-shirt-style top and bright red cigarette pants, an outfit that doesn't look out of place in 2020 or 1953. I feel a shiver of doubt, my stomach giving a horrible lurch. The faint music piped into the lobby is something classical and timeless, and the flowers on the centre table are an elaborate display of pink and white roses. *Were there pink and white roses in the lobby this morning?* It's with some trepidation that I move to the heavy doors of the Polo Lounge.

Strains of Bing Crosby's 'White Christmas' hit me as I step inside, delicate Christmas twinkle lights framing the bar and patio doors to the terrace, and for a moment any doubts I have are stripped away. A man sits at the piano, in a vintage (or not, as the case may be) suit, his hands running over the keys, as he croons softly to the restaurant diners, his hair slicked back neatly away from his forehead. Behind the bar, the bartender has his back to me, his dark blond hair reflecting the glow from the lights overhead. My heart stops in my chest and my tongue feels too big for my mouth. I step forward, intent on ordering a dirty martini that he knows I won't be able to drink, but when the bartender turns around, it's not him. It's not Louis. He isn't here.

Maybe he's on a break. Maybe he didn't start work yet. And then reality crashes in on me, as the pianist switches songs and I recognise the notes that drift through the restaurant. 'Thinking Out Loud' by Ed Sheeran. I'm still here, in 2020. It didn't work.

Stumbling out of the bar, I press my hand to my mouth, sobs rising in my throat. *It didn't work. I'll never get back to 1953.* I had been so reluctant to try without a good reason, and when I saw the article on Evelyn I was so convinced that it was a sign. That Evelyn's death was a strong enough reason for me to be sent back to the past. Suddenly nauseous, I start to run through the lobby, desperate for fresh air and to get away from the hotel before someone sees me crying in this ridiculous dress. As I reach the lobby doors to the red carpet outside, I step on the untied shoelace of my Converse sneaker, the long folds of the dress wrapping themselves around my legs in a tangle.

It happens so quickly I can't get my hands out in time to break my fall, and the last thing I see before the ground rushes up to meet me, my head striking the top step of the hotel entrance, is the valet turning to face me, his mouth open in a shout.

Chapter Three

'Miss? Are you OK? Let me help you.'

The concerned valet peers at me and I blink up at him, before pushing myself into a sitting position. My head throbs and I feel slightly sick.

'I'm... I'm OK. Thank you.' But I'm not. As the valet peers down at me, holding out a hand to help me to my feet, he doesn't look like the same guy who turned as I fell. In fact, this guy's uniform has a distinctly vintage air about it. Allowing him to help me up, I brush myself down, before pressing my palm to my forehead where there is a small bump. *Ouch.* Telling myself it's the bump to the head making me feel dizzy, I slowly turn and take in the lobby. The flower arrangement in the centre... wasn't that pink and white before? Now there is a dazzling display of orange and yellow roses taking centre stage in the reception area, and my heart flutters. They couldn't have replaced that flower display in a matter of minutes, and I couldn't have been knocked out for long, because an ambulance would have been called. When the valet helped me up, it was as though I'd only just fallen.

'Are you certain you don't want me to call you a doctor?' the valet asks, still peering at me. 'You sure did take a knock to the head.'

'No, no thank you.'

'Here, miss, I think you dropped this.' With what I think is a curious frown, the valet hands me my phone, a sharp crack running across the screen, along with the coins and the skeleton key which must have scattered from the sash when I fell.

'Thank you.' Drifting away from the valet, I move through the lobby, glancing at the reception desk as I shove the coins back into my sash. There is no sign of Lyle and his tapping fingers; instead a girl sits there, her hair short and curled, pinned up neatly. I can hear my pulse in my ears and my legs tremble as I walk back towards the Polo Lounge, feeling slightly light-headed. *Concussion? Or time-slip?* At the heavy restaurant doors, I pause, not sure if I want to go back inside. If I walk in and everything is as it was, then I think I probably do need a trip to the hospital – and I'll know for certain that I really can never go back. Taking a deep breath, I shove the doors and step inside, time seeming to freeze for a moment as I take in the scene ahead of me.

There is no sign of the tasteful Christmas decorations that twinkled throughout the Polo Lounge moments ago. Plants wind their way up the walls behind some of the booths, and the whole room feels fresher and brighter. The style of the diners at the well-spaced tables is unmistakeably 1950s, the green leather booths filled with women sporting nipped-in waists and perfectly curled hair, and men in sharp suits, not a polo shirt or crumpled pair of chinos in sight. At the piano, a different musician in a very similar suit to the previous pianist plays Perry Como's 'Some Enchanted Evening', his hair slicked back and parted into that distinctive style known as a 'duck's ass'.

It... worked? It worked! I don't quite understand how but I am here, in the past just as I hoped, and I have to blink away hot tears of relief. It must have been the fall that transported me back – as it did the first time – and I remember my untied shoelace. Stooping to retie it, I use the brief moment to gather my thoughts and get my breathing under control. If it worked, and I really am back in the past, then Louis must be here somewhere. Raising my head I look over at the bar, expecting to see him, cocktail shaker in hand, his hair falling over his forehead as he gives that wicked grin that always makes my stomach turn over, but... he isn't there. A thin, dark-haired man with a pencil moustache stands in his place, chatting to one of the patrons. Combing the room, I search for Louis, hoping I'll see him delivering drinks to a booth or chatting with a guest, but there is no sign of him. I wait, hoping he might reappear behind the bar with a fresh bottle of something in hand, but he doesn't. I might be back in the past at the Beverly Hills Hotel, but Louis is not.

He's not here. I made it back, and yet Louis isn't here. Turning sharply on my heel I hurry out of the Polo Lounge, my stomach churning as I head out of the hotel entrance, bypassing the valet and turning left onto the path that leads out into the street. It had never occurred to me that Louis wouldn't be in his usual position behind the bar. I assumed that time for him had been much the same as it was for me – the same old monotony day in, day out. I'm not sure where to go, or what to do, but my feet instinctively turn towards the boulevard. There is a newspaper stand outside the hotel and I slow as I approach it, glancing back towards the hotel, taking in the subtle changes. The hedges that aren't quite as thick and full, the palm trees that don't tower quite as high, the pink of the exterior that is just that little bit brighter. The daily newspapers are kept on the bar in the Polo Lounge, but once I realised the bartender wasn't Louis, I left without thinking about the papers. I have no idea what the date is. Sliding my fingers under my sash for a coin, I shove it into the slot and pull out the newspaper, a horrid sensation of déjà vu creeping over my shoulders.

SNOWFALL SLATED FOR LA AREA

The headline shrieks out at me, but I don't read the story beneath it. Instead my eyes go to the date at the top. 29 January 1950.

1950. *1950?* Only a little over six months have passed since I was last here, even though it's been eighteen months at home. Black spots dance in front of my eyes, and I squeeze them shut, swallowing hard as I think for a moment that I might be sick. I scrabble in the folds of my dress, searching for the article I printed on Evelyn, but when I pull it out the ink is faded, and the page is unreadable. *Cheap printer toner? Or the leap in time?* The ink is so faded it's barely there, but I hold it up to the sun overhead, trying to make out the year. *1953.* It definitely says 1953, so why am I here, in 1950?

Cars roll by, Cadillacs and Buicks, all more familiar to me from movie sets than the roads, with more than one driver giving me a second glance as I stand on the side of the road in my evening gown. After dropping my useless phone into the trashcan beside the newspaper dispenser, I start to slowly walk towards Sunset Boulevard. The sky is a crisp bright blue overhead and my stomach rolls again, sweat beading at my hairline. Given that the air is chilly, I don't think it's the weather making me feel sick. When I found myself in 1949 the first time, the date had matched the date in 2019, and I had foolishly assumed that it would be the case this time. It seems I have no control over time at all, and there are no rules to manage it. *1950?* How did things go so wrong? And now what do I do?

Out on Sunset Boulevard, I take a moment to get my bearings. Some things look familiar from the last time I was here (there? then?) and although my mouth is dry and I'm in the wrong year, there is a tiny spark of excitement in my belly. Googie's, the diner, is further up the street at 8100 Sunset and my mouth floods with saliva at the thought of hot, salty, crispy fries and a thick chocolate malt, out of the cool January air.

Decision made, I head towards the diner, longing for the familiarity it offers, taking in my surroundings as I walk. The huge billboards that line the boulevard in my own time and which are lit up day and night are gone, replaced by smaller, but still impactful billboards. Instead of advertising *Selling Sunset* and the latest mobile phones, they are decorated with smiling wives and well-behaved children, advertising bread, washing powder, a stable life-style of drudgery and routine. There is less litter lining the streets, and everything feels a little more real than it does in 2020. Less light, less glitter, just *less*. People hurry past on their way to work, home, to collect their children, busy but still *present*. My lips twitch, curving upwards as a young man (again with that hideous duck's ass haircut) tips me a wink and a smile as he steps out of my way. Not a mobile phone in hand, or a set of AirPods wedged into ears in sight.

'Good morning, ma'am.'

'Good... morning,' I reply, as I step past him, the skirts of my evening dress rustling. I can't remember the last time anyone besides Eric wished me a good morning. Certainly no strangers, not in my LA. My heart lifts for a moment, before realisation creeps back in. I am still in the wrong time, with no idea why.

Googie's is open and I pause at the door, peering inside through the slatted blinds. I'm not sure what – or who – I'm expecting to see inside, but even so a wave of disappointment washes over me at the sight of not a single familiar face.

'Ma'am? Excuse me, ma'am.'

'Oh gosh.' The door swings open and I step aside, realising I am blocking the exit. 'I'm so sorry.'

A woman, slightly older than me, steps out, squinting as the sunlight hits her face. She turns and holds the door for me as, with her other hand, she places a large pair of sunglasses on her face. Her blonde hair is tucked up in neatly pinned rolls and her waist, in fitted black slacks, is tiny. I tug my dress down slightly and step inside. 'Thank you.'

'You're welcome.' Her voice is husky, as if she has a sore throat, and I feel for one fleeting moment that perhaps I should know her, but then it's gone and so is she, and I am standing inside a diner that ceased to exist years ago.

'Fries and a chocolate malt, please.' I place my order and then head for a booth in the middle of the restaurant. It's nearly lunchtime, and a steady stream of people enter and leave the diner as I wait for my food, my stomach beginning to growl. It seems even time travel can't dull my appetite.

As I wait, I pull out the article again, smoothing it flat on the table. Evelyn's face beams out at me, and I wrinkle my nose. She really is outstandingly beautiful, but is it awful to say that I understand how someone could want to kill her? I found her utterly infuriating, and it wouldn't take a huge stretch of the imagination to picture her pushing someone too far. It still doesn't explain why I am here now, instead of in 1953.

'Here you go, hon.' A waitress plops a plate of fries and a shake on the table with a weary smile. 'Enjoy your meal.'

'Thanks.' I smile up at her. 'I couldn't borrow that, could I?'

'This?' She plucks the pencil out of her top pocket with a frown. 'Uh, sure. I guess. Just leave it on the counter when you're done.'

'Brilliant. Cheers.' Flipping over the faded article I try to remember everything I can about Evelyn. If I can't find Louis then I might have to do this alone. Squashing down the heavy sensation in my chest at the thought of Louis moving on without me, I think back to the first time I met Evelyn. She was pretty, wholesome, and looked as if butter wouldn't melt in her mouth. Until she spoke, that is. Then she was... caustic, at the very least.

Connecticut. I'm sure she was originally from Connecticut, moving out here in her senior year of high school, but that doesn't help me. I never knew where Evelyn lived in Los Angeles, or whether she worked, so it's not as if I can head over to her house to try and warn her. The article said she lived in Melrose Hill, but has she even moved there yet? If she'd been married to this guy for eighteen months in December 1953, she might not have even met him yet. In my own time it's not unusual to have a long engagement, but I don't think it's the norm for this day and age... and knowing Evelyn, she would have wanted to get a ring on her finger as soon as possible.

Louis's parents' house. That's where I officially met Evelyn for the first time, but I'm not even sure how to get there. I know it's out in Santa Monica, and it's a cute little house with an actual white picket fence and a wraparound porch, but that's as much as I have to go on. Defeated, I rest my head on the cold Formica table. How on earth can I help Evelyn when I don't even know where to find her?

'Lily?' The sound of my name pierces my thoughts, and for a brief moment I wonder if I've fallen asleep and this entire day has been a dream. Because I recognise that voice. 'Lily… is that you?'

I lift my head from the tabletop, my eyes widening as I realise who is standing over me.

'I'd recognise that hair anywhere.'

'Jean.' I get to my feet, a grin spreading across my face. 'Oh my God, *Jean*.' My voice cracks and then she is pulling me towards her for a hug, a world away from the old Jean I used to know – the stiff, buttoned up Jean who worked as movie director Leonard Langford's personal assistant on set, and disapproved of almost everything I did.

'Lily! I can't believe it's you! You never called to say you were in town.' Jean holds me at arm's length, running an appraising eye over me. 'This dress is lovely – although wildly inappropriate for lunch here, of all places – and what did I tell you about those dreadful sneakers?'

I glance down at my battered Converse, powerless to stop the burst of laughter that erupts from between my lips. 'You know me, Jean, comfort over style.'

Jean smiles and slides into the booth next to me. 'Oh Lily, it's so lovely to see you. We were all so worried when you just… *disappeared* like that. What happened? Did you go back to London?'

I feel my face go blank, as I desperately search for the right thing to say. 'Oh, I—'

'Your friend, the barman – Louis – he told Leonard and me that he thought you had to go back to London for a family emergency. Leonard was dreadfully disappointed – I think he was hoping that you would take over my job as his PA, given that it wasn't really appropriate for me to work for him once everyone knew we were together.' She takes a breath. 'I hope everything worked out OK?'

'Yes,' I stammer, the word sticking in my throat. I always wondered what Louis would think about my absence. If he thought I ran away because of what he said to me that last night in the Beverly Hills. 'Everything worked out, I guess. What about you and Leonard?' I flick my gaze towards the huge diamond that sits on her ring finger.

'Well, yes, that's going very well.' She blushes, and I get a glimpse of the old Jean, reserved and ever so slightly prudish. 'We're getting married soon. I didn't know where to send your invitation, so I gave it to Honey, in case you called her. You *are* coming, aren't you, Lily?'

'That's wonderful news. I… of course I'm going to come.' *If I'm still here.* I am genuinely happy for them, and if I am still here in 1950 then there's nothing I'd love more than to be a part of their wedding. 'Listen Jean, I was wondering—'

'Excuse me! Miss? Could we get some iced tea over here?' Jean gestures at the waitress and I wait to ask her if she knows anything about where I can find Louis and Tilda – Louis's sister, who had been a central part of everything that happened with Honey Black the last time I was here – or even Evelyn. 'Now Lily,' Jean turns back to me, her eyes shining. 'Why didn't you call and say you were back in town?'

'I… it was a little unexpected—'

'Oh!' Jean gasps, pressing her hands to her mouth. 'You're here for tonight aren't you? *That* explains all of *this*,' she wafts a hand over my evening gown. 'Oh my gosh, Leonard set this up, didn't he?'

'Um…'

'You're a surprise for Honey!'

'I am?'

'I knew it.' Jean sits back with a small smile of self-satisfaction. 'I knew Leonard would have something planned but I never dreamed it would be *you*.'

Oh boy. Drawing in a deep breath, I rest a hand on Jean's arm until she pauses. 'Jean, hang fire for just one moment.'

'What?' She stops, giving me a quizzical look. 'I know you're ready hours ahead of schedule, which to be frank, Lily, is a *miracle* for you, but you *are* here for tonight, aren't you?'

'I wish I could say yes, Jean, but I honestly have no idea what you're talking about.'

Jean's mouth drops open and for a minute I want to laugh, as her usual poise falls away. 'The *premiere*, Lily. It's tonight. The premiere for *Goodtime Gal* is at the Grauman Theatre this evening. Everyone will be there.'

Oh my God. Is that why I'm here today, instead of in 1953? Surely not. I mean, it's a big deal, but it's still only a movie premiere. And three years is a long time to hang around and wait for Evelyn to get herself in trouble. I am aware that Jean is still talking, but I haven't heard a word. All I can think is that the premiere is tonight and I am here, in Hollywood, in 1950, and so are Honey, and Jean, and Leonard, and…

'Tilda,' Jean is saying, her hands flying as she talks.

'Wait. Woah. Back up for just one second.' I take a sip of my malt, the sweet drink thick and cloying on my tongue, buying time to compose myself. 'Tilda? What about her?'

'She's a friend of yours, isn't she?'

'Yeah, she's a friend.'

'Excellent. So, you can catch up with her tonight.' Jean gives me an excited grin. 'She'll be at the premiere. She's covering it for the newspaper at UCLA. Part of her college course or something.' Jean rolls her eyes, letting me know exactly what she thinks of that. I'm pretty sure the moment Leonard makes it official Jean will pack up work and start popping out babies.

'Tonight?' My stomach lurches and I feel my pulse start to thud, heavy and insistent. 'She'll be there tonight?'

'Sure will.' Jean looks me over. 'And now, so will you.'

Chapter Four

Cameras click as I step out of Leonard's sleek black Cadillac onto Hollywood Boulevard, my initial discomfort at returning to the past dressed to the nines in the vintage evening gown fading away, and I find myself fitting right in with the great and the good of Hollywood. Cars double park outside and crowds fill the sidewalk on either side of the hand- and footprint-filled courtyard to the Grauman Theatre, clapping and cheering, as flashbulbs go off and one gentleman in a pork pie hat, camera around his neck, snaps my photo. Not sure of the consequences of yet another photograph of me taken forty-five years before I was born, I hold up a hand to shield my face, as Jean takes my other hand and leads me towards the ornate entrance to the theatre. Although I've passed the Grauman Theatre a hundred times in my own time, there is something breathtaking about seeing it now, open for not even thirty years. Palm trees on either side of the courtyard sway gently against the bright lights of the theatre. The feeling as we step inside is of walking into an emperor's palace, thanks to the dragon carvings that overlook the entrance, beneath the slanted temple-style roof. There is no sign of Honey, or anyone else I know for that matter.

'Here.' Once inside Jean hands me an old-fashioned, a curve of orange peel licking the glass, and then heads off to mingle while I tuck myself into a corner of the lobby beneath the hand-painted Chinese murals to observe. I let the whisky and orange burn my tongue as I sip and wait, my cheeks growing flushed with booze.

'Hey sweetheart, who are you waiting for?' A man in his mid-twenties swaggers over to me in a fitted T-shirt and jeans, his dark hair artfully arranged over his forehead. 'Can I get you another one of those?'

He is unbelievably beautiful and wildly familiar. I shake my head. 'No, thank you.' All I've eaten today are the fries at Googie's and the alcohol has already gone to my head.

'Are you sure?' He leans in close, and I get whiff of cologne and cigarette smoke. I forgot how everyone seems to smoke here. 'You're too pretty to be standing here all alone this evening.'

'There you are.' A woman with dark curls and a pout on her pretty face glances over me dismissively as she takes the young man by the arm. 'I've been looking all over for you.' She gives me another look that can only be described as salty, as he smirks at me before allowing her to pull him into the crowds of people still milling about the lobby.

'Vivien doesn't take too kindly to being left for a single moment at these things.' Jean appears beside me, a fresh drink in her hand, only hers is clear with a slice of lemon and looks a lot like it's just Perrier.

'Vivien?' I follow her gaze towards the dark-haired woman, who now smiles and nods graciously at the people she passes. 'That was... *Vivien Leigh?*'

Jean gives a low chuckle. 'Something, isn't she? She's just as sharp off screen as she is on screen, don't you think?'

I feel as though someone has dunked me in a bucket of icy cold water. *Vivien Leigh just sneered at me.* Yesterday I was watching her cry out to Clark Gable as he left her standing on the porch at Tara, and today... today she snubbed me. 'So that guy with Vivien...' I blink, speechless for a moment. *That guy* was Marlon Brando. *Streetcar*-era Marlon Brando, the hottest version of Marlon Brando that ever graced our screens. I just got chatted up by Marlon Brando, before he ate his way to 350 pounds and bought himself a raccoon named Emma.

'Marlon?' Jean smiles knowingly. 'Marlon is... a bit of a ladies' man. Vivien and Laurence have been married *forever* but those two are making a movie together and there are rumours. Hell, there are rumours flying all over town about that guy even when he's not making a movie.'

'I bet,' I say faintly and take a gulp of the fiery drink in my hand.

Flashbulbs burst outside the entrance to the lobby and muted murmurs become an excitable chatter as the doors swing open and Billy Walters enters with his wife, Cynthia Lake. Cynthia is no great fan of mine, so I draw back into the crowd as they pass, the floor tilting beneath my feet. Closing my eyes I take a deep breath, trying to ground myself. It all feels so odd, and yet so right to be back here. The chattering becomes a roaring cheer and I open my eyes to see Honey walking in on Joe's arm, wearing an exquisite green dress – thin straps over her shoulders, ruffles at the bust, before it flows like an emerald waterfall to her feet – and her trademark coral-red lipstick. My heart turns over at the familiar sight of her, at the sound of her laugh as Joe whispers in her ear. Dreamlike, I step forward, the people either side of me melting away as she looks up and catches my eye. Her eyes widen and her mouth drops open, a perfectly manicured hand rising to cover her lips.

'*Lily?*' Those famous navy-blue eyes fill with tears and the bridge of my nose starts to tingle as she reaches out and pulls me into a hug.

'Isn't this just the most wonderful surprise?' Jean gushes, appearing beside us. 'Isn't Leonard clever to arrange for Lily to be here? I knew he would have something up his sleeve.'

'It's so good to see you, Honey.' The words come out thick and gnarled through the lump in my throat.

'Oh Lily—'

A disembodied voice with the clipped tones of old newsreels announces that the audience must take their seats, and Honey is swept away by her security team. She turns back and calls out to me, 'Ciro's, after the showing! See you there!'

'Ciro's?' *The nightclub?* I had forgotten Ciro's had ever existed. Now the Comedy Store in my time, Ciro's was *the* place to be seen in Hollywood through the Forties and Fifties, and a shiver of excitement ripples over me. Ciro's is almost worth coming back for on its own. And then I remember Evelyn and the horrible fate that awaits her. There has been no sign of Tilda so far and I'm starting to think that this whole evening will be a bust when it comes to tracking down Evelyn.

'I'm just going to use the ladies' room.' I press my empty glass onto the tray of a passing waiter and step away, but Jean's eyes are on Leonard, who has just entered the theatre. It's too hot in the lobby and there are too many people milling around. I've just seen Honey Black, when I had resigned myself to never seeing her ever again in my life, I'm still trying to get my head around the Marlon Brando/Vivien Leigh thing, and the fact that I am back here, in the past. Everything is too loud, too bright, and feeling overwhelmed, I push through the crowd towards the restroom. The ladies' room is blessedly quiet and I sit on the closed lid of the toilet, waiting for the cool air to calm my flushed cheeks. *Honey.* After all this time, it feels surreal to see her again, after months and months of being too afraid to even google her name. As her eyes lit up when she saw me I felt for the first time in a long time that I belonged somewhere and I shift restlessly on the toilet seat, not wanting to give that too much thought.

After a few minutes, I blow my nose and flush the toilet, and am about to leave when the outer door creaks and voices reach me.

'I already told you; I'm not interested. That's not the way I work.'

Peeping through a crack in the door, I see an older woman swiping a lipstick over her mouth, before straightening a small hat over her hair, her perfect dark waves giving her an almost matronly air.

'Oh come on, you didn't even give me a chance!' A second voice fills the small bathroom and I pull back, hitting the backs of my legs on the cold porcelain of the toilet. I know that voice.

'And nor do I need to. I am a respected columnist. What would people say if I had some... some Girl Friday hanging around all the time? They're hardly likely to take me into their confidence with an extra set of ears listening in.'

'Ms Parsons, I'm not talking about gossip. I'm talking about interviewing. I can get you an interview with Honey Black, I told you that. I just want one chance to interview Frank while he's here, that's all.'

I hardly dare to breathe as I realise who the older woman is. Louella Parsons, the undisputed queen of

Hollywood gossip. A well-known columnist, Louella was adept at appearing slightly vague and uninterested in order to persuade celebrities to confide their deepest, darkest secrets to her, only for her to splash them all over the newspapers. Apparently. I guess I'm about to find out.

'Good Lord, you're worse than that dreadful Hedda Hopper.'

'Wait! Please don't leave.' The other woman's voice is low, filled with a despondent air. 'It would mean so much to me if I could even just *be there* while you interview Frank? I promise I wouldn't say a word. This is all I've ever wanted.'

Hearing the crack in her voice, I can't hide myself away any longer, even though I'd rather our reunion was a little more private. Smoothing down the too-tight bust of my evening gown, I take a deep breath and step out of the stall.

'Hello, Tilda.'

Smiling uncertainly, I watch as Tilda catches sight of me in the bathroom mirror, her mouth falling open, before she spins round and wraps her arms around me.

'Lil? What? Where…?' She holds me at arm's length for a moment and then pulls me back in for another huge hug. 'You're… here?'

Squeezing her hand I turn to Louella, who is watching Tilda's excitement with an amused twitch of her lips. 'Ms Parsons? I'm Lily Jones, an old friend of Tilda's.'

'So I gathered.'

'You must be here to cover tonight's premiere. How exciting.' I give her a wide, toothy grin which she vaguely reciprocates.

'Jones? Aren't you the girl who was involved in all that… scandal a while back? At the Beverly Hills?' Louella gives me a long, hard look as if committing my face to memory.

'It would have been far more of a scandal if Lily hadn't been there,' Tilda says, never taking her eyes off me. It's as if she thinks I'll vanish in a puff of smoke if she looks away.

'I was there, yes,' I say graciously. 'Ms Parsons, I couldn't help overhearing that you're interviewing Frank this evening? I'm assuming you mean Mr Sinatra.'

'You assume correctly.' Louella's bosom puffs up with pride and I thank my lucky stars that my mum was such a huge Sinatra fan. 'After the premiere I'll be speaking with him at Ciro's. Alone.' She directs the final word at Tilda, who huffs theatrically.

'It's such a shame,' I move to the sink and turn on the tap, thrusting my hands under the water, 'that you won't allow Tilda to join you. I've heard such good things about her work at the newspaper at UCLA. Accomplished and auspicious, that's what they're saying about her. But it was nice to meet you, Ms Parsons. I'm sure I'll see you again.'

Tilda says nothing as Louella reaches for the door handle.

'Well Tilda, I guess I'll have to give *you* the snippet of gossip I have on Frank and Ava Gardner, if Ms Parsons is in such a hurry to be away.' I sneak a peek into the bathroom mirror as Louella pauses, her ears pricking.

'Wait a second.' Louella turns, rearranging her expression into something more welcoming. 'What is this about Frank and Ava?'

'Oh no, I wouldn't want to keep you.' I check my teeth for lipstick and make a great show of smoothing my hair down. 'Ready, Tilda? I can't wait to see the movie.'

'*Please.*' There is a desperate air to Louella's voice now and I see Tilda tamp down a smirk. 'Of course Tilda can come with me to interview Mr Sinatra. I never said she couldn't, I just—'

'Really?' The word squeaks out of Tilda's mouth like a deflating balloon.

'So she'll meet with you after the movie?' I say briskly. 'And you'll take her to see Frank?'

Louella nods primly. 'Yes, of course. Tilda, you may sit with me this evening if you'd like. Now Ms Jones, what was it you wanted to say about Mr Sinatra and Ms Gardner?'

'Well, they're dating,' I say, crossing my fingers that I have my timeline correct.

'That's just gossip and rumours,' Louella says, but there is the tiniest hint of doubt in her voice.

'I can tell you, hand on heart, that Frank Sinatra and Ava Gardner are conducting an affair.' Louella blinks and I wait a moment before I deliver the ultimate piece of gossip. 'They're going to get married.'

Tilda gasps and Louella quirks an eyebrow. 'Really?'

'November, next year. They'll be married on the seventh of November 1951; you mark my words.'

'But…' Louella frowns, shaking her head. 'He's already married. To Nancy.'

'Next month they'll announce that they're separating, and by October next year they'll be divorced. You can add that to your column.' I tip her a wink and grab Tilda by the hand. 'Now, if you'll excuse us.'

-

'Oh my word, Lil, I can't believe it's really you. And I can't believe you just bullied Louella Parsons into taking

43

me along on a job.' Tilda's cheeks are flushed, and she can't stop grinning as we make our way through the lobby towards the theatre. 'Wait. I don't want to go in there yet. I want to know – are Frank and Ava really dating? How do you know they'll get married? And where have you…?' She grows serious. 'Where have you been, Lil? You just *disappeared*.'

I reach a hand towards her, but she pulls back, shaking her head. 'You left, Lily, without a word. You didn't even leave a note. Where did you go?'

I bite my lip, not sure what to say or how to say it. Tilda and I had grown so close while we were trying to save Honey Black, and it's almost unbearable to see the distrust in her eyes now. 'I'm so sorry, Tilda. I never meant to hurt anyone, and I promise I can explain but… can we get through the movie first? There's a lot I need to tell you, and I kind of don't know where to begin.'

Tilda opens her mouth, then as something takes her attention over my shoulder she glances back to me and closes her mouth again. I know what it is, before I even turn. My pulse starts to race and something kicks up a storm in my stomach, a tornado of butterflies. Slowly, I turn around in the now empty lobby.

'Louis.' His name is a whisper and I feel my eyes fill with tears. He's here. Standing in front of me, just as I've imagined every day for the last eighteen months.

'Lil?' He takes a single step towards me and it feels like the ground shakes beneath my feet. 'Lily Jones? You're… back?'

I nod, my throat too thick with tears to speak. I wish he would hold out his arms so I could fly into them, feeling him crush me hard against him, the fresh lime scent of him so familiar. Instead he stands stock-still, his eyes never leaving my face.

'You're back.' His voice is oddly flat, and there is no sign that the thrill I am feeling at seeing him again is reciprocated.

'I'm back.' My stomach is in knots and I slide my hands behind my back so he can't see how they shake.

'Well, nice to see you.' Louis gives me a curt nod and holds out an arm to Tilda. 'Come on, Tilda. We'll miss the show.'

Chapter Five

'Wait.' My voice is a croak, barely audible above the opening credits that thunder from the auditorium, and neither of them turn back. 'Wait, Louis, please!' Hurrying after them, I reach out and snag the back of his crisp blue shirt with my fingertips. There is an agonising pause as he stops, waiting a second before he turns.

'What is it, Lily? I'm here to watch the movie.'

I've never heard his tone so icy, cold enough to freeze lava. 'Will you let me explain?'

Tilda glances between us, her brow furrowed. 'Lou,' she says quietly. 'Maybe let her talk. She owes you – *us* – an explanation.'

Louis looks down at his shiny, conker-brown Oxfords, avoiding my eye. 'The movie is about to start.'

'Louis, please. I know I just vanished, and I never meant it to be that way, things just... I can explain, at least I'll try to—'

'Miss Jardine?' A voice hisses urgently from the theatre door, Louella Parsons gritting her teeth in Tilda's direction. 'I thought you wanted to interview Mr Sinatra later on this evening? If that is still the case then I advise you to follow me.'

Tilda gives Louis a stricken look, and he waves her away. 'Go, Til, I'll be fine. We can catch up afterwards.'

'If you're sure?' Tilda gives me a hard stare, before she kisses Louis on the cheek and scurries towards Louella and the theatre door, leaving Louis and I alone.

The space between us grows smaller and I feel as though I can't quite catch my breath.

'You just left,' Louis says softly, running his eyes over my hair, my face. My stomach flips again, and for a moment it feels as if no time at all has passed since the day he told me he and Evelyn were over, right before I ended up back in my own time. 'I waited for you, you know.'

I take a small step back, clearing my throat. 'I'm so sorry, Louis. I couldn't… I wish I'd been able to stay.'

'Why didn't you?' He steps towards me, closing the gap, and I can barely breathe over the crashing of my heart against my ribcage. 'You could have left me a note. Left a message at the hotel reception. I waited all day for you, and the next. I thought something had happened to you.' He runs a finger along my jawline, before lifting my chin so I have to look at him.

I open my mouth, but before I can speak an usher appears, hastily gesturing to us to enter the auditorium. 'After the movie,' I say. 'If you'll hear me out? I'll explain then.'

–

It is the longest hour and a half of my life. As Honey and Billy cavort on screen I am acutely aware of Louis sitting beside me, his thigh just millimetres from my own. Memories hit me one after the other: the memory of watching Honey in her first movie, *Kentucky Queen*, snuggled up on the sofa with my mother before she died, memories of *Goodtime Gal* being made and all the shocking events that occurred during filming, Evelyn's face as she was introduced to me for the first time. The memory of Louis, pressing his mouth hard against mine right before I slipped back to the Beverly Hills Hotel in the present day. *What am I going to tell him about why I had to leave?* I can't tell him the truth – that I had to go back to 2019, to my own time, and that even as I did it, I didn't want to go. That all I've thought about since that day is him, and being back here. My mouth is dry, sour with old bourbon, and I worry at the skin around my nails, fretting over what to say, and whether he'll forgive me. If he doesn't forgive me, if Louis says he never wants to see me again, then I don't know what I'll do. And not just because of what is going to happen to Evelyn. I can barely focus on the movie and feel nothing but relief when the lights go up and the audience gives the cast a resounding round of applause.

As the auditorium empties out Jean sweeps me along with her and Leonard, taking it as read that I'll travel to Ciro's in Leonard's car, and I watch helplessly as Louis gets left behind in the crowd, hoping that he will follow. Ten minutes later, we pull up outside Ciro's, and I feel that familiar sense of discombobulation. We have driven along Hollywood Boulevard, down onto Sunset, passing an empty lot where the Saddle Ranch Chop House sits in my time, and that other famous Hollywood hotel, Chateau Marmont. Instead of the graffiti scrawls of celebrity comedians that adorn the side of the Comedy Store in the twenty-first century, *Ciro's* flows in an elegant cursive script on the smooth black fronting of the building. Paparazzi swarm outside, oversized cameras and flashbulbs ready to capture the glitzy, glamorous stars as they enter.

Sliding from the car, I follow Jean towards the entrance, relieved when I see Tilda and Louella ahead of me. Inside, an orchestra plays on a small stage flanked by heavy curtains, while clusters of small tables surround a tiny dance floor. Most of the tables are already full, the air buzzing with the tuneful hum of stringed instruments and gossipy conversation. It's warm inside, a stark contrast to the cool January air outside, and the air feels thick and humid as I nod an awed hello to James Dean – who no longer wears a waiter's uniform, unlike the last time I saw him – and then Honey is there, wrapping her arms around me.

'Lily, you came! And this dress! You look wonderful.' She kisses me enthusiastically on the cheek, before pulling back and eyeing me critically. 'I thought you'd vanished off the face of the earth.'

'I'm sorry, Honey,' I say, my cheeks flushing. I should have known that I wouldn't be able to slip back to my own time without any questions being asked by the people I left behind. 'It all happened rather suddenly. I didn't get the chance to say goodbye.'

'Where on *earth* did you go?' she asks, her brow creasing as her blue eyes search my face. 'I was so terribly worried when no one could find you the day… well, the day after everything happened.'

'I had to go home. To London. It was a… uh, a family emergency.' I swallow down the lump that sticks in my throat. 'I never meant to upset you, Honey, and I'm so sorry that I made you worry.' I hadn't even let the thought cross my mind that perhaps the people I'd left behind in 1949 would have been concerned about me. Selfishly, I'd been more concerned with wallowing in my own misery at never seeing them all again.

'Really I should be furious with you for runnin' off and leaving us all like that without a word, but I am so thrilled you're back.' Honey reaches out and squeezes my hands, unable to contain the grin that marches across her face. 'Have you seen Tilda and Louis? They're both here somewhere.' Honey leans in conspiratorially. 'Tilda is sitting with Louella Parsons and Frank Sinatra, although I'm not sure for how much longer. I just overheard her ask him if he thinks marrying Ava will launch him back to stardom – the poor thing has had *terribly* bad luck lately – and I don't know *where* she's got this idea that Frank and Ava will ever get married.'

Yikes. 'I did see them both very briefly before the movie. *Goodtime Gal* was wonderful by the way, Honey. You did it. You're a star.'

'I am, aren't I?' Honey presses her hands to her cheeks in glee and I catch an adorable glimpse of the small-town girl from Kentucky. 'Oh, hello darling, wonderful to see you.' She pauses as a handsome man leans in to kiss her cheek.

'Was that…?' My eyes follow him as he weaves his way towards the bar.

'Oh, darlin' Jack Kennedy! Such a peach, for a politician.' Honey follows my gaze, her accent slipping a little. 'He says he'll be president one day, but we'll see. Bless his heart. Goodness knows what he's doing in town.'

'JFK,' I say faintly. 'Right. Of course.'

Louis approaches from the side of the stage, the room seeming ever fuller with actors, producers and musicians. If I wasn't so worried about Evelyn – and so devastated at the idea that Louis might be about to cut me off forever – I might have had the time of my life, but as it is, the heavy stone of worry that seems lodged in my gut is impossible to shift.

'Honey, you were magnificent.' Louis gives Honey a hug and she scurries off, calling out to Marlon Brando, who is now *sans* Vivien Leigh. 'Lily.' He nods his head formally, as if I am someone he met once and didn't particularly like.

'Louis, please don't be angry with me. I need to explain...' My tongue feels too big for my mouth as I realise that I still have no idea how I'm going to explain my sudden absence. 'We need to talk.'

'Yes, we do.' He is unsmiling and it's so unfamiliar to me that I almost feel he is a stranger. 'Lily, I—'

Shouting erupts from across the room as a woman gets to her feet, furiously yelling at a man with neatly slicked-back hair, wearing a suit and tie. 'He *spat* on me,' the woman yelps, as the man is forcibly removed from her table, murmurs of shock rippling through the room. 'He kicked me on the shin and then he spat on me!'

'Serves you right for printing lies about my wife! You shuckster!' the man calls out as he is hustled away towards the exit. 'Put this in your column!'

'You're damn right I will, Franchot Tone!'

'Can we get out of here?' Despite the drama unfolding around us, what I have to say to Louis can't wait.

'Sure. If that's what you want.' Louis grips my elbow tightly, expertly weaving his way through the crowd, but there is nothing romantic or flirtatious about it, I could be his ninety-year-old granny. Once outside, he leads me along Sunset Boulevard, around the corner to where he has parked. 'You didn't want to spend more time with Honey?' he asks as we reach his car.

Christine. I reach out a hand and stroke the smooth paint work of the old Cadillac. Louis's pride and joy. 'I would have liked to, but... it's more important that I talk to you. You painted Christine. She looks all shiny and new.'

A faint smile twitches at the corners of his mouth for the first time. 'Doesn't she look great? If we wait here Tilda will know where to find us.' We both fall silent and the air between us grows thick, pregnant with everything unspoken. I shift in my Converse, my feet cold through the thin soles.

'I'm sorry,' I say quietly. 'For leaving the way I did.'

Louis buffs an imaginary scuff from the car's paintwork. 'Why did you?' He finally raises his eyes to mine. 'I thought... well, I thought we could have something special, Lily. I thought you felt the same way I did.'

I do! I want to shout, but instead I say, 'I never meant to hurt you. I thought I would be there, the day after the arrest, but...' I break off, swallowing hard. How can I explain to him what happened? That I went to the Paul Williams Suite and figured out the way back to my own time, even though part of me never really believed that it could work both ways? That I was devastated to find myself back in my own time, unable to think of anyone but him for the past year and a half.

'It was a mistake,' I say, watching his face. 'I wish I hadn't left, but I had to. I had to... go home.'

'To London?'

I hesitate before giving the tiniest nod. 'I didn't even know I was going until the last minute, I couldn't... there wasn't time to tell you.'

Louis stares at me, his face a granite mask. 'And you couldn't write a letter? Send a telegram? You knew where to find me, you could have written to me and let me know where you were at the very least.'

'I didn't… I couldn't…' The words won't come, and I have to blink rapidly to stop the tears that fill my eyes from falling.

'And Tilda – she was devastated when you left. If you didn't want to write to me you could at least have written to Tilda. You could have let her know that you were OK.'

'It wasn't that I didn't want to—'

Louis shakes his head, looking away. 'Six months, Lil. *Six months* without a word from you, and then just when I think I'm starting to get over you, just when I'm starting to wake up with something other than you on my mind, you come back, waltzing in as if nothing has happened.'

Oh. Oh, God. 'I'm so sorry, Louis. I'm so, so sorry. Please believe me when I tell you I didn't want to go back, that I didn't have a choice. And I'm sorry that I didn't write. I've… I've thought about you every day since.'

Louis's face softens and my mouth is suddenly dry as he takes a step forward, reaching for my hand. As his fingers wrap around mine, a thousand tiny fireworks erupt across my skin, before he lets go just as abruptly.

'You look the same,' I say eventually, glancing up at him shyly. 'For a while, when I got back, I couldn't picture your face clearly, but now I can really see you and you look exactly the same.'

'Your hair is shorter.' Louis reaches out and tugs at a curl, his lips curving as it pings back into shape.

'I went to the Polo Lounge,' I say. 'You weren't there. I thought maybe…'

'Night off,' Louis says, moving back towards Christine as if afraid to stand too close to me. 'For the premiere.

53

Honey invited me, and I didn't want to turn her down. The movie… it reminded me, you know…'

I know. It reminded me too, of all that went before. 'So, you still work at the Polo Lounge?'

'Kind of.' Louis shrugs. 'I've put a band together. Things are going pretty well, but I still do a couple of shifts a week in the bar. I like it there. You know my cocktails make everything seem a little brighter.'

I laugh, the air clearing slightly between us. 'Until the morning hangover, at least.' Growing serious I look down at my battered sneakers. 'I thought you'd left. I thought I wouldn't be able to find you.'

'Lily, I—'

'Oh, thank goodness you waited for me, I thought you folks might have left!' Tilda appears, grinning and slightly breathless. 'Did you see? Franchot Tone *spat* on Florabel Muir's shoes, all because she printed something in her column about his wife. He's being arrested! Louella is phoning it in right now. And I spoke with Frank Sinatra! Seriously folks, that man is an utter dream. Can you believe it, I just interviewed Frank Sinatra! OK, well not *interviewed* as such, but I stood there and took notes while Louella did. And Ava Gardner – honestly, Lily, you've never seen a woman so beautiful. Do you think if Florabel gives up her column there might be space for me? I mean, I wanted to break more serious stories, but everyone starts some—' She breaks off. 'Wait. Is everything swell? More specifically, are you two… all right?'

I sneak a look at Louis. 'We will be. I think. I *hope.*'

Tilda is silent for a moment, as if weighing up the situation, and then she asks the question I've been waiting for one of them to ask. 'So Lily, why are you back?'

Oh boy, here goes. 'It's Evelyn,' I say, my hand going to the sash of my dress where the faded newspaper article burns a hole against my waist.

'Evelyn?' Tilda frowns. 'Our Evelyn? What about her?'

'She's, er...' I swallow, rubbing my hand across the back of my neck. 'She's in trouble. At least, she's going to be. Not yet.'

'In trouble?' Tilda shakes her head as if I'm speaking a foreign language.

'This is your... gift, isn't it?' Louis says, staring at me. I feel my cheeks begin to burn. 'You've seen something about Evelyn, haven't you? That's why you're back.' There is a look I can't read on his face, a look that makes my stomach pitch. '*Evelyn* is the reason you came back.' He looks away, swallowing hard, and I realise he thinks that Evelyn is the *only* reason I came back.

'I didn't come back just for her, but yes,' I say, a chill winding over my shoulders that isn't down to the night air. 'I've seen something about Evelyn, and it's bad. Really bad.'

'Bad like...' Tilda looks pale in the faint yellow glow of the streetlamp nearby. 'Like, Honey Black bad?'

Hating myself for doing this to them both, I nod. 'I'm afraid so. I need to find Evelyn. I need to do something to warn her, to try and stop this from happening.'

'What *is* going to happen?' Louis asks, his tone sharp. 'Tell me, Lily. I've known Evelyn a long time, and I care about her. I don't want you to drip feed me things piece-meal like you did with Honey. I want to know exactly what you think is going to happen to Evelyn.'

So, I tell them.

—

'Tilda, get in the car.' Louis opens the door, throwing her a stern look.

Tilda's face carries a sickly pearly sheen as she slides into the back seat, tucking her skirt in around her. 'I can't believe this. Lily, are you sure?'

'Yes.' I nod, climbing into the passenger seat beside Louis.

'Tell us everything you know.' Louis pulls away from the kerb, and as he turns back on to the boulevard I see the flashes of camera bulbs behind us as someone important leaves the nightclub.

'Just what I told you,' I say, trying to recall as much of the article as I can. If Evelyn had been famous there would have been tons of information, but she's not, she's just a regular woman. 'Her mother will find her dead at home, after Evelyn calls her begging for help. She won't make it to the house in time to save her.'

'Oh gosh.' Tilda's voice is low in my ear as she sits on the edge of the back seat, her hands around my headrest. 'This is terrible. And you say her husband does it?'

I nod, still feeling queasy. 'I think so. He disappears after they find Evelyn's body.'

'Jeez. I know Ev can be all hat and no cattle at times but even so.' Tilda sits back with a thump, her skin still white and clammy.

'All hat…?' Sometimes I am stumped by the things Tilda comes out with.

'You know what I mean, Lil. Evelyn can be so boastful and full of herself and so… so, *infuriating* at times, but heck, she's not a bad person, she doesn't deserve this.' Tilda presses her hand to her mouth briefly, as if finding the news hard to swallow. 'And this was all that was written on Evelyn's page?'

I had forgotten that I gave them that analogy – of 'reading' the future on the page – the last time I was here. I guess technically, I'm not lying.

'What's his name?' It's the first time Louis has spoken since he asked what I know, and I realise he's more shaken by the news of Evelyn's future death than I thought.

I go to pull out the article, the name dancing away from the tip of my tongue, before my fingers slide away, the paper crumpling slightly. 'I want to say Jon or Jim... Jack? And the surname was something Italian sounding.' The shock of seeing Evelyn's fate on the page meant that his name slid out of my mind before I could commit it to memory, and of course now the ink on the article has faded to almost nothing.

Louis's eyes meet Tilda's in the rear-view mirror and she lifts her shoulders in a slight shrug. 'Beats me,' she says. 'I have no idea who this guy could be.'

'I was half hoping you would know something,' I say, not realising until I vocalise it that that's exactly what I was hoping for. That Louis or Tilda would know this guy and we could persuade Evelyn to kick him to the kerb before he even has a chance to propose.

'Well, now you'll get to speak to Evelyn herself and maybe we can figure this thing out.' Louis pulls up outside a house not dissimilar to the one his parents live in, although slightly smaller and neater. 'This is Evelyn's house.'

–

The house looks like something out of a Netflix movie, with a disturbingly well-trimmed lawn and perfectly painted shutters. The neighbourhood is quiet as we walk up the path to the front door, and I feel a prickle of apprehension as Louis knocks with a quick double rap.

'Louis?' The door opens a crack and Evelyn peers out. 'Oh, Louis!'

I cast a quick glance at Tilda as Evelyn pitches forward, one hand holding her housecoat closed as she throws the other around Louis's neck. I had assumed that he and Evelyn had stayed broken up after I left, but maybe I was mistaken. Maybe that's why he was so quiet on the way over here; if he was still seeing Evelyn the thought of her being married to someone else would be painful enough, without also knowing that that person was going to do her harm.

'How did you know?' Evelyn hiccups the words, clouded in sobs. 'How did you know I needed you?'

Louis turns to me, his brow furrowed as he tries to untangle Evelyn's arms from around his neck. 'I didn't, Ev. I didn't know. I came to see how you are.'

'Oh.' Evelyn pulls back and now I see that her eyes are pink-rimmed, and her cheeks are rosy as if she has been crying. She turns away, heading back into the house, and after a bemused glance in my direction Louis shrugs and we follow her inside.

Evelyn's house is just as I would have pictured it, if I had ever thought about where Evelyn lived. Everything is very neat and tidy, the cushions on the dark green sofa neatly plumped, a copy of the newspaper folded sharply down the middle on the coffee table. I avert my gaze from the paper, the date seeming to stand out in thick, bold type. Heavy cream drapes hang at the windows, and a rug in a ghastly shade of lime green sits beneath the coffee table. It is the epitome of early 1950s chic, heavily influenced by the style of Hollywood stars, and I wonder for a moment just who exactly has paid for all of this.

'Ev, I brought someone to see you.'

'Hey.' Tilda steps forward and Evelyn gives her a weak smile, which fades as soon as she sees me.

'Oh. It's you. Iris. Or whatever your name is. I thought you left town.' The air of vulnerability fades as Evelyn radiates her usual hostility and I try not to bristle, even though just the sound of her voice is like nails on a chalkboard.

'It's Lily, and you know that very well.' I smile, trying to diffuse her chilliness. 'Hello Evelyn, it's been a while.'

'It could have been longer; I wouldn't have minded.'

Tilda bites her lip, amusement flickering across her features as Louis shakes his head. 'Evelyn, there's no need to be rude to Lily. She's here to help you.'

'She is?' The scowl drops from Evelyn's face, and I see how Louis could have found her attractive. 'But how did you know? I only found out myself a little while ago.' Her eyes fill with fresh tears, and she presses a tissue to her nose.

'Found… out? Found out what?'

'Why, about Sonny, of course!' Evelyn cries, a fresh wail of despair renting the quiet suburban air. 'He's been *arrested*, Louis!'

Tilda mouths '*Sonny?*' at me, as I mouth back, '*Arrested?*' and Louis wraps an arm around a distraught Evelyn and guides her towards the sofa.

'What has Sonny been arrested for, Evelyn?' I ask, as Louis gets her settled against the cushions and Tilda moves to the drinks cabinet in the corner and pours her a stiff gin.

Evelyn takes a huge gulp of her drink, letting out a shuddering breath before she answers. 'Murder. My boyfriend – my Sonny! – has been arrested for murder.'

Chapter Six

'Murder? Jeez, Ev. Who is he supposed to have offed?' Tilda asks, her eyes wide.

'*Til,*' Louis hisses. 'What Tilda means is, what happened? Who is Sonny supposed to have killed?'

Evelyn takes a deep breath, but even so her words are washed away on a wave of sobs. '...Some girl... casino... for lunch and then... *arrested.*' She lets out a wail that makes me wish I had earplugs.

Oh blimey. 'Evelyn. Take a deep breath and start at the beginning.' Ignoring the look she shoots me – full of vinegary dislike – I perch on the sofa next to her.

'Wait a second. Sonny's your boyfriend?' Tilda frowns. 'I thought you were going with Paulie Brooker?'

'And the last I heard she was going with Mickey Halfender,' Louis murmurs in my ear, and I give Evelyn a quizzical look.

'Evelyn?'

Wiping her eyes, Evelyn sips at her drink prudishly and looks up at Tilda. 'I went on two dates with Paulie Brooker, that's all. He wasn't for me.'

'Not the marrying type,' Louis mutters under his breath, and I press my lips together.

'And Mickey... well, Mickey wanted to marry me, but it turned out that he wasn't—'

'Rich enough? Handsome enough?' Tilda rolls her eyes.

'He had no ambition,' Evelyn snaps, glaring at Tilda. 'And then I met Sonny, and he was... he was just *perfect*.' Her eyes fill with tears and Louis reaches into his pocket and hands her a handkerchief, coming to sit beside her. 'He's handsome, and charming, and he always takes me to beautiful restaurants and the most glamorous parties. He's everything I ever wanted.' She casts a sly glance in Louis's direction. 'And now it's all...' A sob hiccups out of her mouth. 'It's all *ruined*.'

'So, Sonny has been arrested for murder? When did this happen?' Louis asks, concern drawing his brows into a sharp V.

Evelyn nods, pressing Louis's handkerchief to her eyes. 'Yes, the police arrested him this afternoon. We went out for lunch – Sonny took me to the most darling little place along from Musso's, so exclusive you wouldn't believe it – and we'd only been there a short while before it happened,' she hiccups a sob. 'The police came barging into the restaurant, they didn't even care that we were only on our appetisers! They said they were arresting Sonny on suspicion of murder and dragged him away and into a police car in full view of everyone. I can't show my face in town.' Another dramatic sob escapes. 'Oh Louis, what am I going to do? If Sonny is found guilty at trial, you know what the punishment is!'

'Life imprisonment?' I say, watching as Evelyn's hand sneaks into Louis's.

'Death!' Evelyn wails, burying her face in Louis's shirt as he meets my gaze over the top of her head. Tilda looks stricken, her face losing the faint hint of colour that had just started creeping back into her cheeks.

'First degree murder means death row, if found guilty,' Louis says quietly, and the hairs on the back of my neck prickle, as if someone has just walked over my grave. *Holy shit. This is serious. Hell, just being arrested for murder is serious business, let alone the potential for being sent to death row if found guilty. I've seen those Louis Theroux documentaries – I wouldn't want to spend a single minute in regular jail.* My pulse skips as I realise that perhaps there is going to be more to saving Evelyn than I first thought.

'Lily.' Louis's voice breaks into my thoughts and I throw him a distracted smile. 'I was just saying to Evelyn that perhaps she could tell us a little bit about what happened with Sonny? How all this came about.'

'Yes. Of course. Absolutely.' I glance around the immaculate sitting room, but can see no sign of Sonny's presence here. If Evelyn wants us to help, then we need to know as much as possible about him and his habits. There is still the lingering thought at the back of my mind that I am here to save Evelyn – and if that means helping Sonny, then so be it. Maybe then Evelyn will marry Sonny and get a happily ever after after all. 'Does Sonny live here? With you?'

Tilda gives an audible gasp, as Evelyn turns a shocked face towards me. 'What exactly are you insinuating? Of course Sonny doesn't live here.'

Yikes. Of course Evelyn and Sonny wouldn't live together – it's 1950, for Pete's sake. I had spoken without thinking, and now I feel a fierce heat creep up my neck and over my cheeks as Louis looks at the floor.

'What I meant was… does he spend a lot of time here?'

Evelyn looks demurely down at her knees. 'Some. Obviously my parents are here most of the time, but they're on vacation at the moment. They've gone to Palm Springs for a few days.'

That answers one of my questions, at least. Evelyn lives here with her parents. 'And if you're not here, where do you guys spend time?'

'Over at his place, occasionally. He has a small apartment over on Vine.' A tiny smile plays on Evelyn's lips. 'Mostly, we go out. Restaurants, parties, that kind of thing. Sonny travels a lot for work, so we have to make the most of the time we do have together.'

'What does he do?'

Evelyn preens a little, her hand going to smooth her hair. 'He's an insurance salesman. A very successful one.'

I pause for a moment, letting my eye catch Louis's. 'Evelyn, do you think you could tell us exactly what happened? You said he was dragged out of the restaurant by police, but why do the police think he has committed a murder?' Evelyn was so distraught earlier that I still have no idea who Sonny is supposed to have murdered.

Evelyn heaves a dramatic sigh as her eyes fill with fresh tears. She pulls her housecoat tight around her body, even though the house is warm, and looks up at the ceiling. 'I don't know the full story,' she says eventually, 'only the tiny pieces of information I could get over the telephone once they'd taken Sonny away.'

'Tell us,' Louis urges. 'We want to help, right Lily?'

'Right.'

'It's a big, horrible, terrible mess,' Evelyn says, her voice wobbling. 'A woman was murdered, and they're saying Sonny did it. Greenwood, that's her name. Bess Greenwood. Some casino bunny from Vegas.'

I rack my brains, wondering if I've ever heard the name before, if I've caught a moment here or there of a true crime documentary about her on Netflix, or if any of the podcasts have covered her, but it doesn't ring any bells.

'She was found on a small ranch, out in a town called Baker, just this side of the California–Nevada border.' Evelyn pauses, wiping at her eyes again. 'They said she'd been strangled with some sort of soft ligature and that they knew Sonny was there – they're saying he killed her! They… they're saying that he strangled her with his tie. But I know he didn't do it! He would never do anything like that, never!' She sniffs delicately. 'Sonny is a respectable, decent man, the furthest you could ever imagine from a murderer. And he would never be running around with another girl – certainly not a girl like that!' Evelyn bursts into fresh sobs, loud and ragged, as Tilda gives me a bewildered look over her head.

'Tilda?' Louis extricates himself from Evelyn's grasp and gets to his feet. 'Perhaps you could take Evelyn to the bathroom and once she's feeling calmer, wash her face? Pour her a fresh drink?'

Tilda nods. 'Sure. Come on, Evelyn.' She wraps her arm around Evelyn's shoulder and leads her out of the sitting room, leaving Louis and I alone. I let out a long breath.

'Blimey. This is bad, Louis. Really bad. Do you know this Sonny?'

Louis shakes his head. 'I've never heard of him. Like I said, the last I knew Evelyn was seeing Mickey Halfender.'

'And Paulie Brooker.'

'Don't think badly of her, Lil.' Louis's tone is soft. 'She was really hurt – I really hurt her – when we broke up. All she ever wanted was to settle down, to get married and have babies. She was just looking for the right guy.'

'And now she thinks Sonny is the right guy?' I move away, running a hand over the ornaments that line the mantelpiece. 'I mean, maybe he is. This could all be a huge mistake and Sonny is innocent. Evelyn certainly seems to be convinced that he is.' *Maybe that's why I'm here, three years too early.* 'Maybe if I don't help, Sonny will go to prison, and then Evelyn will end up meeting the guy who's going to murder her.'

'Keep your voice down,' Louis hisses. 'This *is* why you came back, Lil. Maybe this is how you help Evelyn.'

I nod thoughtfully, even as a faint fluttering of fear makes my limbs feel liquid and loose. Maybe Sonny *is* the reason I ended up back here just six months after I left, instead of three years later… maybe Sonny is the key to saving Evelyn – but even if that is the case, I still feel lost at sea. Honey was different, I had inside information. This time I have a single article, the print so faded I can no longer make out the words – I'm going in blind. 'This is all Evelyn knows, what she's told us?'

'I guess so.' Louis reaches out, placing a hand gently on my arm, a thousand volts zooming along my veins. 'Lil, do you know anything? Could you see anything else at all on… ahh… Evelyn's page?'

'Nothing. Just the bare facts that we talked about earlier.' I shake my head. 'I don't recognise the name Bess Greenwood at all.'

'Why would you?' Evelyn's voice is stronger now as she reappears in the doorway, her eyes lightly rimmed with pink, but altogether much more her usual acerbic self.

'We were just tossing some thoughts around. You know, trying to see what we can do to help you.' I smile, but it's forced.

'Well, thank you. I'm sure I'm very grateful.' Evelyn has the good grace to look a little sheepish.

'Can you tell us anything else?' Louis asks.

Evelyn shakes her head. 'That's really all I know. I don't know why the police are so convinced that Sonny was there, that he's responsible. I'd never heard the name Bess Greenwood before that night, and we've certainly never been to Baker.' She begins to pace, wringing her hands together. 'I can't believe this is happening! This just isn't fair! Sonny and I… we're so happy together, and now I'm going to be all alone, again.'

Tilda frowns, pursing her lips as I shake my head, so slightly that only she notices. 'You won't be alone, Evelyn. I told you in the bathroom that Lily will help you. She's great at this kind of thing.'

Oh yikes. 'Evelyn, if you don't know any more than that, then we really need to speak to someone who does know what's going on.' I glance up at Tilda, remembering her fiancé's cousin had been in the police force. 'Reggie's cousin, what was his name? The police officer?'

'Frank?' Tilda bites her lip, regret written all over her face. 'He left the precinct. He moved to New York not long after you went back to London. I don't think there's any way he can help us.'

'Shit.' Rubbing my hands over my eyes, I ignore Evelyn's shocked expression at the expletive and move over to the small table that holds the telephone and a black address book. 'There must be someone who can help, someone who can get us the information.' I'm sure in 2020 there would be a way of finding details online, court records, Facebook posts, TikTok videos about madcap conspiracy theories as to what the real story surrounding Bess Greenwood could be. Here, though, I have no idea where to start. I thumb through the pages of the address book mindlessly, barely paying any attention to the immaculately neat writing that fills the pages until I land on L.

'Archibald Lemon. Attorney.' I look up to catch Louis's eyes on me as Evelyn still paces uselessly, her hands growing red from where she has wrung them like an old dish rag. '*Attorney*, Lou.'

'It's our best shot.'

'What? *What* is your best shot?' Evelyn wails, glancing between us as I see a lightbulb go on over Tilda's head.

'Who is Sonny's lawyer?' I ask. 'He might be able to give us more details – maybe if we explain that we think we can help, he can give us more information as to what they think Sonny actually did…'

'His lawyer is a man called Benjamin Fry,' Evelyn says, finally stopping her pacing. 'And I guess you could speak to him. We'd have to get Sonny's permission for him to tell you anything, I should imagine.'

'Well, let's do that,' Tilda says, her eyes sparking with excitement, fired up by the thrill of the chase.

'Or you could just…' Evelyn trails off, glancing towards a photo frame on a bookcase that I hadn't noticed before. It holds a photo of a beaming Evelyn, alongside a handsome man with slicked-back dark hair, wearing a suit and tie. His arm wraps tightly around her waist, with a smile that doesn't quite reach his eyes. 'You could just speak to Sonny himself.'

Chapter Seven

'Is that allowed?' Tilda looks confused, and I shrug. I have no idea. I'm seventy years behind as it is, and I don't even know the rules in my own time.

'When his lawyer called earlier he said he'd try and get it agreed that Sonny could call me,' Evelyn sniffs, once again yanking out the now soggy handkerchief. 'He's being held in Lincoln Heights Jail right now, but if he's charged and found guilty at trial then he'll be moved to San Quentin.'

Goosebumps sprout over my arms, as an icy finger strokes my spine. Even in my own time San Quentin is notorious. I glance at the clock on the sitting room wall. It's getting late, and I wonder how realistic it is that Sonny will call tonight. 'Louis? What do we do?'

'I vote we wait,' Tilda says, before Louis can speak. 'We don't know whether Sonny will get the chance to call again, and if we aren't here tonight and he *does* call...'

As if on cue, the shrill ring of the telephone pierces the room. We all look at each other, before Tilda nudges Evelyn. 'Go on, answer it.'

Evelyn moves quickly across the room, her fists clenched, as the air in the room seems to grow thin. I can't stop thinking about the fact that I potentially hold the fate of both Evelyn *and* Sonny in my hands. I know it's not dissimilar to what happened with Honey a few months ago, but something about it feels different – perhaps because the whole thing with Honey was accidental. This time I've come here deliberately. A horrible thought strikes me as Evelyn lifts the receiver, putting an end to the nerve-shredding shriek of the phone. *What do I do if Sonny isn't innocent?*

'Hello?'

A frantic tattoo of butterflies beats in my chest as I watch Evelyn's face change, and I step forward to take the receiver. She shakes her head.

'Hi, Mom.' It's as if we all let out a collective breath, but whether it's of relief or disappointment, I couldn't tell you. 'No, everything is... fine.'

'*Her parents don't know yet?*' I mouth at Louis, who shrugs.

'No honestly, everything is just peachy. I'm...' Evelyn casts about the room, running her eyes over the coffee table. 'I'm just reading the newspaper and then I think I'm going to turn in for the evening.' A pause. 'No, no Sonny tonight. He's... out of town.'

My gaze wanders back to the photograph on the bookcase, as Evelyn struggles through idle chat with her mother. It looks to have been taken recently, as Evelyn's hair is a similar length and she wears a fur coat, a grinning Jack O'Lantern on the porch behind her. Sonny on the other hand wears only a sports jacket, his gaze on Evelyn as she smiles at the camera. I wonder who took the photograph, what her parents think about him, and whether I really can stop the dreadful event that is currently written in Evelyn's stars.

'Oh gosh.' Evelyn hangs up and bursts into fresh tears. 'That was so hard. I've never lied to my mother, before.

Never. She's going to be so upset when she finds out what has happened.'

'It will be fine, Ev.' Louis wraps his arm around her shoulders and I shift, trying to ignore the tickle of jealousy that burrows under my skin.

'So you're not going to tell your parents that Sonny has been arrested?' I ask, briskly. 'What about when they come home? Surely you'll have to tell them then?'

Evelyn shakes her head, hesitating for a moment. 'No, I'm not going to tell them. Not yet. I didn't want to tell them tonight and ruin their vacation. My mother would rush straight home, and I don't want that.'

The newspaper article presses hotly against my skin through the fabric of my dress. I picture Evelyn's mother receiving the frantic, desperate phone call from Evelyn, rushing across town to get to her dying daughter, not making it in time. Looking up, I catch Louis's eye and know that he is thinking of the same thing.

'Look, maybe you should go on up to bed, Evelyn,' Louis says, gently. 'You must be exhausted. It's getting late, and we're not even sure that Sonny will call. Maybe tomorrow we can contact his lawyer, this Benjamin Fry, and see if we can get the chance to speak with Sonny.'

Evelyn nods and Tilda leads her back up the stairs, murmuring to her softly in a very un-Tilda-like fashion, leaving Louis and I alone once more.

'Are you all right?' He steps closer and I can smell his aftershave, with a faint tinge of the rosewater perfume Evelyn wears. 'I don't think Sonny will call, do you?'

I shake my head, wishing I could just lean into him and close my eyes, whisk us away fairy-tale style back to Beverly Hills, away from Evelyn, and Sonny, and everything that lies ahead. Instead, I say, 'No, I don't think so. I think we just have to wait until morning.'

Tilda hurries downstairs once Evelyn is settled, clutching the telephone number for Benjamin Fry in one hand, and as we all climb into Louis's car I get the sensation of time slipping away, unravelling like ribbon.

'Where to?' Louis looks at me expectantly, as he turns the key in the car's ignition.

'Where…? Oh.' My cheeks burn hot and red, as I realise what he is asking me. I guess I had hoped that either Louis or Tilda would invite me to stay with them, but then, naively, I hadn't been expecting them to be so mad at me for leaving. 'The Beverly Hills, I guess.' I don't have a room there obviously, but I know I can sneak into the laundry room. I've slept in worse places – Eric's sofa bed had bugs once, and it never smelled right again after the fumigator came out.

'Beverly Hills it is.' Louis glances in his mirror and moves to pull away from the kerb.

'Wait, Lou.' Tilda's voice is low, and I busy myself with the sash of my dress, pulling it tighter around my waist and retying it. 'Lily should stay with us. With me. At Mom and Dad's.'

Louis says nothing for a moment, his jaw tightening. 'Tilda, Lily has said she's staying at the Beverly Hills. I think it's best if I just drop her off there and come back to collect her in the morning.'

'For Pete's sake, Lou. Come on. Lily can't stay there, it'll cost her a fortune. She can't afford that. No one can.'

'We don't know that.' Louis doesn't take his eyes from the road, and I feel sick at the way he's avoiding my gaze. *He hates me. We'll never get back to how we were.*

'You're acting like a brat,' Tilda snaps. 'Yes, Lily upped and left without a word and that was wrong. Lily, that was a real... a real lousy thing for you to do. And not to write or send a telegram? Even worse. The least you could have done is let us know you were all right.'

'I really am sor—'

'I'm not done.' Tilda sniffs and tosses her hair back. 'My point is, Lou, she's still our friend. And she's back – she's really here, when we both thought we might never see her again.' Her voice softens and once again I have to blink away tears. 'I, for one, want Lily to stay at our house tonight, even if you don't. Because at the end of the day, Louis Jardine, if you wanted to, you could have tried to track Lily down yourself. London isn't on a different planet.'

Tilda sits back with a thump, folding her arms across her chest, while Louis continues to keep his eyes on the road. I swallow, not wanting to break the heavy silence that fills the car, half of me thanking God that Louis didn't make any attempt to find me. The thought of him arriving in London in 1949, looking for a Lily Jones that won't be born for another forty-five years, makes me break out in a cold sweat.

Louis doesn't speak for the rest of the journey, and when he does pull up to the kerb, it's with an over-whelming sense of gratitude that I realise we are outside his parents' house, the porch light casting a soft yellow glow over the front yard.

'You win,' he mutters to Tilda, as he gets out of the car and comes around to open the door for me. He might be mad, but he still has manners.

'Thank you,' Tilda says with a shit-eating grin, as I follow them both to the front door. All the other lights in

73

the house are off, and my pulse increases at the thought of spending a night across the hall from Louis. A thought that is soon squashed.

'I'm going to stay at my apartment tonight. I'll pick you up in the morning,' Louis says, stooping to kiss Tilda on the cheek. 'Make sure you call Sonny's lawyer as soon as you can.'

'Sure will,' Tilda says, giving him a stiff salute and stepping inside the house.

'Thank you,' I say, as I pause on the doorstep. 'For agreeing to let me stay here.' My heart crashes against my ribcage as Louis turns to face me, and I wonder if he'll kiss my cheek too.

Louis stares at me for what feels like a long time, his eyes raking over my face. 'Good night, Lily,' he says, and then he turns and walks back to his car without a backward glance.

Tilda is tucked into bed by the time I have used the bathroom, stepping into a frilly, flimsy nightdress she had left on the dresser for me. At the end of the other twin bed in her room is a set of clean clothes – a pale blue striped dress, with matching cardigan.

'I thought maybe an evening gown wasn't quite the right attire for a lawyer's office… but I didn't bother with shoes,' she grins as I thank her. 'I know how you love those terrible sneakers you wear.'

Forcing a smile, I slide into the twin bed, pulling the blankets up to my chin as Tilda reaches over and switches off the lamp.

'Til?'

'Yeah?'

'Are you still really mad that I left the way I did?'

There is a rustle of blankets, and then the lamp goes back on and Tilda is facing me, propped up on one elbow. 'Truthfully? Yeah, I kind of am. But seeing you back here… you're my friend, Lily, and I missed you.'

A lump rises in my throat, so big I can barely breathe. 'I wish I'd never left,' I say, tears spilling down my cheeks. 'Do you think he'll ever forgive me?'

There is a moment of silence as Tilda stares at me. 'Yes,' she says after a lengthy pause. 'He will forgive you eventually, but you really hurt him. You can't expect to come back and for him to behave as if nothing happened. It's going to take time for him to trust you again.'

I nod, knowing that what she's saying is true. I would have felt the same way if it had been the other way around. I *had* felt that way, when Louis wasn't behind the bar where I expected him to be – it had been like a kick in the stomach to think of him moving on without me. The room goes dark as Tilda switches out the light again.

'Lily?' Tilda's voice is low in the thick, inky darkness.

'Yes?'

'I love you to pieces, but if you hurt him again, I'll kill you myself.'

Chapter Eight

The following afternoon, after a phone call taken by Benjamin Fry's snippy assistant, we pull into a small, unswept parking lot, dirt and weeds collecting in the cracks in the concrete. Despite the unkempt parking area, the building that houses Benjamin Fry's office is large and imposing, row after row of darkened windows looking out over the dusty car park. It's in view of the Lincoln Heights Jail – a depressing vista of bars across windows and crumbling concrete – and there is an undeniable sense of desperation and despair as Tilda and I slide out of the car, leaving Louis at the wheel.

'Are you two sure you'll be all right? It doesn't feel right not going in with you.' Louis frowns, squinting as the sun hits his eyes.

'We'll be fine,' Tilda says, with a roll of her eyes. 'It's Benjamin Fry, attorney-at-law we're meeting, not the Black Dahlia killer.'

'Benjamin Fry, who you've never met. Who could be the Black Dahlia killer for all you know. And who might be a wacko at the very least.'

'He's a lawyer, Lou, he can't be that much of a wacko.'

I say nothing for a moment, thinking of all the corrupt lawyers that have reared their heads on the various true-crime podcasts I devour while I'm cleaning the Beverly Hills Hotel bungalows. Louis raises his eyebrows in my direction and I sigh. 'Listen,' I say, 'we're going to a lawyer's office, to meet a lawyer. There'll be other lawyers around. I'm sure Ben Fry is a nice guy, you don't need to worry.'

'And anyway it took a lot of persuasion just to convince Fry to let the two of us meet with him. There's no way he'll let you in, too,' Tilda says. Fry had flat-out refused us access to Sonny in prison, so meeting with him at his office felt like a win – a small, disappointing win, but a win all the same.

Louis grumbles under his breath as Tilda nudges me. A red station wagon pulls into the parking space next to us and a man almost explodes from the driver's seat. He's big – really big – his suit straining at the seams, and with his double chin and small moustache, hat perched atop dark hair, he brings Oliver Hardy to mind.

'Tilda Jardine? Benjamin Fry.' He is slightly breathless, his palm sweaty as he grabs my hand and pumps it once, twice. Grease spots his shirt and there is a tiny piece of what looks like lettuce stuck in his teeth.

'Lily Jones. This is Tilda.'

Tilda reaches forward and shakes his hand, her mouth twisting in a slight grimace as she slides her hand across her skirt when he drops it.

'Nice to meet you. Shall we?' Fry gestures towards the office building and with a nervous glance at Louis, Tilda and I follow him. 'I don't have long, so let's get this over with.'

'Thank you so much for agreeing to see us at such short notice.' It's Tilda's turn to be slightly breathless, as Fry marches us up the front steps to the office. For a larger man, he's surprisingly speedy. 'We really appreciate it.'

'Well, don't expect too much. I'm not sure I can tell you anything you don't already know.'

Tilda throws Fry a dazzling smile as he holds the door for her and we slip inside his dark, gloomy office. She had called him early this morning, explaining that we knew Evelyn, and he hadn't seemed too inclined to help – until Tilda mentioned she was a reporter. As Ben Fry hefts his bulk behind his desk, leaning forward on steepled fingers, my veins ping with adrenaline and my mouth is dusty and dry.

'What exactly is it that you ladies want?'

'We want to talk to you about Sonny. As we said, we're friends of Evelyn, and she's convinced he didn't do it,' Tilda says, sliding her notepad from her pocketbook.

Fry lets out a gusty laugh, tainted with the scent of pastrami and mustard. 'That's what all the wives and girl-friends say.'

'Are you saying you think he did it?' My tone is unintentionally sharp. 'I mean, what's your take on it all? You are defending him after all.'

'He *says* he didn't do it.' Ben Fry opens up a file bearing Sonny's name and my eyes are drawn to a mugshot clipped to the front page. Even in the unflattering light of jail, there's no denying that the man in the mugshot is handsome – and very charming, I'm sure – but Sonny isn't anything like I imagined. There is a hardness around the eyes, although that could be from the stress of being arrested for something he allegedly hasn't done. Who knows? The closest I've come to being a criminal is running away from Pizza Hut without paying when I was fourteen.

'That's exactly why we're here, Mr Fry,' Tilda huffs in frustration. 'Evelyn is utterly convinced that Sonny didn't commit this murder – and if she's right and Sonny *really* didn't do it, why is he sitting in jail for it, and why is no one trying to track down the real killer? If Sonny is innocent surely someone should be trying to figure this out.'

'And you two dolls reckon *you* can do it?' Fry lets out another fragrant laugh. 'There is overwhelming evidence against Sonny, and I'm the best lawyer in town, believe it or not…' he shrugs. 'Don't you dames have socks to darn or something?'

'What is the evidence?' I ask. 'You say there is "overwhelming evidence", but what is it? Why are the police so convinced that Sonny is the one responsible for the murder?'

Fry sits back, shaking his head. 'Are you for real?' He sighs, and I narrow my eyes. 'OK, OK. There was a witness, all right? There was a witness who saw Sonny running away from the scene.'

'A witness? Who was it?'

'Nope. No. I'm not at liberty to tell you that,' Fry says. 'I can't have you privy to confidential information that might harm this defence.'

'Listen, buster, do you want our help or not?' Tilda hisses across the table. 'Last year Lily solved the biggest Hollywood scandal in decades, and she could stop an innocent man from going to death row, if you'll just speak to us.'

I close my eyes briefly, wishing I had persuaded her to let Louis come instead. 'What Tilda means is…' I lean in now, forcing myself to meet Fry's greasy gaze. 'We'd really like to help you with this case. Not that we doubt your ability at all, but it's important to our friend, Evelyn.' *And potentially will save her life.*

'Well first off,' Fry bustles, shuffling the file in front of him and slamming the cover closed, 'I really don't need the help of two amateur sleuths who've read too much Chandler. I don't think you gals quite realise what you're trying to get yourselves mixed up in.'

'Could we just ask you a few questions?' I can feel him slipping away as he glances at the clock on the wall over our heads. 'So we can tell Evelyn what's going on. She's at her wits' end sitting at home not knowing what's happening.' I let my eyes fill with tears and wring my hands together.

'Oh jeez. OK. Five minutes. But then you gotta leave. I've got things to do.'

Tilda licks her pencil and leans forward, as my tears miraculously disappear. 'Bess Greenwood. Did Sonny know her at all?'

'No,' Fry shakes his head. 'He says he never met her.'

'Do you know how she died? Have the police given you any details?' Tilda's pencil scratches across her notepad.

'Only that she was strangled, at a ranch in Baker. Someone said they saw Sonny running from the house, but Sonny never went to Baker that night.'

'So, where was he?'

Fry frowns and I think for a moment he's about to throw us out. 'He says he was in Vegas,' he says after a drawn-out pause. 'For work. A convention, apparently. He says he spent that evening playing the slots before he went up to his hotel room completely alone, without even a… lady guest. No room service, no nothing. He went to his room at around midnight that night, and then checked out of the hotel and left Las Vegas early the next morning to get home to his girl.'

'A convention?' Comic-Con springs to mind, and despite the circumstances, I smother a grin at the thought of Sonny dressing as Gandalf for the weekend.

'Right. A convention. For work.' Fry shifts in his seat, stifling a burp, and glances at the clock on the wall again. Time really is sliding by, and we only have a few more minutes. 'I don't know what else I can tell you, ladies. Sonny says he wasn't in Baker; he doesn't know Bess Greenwood and certainly never laid his hands on her. Apparently. But it's for a jury to decide.'

'Can't anyone vouch for his alibi?' Tilda asks, frowning as her red hair falls over one eye. 'I mean, someone must be able to tell the cops that he was at a convention, there must have been hundreds of people who saw him. Same with him playing the slots all evening – someone must have noticed him.'

'Clearly you dolls have never visited Vegas before – the folks there are focused on their own gambling, not paying any mind to anybody else. Now, if you'll excuse me, ladies, I've answered your questions.' Fry lumbers to his feet, casting a thick shadow over the table. 'Believe me when I say I am here to do the job I am paid to do – you gals can rest assured on that.'

Something tickles at the back of my neck, like a whisper of breath, or the lightest stroke of a fingertip. 'And you have no idea who would have wanted to place him at the scene? No clue as to why someone would say he was there, when he claims he wasn't?'

'Miss Jones, there are plenty of reasons why someone would say that.' Fry opens the door and gestures for us to leave. 'But usually there is only one main reason. Now, if you'll excuse me. It would be in everyone's best interests if I don't see you again.' He pauses as we step out into the corridor. 'One more thing. I'd better not see anything we've discussed in print, or there really will be hell to pay.'

–

'How'd it go?' Louis is leaning against the car as Tilda and I hurry across the parking lot towards him. The huge building casts a chilly shade across the lot, and I shiver, still feeling slightly uneasy.

'According to Fry, Sonny knows nothing, saw nothing, did nothing, although the cops are saying that a witness saw him running from the ranch where Bess was found.' Tilda sighs, throwing her notebook in the open car window.

'Really? A witness? That doesn't sound good for Sonny.' Louis turns to me. 'Lil? What did you think?'

I pause for a moment, not sure I want to voice my feelings out loud. Turning back to look at the lawyer's office, my eyes go to the top-floor window, where movement catches my eye. It's as if someone has pulled back, away from the dusty glass, and the sensation of being watched is like thousands of tiny ants crawling over my skin. 'Honestly? I feel as if something isn't right, but I don't know what. I know he's a lawyer, but Fry was very cagey – he told us there was a witness, but he said he couldn't tell us anything about them, and he certainly wasn't happy at the thought of us poking around in things.'

'Something definitely stinks,' Tilda agrees. 'You were right, Lou, even though I hate to say it. Fry might not be a wacko but there was something very *unsavoury* about him.'

'Where is Baker, anyway?' I ask Louis, as he reaches into the car and pulls out a map. Blimey, it's been years since I saw an actual map, and as his finger slowly traces the worn paper, I long for the speed and simplicity of Google Maps.

'Right… *here*.' Louis jabs his finger at the page, and I raise an eyebrow. 'Right before the Nevada border. Maybe a three-hour drive from here?'

'And from Baker to Las Vegas?'

'I don't know… an hour, hour and a half maybe?'

Tilda looks up and I recognise the glint in her eye. The glint that says there's a story, and she's going to find it. 'We have to go, right?' She looks from me to Louis. 'We have to go to Baker, have a look and see where Bess's body was found. And while we're over that way, we might as well go to Vegas, don't you think?'

Chapter Nine

'Evelyn was happy with us leaving her behind? She knows this might take us a few days, right? If not longer.' Louis glances in the rear-view mirror as we pull away from Evelyn's home the next morning, having briefed her on what Benjamin Fry had told us. It's my third day back in the past and I feel itchy with anticipation and the sensation that time is moving too swiftly.

'Not happy exactly,' I say and Tilda scoffs from the back seat.

'She's furious, Lou,' Tilda says with a smirk. 'But I told her things could get dangerous, and I didn't want her to get shot so…'

'Shot? Good Lord, Tilda.'

'So, our plan is to head out to Vegas to see if we can find a way to prove Sonny's innocence?' Tilda says, thought-fully. 'Lil… forgive me if I'm getting this all wrong, but you say that the person who's going to hurt Evelyn is her husband, so why aren't we looking for that guy instead of keeping Sonny out of jail?'

Tilda has a very good point. In 2020 it probably would be the easiest way to keep Evelyn safe – find the guy who's supposedly going to murder her and make sure that Evelyn doesn't come into contact with him. In 1950, though, it's not so easy. With no Google or social media, it's practically an impossible task.

'Honestly?' I say. 'The truth is I have no idea where to start looking for Evelyn's future husband.' The shock of reading what was written in the stars for Evelyn means that try as I might, I can't remember his name. All I remember is feeling numb as I realised what I was reading, my tongue pressing unfeeling against my lips as a wave of nausea washed over me. Even if I could remember who he was, I don't have the first idea about how to go about finding someone Evelyn hasn't even met yet. 'I'm not sure of his name, how they're going to meet or where he's from. But the one thing we do know is that Evelyn is in love with Sonny right now – if he is innocent and we can keep him from going to jail, maybe Evelyn will marry him instead and she won't meet the guy who's going to hurt her.'

'And if Sonny *is* in jail, then Evelyn is free to be swept off her feet by this other guy,' Louis says.

'Jeez,' Tilda grumbles, 'I don't know who I feel sorrier for right now – Ev for getting tangled up with this other guy or Sonny for having to spend the rest of his life with Evelyn.'

I turn my head to the window, stifling the smile that creeps over my face. I catch Tilda's eye in the wing mirror and she smirks back, before shifting in her seat and resting her head back. It's a matter of minutes before she's asleep. Tilda has never been a morning person.

'You picked up the paper?' Louis asks, never taking his eyes from the road.

'Right here.' Unfolding this morning's newspaper across my lap I turn to page five, searching for the small article that Evelyn had pointed out to me as we arrived at her place this morning.

'What does it say?'

'Not a lot, really.' I run my finger over the words, enjoying the way the ink feels beneath my fingertip. No one reads newspapers anymore. You see scruffy copies of the *Metro* left on the tube at the end of the day, but I don't remember the last time I saw anyone actually reading a newspaper. They'd rather scroll mindlessly on their phones for the entirety of their commute, sucking up gossip on the Real Housewives, or watching TikTok. 'It says that police have arrested a suspect for the murder of Bess Greenwood – a waitress at Vegas's biggest casino – but it doesn't mention Sonny by name, which is good for Evelyn I guess. Especially as she hasn't told her parents.'

'That's kinda weird, huh?'

'That she hasn't told her parents? I guess, but I don't know what kind of relationship they have.'

'Close. With her mom, at least.' That fits with Evelyn calling her mum before the police when she was – is going to be – brutally attacked. 'I guess I thought she would have called her mom straight away. Let's be honest, Evelyn wouldn't usually be worried about ruining her parents' vacation.'

'True.' I pause for a moment, mulling things over. 'Maybe she thinks this will all be over before her parents get home – maybe she genuinely doesn't want to ruin their holiday. She is pretty convinced that Sonny is innocent.'

'And what do you think?' Louis glances at me, but I stare straight ahead out of the windscreen, at the long, dusty highway ahead of us.

'Me?'

'Come on, Lil, you met with his lawyer.' Reluctantly I turn to face him, taking in the way the sun bounces off his hair, the way his arm muscles move beneath his T-shirt. He glances back at me, making my breath catch. 'You must have some thoughts about Sonny, about how Ben Fry spoke about him. Caginess aside, did Fry seem like a decent lawyer? The kind an upstanding citizen would want to represent him? You're a pretty good judge of character.'

Thinking about previous experience I'm not sure that's true. 'Something definitely felt off.'

'Off? How?'

'I can't put my finger on it. He didn't give us a lot, but from what he did tell us, it felt like... there was something he wasn't saying. Or something he said that made me pause for a moment, you know? My mum used to call it the *vibe*.'

Louis gives a small smile. 'The vibe. I like that.' He pauses for a moment, the only sound the purr of the Cadillac's restored engine, and the rush of tyres on the road.

'There was something else,' I say, after a moment of silence.

'What?'

'Ben Fry... I didn't like him.'

'Why not? He did come across as kinda slimy, but I thought all lawyers were like that.'

I think of the lawyer, turning up late after his lunch break, the way he talked down to us, belching out gusts of meaty breath. 'I don't know. Fry reckons he's meant to be one of the best in the business, but if I were Sonny I don't think I'd be so reliant on him.' Dust whips across the windscreen as a truck overtakes. 'I think... perhaps Benjamin Fry thinks Sonny did it.'

'You do? Jeez.' Louis glances at me, his face pinched. 'That's pretty sorry for Sonny, if even his lawyer isn't convinced he's innocent.'

'If he is innocent, it just means there's more pressure on us to prove it.' We fall silent, and I wonder if Louis is also wondering how on earth we're going to do that.

'When you left I told everyone there was a family emergency. I didn't know what else to say.' Louis's voice is quiet, and I strain to hear him over the rush of tyres on the road.

I shake my head, turning away as I blink rapidly. 'Oh.' Now I don't know what to say. I did go home, just like Louis told people. But to my own time, not London. And it was more of an accident than an emergency – part of me had thought it would never work. 'It was something like that.' I shift in my seat, prickly at the thought of lying to Louis. 'I'm glad to be back.' I swallow, my mouth suddenly dry.

'For Evelyn.'

'What?'

'You're glad to be back for Evelyn.' Louis still doesn't look at me, and my stomach drops away. 'I suppose part of me was hoping that you came back for me.'

I have that unsteady sensation you get on a roller-coaster, as if the ground might drop away from beneath my feet at any moment. 'I didn't just come back for Evelyn, Louis. If you must know, I came back because I wanted to see you. I missed you.'

There is a thick, heavy pause, and part of me wishes I could snatch the words back. I know Louis is angry with me, but I couldn't bear it if he rejected me outright. 'LA certainly wasn't the same without you,' Louis says eventually, giving me a sideways glance. 'So, did you meet anybody? When you went back home?'

'No.' I shake my head. *LA wasn't the same without you.*
What does that mean? It feels as if all the air has been sucked
out of the car.

'No... dating?'

'No.' Heat creeps across my cheeks and I make a show
of glancing in the mirror, pushing my hair out of my eyes.
The windows are open, the air hot and dry and dusty,
but it's better than having no air in here at all. *How did*
people here ever survive without air conditioning? There are
some things – air conditioning, and a decent sunscreen to
name but two – that I really miss from the twenty-first
century. 'You?'

Louis shakes his head. 'I've been busy practising my
music, putting a small band together, plus I'm still the best
bartender in Beverly Hills. There's only so many hours
in a day.' He looks at me and finally grins. 'Remember
the Palomino? We played there two weeks ago. Only a
warmup, but it's something.'

'That's fantastic!'

Louis shrugs, but there's no hiding the gleam in his eye.
'Yeah, things are looking up.' He reaches down and links
his fingers through mine, squeezing briefly before letting
go, as my heart swoops and dives. In the wing mirror I see
Tilda's eyes snap closed and press my lips together, trying
not to smile. A road sign, thick with dust, tells us we are
fifteen miles outside of Las Vegas and I sit up, pointing to
the sign.

'Almost there.'

'Yeah.' Something thick and unsettling sits around my
shoulders, a lead blanket, as I remember the thought that
crossed my mind when Evelyn answered the telephone,
and again in Fry's office when I asked why someone would
say they saw Sonny running from the scene. *There are*

*plenty of reasons why someone would say that… But usually
there is only one main reason.*

The truth. That's the main reason why people say those
kind of things.

What do we do if we find that Sonny really did do it?

–

Las Vegas in 1950 is nothing like the Las Vegas I visited
with Eric in 2019. We flew out for a long weekend with
a few of his friends so I didn't have the experience of
driving the winding, orange-dust-coated Highway 91,
which would eventually become the Las Vegas Strip.
Leaning forward in my seat, I see pink neon on the right-
hand side, announcing the Flamingo Hotel, a gasp sliding
from my lips.

'You've been here before?' Tilda sits forward, her hands
grasping the back of my seat.

'Yeah. A while ago. It didn't look like this though.'
The Flamingo was where Eric and I had stayed, but today
– now – it's decidedly less flashy. The pink neon is similar,
but lacks the flashing feathery display it has in the twenty-
first century. The parking lot is filled with cars, Cadillacs
and Fords showing off their soft curves and startled headlights. The surrounding area is… well, flat is the only way
I can describe it. Flat, dusty, *desert-y*.

'It was… different,' I settle on, my face still pressed to
the window. The strip looks odd without the pyramid
of the Luxor Hotel, without the gondola-filled canal of
the Venetian, without the bright lights of the electronic
billboards advertising the latest Caesar's Palace residency.

'Smaller, I bet. And less fancy,' Tilda breathes, her
eyes wide. She peers out of her window, mimicking me.
'Although right now, it seems… kind of tacky.'

I want to tell her that Vegas is just as tacky in my time, but she's right. Ahead of us, a long neon strip light announces our arrival into Las Vegas and a little further along, a bright yellow sign flashes, 'GOLDEN NUGGET GAMBLING HALL'. Everything is slightly dull and grimy in the daylight, despite the flashing neon signs and promises of excitement and glamour. Without the many, many hotels pressed side by side along the Strip, without the tourists and gamblers filling the sidewalks day and night, Las Vegas just seems what it really is in the early 1950s. A small, dry, desert town, clawing its way towards notoriety.

'I don't get why we came here first.' From the back seat Tilda stretches and yawns. 'Baker is back that way—' she jabs her thumb towards the rear windscreen. 'Shouldn't we have gone there first?'

'It was Lily's idea,' Louis says, as we crawl slowly along what will eventually be the Las Vegas Strip. 'It'll be better to drive from here to Baker in the evening, so we can see exactly how long it would have taken Sonny, if it would have been possible for him to do it with the times given around his alibi. After all, he said he went to his room at midnight, but was back in Los Angeles by early morning to see Evelyn after checking out of his hotel. And—' he pauses for a moment, attention caught by a minor scuffle breaking out between two men in the doorway of a pawn shop. 'I think we should head out to the ranch at night.'

'Oh, I like this Louis. He's much more fun than the usual Louis.' Tilda waggles her eyebrows and I laugh.

'Seriously though,' I say, 'we don't know how isolated the ranch is. I thought about going over there first, on the way to Vegas, but Louis pointed out that if there are neighbours nearby and we're over there snooping around in broad daylight, we're likely to be carted off by the police.'

'And we won't if we're stalking around in the dark with flashlights?'

'Til, you're supposed to be an investigative journalist – we're going to be investigating, right? If the ranch is isolated enough we'll be OK with the flashlights – and if there are neighbours, hopefully they'll be tucked up in bed – but we don't want to risk snooping in the day in case the cops are still about,' Louis says.

'I didn't want to waste an entire day waiting,' I say, throwing the newspaper in Tilda's direction. 'I figured we could use the time today to ask around about Bess, find out what she was like, the kind of people she ran around with. Anything, basically, that might give us a lead on what has happened to her. We can also start asking around about Sonny's alibi. If there was a convention held in town then surely the hotel management must have some idea where – there can't be too many places for it to be held, it's still a small town.' The word *still* slips out before I realise and I hurry on, hoping neither Louis nor Tilda finds my choice of phrasing odd. 'If Sonny really didn't do this, then someone else is responsible, and somebody somewhere here must have some idea of the truth. The paper says Bess was a waitress at the largest casino in Las Vegas.' I tap Louis on the arm. 'Louis, slow down. Here.'

The Desert Inn – the sign overhead actually proclaims it 'Wilbur Clark's Desert Inn' – sits on the site where you would find the Wynn Hotel in the twenty-first century. Instead of the tall, elegant, curved Wynn, with its lush tropical greenery out front and crystal-blue lake that greets guests on arrival, this is a long, squat building, flanked by young palm trees and shrubs, with a parking lot already half-filled with cars. A stark contrast to the modern hotel.

'Wow,' Tilda breathes as Louis pulls into a parking space and kills the engine. 'Look at this place, Lil.'

The hotel/casino is long and low, with a white chip tile roof and a green and Bermuda pink exterior. It almost feels like the poor, hick cousin of the Beverly Hills Hotel, or at least it would if the front of the hotel wasn't dominated by a huge fountain.

'Well, it's the biggest casino here, so Bess must have worked here, right?' Stepping out of the car, I feel the stretch in my hamstrings after being cooped up for hours and we all stand in the parking lot, our eyes on the hotel. Despite it being late January, the sun is warm, warmer than Los Angeles for sure, and I feel the tickle of thirst at the back of my throat. 'I vote we head inside.' I pull out the hundred dollar bills that Evelyn had pressed into my hand before we left. 'In case you need them,' she'd whispered.

'If we head to the bar we can have a drink and people watch, get a feel for who works here,' I say, feeling a prickle of sweat under my thin blouse. 'We can start asking around about Bess. Someone must know her here.'

'Yeah,' Tilda says, distractedly, her eyes on the buildings across the street. 'Listen guys, you go ahead and get a drink – I'll meet you back here in a little while.'

Chapter Ten

'I guess we leave her to it,' Louis says, as Tilda grabs her pocketbook from the back of the car and starts to head across the street.

'She knows what she's doing,' I say, as she strides away from us in her red pencil skirt and black blouse, her shoulders back and her hair flying as she looks both ways before crossing the street. 'She's more accomplished than you give her credit for.'

'She's a college student,' Louis says, 'not Walter Cronkite.'

I let out a laugh, even though I'm not entirely sure who Walter Cronkite is or whether Louis is joking, and follow him towards the entrance to the hotel. While it may appear to be a poor relation to the Beverly Hills Hotel on the outside, inside is another story.

'Wow.' Louis's eyes are huge as we walk through a reception area clad in redwood, our footsteps ringing out as we walk across the flagstone floors. I feel as if I have stepped on to the set of *Ocean's Eleven*, and I surreptitiously pinch myself on the arm, just to double-check that this is indeed actually happening and I've not fallen asleep in front of TCM to the strains of Sammy Davis Jr singing 'Eee-O-11'. This is a completely different style of luxury compared to the Beverly Hills; something more rustic, with a hint of something wild and untamed bursting to get out. To get to the bar we have to pass the reception desk – with a small queue of patrons waiting to check in – a coffee shop and a beauty parlour, and once we lay eyes on it the bar doesn't disappoint. It's huge – much, much bigger than the tiny bar at the Polo Lounge. A beautiful, curved bar runs the length of the room, with a row of identical stools beneath it. On the walls, backlit framed photographs showcase the celebrities that have graced the casino with their presence since its opening a little over a year ago, and in the centre of the wall there is a full-sized roulette wheel.

'Lily, look at all those bottles. Just think of the cocktails I could create…' Lost in his own world Louis wanders towards the bar, running his eyes over the hundreds of bottles that sit on the back shelf.

We slide onto two of the immaculate white bar stools and wait for the bartender to serve us. The rest of the room is filled with tables surrounded by pale mauve bucket-style chairs, and maybe a third of them are occupied. It's still early for Vegas – only late afternoon – and any chatter is mild and subdued, but there is the promise of more on the air, once the sun goes down. The clanging ring of slot machines brings a thread of excitement as I cast my eyes around the room, looking for anyone who might be able to give us some information on Bess.

'Help you guys?' The bartender appears, a welcoming smile on his face. He's maybe mid-forties, with skin that is lined and tanned as if he's spent hours out in the sun, and I can imagine him sitting out on his porch with a beer, watching the sun go down.

'Just a juice for me,' I say, the memory of Louis's cocktails bright in my mind. I want to stay clear-headed while I'm here.

'I'll take a beer.'

The bartender hands over our drinks, and smiles. 'So, new faces here at the Desert Inn. Where are you guys from?'

'Los Angeles,' Louis says.

'You don't sound like you're from LA.' The bartender rakes his eyes over me, lingering slightly too long, and I feel a prickle of unease.

'No, I'm British,' I say. 'But I live in LA now.'

'Fascinating.' He picks up a glass and starts to polish it. 'So, you guys here on vacation?'

'Something like that.' Louis sips his beer, keeping his eyes on the bartender. 'We were actually hoping to run into a friend of ours. Maybe you know where we can find her?'

'Maybe. What's her name?'

'Bess. Bess Greenwood. Do you know her?'

There is a pause, pregnant with something I can't quite name, before the bartender shakes his head slowly. 'Can't say that I do. Sorry, pal.' He throws down the towel he was using to polish the glasses and moves to serve two men at the other end of the bar, one in his fifties, the other younger and almost bursting out of his suit his arms are so muscular. They both wear sharp suits and polished shoes.

'Did you get the feeling that he wasn't being quite straight with us?' I turn to Louis, my mouth feeling dusty and dry. I sip my orange juice, wincing slightly as the cold, tart juice hits my tastebuds.

'I don't know, he seemed like a nice guy. Maybe we're just reading too much into it.' Louis glances down the bar and I follow his gaze to see the older gentleman and the bartender staring at us. The gentleman raises his martini glass in a salute in our direction, his stare unwavering. I raise my juice glass in return, not sure why my stomach gives a sickening lurch.

'Actually, yeah. Maybe you're right.' Louis slides off his stool and holds out his hand. 'Maybe he wasn't being quite straight with us.'

'Perhaps the news has already hit Vegas and he didn't want to tell us that Bess is dead,' I say. 'Either way, I think we should get out of here.'

As we head out towards the pool, the light is fading but the air is still warm. The pool area is impressive – loungers surround a large figure eight swimming pool and while the sun is beginning to go down, guests are still relaxing by the water, a group of men showing off to their wives (or, more likely, girlfriends) by diving gracefully from the dive board. It's busier out here than in the bar, and I let my shoulders relax.

'Is that Judy Garland?' Louis nods his head in the direction of a petite woman in a red and white bathing suit, her dark hair perfectly curled and pinned. She sits on the edge of a lounger, drink in hand, as two men vie for her attention. She gives them an enigmatic smile, before lowering her sunglasses and reclining back.

'And over there, isn't that Frank Sinatra?' I know it's him, having seen him just two nights ago at Honey's premiere. There is still no sign of Nancy, but Ava Gardner sits beside him, a pretty but vacant smile on her face. 'Who's that guy sitting beside Ava?'

'That's Jonny Valentine.' Louis turns to me with an incredulous look as I pull a face and shrug. 'You've never heard of Jonny Valentine? He's more famous than Frank will ever be!'

My future knowledge says otherwise, but I just raise my eyebrows and shake my head. 'There's a hefty clientele here, huh? I wonder if any of these guys would have known Bess?'

'I doubt it. I mean, speaking as someone who works in this industry, I'm pretty sure that half the movie stars I've served would never recognise me again, and they certainly wouldn't know my name.'

Louis has a point, and I feel a pang of sorrow for Bess. There was no mention of family or loved ones in the newspaper article, and I wonder whether anyone is missing Bess now. *I wonder if Eric has missed me yet? Or have I only been gone for a matter of minutes?* The thought rises and I push it away.

'Lily?' Louis nudges me, and I see a waitress in a form-fitting uniform with huge buttons and a white frilled apron hurrying towards Frank and Ava with a tray of drinks. Louis steps away from me, timing it so that he crosses her path just as she delivers the drinks and turns back towards the hotel.

'Oops, I'm so sorry.' I watch as Louis smiles down at her and she grows visibly flustered. 'My wife and I were wondering if we could get a drink?' He gestures in my direction and I raise a hand.

'Of course. What can I get you?' The girl pulls out a pencil as Louis guides her towards me.

'Just juice is fine for me,' I say, peering over her shoulder. 'Wow, I knew this place was fancy but I wasn't expecting to see movie stars around the pool!' I adopt a starry-eyed expression as Louis throws me a puzzled frown.

'Oh, yeah.' The girl glances behind her towards Judy Garland, before lowering her voice. 'We see a few actors and actresses here. But we're not really supposed to talk to them.'

'Exciting though, huh?' I go on. 'You must have met some really fabulous people while working here, even if you aren't supposed to speak to them.' I smile at her. 'Have you worked here for a while?'

'A few months. Since last October.' The girl frowns.

'Mr Sinatra seemed impressed by you.' I smile as she flushes a deeper red. 'So, if you've been here since October you must know quite a few of the other girls who work here?'

'Yeah?' Suspicion dawns in her eyes and she pulls back. 'Hey, listen, I'm not into any funny business, you know? I'm just a hostess, nothing else. I know what they say happens at some of these wild parties – Hollywood people coming down here and acting all crazy – that's not for me. I'm just sayin'.'

'What? No! That's not what I'm getting at!' Aware of heads turning in my direction I lower my own voice. 'I'm looking for someone who might have known Bess Greenwood. I think she works – worked – here.'

'Bess Greenwood?' The girl shakes her head. 'I'm sorry, but I never heard that name. There's a high turnover of hostesses in places like these. There seems to be a new girl starting every week. I don't know all of the hostesses, but I know the girls who work out here and none of them are named Bess.'

'What about a convention?' Louis says. 'Did you hear anything about a convention being held here in town recently? For insurance salesmen?'

The waitress frowns and shakes her head again. 'I have no idea what you're talking about. I just serve the drinks.'

Disappointment ripples through me, but it doesn't mean we've hit a total dead end. Just because this hostess doesn't know Bess, doesn't mean she didn't work here, and it doesn't mean that any of the other hostesses don't know Bess. Seeing the gentlemen from the bar step out on to the terrace, I thank the girl and wave her away.

The older man walks over to where Frank Sinatra sits with Jonny Valentine, removing his jacket and slipping into the one vacant seat at their table. As he does, he looks up and catches my eye. I look away quickly, reaching up and putting my arms around Louis's neck.

'What…' Louis is silenced as I press my mouth against his, before pulling away slightly with a coy giggle and a sly glance towards Frank's table.

'Lily, what are you doing?' Shock makes Louis's voice rough, but there is no mistaking the spark of electricity that leaps between us.

'That guy – the one from the hotel bar. He and his friend have just come out to sit with Frank Sinatra and Jonny Valentine, and he was watching us. Just play along.'

Pausing just long enough for my heart to double skip painfully against my ribs, Louis leans down, running his hand over my hair in a way that sends shivers down my spine, before gently lifting my chin and tilting my face towards his. My breath stops in my throat and all I can hear is the pounding of my pulse in my ears as he leans in.

'Woah! You two should come with a warning.' Tilda's voice is like a bucket of cold water as I jerk back, and Louis swipes a hand over his mouth. A swift glance across the pool shows that Suit Guy is fully engaged in conversation with Jonny Valentine and is paying absolutely no attention to us at all. 'I was going to ask what I missed, but clearly I missed *everything*.'

'Tilda, stop. It's not what it looks like.' I smooth my hands over my thighs, running my damp palms over the bottom of Tilda's borrowed dress as Louis moves to an empty table by the pool and pulls out a chair for each of us. 'See that guy over there?' Tilda cranes her neck as she sits and I roll my eyes. 'Be subtle, jeez.'

'The old guy? With the tie? Got a big muscly goon standing behind him?'

'Yeah. He was at the bar when we asked about Bess, and the barman seemed a little... off. Then he was watching us when he came out to the pool.'

'So we played the part of the newlyweds, enjoying their honeymoon,' Louis chimes in.

'Big stretch, Lou,' Tilda smirks, but before I can ask what she means Louis is questioning her.

'Where the hell have you been? You just jumped out of the car in the parking lot and disappeared.'

'I didn't *disappear*, I went to *investigate*.' It's Tilda's turn to roll her eyes, and then she pulls out her pocketbook, throwing it on the table. 'I went across the street.'

'To the casino?' I had noticed a smaller casino across the street when we pulled into the parking lot of the Desert Inn, part of a cluster of stores and bars. Smaller, but gaudier, with a giant shoe atop the sign proclaiming it to be the 'Silver Slipper'.

'You guys just assumed that this place must be the biggest casino in town purely because of its size, but if you actually *look* you would have seen that the Silver Slipper is part of something even bigger than this hotel – the Last Frontier Village. You guys were set on coming in here so I thought maybe I'd just wing it and head over there to see if anyone who might have known Bess worked across the street.'

'And?' Louis asks. 'Did you find anything?'

'I did.' Tilda smiles, and flips open her notebook, pointing to a page with a scrawled note. 'Bess didn't work at the Desert Inn, although she was partial to an after-show drink here. She worked at the Silver Slipper. And she wasn't a waitress.'

Chapter Eleven

'If she wasn't a waitress, then what was she doing here in Vegas?' Louis frowns as he asks the question that rises on my own lips.

'Let's just say our Bess was leading a slightly more glamorous life than that of a waitress. Come with me.' Tilda gets to her feet. 'There's something I want you to see.'

As the night draws in and stars prickle above our heads, we make our way from the pool through the hotel and out on to the sidewalk outside. The streets are busy now, people milling about in their best clothes, their chatter and laughter carrying on the air. The night is full of fur stoles, red lipstick, and the clatter of heels on the sidewalk, the air fragranced by heavy perfume and cigarette smoke. From the hotel comes the ringing of the slots, the chink of coins dropping from the machines into cups, held out greedily by gamblers. Las Vegas is coming to life.

'Woah.' Tilda comes to an abrupt stop in the courtyard as music strikes up and the huge fountain in front of the Desert Inn erupts into life. Jets of water leap towards the sky, choreographed to the music that echoes tinnily in the night air, as hotel guests pause and gasp at the display. It's like the show at the Bellagio in my own time, only a smaller version. I smile as Tilda's eyes widen, her hand going to her mouth.

'Tilda, come on.' Louis yanks impatiently at her hand and she tears her gaze away.

'Isn't that *incredible*?' she gasps. 'How do they even do that?'

Louis tugs her away and we cross the busy street, weaving our way between the throngs of people on the sidewalk, ignoring the toot of car horns as we head for the Last Frontier Village. Tilda was right; this place is huge, far bigger than the Desert Inn. Walking in under the huge entrance sign, the Silver Slipper is on our right, neon signs lighting up the frontage. Above our heads, dancing precariously atop the Silver Slipper sign, is that giant slipper, reminiscent of something Cinderella would wear, the outside a bright metallic silver, the underside a deep red. The world's earliest Louboutin, maybe. Along-side the casino is a gun shop, the Frontier Museum, and a saloon. Music fills the air, the tones of Bing Crosby ringing out, and I feel a flash of déjà vu, remembering the way he played the piano at Honey's birthday party six months ago. The scent of cigarette smoke and hops pours from the open doors of the saloon and there is an undeniable party atmosphere as people jostle and laugh, one more suited to the festive season than late January. It's easy to see why Vegas grew into what it is in my own time, and easy to see how it all could become corrupted.

My feet slow as a poster on the exterior wall of the saloon catches my eye.

'*Desert Dancers*,' I read. 'Is this what I think it is?'

Tilda nods. 'Yep. These are the showgirls, and there…' she points a finger at a smiling girl in a feathered headdress and sequinned leotard, '…is our Bess Greenwood.'

'She was a dancer, not a waitress.' Louis peers closely at the black and white poster. 'What kind of show is this?' His cheeks pinken. 'I mean… is this something…?'

'These girls introduce the main acts at the Silver Slipper,' Tilda says. 'It's supposed to be tasteful, but I guess you could call it a burlesque show.'

So Bess really wasn't a waitress. She was a burlesque dancer. A Vegas showgirl. I realise that it makes sense now. The way the police have accepted Sonny as the culprit in her murder. She's just a burlesque dancer, and if they can put Sonny behind bars they don't need to waste police time and money on a proper investigation. The thought makes me feel sick, the way Bess has been filed away as 'solved'. It's the same in 2020, although better hidden in my time. Attitudes haven't changed towards women in decades, and the more time I spend here in the past, the more shockingly real it becomes to me, especially as it is so wildly overt here. I reach out, running my finger over Bess's face.

'Lily? Are you ready?' Louis taps my shoulder. 'Tilda found out this afternoon that the show – Bess's show – is opening for Jonny Valentine at the Silver Slipper tonight. If we hurry we can catch the start, and then perhaps we might be able to speak to some of the other dancers afterwards, see if they know anything.'

I drag my gaze away from Bess's smiling face and follow Louis and Tilda as they weave through the crowds, joining the ticket line for Jonny's show. It winds around the side of the building, moving slowly towards the ticket office and I realise Louis was right about Jonny.

'He's really popular, huh?' I crane my neck, trying to see the front of the line.

'Popular?' Tilda yelps. 'Lil, Jonny Valentine is the cream of the crop. His last three songs have all topped the Billboard charts!'

And yet, in 2020 no one has ever heard of him. I wonder what happened to make Jonny Valentine fade into obscurity, while Frank Sinatra's star went on to rise back to the top.

'Three, please.' Finally we reach the front of the line and Louis digs in his pocket for a ten dollar bill.

'Sold out,' the gravel-voiced woman behind the counter says, a lit cigarette wiggling at the corner of her mouth. Her blonde hair is piled up on top of her head, and thick make-up folds into the creases around her eyes.

'*Sold out?*' Louis's shoulders slump. 'We really need to get into this show. We were in line for over an hour.'

'Shoulda bought ahead of time.' The woman shrugs, reaching above her head to pull down the counter shutter. 'What can I say? It's Jonny Valentine. You'll have to try again tomorrow.'

We don't have time to wait until tomorrow. Every day wasted is a day closer to Sonny going to trial. A day closer to Evelyn being murdered.

'Excuse me, ma'am.' Tilda shoulders her way past Louis, pasting on a brilliant white smile. 'I don't think you realise. I'm press.'

'Press?' The woman frowns.

'Do I need to spell it out?' Tilda leans in, plucking a white card from her pocketbook. She flashes it in the woman's direction, before turning and gesturing to me and Louis. 'Louella Parsons sent me. I'm here to interview Jonny for Louella's column, and these two here, they're my assistants.'

The woman stubs her cigarette out and takes the card, running her eyes over it. I catch a glimpse of Louella's name on it in curly script as she hands it back to Tilda. 'Well, why didn't you say so before? You know press don't have to queue for tickets, although… press night was last week.'

'I was in Los Angeles interviewing Frank. *Sinatra*,' Tilda whispers, tipping her a wink. 'Thank you so much, ma'am.' She shoves the card back in her purse and we follow the woman through a side door, straight into the casino's auditorium. It feels like a Dorothy moment, when the Wizard of Oz opens the gates to the Emerald City to her, once he realises who she is.

The auditorium is darkened, a spotlight on the empty stage heralding the start of the show, when we slide into seats at a front row table at one end of the theatre. Glancing over at the other tables that line the front row, I make out Frank and Ava sitting close together, cocktails on the table before them. I had thought Ava Gardner was beautiful when I watched her in *Showboat*, curled up on the sofa with my mother not long before she died, but in the flesh she is stunning, and I have to remind myself not to gawp. No wonder Frank will leave Nancy to marry Ava next year. Also at their table, a large martini in front of him, is Dean Martin, and a blonde woman who looks vaguely familiar, a blue haze of smoke around her head from her cigarette. She pulls out a lipstick and applies it expertly without a mirror, not taking her eyes from the stage ahead of her. I know her from somewhere, but I can't think where, and the dim lighting makes it difficult for me to make out her features clearly.

Music swells to fill the auditorium, the spotlight moves, and I tear my eyes away as the dancers kick their way on to the stage. Whistles and cheers fill the air, several tables getting to their feet and clapping as the girls move across the stage. It's far more rowdy – and a lot more glitzy – than I was expecting, but the girls' smiles are fixed on their faces as they look out into the audience, their arms linked behind their backs while they kick their legs high into the air, in some semblance of the can-can.

'That's who we need to speak to.' Tilda discreetly gestures towards the stage, her voice a low murmur in my ear, as a hostess in a shorter than average skirt brings over a tray of drinks.

'One round of Atomics.' The hostess smiles, and Louis presses a coin into her hand as a tip.

'Yikes. What the hell is in this?' I take a sip, wincing at the burn of alcohol on my tongue.

'Brandy, vodka, a dash of sherry, strained then mixed with brut champagne.' Louis takes a mouthful of his own. 'Named for the testing, out in the desert.'

I had forgotten about the atomic testing carried out just outside the town, and with good reason if this is how they celebrate it. 'Who do we need to speak to, Tilda?' My eyes go back to the stage, where the girls smile rigidly at the crowd, their faces blank as the lights catch the glint of sequins on their matching mauve leotards that leave nothing to the imagination. They break formation, splitting into two lines, the girls at the front shimmying and shaking their way across the stage, making a flimsy attempt to cover their modesty with huge, mauve feathery fans.

'See that girl? Right on the end in the back row?' Tilda lifts a finger in the direction of a young woman at the end of the row. She is barely more than a girl, her auburn hair pulled tightly away from her face, her purple and silver feathered headdress bobbing as she kicks her legs into the air. 'That's Cassidy Clark. She was Bess's best friend. At least, that's what I've been told.'

I don't ask where Tilda got her information. 'She might know what Bess was doing the night she was killed. Do we even know why she was in Baker in the first place?'

'We don't, but Cassidy might.' The lights go down and the audience clap, a few wolf whistles renting the air, and then in the glare of a single spotlight, Jonny Valentine appears on stage.

Ninety minutes later, it's easy to see why Jonny has so many female fans. He is charming, entertaining and funny, with a voice to crack hearts. He dedicates a song to his 'beautiful, wonderful wife, all the way out here from Florida to watch me sing,' the spotlight resting on the blonde woman sitting beside Dean Martin as she smiles graciously and raises her martini glass. A talented showman, Jonny holds eye contact with the front row, leaning down to pass Tilda a flower that she clasps to her chest rather too tightly, but also engages those at the back, calling out to them and blowing kisses at the end of his set. What's not so easy to understand is why he will vanish into obscurity, leaving a space that Frank Sinatra will fill. The crowd is on its feet, us included, clapping until our hands are sore as the spotlight on Jonny fades.

'Come on, let's get out of here. We need to catch Cassidy before she leaves for the night.' Louis skirts around the edge of the table and I follow him and Tilda around the side of the stage, through a door that takes us into a chilly, empty corridor backstage. Passing a door with Jonny's name on, I can't help but peep in where the door stands half open, catching a glimpse of Jonny loosening his tie and accepting a glass of whisky from his wife. She smiles up at him as he frowns and takes the glass without a word, turning his back on her. As she looks away she meets my eye, stilling as she notices me in the doorway, her eyes wide. I give her a small smile before quickly moving on, feeling as though I have intruded in some way. At the end of the corridor is the girls' dressing room, muted shrieks and laughter coming from the half-open door. Stepping inside, it's a whirlwind of lipstick, feathers, sequins and tights, and I smother a grin as Louis tries to look anywhere except at the bounty of flesh on display.

'Can I help you?' A cool blonde turns as we enter, her mouth drawing into a pout as she eyes Louis. 'You looking for me?'

'Uhhh, I don't… think… so,' Louis mutters, his cheeks burning a bright, flaming red.

'Sure you are, sugar,' she smirks, reaching out to run a hand over his shoulder.

'Yeah, we're not looking for you,' Tilda says briskly. 'Unless you can tell us where we can find Cassidy Clark?'

'Cassidy?' The blonde drops the smirk and turns back to the mirror, swiping at her lipstick with a tissue. 'What do you want with her? She dances at the *back*, for Pete's sake.'

'We want to talk to her about Bess Greenwood,' I say, watching as the girl stops scrubbing at her mouth for the briefest of seconds.

'Bess? She left.' Looking down, the dancer rummages for cold cream, avoiding my eyes.

'Can you show us where Cassidy is?' Tilda asks again, her voice steely as she stares hard at the girl. The girl shakes her head and mutters something under her breath. 'Louder for the folks at the back.'

'Over there. Back of the dressing room.' The girl points, and then winks and blows Louis a kiss as we manoeuvre our way past racks of glitzy, bejewelled costumes and feathered headdresses.

'Cassidy?' Tilda stops in front of a mirror lit by bright bulbs that cast a too-white glow across the girl's face as she tugs at her false eyelashes. 'Can we talk to you?'

'Uh, sure. You want me to sign something?' Cassidy roots through the pile of make-up bottles and tubes that litter the table in front of her, looking for a pen. 'We don't get asked often, but if people can't get hold of the main act—'

I slide into the empty seat beside her, moving a ruffled, glittery gown out of the way. 'We don't want an autograph. We wanted to speak to you about Bess.'

'Bess?' Cassidy's eyes meet mine in the mirror, as she slowly swipes a tissue over her lipsticked mouth. 'She's… Bess is gone.' Her eyes grow damp and she blinks rapidly before beginning to scrub at her thick make-up with a flannel cloth.

'We know.' Tilda rests a hand on Cassidy's shoulder. 'And we're so sorry. You knew her well, didn't you?'

Cassidy shifts slightly under the weight of Tilda's hand, her eyes flicking towards the door. The other dancers are leaving and only a handful remain, sliding their feet into comfortable shoes and pulling sweaters over their heads. 'Yes, Bess was my friend.'

'We want to help,' Louis says gently. 'We want to make sure there is justice for Bess.'

'They arrested someone already,' Cassidy says quietly.

'He says he didn't do it,' I say. 'Do you know him? Do you know Sonny? If you could just tell us whether he and Bess—'

'Cassidy!' Her name floats from the open door into the corridor, and she looks at me in horror. Moments later, the suited man with the big muscles from the bar earlier appears in the doorway, peering around the rail of show clothes. 'Cass? Are you still in here? Let's go.'

'Coming! One minute!' Cassidy gets to her feet, wrapping a cardigan around her shoulders. 'Don't leave until I'm gone,' she says in hushed tones. 'I can't talk now, but meet me tomorrow morning, at eleven o'clock, out at the diner on Highway 91. Don't tell anyone else.'

Chapter Twelve

'That was the guy, wasn't it?' Louis says, his voice low. 'From the bar earlier. He was stood with the older fella. I wonder if maybe he was a bodyguard or something.'

I nod, that creeping sense of unease growing stronger. I rub my hands over my arms, goosebumps sprouting despite the warmth of the dressing room. 'It might be nothing, but it doesn't feel like a coincidence that he was over at the Desert Inn, and now he shows up here and he knows Cassidy.'

'Did either of you get the feeling she was afraid of him?' Tilda says, her voice muffled as she rifles through the show costumes, running her fingers over glitter and sparkles.

'She definitely didn't want him to know we were here.' I peer out into the corridor, checking the coast is clear. 'If he knows Cassidy then there's a chance he knew Bess too.' I wave the other two into the corridor and we make our way towards the exit. The corridor is still empty, but it's a different kind of empty. Creepy, almost, as dark shadows gather in the corners of the dressing room doorways. The overhead lights are out and there is only the faint glow of the emergency lighting as the hallway stretches out ahead of us, our footsteps echoing on the concrete walkway.

'You think Cassidy might know who this eyewitness might be that saw Sonny apparently leaving the ranch?' Louis asks.

'She might,' Tilda says. 'Fry was very reluctant to give us a name, but if it's someone Bess knew Cassidy might be able to help.'

'Shhhh.' I pull up short, gesturing for the others to stop. 'Did you hear that?'

'Hear what?' Tilda whispers.

'I thought I heard a door close.' My heart is hammering in my chest, and now in the darkened, silent corridor I second guess myself. 'As if someone just sneaked out ahead of us.'

'You think someone was still here? That they might have been listening to us?'

'I don't know. Maybe. Maybe I was imagining it. This place is creepy in the dark.' Full of doubt, I shake my head and lead us on towards the exit, glancing over my shoulder one last time as we reach the door.

'I think we should get out to Baker as soon as possible,' Louis says as we step out into the bright lights of the Last Frontier Village. Someone whoops as a slot machine chings out a celebratory tune and the sound of coins hitting cups fills the air. 'We can do the run out there tonight. It'll give us a good indication of how long it would have taken Sonny to get there and back, and if it works with his alibi.'

'The alibi of sitting in his hotel room alone, without even ordering room service,' Tilda says gloomily.

I know Sonny's alibi is useless, but I want to see the ranch where Bess was found. The police have been working on a tip that someone saw Sonny fleeing the scene, so how well will they have searched the property? They certainly don't seem to have looked at anyone else as a suspect. I want to see the place for myself, hoping that maybe I'll spot something the police haven't, given I have a more open mind about this than the county sheriff's office.

'Let's head to Baker now, if you're not too tired to drive out there, Lou?'

Louis nods, even though there are faint purple smudges beginning beneath his eyes. 'I want to get out there as soon as possible. Before other people have the same idea.'

I hadn't thought of that. Assuming Sonny is innocent, then Louis is right, there is a chance that the real culprit could return to the ranch. Not to mention the press. 'If we leave now we should have time to catch some sleep before we meet Cassidy at the diner in the morning.' Tilda and I both step off the sidewalk at the same time, but I don't see Tilda step back until it's too late.

'Lily!'

I turn, squinting as headlights dazzle me, but I'm too late and the next thing I feel is the impact of the car against my legs as it clips me.

'Oh my God. Lily! Lily, are you OK?'

Opening my eyes, I see Tilda's face hovering above me, pale and wide-eyed. 'Yeah. I think so.' My hip aches, but when I push into a sitting position it's my ankle that throbs most fiercely.

'Jeez Lil, you could have been killed.' Louis's hands are cold as he crouches beside me, pressing his fingers lightly against my skin. 'Wiggle your foot.' I oblige, screwing up my nose at the sharp pain that radiates along my ankle. 'I don't think it's broken. Sprained, though. What an asshole.'

'He didn't even stop.' Tilda tuts, as she and Louis help me up. The rose that Jonny Valentine handed Tilda lies crumpled on the sidewalk, petals crushed. 'You sure you're all right, Lily?'

'Yeah.' I nod, testing my weight on my sore ankle. 'I don't even really know what happened.'

'You stepped off the kerb and the car just appeared out of nowhere,' Tilda says, her voice shaking. 'He was going too fast and didn't even stop, just clipped you and drove away.' She tucks one hand under my arm and Louis takes the other and together they help me limp across the street, into the Desert Inn.

'Sit here.' Louis parks me on a stool at the bar and waves the bartender over. 'Brandy for the lady, please.'

It's the same guy from this afternoon, even though it's past midnight. 'Sure.' He pours a hefty double and slides it in my direction. He catches my eye for the briefest of seconds, but long enough for me to realise that he recognises us from earlier. 'Everything all right?'

'Our friend just got clipped by a car,' Tilda says. 'Do you have a first aid kit? She's going to need to strap her ankle.'

I try to wave her away, but she shoves the brandy glass into my hand and forces me to drink. I choke down a mouthful of the strong liquor, relishing the burn as it slides down my throat. 'I'm good.'

'No, you need to strap it,' Louis says, 'and I think we should probably call the police. Did you catch the licence plate? It looked like a Chevy to me.'

The bartender looks up from the undercounter of the bar, where he pulls out a first aid kit and hands it to Louis, who immediately starts to wrap my ankle. 'You're not really hurt though, right? Just a clip? To be honest, it would be a waste of your time, calling the cops.'

'The guy hit her and drove away!' Tilda hisses, outrage making her cheeks flush pink. 'Isn't that illegal here in Nevada?'

The bartender holds up his hands. 'OK lady, relax. I didn't mean it wasn't a wrong thing to do, all I meant was, this is Vegas. The cops have plenty to do every night, and they won't make you a priority. Kids drag up and down Fremont all the time – almost every night. Some of them can't drive as well as they think they can. You call the cops, they're just gonna get mad at you for wasting their time – the kid will be long gone.'

'No. Uh-uh.' Tilda shakes her head, folding her arms across her body.

'Til.' I reach out, pressing my hand against hers. The brandy has made me feel tired and a little woozy. 'Leave it. It's just a sprain, nothing serious. We don't have time to call the cops, you know that.'

'You need to rest,' Louis says. 'I'm going to see about rooms here for one night at least, maybe more. We can head out tomorrow.'

I open my mouth to protest but Tilda gives me a hard stare. 'OK. Tomorrow. And no cops.'

The bartender smiles, tipping another dose of brandy into my glass. 'On the house.'

I sip, my eyes never leaving his face. I can't help but feel that his generosity is down to the fact that I agreed not to call the police, rather than concern for my well-being. Because the car *was* a Chevy, but it was a station wagon – not the kind of car kids drag race at all.

–

'Here we are.' Louis opens the hotel room door with a flourish. 'This here is you gals, and I'll be just down the hall.'

'What?' Tilda's voice is as sharp as razorblades as she turns to Louis, open-mouthed. 'You can't leave us here alone.'

'What do you mean?'

'We can't sleep here alone, Louis. We're two girls on our own, and in case it escaped your notice, your friend was just swiped by a car.' She puts her hands on her hips and stares him down.

'I was stood in the road,' I say weakly, the booze making my head spin.

'Tilda, we can't all sleep in one room,' Louis says with a sigh. 'It's not…' he glances at me, '…proper. What would people think?'

Tilda lets out an outraged snort. 'I'll tell you what they'd think. They'd think we're in town looking for a dead girl, and we've put ourselves in danger already by stirring up a hornets' nest in asking about Bess. They'd think what kind of a man lets his sister and the girl he l—'

'Tilda!'

'It's OK.' My ankle throbs, the pain pulsing up my shin, and I just want to lie down and go to sleep. 'I don't care what anybody thinks either. Tilda's right, Lou. I think it's better if we all stay together.' Even though the thought of sleeping in the same room as him makes me go hot and cold.

With a resigned shrug, Louis sighs, stepping aside to let Tilda in, before carrying in the overnight bag she packed for us.

'I'll be your chaperone, don't worry,' she says with a sweet smile, patting him on the cheek. Honestly, sometimes I think she's a psychopath.

Stepping inside, I take in the room. It's more basic than the suites at the Beverly Hills, the décor less luxurious, but it's still pretty fancy. Twin beds sit side by side, separated only by a small bedside cabinet, and a roll-away cot is pressed against the wall beneath the short drapes. Louis takes my hand and leads me to the bed closest to the ensuite bathroom.

'Here, you can use the bathroom first,' he says. 'Tilda, you take the other bed and I'll take the cot.'

'Absolutely not,' Tilda says. 'You've been driving for hours today, and there's no way I'm taking the wheel all the way to Baker tomorrow because you're exhausted. You take the bed; I'll take the cot.'

Plucking the wash bag from the small overnight case, I limp into the bathroom, closing the door firmly as they argue it out. The day has been long and tiring and my ankle throbs, despite the strapping. Closing my eyes, I picture the glare of headlights, the roar of the engine as my heart rate triples at the realisation that I don't have time to get back onto the sidewalk before the car will hit me. *There was no other car.* As I unwrap a new toothbrush, I feel nauseous. *There was no other car on the road, so how could it have been kids drag racing?* Briskly I brush my teeth and rinse my mouth out with water, my stomach rolling. *I don't think it was an accident.* Things happened so quickly that I couldn't testify to it, but I think at the last moment the car swerved *towards* me, not away from me. I think that this might have been a warning.

–

Who knows if it's the throbbing of my sore ankle or the close proximity to Louis that keeps me from sleeping, but what I do know is that I have tossed and turned all night. Tilda won her argument and Louis sleeps soundly in the twin bed beside mine, his breathing soft and regular. I won't lie, I had thought about what it would have been like to spend the night beside Louis when I went back to my own time, but I never dreamed about it being like this. At least, I never fantasised about having a fat, swollen ankle and his sister sleeping on the cot on the other side of us. His eyelashes flutter on his cheeks as he dreams and I have to resist the urge to reach out and touch his hair. The moment he crouched beside me after the car struck me had almost felt like before, as though he had forgotten just for a moment to be angry with me, and I wonder exactly what it will take for him to forgive me. I know I should have tried to explain things to him before I left, but what could I tell him? And if I'm honest, I'd been half hoping it wouldn't work, that I wouldn't be able to return to 2019. Rolling over, I punch the pillow into shape and close my eyes, regret and worry making my brain itch.

I doze on and off, seeing the first pink fingers of dawn pressing against the curtains after a particularly fierce dream that wakes me with a gasp, before I am pulled under again. When I wake for the last time, the room is filled with bright sunshine, the curtains wide open.

'Hey.'

The whisper comes from Louis, who is lying facing me, his hair rumpled, one hand tucked under his cheek. Despite the bedside cabinet between us I could still reach out and touch him.

'Hey. How did you sleep?'

Louis's eyes run over my face, and I swallow, hoping I don't have rotten morning breath. 'A little. Not well.' His gaze dips to where the blanket has slipped, showing the tiniest glimpse of skin across my chest. I tug it up, flushing hot.

'I kept seeing the car... the way you fell.' Louis keeps his eyes on me, and I shift slightly, aware of the fact that apart from the bedside cabinet, only a blanket and Tilda's flimsy nightgown separates me from him. 'I could have lost you, Lil. You could have died if that car had been any further over. I don't know what I...' He reaches out, hooking a finger under a curl that lies across my forehead, gently moving it back into place, before he seems to realise what he's doing and pulls back. 'Thank God you're OK, that's all. Did you sleep well? You seemed restless.'

I *could have lost you, Lil.* I, *not* we. Trying not to read too much into things, I give a non-committal hum, not wanting to talk about the horrors that plagued my dreams. 'Just my ankle playing up.'

'You guys aren't up yet? I figured the sunshine would get you out of bed.' The door crashes open and Tilda stands there, juggling three cups of coffee in her hands. 'Lou, give me a hand, would ya?'

'You're a terrible chaperone, but I'll forgive you if that coffee is still hot.' Louis slides out of bed and I take the opportunity to slip into the bathroom and hastily scrub at my teeth, wash my face, and put my clothes on. Stepping back into the room, Tilda looks up and smiles brightly, and I sense – not for the first time – the unmistakeable feeling that they have been talking about me.

'Get this down you and then we need to hotfoot it out of town.' Tilda passes me a cup of lukewarm coffee. It tastes like dirt and leaves grit in my mouth, but I slug it back anyway.

'Shit! It's ten thirty. I didn't realise it was so late.'

'We've missed your potty mouth, Lil,' Louis smirks, as he tosses the car keys into the air and swings the hotel room door open. Tutting, I roll my eyes and follow him out to the car, trying not to limp too heavily as my veins fill with a warm fuzzy feeling. Maybe Louis is coming around, just a little.

Twenty minutes later, we roll to a stop outside a dusty-looking diner, just off the highway. A couple of trucks are parked up in the parking lot – if you can call it that. It's more a patch of earth outside the diner, dustier and more worn than the surrounding area. The diner itself has seen better days. The sign that spins lazily outside boasts 'Best Burgers in Nevada' in red and yellow paint, cracked and peeling as if blowtorched by the sun, and the glass in the window at the far side is spider-webbed, a criss-cross of duct tape holding it in place.

'This is it? You're sure?' Tilda squints as she steps out of the car, desert wind sending her skirt flying.

'Cassidy said the diner out on Highway 91.' I glance down at the map, before shoving it into the glove compartment and getting out of the car. 'This is Highway 91, and we didn't pass anything else on the way out here.'

'This is definitely the place.' Louis gestures to the grimy window, and peering in, I see the dancer sitting at a table alone, staring blankly at a menu, a single coffee cup beside her.

Cassidy looks up as we enter, the bell above the door heralding our arrival over a jukebox playing an old Vaughn Monroe song. 'You came.' Her voice is flat, her face pale, and as she pushes her hair back I see the dark smudge of a bruise on her wrist.

'Of course we did.' I ease myself into the booth opposite her, wincing as my foot hits the table leg. 'Sorry for accosting you in your dressing room last night, but we really wanted to speak to you about Bess.'

'What happened to your foot?' Cassidy stares at me boldly as I shift, trying to get comfortable.

'Nothing. Just a sprain.'

If looks could kill, Tilda would have me splattered all over the diner. 'She got hit by a car, leaving the casino last night. Bartender said it was kids drag racing, but… I don't think so somehow.'

The remains of any colour drains from Cassidy's face. 'Anybody know you're talking to me?'

'Uh, no,' Louis says. 'We haven't told anyone we're here.'

'How do I know I can trust you?'

'Our friend…' Tilda says quietly, '…it's her boyfriend who has been arrested for Bess's murder.'

Cassidy pulls back, eyes wide with shock.

'No, wait,' Tilda says, reaching out to clasp Cassidy's hand. 'He didn't do it… at least we don't think he did. We want to find out who is responsible for hurting Bess just as much as you do.'

After a long pause, Cassidy gestures to the waitress to bring a pot of coffee and then leans in, lowering her voice. 'I'll tell you everything I know, but you might not want to stay in Vegas once I've finished.'

Chapter Thirteen

'What was Bess like?' Tilda asks gently.

Cassidy smiles, her face lighting up. 'Oh, she was beautiful. Funny. Smart. She always had a quick comeback if someone snarked her. People tried to get the best of her, but Bess always got the last word.'

'Was there anyone in particular that she liked to get the last word with?'

'Daisy. Daisy always had something to say to her.' Cassidy looks up and meets my eyes. 'Daisy is the first dancer – front row and centre every night. Bess was better than her; Bess should have been the one dancing in that spot and both of them knew it. Daisy told Bess that she was going to be the next Lili St Cyr, and Bess laughed in her face. She told Daisy that if she wanted to be like Lili she needs to learn how to loosen up a little and maybe do something about her saggy bosom.' Cassidy gives a short laugh, before her face drops.

'Did they argue a lot?' I ask, wondering if Daisy is the blonde dancer with the saucy attitude.

Cassidy shrugs. 'A little. I never really thought much about it until…'

'Until?' I prompt her.

'That last day.' Cassidy blinks and a tear sticks to her spiky mascara-ed lashes. 'They had a terrible fight that last day. Bess came back to our apartment and she was furious, saying that she was done with Daisy… Daisy said she was going to find a way to see the back of Bess for good.'

Tilda's eyes meet mine and I pause for a moment, wondering what Daisy and Bess could have fought about so bitterly. 'Why would Daisy say that?'

Cassidy shrugs. 'I don't know, Bess didn't say. Daisy was the least of Bess's problems.'

'What do you mean?'

'I don't know much about what Bess was up to, but she wasn't just a dancer. Bess wasn't the girl I thought she was.'

Tilda has been scribbling wildly on her notepad and now she licks the tip of her pencil as I lean in closer, afraid I'll miss something, Cassidy's voice is so quiet.

'You knew Bess well, didn't you?'

Cassidy nods, plucking a napkin from the dispenser on the table. She glances over my shoulder, as the bell over the door rings signalling another customer, and when it's no one she knows she turns her gaze back to me. 'I thought I did. We both ended up in Vegas around the same time. Bess went to California originally – she'd met a man who told her he could put her in the movies, only it wasn't the kind of movies she wanted to star in, if you know what I mean. Bess wasn't a prude, not by any means, but she wouldn't do anything that could come back to haunt her.' The diner falls silent as the jukebox switches record, the mechanism whirring. 'Well, until now.'

'How did you end up out here?' Tilda asks. There is a messy scrawl across the page of her notebook that I assume must be shorthand, because it's completely indecipherable to me.

'The usual.' Cassidy shrugs, looking even younger than she appeared on stage last night. 'I hopped on a train out of town and ended up here, but it could have been anywhere, I wouldn't have cared.'

'How did you meet Bess?'

'In a launderette,' Cassidy smiles at the memory. 'She didn't have the right change. I gave her a quarter.'

'And then you ended up dancing at the Silver Slipper together? How did that happen?' I watch as Cassidy shreds the napkin, reaching to pull out another, the pile of white tissue in front of her growing ever bigger.

'A girl Bess knew told her about the audition, and she asked if I wanted to go along with her. Obviously we both got the job – the Silver Slipper are always looking for hostesses and dancers – and we got along so well that Bess asked me if I wanted to move into her apartment with her. That was a little over a year ago.'

Louis sits back, frowning. 'That's not it though, is it? You said Bess wasn't the girl you thought she was?'

Cassidy looks up at him, her face pale. There are dark shadows under her eyes, and I get the impression that I am not the only one who didn't sleep well last night. 'Bess changed. The last couple of months.'

'Changed how?'

Cassidy shifts in her seat, her eyes going to the door again. A lone car drives past, kicking up dust as it goes, and I almost expect a tumbleweed to roll by the window. Despite the empty highway and the new record that has slotted into place on the jukebox covering our conversation, Cassidy is still rigid in her seat, her shoulders tight, her voice cracking. 'Bess was a good girl really. She might have been sassy and smart with her mouth, but she was good. I just want to make that clear. No one seems to realise that. Did you know they've replaced her on stage already?' She sniffs. 'I got there last night and there was another girl putting Bess's costume on. It's like no one is bothered by her death, no one has even noticed that she isn't there, and now you're saying they might have arrested the wrong fella?'

'That's why we're here,' Louis says, firmly. 'To find out what happened to Bess and who is responsible.'

Cassidy gives a slow nod. 'Bess was shrewd. In the beginning she seemed happy enough but after a while… dancing was never going to be enough for her. She loved working at the Silver Slipper, but she loved the other things more. She was never going to be just a dancer, that's why Daisy's jealousy was so ridiculous.'

'Other things?' Tilda frowns, catching my eye.

'After the shows, we would quite often head across the road to the Desert Inn. There are always men at the bar who've been to the show, or they're in town without their wives. They're usually more than happy to buy the dancers a few drinks, spot them a few cigarettes. Before, Bess would always leave when I left and we'd get the bus back to the apartment together, sit up for hours talking about the men we'd met, but just lately…'

'Lately?' I prompt when she falls silent.

'Lately she wasn't leaving. Very often when I wanted to leave she would be nowhere to be found. The first time I thought maybe she'd gone on back to the apartment without me.' She pauses for a moment, as if not sure she should go on. 'She… she liked the attention of the men, and who could blame her? She was beautiful. Before, it all seemed innocent – some drinks, dancing, a little flirting, but the last few months…' Cassidy breaks off and swills down the now cold coffee in front of her. 'She wasn't coming back until the early hours of the morning, some-times not at all – that's why I wasn't too worried initially when she didn't come home that night. Bess had more money too, and when I asked her about it I couldn't get a straight answer. She just said that she knew something that changed everything. Something that could set her up for life.'

'Yikes.' Tilda sits back against the booth, flapping her hand. Her pencil is worn to a thin slant of lead and her notebook is filled with her sprawling handwriting.

'What do you think she was involved in?' I ask, as Cassidy swipes beneath her eyes with the one napkin she hasn't shredded, the tissue coming away black with mascara.

She shrugs. 'I have no idea. I barely saw her the last couple of weeks, except for during the shows. She was home long after I went to bed most nights.'

'Do you think she could have been seeing someone?' Louis asks, echoing my own thoughts.

'I think so.' Cassidy gives a slow nod. 'She definitely had a lot more cash, and why else would she stay out all night?' She gives a coy glance towards Louis. 'Both of us had stayed out once or twice, but never regularly.'

'Did she know a guy called Sonny? An insurance salesman?' Even as I ask, I think I know the answer.

'I don't think Bess ever mentioned anyone by that name.'

'What about Baker?' Tilda asks. 'Did Bess ever mention anything about going out to a ranch in Baker?'

'The place where she was found?' Cassidy pauses, pushing her empty coffee mug away. 'No, I'm sorry. She never mentioned Baker or a ranch.'

'And you haven't heard any talk about an eyewitness who saw Sonny leaving the ranch that night? I'm sorry if this is upsetting for you, Cassidy, but we have to ask you these questions,' I say, as Cassidy swallows, her eyes wide.

'I'm sorry, I've told you everything I know.' She fumbles for her bag as she gets to her feet, stumbling in her haste to leave the booth. 'I have to go. I shouldn't be here.'

Cassidy leaves, climbing into an old beat-up car parked around the back of the diner. I think I see a man behind the wheel as she peels away in a cloud of orange dust, but it's hard to tell. Once she's gone, I gesture to the waitress to bring us a fresh pot of coffee and turn to Tilda and Louis.

'So, what do we think?'

'Bess was definitely mixed up in something she shouldn't have been,' Louis says. 'Whether that was a relationship with a married man, or something more sinister.'

'And she definitely wanted to keep Cassidy out of it – maybe to protect her?' Tilda chimes in. 'Why else would she be so secretive?'

'I guess that depends exactly what it was that Bess Greenwood was involved in.'

'It would be helpful to try and speak to this other dancer, Daisy, about her fight with Bess,' Louis says. 'Could she be behind Bess's death? After all, Cassidy said Daisy told Bess she would make sure they'd seen the last of her.'

'There might be other dancers who witnessed the fight, depending on where it took place. And if it took place at the Desert Inn then maybe someone there saw something.' I think about the two men from the bar, in particular the thuggish-looking one who called out to Cassidy. He didn't seem terribly approachable. 'I'm not sure that all of the clientele at the Desert Inn will be forthcoming about knowing Bess, if there's any truth to what Cassidy told us.'

'I wonder if Jonny Valentine knew Bess.' Tilda looks up from her notepad. 'If he's playing at the Silver Slipper every night, and possibly staying at the Desert Inn – given that we've seen him there already – then there's a chance he might know Bess, by sight at least.'

I scrub my hands over my face, already feeling weary. My ankle throbs and my temples pulse in sympathy. This whole thing is a huge mess, and I can only hope that we can prove Sonny's innocence at the end of it. I dread to think how Evelyn will react if the answers we find aren't the ones she's looking for.

Chapter Fourteen

A group of twittering fans surround Frank and Ava as they leave the Desert Inn later that evening, Frank's famous blue eyes shining as he takes pen after pen, scrawling his signature on various items.

'I don't get it,' Tilda sighs. 'Jonny is far more charismatic. If it wasn't for all these rumours flying around about him and Ava I think most people would have forgotten all about Frank.'

I bite back a smile as Louis brings the car around, avoiding the crowds, and I slip into the passenger seat, Tilda sliding in behind me as music starts up and the Desert Inn fountains spring into life once more.

There is a chill to the night air, the clear sky overhead dotted with stars, and as we head back onto the highway the bright lights of Las Vegas fade into the distance, leaving only the glow of the headlights ahead of us.

'There's nothing out here,' Tilda marvels as she stares out of the window into the inky darkness beyond. The car headlights pick out the scrubby, dusty shrubs that line the highway, but now the neon glitz of Vegas has been left far behind in the distance, we can't even see the line of the mountain range that sits behind the town. 'Kinda creepy, huh?'

I can well imagine this highway being the perfect hunting ground for serial killers. We haven't passed a single car since we left Las Vegas, and now, as we cross the state border into a town literally named 'State Line', there is still a marked absence of human occupation. A gas station sits on the side of the highway, its pumps closed and the store dark.

'Anyone else getting serial killer vibes?' I say, as we pass the gas station and head on into the darkness. 'It wouldn't surprise me to find a ton of bodies buried out in this desert.'

'Jeez, Lily, what a thing to say.' Louis pulls a face.

'Sorry. It's just… this whole area has a big *Texas Chainsaw Massacre* vibe. I'm half expecting a hitchhiker to flag us down just so they can chop us into tiny pieces.'

'A chainsaw massacre? In Texas?' Tilda claps a hand over her mouth, her eyes wide. 'When did this happen, Lily? Oh *no*, did you see that written on one of your pages? Is there going to be an actual *massacre*?' She looks like she might be sick.

Oh, hell. 'No! No massacre. I swear. I just meant… this place is desolate. Anything could happen. No one would be around to hear a thing.'

Reassured that no one is about to be sliced up with a chainsaw, Tilda sits back in her seat, and I clamp my mouth shut until a sign up ahead announces BAKER POP. 273.

'This is it. This is the town.' I reach for the map, angling it towards the puddle of moonlight that seeps in through the window. 'There should be a turning, just off the highway a little further along.' Wishing I had my phone with its bright torch and, more importantly, Google Maps, I squint at the map, my eyes straining in the dim light.

'There!' Tilda points to a shadowy opening on the left and Louis swings the car in, tyres crunching. The dry lane, flanked by the same scratchy thin shrubs that dot the desert landscape beside the highway, serves as a driveway to the ranch that sits ahead of us. There are no other houses and as we pull up outside a chill works its way down my spine. It's so isolated, and I know if I were Bess I wouldn't have felt comfortable staying here alone. I rub my hands over my arms, feeling as though I am missing something.

'Maybe pull in over there.' I gesture towards the side of the house, where a garage is attached. Beside the garage is a small nest of trees with thin trunks but a vast expanse of leafy branches that presumably throw out shade during the day. By night, they will stop the reflection of moonlight on the car perfectly. The trees snake their way away from the house, marking the boundary to a thin dusty track on the other side that presumably leads to the back of the ranch land.

Stepping out, I run my eyes over the house where Bess's body was found. At the front there is a paved area, with a circle of grass in the centre, an American flag flying proudly from the middle of it. There is another patch of grass to the right of the house, and four leafy bushes sit in front of the porch. The greenery does something to dispel the dry, dusty surroundings, tricking the dweller into thinking they are somewhere more country than desert. The house itself is grand, even by twenty-first century standards. A wraparound porch with a sloping green roof hugs the house, which is a rich red timber, the roof of the top storey a matching green, giving the impression of forests and life. A large arched window sits above the front door, and I wonder if Bess looked out on her killer as they travelled up the drive, their headlights dazzling her.

'Lily? We should see if there's a way in.' Tilda's voice breaks into my thoughts and I nod, stepping up onto the porch. Despite the horror that occurred inside the house, the porch feels cosy, a swing seat at one end holding a soft-looking mohair blanket.

'There's no crime scene tape,' I say, walking up to the thick, solid wood front door.

'No what?' Tilda frowns, as she cups her hands and peers in through one of the front windows.

'No police tape, no barriers.' I mimic her, pressing my face against the small pane of stained glass in the front door. The hallway is dark, no signs of life. 'Nothing to stop anyone from coming in and looking around.' As I speak there is the tinkle of breaking glass from the rear of the house.

'Shit! What was that? Where's Louis?' My pulse triples, my breath coming fast as all kinds of things run through my mind. *Raccoons. Texas Chainsaw Massacre. Bess's killer.*

'Language, Lily.' Louis appears at the edge of the porch, grinning and slightly breathless, his hair falling over his forehead. 'I've found a way in.'

Louis has wrapped his hand in his shirt and smashed a small pane of glass by the rear doors of the house. *Louis. The guy who flinches if I curse.*

'Wow. You really did find a way in. *To jail*,' Tilda says with a quirk of her eyebrows.

'We need to get inside,' Louis says, a little sheepishly. 'I checked under the pots but there was no key, and then I saw it was in the lock of the back door so...' He shrugs, then slips his hand through the broken pane, reaches in, and unlocks the door.

'I hate to say it,' I whisper to Tilda as Louis steps into the kitchen, 'but Lawbreaker Louis is kinda hot.'

'Please,' Tilda rolls her eyes. 'You think that's bad? I've got plenty worse than that up my sleeve.'

I smirk and follow her inside as Louis flicks on a flashlight he found in the trunk of his car, scanning the kitchen. 'Couldn't we turn on some lights? It's not like there are any neighbours to see us.'

Again I feel a flicker of uncertainty, a sensation that I am missing something as Tilda switches on the kitchen light and I take in the scene. The countertops are clear, apart from two brandy glasses that sit side by side on a draining board, a tiny smudge of lipstick on the edge of one. Opening the fridge, I see a block of butter, some milk that smells a little dubious, and a bottle of champagne.

'Well, she wasn't planning on staying long,' Tilda says, as she peers over my shoulder. 'You think she met a man here?'

'Maybe, after what Cassidy told us.' Closing the fridge, I move to the cupboards, opening them one by one to reveal plates and glasses in the cupboards above the sink, and cleaning products and a box of Rat-Away in the ones below. Tilda opens the bin, peering in with a grimace.

'She ate here,' she says. 'There's an empty strawberry punnet and what looks like a cheese rind. And this.' She pulls out an empty brandy bottle. 'It all says romantic to me.'

I wander into the living area, where Louis is surveying the room. Cushions on the sofa have indents in them, as if someone has slouched against them, and there are cold ashes in the stone fireplace. *Champagne, brandy, a fire, strawberries.*

'Did you look upstairs?'

Louis shakes his head. 'Not yet. It looks kind of… peaceful in here though. Evelyn said she was found at the ranch, but she didn't say where. It doesn't look as if there has been a struggle, not in this room at least.'

He's right. The room looks as though it has been used, but there is nothing broken, nothing out of place, no sign that there might have been a struggle. Louis heads for the stairs and as I step forward to follow him, something glints beneath the sofa. Curious, I get on my knees and grope in the tiny gap between the sofa and the hardwood floor, closing my fingers around something cylindrical.

It's a lipstick, presumably belonging to Bess. Removing the cap, I twist it up, a faint, waxy scent rising. It's a bright orange red, the same colour that stains the rim of the brandy glass in the kitchen, and with Bess's dark hair it would have looked striking on her. I imagine her applying it, sipping brandy as she waited for her lover to arrive, and slip it into my pocket before hurrying after Louis.

The staircase brings to mind Tara in *Gone with the Wind*. Polished wood, the stairs are wide and spiral up to a huge hexagonal landing. Large arched windows sit at the front and back of the house, the front looking out on to the winding driveway, the rear looking out over the land at the back of the property. I pass the master bedroom, the room immaculately presented with no sign of anyone staying in it, to stand at the rear window and look over the land below. Peering out, I see a vast lawned area, the treeline to the left shielding it from the road and any prying eyes. At the far end of the garden, almost obscured by the trees, moonlight reflects off the tin roof of what could be a barn.

'Lil?' Louis calls to me from one of the rooms that branch off from the main landing. 'Come and look at this.'

The bedroom Louis and Tilda stand in has clearly been used; the pristine white covers of the bed are mussed, the pillows squashed, and I wonder if Bess was found here, her body splayed out across the downy bedspread. The thought makes it difficult to draw a breath.

'It still doesn't look as if there was a struggle though,' Tilda says as she enters the room behind us. The lamp on the nightshade is upright, and the sheepskin rug beside the bed is perfectly lined up. 'I think whoever Bess met here… she knew them.'

'Either that or she wasn't expecting them, and they caught her while she was sleeping.' But even as I say it, my thumb rubbing over the cap of the lipstick in my pocket, it doesn't feel right. Even if Bess was sleeping when the killer arrived, surely she would have put up some kind of fight when she realised what was happening.

'I really hope Cassidy was telling the truth when she said Bess didn't know Sonny.' Tilda's voice is solemn and my stomach gives a lurch. Just because Cassidy had never heard Bess mention Sonny, it doesn't mean she didn't know him.

'There's no indication that anyone even lives here,' Louis says, as he turns from the empty wardrobe. The doors are open wide and the empty hangers jangle as he closes them. 'No food in the fridge, empty wardrobes…'

'It could be a second home,' I say, 'or a rental.'

Louis's eyebrows raise at the mention of a second home and I wonder if I've put my foot in it again. Do people have second homes in the 1950s? Rich people must do. Skimming over it, I peer under the bed, but there aren't even any dust bunnies.

'You hear that?' Tilda stands stock-still, her head cocked towards the window. 'Louis. Turn out the light.'

As Louis snaps off the bedroom lamp, I hear it. The sound of tyres on the gritty, sandy track that leads to the ranch. I throw a panicked look at Louis as the sweep of headlights fills the room, followed shortly after by the sound of a car door slamming, and footsteps crunching their way up to the porch.

'Oh hell.' My ribs feel as if I am being squeezed in a vice, my breath short and shallow in my ears. 'They're coming inside.' There is the sound of the front door opening, a swish as it is pushed closed, followed by the murmur of voices. 'What are we going to do?' I hiss, my voice a frantic whisper.

'This way.' Louis grabs my arm, pulling me towards the empty wardrobes. 'Tilda, come on.'

'Hello?' The word is gruff, spiky, carrying up the timber staircase to the upper rooms. 'We know you're here. Best thing you can do is come out before it's too late.'

Louis pushes me into the cramped space, my body pressed against the back wall of the closet to make room for Tilda.

There is a creak, the sound of a boot being placed deliberately at the foot of the stairs. 'We saw the lights on. Best to come out now.' I hear a click, and my heart goes cold. I've only ever heard that sound in movies – the click of the safety being removed on a gun.

'Tilda, *now*!' Louis hisses, his grip on her tightening. 'Get in the closet – he has a gun, for Pete's sake! I'll go down there and speak to them, explain it away somehow.'

But the footsteps have reached the top of the staircase and Tilda doesn't have time to reach the closet without being seen. Instead, she twists away, throwing me a panicky glance before she falls to her knees and pushes her way under the bed. As Louis tucks himself into the closet beside me, a shadow falls across the bedroom door and my heart leaps into my throat, strangling me as I see it. Bright red against the cream rug and wildly visible to anyone who steps into the room. Tilda's skirt, puddling out from beneath the bed frame.

Chapter Fifteen

'Tilda!' Louis's voice is a strangled whisper as we hear the tap of footsteps on the parquet floor of the bedroom. He twists, jabbing an elbow into my ribs, causing me to wheeze.

'Bloody hell, Louis. Keep still.' I grab him, pressing my hand over his mouth. 'And keep quiet. We have to stay silent. They're *right there*.'

Louis stops wriggling, his breath hot against my palm. My heart pounding, I slowly draw my hand away and allow him to tuck his arm around my waist. The closet is smaller than it looks, and my body is pressed against the length of his.

There is the clunk of footsteps as someone walks across the bedroom. Two people, by the sound of it, both equally heavy-footed and neither of them bothered about being heard. A faint chink of light comes from the hall, and I shift round inside the closet to see through the crack in the door.

'There ain't nobody in here, Ralph.' The voice is deep, the sound of smoky whisky and rough hands as the bedroom light goes on. 'I told ya, nobody would dare come out here.'

'Can it, Rocky.' The second voice is higher, laced with spite and something bitter. The voice of a chihuahua. 'The lights are on downstairs, dimwit. Someone's been here.' A pause. 'Come out, come out wherever you are. We won't hurt ya.'

The snort that erupts from the first voice – Rocky – tells me this isn't true. I can still see the corner of Tilda's skirt peeping out from under the bed, and I pray that they leave without checking further. Prayers that are shattered when the men move deeper into the room.

'What's happening?' Louis's voice is a breath in my ear, and I hold up a hand before pressing my finger to my lips.

The silence that fills the room is deafening, and my nerves scream as a shadow moves across the slight gap in the closet door, blocking my sight for a moment. My chest tightens and I battle the urge to close my eyes as one of the men moves to the other side of the room. And then it happens. The inevitable. He looks down at the rug, and the red fabric that puddles there. A strangled shriek erupts as he leans down and deftly yanks Tilda out from under the bed.

'I told you.' Both men come into my line of sight as Tilda gets to her feet, dishevelled and panting, her face a sickly cream. One of the men is significantly larger than the other – Rocky, with the smoky whisky voice – but it's all muscle. Think Dwayne Johnson, but with that hideous duck's ass haircut and two-tone brogues. His suit strains around his biceps, and he holds a gun, keeping it trained on Tilda. The other man is small and wiry – Ralph, with the chihuahua voice – his hair a jet black, with a matching wispy moustache. His suit fits him perfectly, and he wears an overpowering amount of aftershave.

'Don't shoot, fellas.' Tilda's voice is low, thick with the threat of tears. 'Please. You don't need to shoot me.' Shifting slightly, aware of my thigh pressing against Louis's, I inch the closet door open a crack and peer out.

Tilda stands by the small vanity table beside the bed, her hands in the air.

'It's just me. I'm alone.' She tosses her fiery red hair back, as Ralph steps forward and grabs her roughly by the arm, making her gasp in fear or pain, I'm not sure which.

'It's him,' I whisper to Louis, pulling back so he can peep out at Rocky with the big muscles. 'The bodyguard guy from the bar. The one who came to the dressing room to fetch Cassidy.'

Rocky gives Tilda a lingering once-over and I realise that an extra button has popped open on her blouse. Yikes.

'Keep your hands up. You're lucky ol' Rocky doesn't shoot you right now,' Ralph says, tightening his grip. *I can't believe this muscled goon is really named Rocky – talk about clichéd*. If a gun wasn't pointed at Tilda's head I would have laughed.

'Rocky? You wouldn't… would you?' Tilda's voice trembles and Rocky stares at her, his hand steady. 'You wouldn't shoot a gal like me, surely? And a guest here, too.' She looks up at him from beneath her eyelashes, her hands still in the air.

'A guest?' Rocky looks at his sidekick, who shakes his head.

'Lady, we weren't born yesterday.' Ralph throws a glance in Rocky's direction, as if perhaps not too sure on that. 'Ain't nobody meant to be out here.'

'How did you even know I was here?' Tilda blinks up at him, her eyes wide.

Rocky's eyes go to the open button on her shirt, before he drags them reluctantly back to her face. 'We got people keeping an eye on the place.'

'And no one told you I was staying here? That's too bad.' Tilda gingerly lowers her hands, keeping her eyes on

Rocky and the oily black pistol he holds. 'I was just about to get ready for bed.'

Rocky smirks, and Ralph pulls her roughly towards him, knocking her breath from her body. I can see cuts and grazes over his knuckles, as if he's recently hit something. Or someone. 'Cut the crap, lady. I know you're lying. You were hiding under the bed, for Pete's sake. Rocky, just do it.'

'Do what?'

'Shoot her. Jeez, what did you think I meant?'

'But maybe Mr Z knows her. She could be telling the truth,' Rocky says, gesturing to Tilda to raise her hands again as he keeps the gun steady. I let out a breath, as Louis whispers, 'Can you see her? What's going on?'

'Tilda's talking to them.' I press my face against the crack in the door again. I don't dare tell Louis they're holding her at gunpoint. Tilda has her hands back in the air, her teeth biting down on her lower lip as she fights to stay calm.

'I've seen her at the Slipper, so she could know Mr Z,' Rocky says, his voice low, but not low enough.

'Nah. I don't buy it,' Ralph says. Tilda winces as he grabs her jaw and inspects her face closely. He is only just Tilda's height, but there is something sinister and intimidating about the way he looks her over, as if wondering how long it would take to dig her grave. 'I'd know if someone was meant to be here.' He gestures to Rocky, who steps forward and smoothly presses the gun to Tilda's forehead. I clap my hands over my mouth, as a strangled moan threatens to emerge. *Have I ruined everything? Instead of saving Evelyn, have I just got Tilda killed?*

'Oh my God.' Louis nudges me aside, pressing his face to the gap. 'I have to get out of here.' He struggles to pull his arm from around my waist, but I hold on to him tightly. 'Lily, let me go,' he hisses. 'That's my *sister*.'

'*Wait*,' I hiss back. Him bursting out of a closet is only going to get Tilda shot even quicker. 'Just wait one minute.'

'Fellas,' Tilda's voice shakes, but is still considerably more stable than mine would be if I was the one with a gun pointed at my head. 'You got me, OK? I'm not meant to be here.'

'I knew it.' Ralph lets out a bark of laughter, his hand dropping from her face and going to his waistband. He pulls his jacket back, revealing another gun sitting snugly on his hip. 'You must be really looking for trouble. Do you know who owns this joint?'

'No,' Tilda whispers, 'but you could tell me, if you wanted?'

Rocky smirks and just for a moment, the gun wavers. I see Tilda's shoulders rise as she draws in a deep breath, the slight tremble of her knees giving away the fact that she's not feeling as confident as she appears.

'Listen, I'm going to be honest with you, but first I really need you to put the gun down. Please?'

Ralph looks at Rocky, then at Tilda, and gives a short nod. 'One step outta line and you're going in the trunk. Got it? You wouldn't be the first one in there, if you get what I mean.'

Tilda exhales and nods, swiping her palms over her skirt. 'I'm a reporter,' she says. She points at the pock-etbook by her feet and Rocky leans in and picks it up, pulling out her stubby pencil and notebook. He hands it to Ralph who flicks through it, screwing his nose up at the scrawled pages. 'At least, I'm trying to be. I'm a trainee. I heard about Bess Greenwood, and I wanted to get the story.' She pauses, giving Rocky a coy glance. 'I knew no one would let me in here, so I thought I'd break in and see where Bess was found.'

Ralph looks at her askance. 'You're sick, you know that? Wanting to see where a dead body was found?' Judging by the gun on his hip and the cuts on his hands, Ralph looks like he's seen his fair share of violence in his time, and there is the faintest hint of admiration in his tone.

'I'll admit it's a little... voyeuristic, but I thought if I could get the jump on this story, then maybe I might start going places. My boss doesn't have any faith in me, and I guess I was hoping this might be my big break.' Tilda blinks and a fat tear rolls down one cheek. 'And now all I have to show for tonight is making you guys mad at me.'

'God, don't cry. I hate it when broads cry.' Ralph hands her a handkerchief.

'Thank you.' Tilda sniffs and dabs at her eyes. Ralph glances at Rocky, who raises the gun back to Tilda's forehead. Her eyes narrow and the tears miraculously dry up. 'So anyway, the point I was making... I'm a reporter. My editor at the newspaper knows I'm out here, looking into this story.'

'Good for him.' Ralph flicks his fingers in Rocky's direction and the goon steps closer to Tilda.

Tilda's eyes flick towards the closet as she takes a matching step back. 'You boys might want to reconsider shooting me is all I'm saying. People know I'm here. When I don't go back to my office to call in my story later tonight they'll raise the alarm. Call the police. And then not only will the newspaper be digging into the story of Bess Greenwood, but they'll be looking into my disappearance too. After all, it's easy to explain away one dead woman being found in this house… but rather more difficult to explain away two, don't you think?'

Rocky wavers, the gun in his hand lowering slightly as Ralph frowns. 'That's the line you're taking? You think we couldn't get away with it if we offed you?'

'I'm just suggesting…' Tilda's eyes never Ralph's face as my heart threatens to burst out of my chest. I don't know what she's doing, but I am praying with all my might that it works. '…that perhaps we could come to an agreement.'

'An agreement?' Ralph smirks, and Rocky sniggers. 'Depends what kind of agreement.'

Despite her fear, Tilda still manages to roll her eyes. 'How about I drop the idea of digging into Bess Green-wood's death and you drop the idea of killing me? That way we both win.'

'Nah. I don't think so.'

Tilda's eyes widen and I feel my stomach drop away, as a gasp of fear threatens to bubble out of my mouth. *She's not going to get out of it this time. We're done for.*

Rocky leans in and whispers something into Ralph's ear that makes Ralph give Tilda a thoughtful glance. There is a long, drawn-out pause, long enough for all of us to ponder on what Ralph might do to Tilda, before he eventually breaks the silence. 'Second thoughts… maybe that could work.'

'Really?' The word squeaks out of Tilda's mouth in a rush of relief.

'Look, I shoulda just shot you the moment I pulled you out from under the bed…'

Tilda swallows hard, her skin taking on a clammy sheen in the dim bedroom lighting.

'…But I already had enough crap to deal with here, and you look kinda like my sister. If you agree to drop the story about Bess – and you stop poking around in things that don't concern you – then I'll consider your offer, but let me warn you this is a one-time offer only. You see this?' Ralph reaches inside his shirt and pulls out a gold ring on a chain. 'This ring was still attached when I removed it... attached to the guy's *finger*. If you don't wanna find out where the finger is, you need to get outta here. You shouldn't be here, and if it was anyone else that caught you... let's just say they wouldn't be giving you a handkerchief and sending you on your way.' Ralph looks her over. 'Don't you write no story about Bess, you got it? Just forget about her. If I see one word about this in print your fingers will be the next ones I chop off.'

Tilda's shoulders straighten and I want to groan. I recognise that stance. 'Did you know Bess?'

'No,' Ralph says shortly, grabbing Tilda by the upper arm and leading her towards the staircase, Rocky and his gun following behind. 'Best you don't mention her name again. And don't you dare come back here, or I won't hesitate next time. The last face you'll see will be mine, and then I'll make you disappear. For good.' He shoves her towards the stairs, and she vanishes from sight.

'Shit.' I pull away from the gap in the door, straight into Louis. 'Ouch. Sorry.'

'What happened? Where did they take her?'

I shuffle round in the tight space, so Louis and I are standing face to face. 'They disappeared downstairs, but you heard what that guy – Ralph – said. It sounds like they're going to let her go.' I don't mention Ralph's tight grip on her arm as he marched her away, and I hope that he really did mean what he said, and it wasn't just a ruse to get her outside where they could bundle her into the trunk of their car, never to be seen again.

'Thank God. Seriously, I could kill her myself sometimes.' Louis looks down at me, and I am suddenly horribly aware just how small this closet is. 'Are you all right?'

I nod, swallowing hard. I am pressed against him, his arms either side of me. This is the closest we've been to each other since we kissed at the pool.

'We should wait here for a moment,' Louis says, and my stomach flips. 'Let the bad guys leave before we show ourselves.'

I nod, my mouth dry. The roar of an engine comes from below, and I think I hear Tilda call out a goodbye. 'Sounds like they're leaving.' There comes the sound of a second car starting and I look at Louis in alarm.

'That's my car,' he whispers. 'She's pretending to leave. Give her a few minutes and she'll come back for us once she knows they're gone.'

'We should wait downstairs.' I grope behind me, fumbling for the door catch.

Louis reaches out and stops me, holding my hand tightly. 'Wait. One more minute.' He's so close I can feel his breath on my face, and I hope my palms aren't sweaty.

'I can't believe you were just going to burst out of the closet,' I whisper with a half laugh. 'You would have got yourself killed.'

'Rather me than either of you.' Louis holds my gaze, and my stomach does another of those slow, lazy rolls. 'I'd never let anyone hurt you, Lily.'

Oh yikes. Who even knows how long I'll be here for this time? I know I shouldn't do it, but trapped in a tiny closet inches away from being killed, pressed up against the man I've thought about non-stop for almost two years, I tilt my face to his. He must have the same thought because before I can even think about it his mouth is on mine and he kisses me until my knees are so weak I think I'll fall.

Louis pulls away and I press my hand to my mouth, still feeling his lips on mine. 'Oh God, Louis, I'm so sorry. I shouldn't have done that. I know you're still angry with me, but I really am so sorry for everything... not just—'

'Lily, stop.' Louis's tone is sharp and I close my mouth abruptly, hoping I haven't damaged things between us even further. 'Don't. Don't apologise.'

'But—'

'I was – I *am* – angry with you,' he says. 'I was so hurt by the way you left, by the way you never bothered to get in touch. But then... you came back, and now I don't know how I feel. Everything was so bland and boring when you weren't here, and then all of a sudden you blew back in like a hurricane and now I'm in Las Vegas, looking for a dead girl, and my sister just almost got shot.'

'I'm sor—'

'Part of me is still furious with you, but the other part of me... the other part of me wants everything to be like it was before, and if you didn't mean to kiss me, if you're sorry that you did it...'

A gasp of laughter bubbles out of my mouth, and I am slightly breathless with the idea of being forgiven. Of things going back to the way they used to be. 'I'm not sorry at all. I mean, I am for all the other stuff, but not for kissing you just then.'

'In that case, neither am I.' He dips his head again and pulls me close, winding his hands through my hair. It's all perfectly dreamy, until the closet doors are wrenched open, and we yank apart, squinting in the light.

'Clearly I should almost get shot more often.' Tilda eyes us, her tone dry. 'You want to step out of there or should I come back when it's more convenient?'

Louis bites back a smirk as we step out of the closet, my cheeks a fiery pink. 'I don't know about you two,' he says, 'but I think the sooner we get out of here the better.'

Chapter Sixteen

'How did they know we were here?' Louis asks as we descend the fancy, winding staircase in the dark.

'I have no idea. They said they had people watching the place, but there was no one else around and there aren't any neighbours nearby. Maybe they're just driving by and keeping an eye on the place? A woman was murdered here after all... and clearly they don't want anyone snooping.' I thank God we are not living in a time of CCTV cameras and Ring doorbells.

'Wait...' Tilda slows as she approaches the bottom of the staircase, and then she puts her finger exactly on the thing that I couldn't figure out earlier. 'If there aren't any neighbours... how was there an eyewitness to Sonny leaving the property the night Bess was murdered?'

I knew something felt wrong the moment we pulled up to the ranch. The place is so isolated that surely if someone saw Sonny leaving they shouldn't have been here either.

'You think the eyewitness thing was a lie?' Louis asks.

'I think that's a possibility, and it bodes well for Sonny. *If* we can prove it,' Tilda says. 'Either that or someone else was here who perhaps shouldn't have been.' She exhales shakily. 'Things got a little hairy there for a moment, huh? I don't think I've ever met a guy who wears a ring from a severed finger around his neck before.'

'Blimey Tilda, I don't know how you kept it together. You were magnificent.' I peer out towards the window on to the darkened driveway outside. 'Do you think they had something to do with Bess's murder?'

'I think they might know who did have something to do with it, at the very least.' Tilda raises an eyebrow.

'Those guys,' I say, a gut feeling growing stronger the more I think about things. 'Do you think that perhaps... they might be mobsters?' I wait for them both to laugh at me, but Tilda gives a slow nod and Louis simply stares at me as if waiting for me to elaborate. 'The whole ring on the chain thing? The scrapes on Ralph's knuckles. The insinuation that they could get rid of you and get away with it...'

'Whoever they were, they aren't nice people,' Louis says, his eyes going to the front door as if half expecting them to come barrelling back through it, 'and I think we should get out of here in case they come back.'

'Do you think it's safe to leave?' I move to the front door, the hall cloaked in darkness. Outside, shadows fall across the front of the house from the group of trees to the side, making the already velvety blackness outside seem even thicker.

'They headed back out onto the highway,' Tilda says, reaching for the door handle. Slipping through the open door, the three of us hurry to the car, my ankle throbbing as I lurch towards the vehicle. Louis turns the ignition over and for a moment my heart stops, as nothing happens.

'Try again,' I urge, my hands clammy. Although there are no other houses that I can see and we didn't see any other vehicles, those men knew we were here somehow. The spot between my shoulder blades prickles as if someone is watching me and I crane my neck, peering out of the passenger window to see if there is any sign of movement. Headlights appear out on the highway and panic clutches at my throat. *Please don't let it be them coming back*. 'Tilda told them she was alone – we have to get out of here before they realise she was lying.'

Louis nods, a bead of sweat forming on his brow as the car ticks over again, before finally catching with a throaty roar.

'Drive!' Tilda squeals, as Louis throws Christine into reverse and then peels away from the house, a grey cloud of dust pluming behind us as we career down the bumpy, uneven track towards the main highway. It feels as if none of us breathe until the track leading to the ranch has disappeared from the rear-view mirror.

'Well, that was exciting,' Tilda says eventually, as I turn to her open-mouthed and Louis shakes his head.

'Exciting?' I screech, twisting round in my seat. 'Are you kidding me? You had a *gun* pointed at your head tonight. Christmas is exciting. Movie premieres are exciting. Bloody hell, the last episode of *The Sopranos* was exciting. *That*, back there, was terrifying, not exciting.'

'What are the sopranos?' Tilda asks mildly, as I turn to face the road, adrenaline still rushing through my veins at a hundred miles per hour. 'Anyway, did you hear what those guys said?'

'What? Before or after they threatened to kill you?' Louis catches Tilda's eye in the mirror. His knuckles are white on the steering wheel.

'Before, wiseass. Rocky said he'd seen me at the Slipper – that's got to be the Silver Slipper, right? – and then he mentioned someone named Mr Z. He asked if Mr Z knew I was here. Whoever Mr Z is, he has something to do with this place, and therefore it stands to reason that it's likely he's had something to do with Bess.'

'If this Mr Z is connected to the Silver Slipper as well, then there's every chance he knew her.' Everything is pointing to the Silver Slipper as being important in the discovery of the truth about what happened to Bess Greenwood.

'Everything keeps coming back to that place,' Tilda says, just as I am thinking it. 'We have to find an in. We have to find a way to integrate ourselves into the casino, so we can poke around freely.'

'I don't think it's going to be as easy as that,' Louis says. 'If Lily is right and there is some kind of mob connection here, we aren't going to be able to ask around about this Mr Z without some sort of consequences. And we've already seen tonight that these guys don't mess around.'

A spark of inspiration brings a smile to my lips. 'I have an idea. If we can't poke around without rousing suspicion then we need to go undercover.'

'Yes!' Tilda cries as Louis frowns, pressing his lips together.

'I don't know, Lil—'

'No Louis, don't spoil it.' Tilda is almost bouncing in her seat with anticipation. 'This is perfect, Lily – if we can just figure out exactly *how* we can go in undercover, given that some people already know we're asking around about Bess.'

We fall silent, the only sound the throaty hum of Christine's engine. The motion of the car is strangely soothing after the tension back at the ranch, and now I've taken the weight off it, my ankle doesn't seem as painful. It's only as the bright, neon lights of Las Vegas twinkle on the highway ahead of us that the silence is broken.

'Jobs,' Louis says, his eyes never leaving the road. We cross the town limit, the lights becoming ever brighter. He slows and pulls into the parking lot at the Desert Inn. 'We need to get jobs at the Silver Slipper. That's the perfect way to get access.'

Slipping out of the car we head into the Desert Inn, Tilda locating a booth in the bar that is relatively private. 'The hostess at the pool,' I say to Louis, 'she said something about there being a high turnover of hostesses in places like these. She said, "There's a new girl starting every week," so maybe that could work? I could ask if they have a position for a hostess. That would give me a chance to watch the casino floor – maybe figure out who this Mr Z is and what he has to do with the ranch.'

'If Lou could get behind the bar, that would cover the most frequented parts of the casino,' Tilda offers up. 'People talk after a few drinks, right? Who better to listen than the guy pouring the drinks?'

Louis nods. 'And you, sister dear, can work the reporter angle.'

'You've got Louella's card,' I say, 'those… *goons* already know you're a reporter, so if they pop up you just need to be very, very careful given the fact that you told them you were going to drop the story.'

'I'm also going to get an interview with Jonny Valentine. He could be the perfect cover for me – I'll say I dropped the Bess story in favour of covering Jonny and his showbiz lifestyle.'

I had forgotten all about the charming crooner. He must have known Bess, at least by sight – his dressing room is next to the dancers' dressing room. As if we've conjured him up by mentioning his name, Jonny Valentine appears at the entrance to the bar, with what can only be described as an entourage surrounding him. Tilda stands, smooths her hair down and then glides towards the group, incorporating herself into the edges of Jonny's crowd.

'Time to head over to the Slipper?' Louis holds out a hand and gently tugs me to my feet. It seems as though since our talk in the closet moments after Tilda was almost shot something has shifted between us, the balance tilting back ever so slightly to the way things were before, and I feel an overwhelming sense of relief. We walk slowly over to the other side of the street, where Duke Ellington singing about taking the A train blares from the saloon in the Last Frontier Village. Passing beneath the giant silver shoe atop the casino, we head into the lobby of the Silver Slipper. Jonny's show is finished for the night, and groups of people fill the lobby of the casino, making their way from the auditorium to the slots and tables. Despite the late hour, it feels as if Vegas is just getting started.

'I'll leave you here,' I say to Louis at the entrance to the bar. I've spotted someone on the casino floor – a suited man with a name badge proclaiming him to be the general manager – and I want to catch him before he disappears. 'Meet me back at the Desert Inn?'

Louis melts into the crowd in the bar and I set my sights on the casino manager. He is tall and gaunt, with a look of Vincent Price about him. Hoping he doesn't want to suck my blood, I take a leaf out of Tilda's book and pop open a button on my blouse, fluffing out my hair.

'Excuse me, sir?' Laying a hand on his arm, I switch on a mega-watt grin, channelling Sharon Stone when she played Ginger McKenna in *Casino*.

'Ma'am, if you need more chips you need to head over to the cashier.' He barely looks at me.

Resisting the urge to grit my teeth, I push out my chest and let out a laugh that tinkles through the sounds of drunken gamblers. 'Oh no, I don't gamble. I was hoping you'd be able to help me.' The breathy laugh and tiny glimpse of lacy bra at the opening to my blouse does the trick. He stops what he's doing and runs his eyes over me.

'What is it, ma'am?'

'I'm new in town, and I'm looking for a hostess position. A friend of mine pointed me here, she said it's the best casino in town.' I cross my fingers that he doesn't ask me who.

'What's that accent you got there? British?'

'Err... yes. I'm from London originally.' I find myself becoming *even more British*, if that's at all possible.

'London, eh?' He gives a slow nod. 'OK. Maybe that could work.'

'So you can help? You have a position for me?' Wings of anticipation beat in my chest at the thought that it might be that easy – I might have a route in to finding out about the mysterious Mr Z... and what happened to Bess.

'Hostess position you say? I can offer you a trial, if you've got experience. Punters always love a little bit of something exotic on the casino floor.'

Ew. And I'd hardly say Peckham is exotic. 'I have tons of experience.' My feet throb at the memory of hours waiting tables at the Saddle Ranch Chop House. 'Years of it.'

The manager rakes his eyes over me again, and gestures for me to follow him through to a tiny back office where he throws me a black hostess uniform. 'We're short-handed. Trial starts now,' he says, turning back to face me as he reaches for the door. 'Keep circling the tables, make sure their drinks are full. The more they drink, the more they spend... errr?'

'Lily,' I say, then wonder if I should have given him a fake name.

'Lily. And smile, OK?' And then he is gone.

—

Heading back out on to the casino floor, tray in hand, I feel as if I've stepped forward in time, back to the Chop House on a Saturday night, only slightly more glamorous. The hostess uniform the manager handed to me is risqué by 1950s standards. Made of an itchy black fabric, it's an off-the-shoulder number, fitted over the bust and waist with a cute little flared skirt that barely scrapes mid-thigh. It's not something I would feel comfortable wearing in the twenty-first century and I feel even less so donning it in 1950. My shoes don't match at all, but there isn't much I can do about it, and I hope the guests will be so dazzled by my accent that they forget to look at my feet. The tables are filled, men in sharp suits sitting at blackjack and roulette, elegant women by their sides in evening dress complete with jewels that dazzle as they catch the light. The way the women flirt and reach out to touch the men they are with makes me think that wives are not necessarily in attendance.

'What can I get for you, sir?' Spying an empty glass, I swoop on an older gentleman who sits at the roulette table, his arm around a thin, blonde girl.

'Martini, on the rocks,' he barks without looking at me. He doesn't order for the woman, and when I glance at her, I realise it's one of the dancers from the show the previous evening. Hurrying to the bar I keep my head down, hoping she hasn't recognised me.

'Hey! Drinks over here!' A shout goes up and I see Jonny Valentine and his group have migrated over from the Desert Inn, and he is waving a hand in my direction. 'Hey sweetheart, how about a drink?'

There is no sign of Tilda, and I paste on a smile. 'Of course, Mr Valentine. What can I get you?'

'Jack Daniels. Two fingers, and a cube of ice,' he winks at me. 'Simon? What about you?' The small bespectacled man sitting beside him shakes his head, desperately trying to keep Jonny's attention. There is a diary on the table between them, and it appears as if the bespectacled man – Simon – is trying to pin Jonny down to a date for something. It seems an odd time to be trying to do business, but what do I know? I'm just a hostess. Jonny doesn't order for his wife, who sits quietly to one side, sipping on a clear drink that could be water or gin.

'Ma'am? Could I get a drink?' A hand plucks at my sleeve and I realise Dean Martin is also at the table. He beckons me closer, so I have to lean down to hear him. 'Apple juice, that's all. Two fingers in a whisky glass with some ice.' He casts a glance at Jonny, his rich, deep voice a low murmur. 'And a whisky for my friend too. Put it on my tab.' Clamping a fresh cigarette between his teeth, Dean nods at Frank Sinatra, who sits across the room with Ava Gardner. I tighten my grip on the tray, suddenly feeling a little woozy. *I thought things were crazy last time when I met Jessica Parks, but this is something else!*

At the bar, Louis sits at one end, a large drink in front of him. I am about to catch his eye when one of the dancers from the burlesque show slips into the seat beside him. It's the blonde girl, front row and centre. *Daisy.* He slides the drink across to her and says something that makes her laugh out loud, her hand landing on his arm. Turning away, I take a deep breath. *He'll be getting to the bottom of the row with Bess, that's all*. Even so, there is a twinge of jealousy shooting barbed green thorns that wrap around my heart. Taking the fresh drinks from the bartender, I head back to the tables without looking in his direction again.

'Mr Sinatra,' I place the whisky tumbler on his table. 'From Mr Martin.' Frank lifts his glass with a smile and raises it in Dean's direction.

'Your whisky, Mr Martin.' Dean Martin gives me a wink as I pass him his drink, and then squeeze my way between gamblers and girls to Jonny's seat. As I manoeuvre myself next to Jonny, my eyes wander to the diary on the table, Simon's finger jabbing at the page.

'People are asking *questions*, Jonny,' Simon is saying, muted fury in his tone. 'Look—' He rifles back through the pages, filled with appointments. 'I leaned on the girl, and she doesn't know anything, but I'm concerned—'

Jonny reaches out a hand towards the diary, stopping Simon from flipping the pages. 'There's nothing to be concerned about. Just, please… we'll discuss it later. I'll deal with it. And where's Antonia? Send Antonia over.'

As I lean forward to place Jonny's drink on the table he pulls his hand back, catching the bottom of the glass and sending whisky flying all over the diary, his trousers and the skirt of my uniform.

'Oh my gosh. I'm so sorry, sir.' Frantically I snatch at a napkin as Jonny leaps to his feet with a roar. Glancing down as I dab at the damp pages of the diary my eyes widen. The diary is open on 25 January, three days before Bess was found dead. And scrawled in pencil at two p.m. is *Lunch (Slipper) – Bess G.*

Chapter Seventeen

'For Pete's sake!' Jonny is on his feet, knocking my hand away as he tugs the wet fabric of his trousers away from his skin. 'Look what you did! This suit cost me a thousand dollars!'

'I'm so sorry, Mr Valentine. So, so sorry.' My mouth suddenly dry, I back discreetly away from the table, my heart hammering in my chest. Antonia gets to her feet, reaching for more napkins to pat at Jonny's trousers as he pushes her hand away, shoving his chair back and stalking away towards the elevators.

'Sorry,' I whisper again, hurrying back to the bar, my face blazing as I try and process exactly what just happened.

'Miss?' The voice is quiet in my ear and I look up, my cheeks burning. 'Miss? Are you all right?' Antonia Valentine stands beside me, fresh napkins in hand, as she looks at me with concern.

'I… yes, I think so. Thank you.' I take the napkins and brush at the fabric of my skirt. It's some itchy, light wool fabric that seems to have soaked up as much alcohol as it possibly could and the smell of whisky rises, drowning out the scent of Antonia's floral perfume. 'I'm so sorry, Mrs Valentine. I'll take care of the dry cleaning.'

'Oh, no.' Antonia Valentine flaps a hand with a smile. 'Don't be silly, dear, Jonny can afford to take care of his own dry cleaning. I saw exactly what happened. That clumsy oaf knocked the glass clean out of your hand.'

'Even so…'

'You won't get in trouble, will you?' Antonia peers at me, worry making her brow crease. 'It wasn't your fault. Jonny can be… well, he can overreact sometimes. Get angry over the smallest things.' Almost unconsciously she rubs her wrist with her other hand, and I think I catch a glimpse of purple on her skin before she tugs her sleeve down over her hand. 'Let me order him another drink and I'll take it over to him, save you having to do it.'

'I should take it over, it's my job.' Part of me doesn't want to face Jonny's wrath, but the other part of me wants to get another peek at that diary page.

'I insist.' Antonia leans in, her voice low. 'Trust me. It's better if I deal with him right now.' She casts a glance over her shoulder, where Jonny is emerging from the elevator in a fresh pair of trousers.

I hand her a fresh glass of whisky and give her a grateful smile. 'Thank you, and I'm so sorry again.'

Antonia returns my smile as she winks, and turns towards her table. 'You can owe me one.'

I wait until Antonia has returned to her table and handed Jonny his drink before I turn and hurry out into the lobby, where I pull around the corner out of sight. *Jonny did know Bess, he arranged to meet her for lunch before she died. Maybe we also need to be looking into Jonny more closely while we try and track down Mr Z?*

Something crawls up my spine, raising the hairs on the back of my neck. Finding Mr Z is important, but this new information about Jonny isn't something I can just ignore. Poor Bess. *Why did Jonny meet her? Is he responsible for her death?* My eyes go to the darkened restaurant. If I challenge

Jonny about meeting Bess, about knowing her, surely he will just deny it, and part of me is reluctant to confront him after the way he just blew up at me. I need some sort of proof that he arranged to meet her.

The lobby is quieter now, and glancing at the clock behind the reception desk I see it is almost two o'clock in the morning. Any exhaustion I feel drains away as my gaze goes back to the restaurant. It's been closed for several hours, but as staff, maybe I can find a way in. They must have some sort of record of reservations.

The hostess uniform has a superpower – despite the revealing top half and the skimpy bottom half, it makes me invisible. Jonny only saw me when his glass was empty, and now, as I glance around the lobby, I see no one is looking at me at all. *People are asking questions, Jonny.* About what? About Bess? Sidling closer to the restaurant doors, I press down on the handle, but of course, it's locked. Peering in through the window, I see a faint golden glow coming from the back of the restaurant. *The kitchen.* I think I might know a way in.

Grabbing an empty tray I march purposefully through the lobby, towards the back of the casino. There are rear doors that are for staff use only, some leading to staff quarters and offices, some leading directly out into the dusty, gritty lot at the back of the casino. I push through one of these doors, discarding the tray, and head through the lot towards the back kitchen door, hoping my hunch is right. It is, and whistling reaches my ears as I creep towards the open door to the galley. A lone porter – the one who presumably drew the short straw – is bagging up the last of the garbage, swinging the hefty bag up onto his shoulder as if it weighs nothing. Drawing back into the shadows, my nose wrinkling at the smell of rotting food, I watch as he heads towards the large dumpsters at the end of the lot. The door is still cracked open, yellow light puddling out on to the dirt, and I take my chance. Lurching out of the dark on my busted ankle I hurry into the kitchen, warm air scented with garlic and stock hitting me in the face as I hurry through the unfamiliar space towards the restaurant.

Oh crap. My hip catches a pile of saucepans stacked high on a draining board as I squeeze past, and they crash to the floor with a clatter as I scoot away, cursing under my breath. There is a muffled shout as the porter hears the commotion, and holding my breath, I shove through the swing doors into the main restaurant.

The restaurant is dark, the only light the muted shades of green, red, and purple that leach in through the darkened windows from the slot machines on the other side. I can hear the muffled cheers as the slots pay out, and Vaughn Monroe's mournful voice singing about riders in the sky through the speakers in the lobby. Heart pounding, my mouth dusty with panic, I press myself against the wall hoping the kitchen porter thinks the pans just fell, until finally, *finally* he turns out the light and there is silence from the kitchen.

Moving along the wall in the safety of the shadows, I creep towards the hostess desk, leaning on it with relief when I eventually reach it, my ankle throbbing from my mad dash through the kitchen. The top of the desk is clear, neatly tidied for the breakfast rush in a few hours, so I reach underneath, searching for the reservations book. There must be one. Nothing is online or digital yet obviously, and it's just a reservations book – surely it wouldn't be locked in the office? Groping around in the dark, my fingers brush against a used napkin (gross), a name badge reading 'Sylvia' and then, finally, at the back of the shelf I feel the solid, square cover of a reservations diary. Pulling it out, I rifle through until I find 25 January. The page is covered with names, most with a thick line through them. Presumably they are the people who showed for their reservations. I feel a twinge of homesickness. That's exactly the way we do things at the Saddle Ranch. I roll my eyes, feeling ridiculous. I hate that waitressing job. Tilting the book towards the dim light of the slots, I strain my eyes, searching for two p.m. And there it is, the names marked with a thick, black line. Even so, I can still just about make out the name *Valentine* and then *+1 (Greenwood)*.

Bingo. Proof that Jonny knew Bess, and met her for lunch days before she was found dead. Preparing to rip the page free of the diary, I freeze as the shaft of light across the page grows larger.

'Anyone in here?' A flashlight flickers at the doorway and I duck down beneath the desk, my pulse crashing in my ears. *Oh God. The porter must have called security after all.* 'Hello? Whoever you are, you shouldn't be in here. Restaurant closed hours ago.'

I hold my position, crouched behind the desk. My thighs are screaming and I feel the horrifying sensation of a hiccup about to erupt. Pressing my hand against my mouth, I hold my breath, squeezing my eyes closed and praying that whoever it is leaves.

Footsteps ring out across the restaurant floor; the beam from the flashlight swishing across the room. I tuck myself into a ball, barely able to hear the man over the crashing of my pulse in my ears, the smell of whisky rising from my skirt and hitting the back of my throat. Just as I have made the decision to reveal myself, pretending I am here for a lovers' tryst, one speaks.

'There's no one in here, Bob.' Another voice comes from the door and I inch my eyes open. Peering around the frame of the desk, I see two security guards, one holding a flashlight, the other a pack of cigarettes. 'Let's move on, I haven't had a cigarette in forty minutes.'

Praying Bob agrees, I shift position slightly, my ankle begging for me to take the weight off it. I only let out my breath when I hear the door gently snick closed, followed by the unmistakable sound of a key being turned in a lock.

Hardly daring to breathe I wait until I am certain the security guards are gone, and then I limp towards the kitchen, the torn diary page in one hand. I might have succeeded in my mission to find proof that Jonny knew Bess, but it's not going to do me much good if I'm trapped in here. *There has to be a way out.* Maybe the porter didn't lock the door. Maybe a window has been left open for ventilation. I know deep down I'm grasping at straws, and this is confirmed when I enter the darkened kitchen. The pots are all neatly stacked, the surfaces gleaming, and I would be impressed if I hadn't already spotted an issue with my potential escape. The windows can be opened, but screens cover the exterior, meaning they only open a few inches and there's no way I can squeeze out. The door handle twists in my hand, but the door doesn't budge. The whole place is locked up tight for the evening. I am locked in.

'Miss? Excuse me, miss?' A voice murmurs close by my ear and I jerk upright, my muscles screaming. 'You shouldn't be in here.' The voice is low, and I squint in the bright light of the now illuminated restaurant.

Locked in. The security guards locked the door when they left. I must have drifted off. 'I'm sorry.' I swallow, my throat dry, and haul myself up using the hostess desk as leverage. 'I—'

'What were you doing in here?' A woman in a pale pink skirt suit, her waist impossibly tiny in the girdled blazer, stands beside the desk, her arms folded across her body.

Before I can answer I hear my name being shrieked from the restaurant doors. 'Lily! Oh Lily, thank goodness we found you.' Tilda hurries across the floor, her cheeks flushed, and her hair scraped back into a high ponytail. 'Thank you, ma'am. I'm so relieved you found my friend.'

'But I still don't understand why she's here.' The woman turns a stern gaze on me, arching a perfectly groomed eyebrow. I feel grubby and wrinkled in comparison. 'Are you… a hostess here?'

Sheepishly, I nod, hoping no one can hear the crinkle of the reservations page where I tucked it into the top of my uniform last night after realising I really was locked in and there was no way out. 'Sorry, I came here for…' I cast a panicked glance behind her, to the coffee machine on the counter. 'For coffee. Last night. There wasn't any at the bar, so I thought I could grab a cup here for one of the…' *What was the term?* 'High rollers! One of the high rollers, you know how we have to make sure they're kept happy…'

'Stop babbling. Whatever the reason, you shouldn't have been in here.' The woman eyes me with distaste. 'You need to leave. I'm expecting customers.'

'Come on, Lily. Let's get you washed up.' Tilda takes my arm and guides me gently to the lobby, where she whirls on me. 'What the heck, Lily? We've been so worried about you. When you didn't come back to the room last night...' she trails off, biting her lip.

'I got locked in; it was an accident. But I did get this.' Slipping my hand inside my uniform, I fish out the page I tore from the reservations book, pointing to the two p.m. slot. 'Look. Jonny Valentine met Bess Greenwood for lunch three days before she died.'

'What!' Tilda snatches the page from me and peers at it closely, running her finger over their names. 'So, he did know Bess.'

'Did you manage to speak to Jonny last night?'

Tilda shakes her head. 'He had a bodyguard hanging around, and his wife was there too.' She rolls her eyes. 'I hovered on the perimeter for a bit, but getting close to Jonny is proving a little difficult.'

'I met her last night,' I say. 'The wife, I mean. Antonia. I spilled a drink on Jonny and he got kind of mad... she was very sweet to me, although I got the impression that Jonny isn't always a terribly pleasant guy.' The memory of Antonia rubbing absently at the bruise on her wrist rises in my mind and my stomach turns a little. *Was Jonny the one who hurt her wrist?*

'Lily!' Louis approaches from the lobby, concern written all over his face. 'Where were you? We've been looking all over for you. I thought something had happened... you know, *Ralph* might have seen us leaving the house after all.' He lowers his voice.

'Ha!' Tilda barks. 'Lily's night was definitely less exciting than that. She got locked in the restaurant.'

Louis gives me a quizzical look, and I shake my head, not wanting to explain. 'I did get proof that Jonny at least met Bess, even if they weren't well known to each other.' I show him the page from the reservations book.

'Good job, Lil. Although it can't have been fun spending the night in the restaurant,' Louis says with a frown. 'I'm just glad you're all right and you haven't been carted off by gangsters.'

'Not yet,' Tilda says cheerfully. 'How did you get on, Lou?'

'Let's talk where we won't be overheard.' Louis gestures to a table in the far corner of the lobby, out of sight of the reception desk and bar. We squeeze in, and I fight back a yawn as Louis tells us about his night.

'The bar was busy,' he says, 'but they didn't want to take me on as a bartender, they told me that straight off. Said they didn't need anyone.' His shoulders lift in an unconcerned shrug. 'So I just stayed for a drink, and it wasn't a wasted evening.'

I think about the dancer who slipped into the seat beside him, her head tipping back as he made her laugh, and my stomach curdles.

'Oh?' I try to lighten my tone, but Louis still frowns as he turns to me.

'Yeah, it was quite informative, actually. As it turns out, our dancing queen Daisy – remember, front row and centre? – was supposed to meet someone in the bar, but they didn't show, and the only available seat was next to me.' Tilda lets out a gasp. 'We got to talking and I mentioned Bess, but she clammed up. I didn't want to push it so I changed the subject and bought her a couple of drinks, hoping it would loosen her tongue.'

'And did it?' Tilda's tone is sharp as she leans forward in her seat.

'It did.' Louis grins, his face lighting up. 'Cassidy was right when she said Daisy and Bess fought that day. Daisy caught Bess coming out of Jonny's dressing room that morning. She accused Bess of having an affair with Jonny, and Bess denied it. Bess refused to tell Daisy what she was doing in the dressing room, but it's common knowledge among the dancers that Jonny doesn't like anyone being in there. Daisy told Bess that she'd tell people – Jonny's people, I guess – that she saw her coming out of there, and that would be the end of Bess. She would make sure Bess was fired.'

'*A way to see the back of her for good,*' Tilda says, slowly. 'She meant she'd get her fired, not kill her.'

'Then the conversation moved on to Jonny Valentine, and my new friend turned out to be even less discreet after the vodka sodas really kicked in. Apparently the rumour in Las Vegas is that Jonny isn't the saint his publicity manager would have you believe, and this could have everything to do with Bess. The rumour is, Jonny *has* been playing away.'

Chapter Eighteen

'Playing away?' Tilda claps her hands over her mouth. 'But... oh gosh, Lil, men are all the same, aren't they?' She slumps back in her chair, disappointed.

Poor Antonia. 'What exactly did she say?'

'Just that Jonny is not as faithful as the newspapers report. Lil, you've never heard of Jonny before, but he has this reputation as... as a *good guy*. He's devoted to his wife and their kids; he sings about love and romance. To his fans, he's the dream guy.'

Tilda nods in confirmation. 'Sinatra's the bad guy,' she says. 'He's the playboy who cheats on Nancy and loves whisky and women. Although maybe if he does marry Ava, she will calm him down.' She sniffs, clearly not convinced.

'So Jonny cheats on his wife?'

Louis shrugs again. 'It sounds like it, unless it's a bum rap.'

'Bum...?' I can't hide my confusion.

'Unless it's not true,' Louis says. 'I mean, she could have made it up but... something about the way she checked no one was listening tells me she wasn't. And if it is true, it seems to be very discreet – she said it's not a well-known secret and that I shouldn't tell anyone, but she was pretty buzzed.'

'We're not *anyone*,' Tilda says wryly. 'So, Jonny met Bess for lunch before she died… and with this rumour from you, Louis…'

'Maybe Bess and Jonny *were* having an affair. Of course Bess would have denied it to Daisy – she hated her.' A chill works its way down my spine. *Jonny cheats on Antonia. His wife, who has a thick purple bruise on her wrist, possibly put there by Jonny, who she says sometimes overreacts.* Could Jonny have killed Bess? Where does Sonny come into all this? Everything feels huge and unwieldy, like trying to secure a dying tree in a storm. Yawns tug at my throat and I have to admit defeat. 'I'm sorry. I'm exhausted and I don't think I can think straight anymore.' I get to my feet, ready to head across the street to our room at the Desert Inn. 'I need to catch up on some sleep before I can try and piece all of this together.'

'Just one thing before you go,' Tilda says. 'I didn't have a total bust yesterday evening. Once I got kicked out of Jonny's entourage, I asked around about the insurance convention Sonny was supposed to have attended.'

'And?' In all the excitement about Jonny's lunch with Bess, and the mobsters at the ranch house, I'd forgotten about Sonny's alibi.

'Nothing. Nobody knows anything about it. It's almost as if there wasn't a convention here at all.'

–

Tossing and turning, I don't think I'll ever fall asleep, but what feels like moments later Louis is gently shaking me awake and the sunlight that slants in through the thin curtains is a muted shade of indigo and pink. I've slept the entire afternoon.

'You should have woken me earlier.' I struggle into a sitting position, aware that my breath is probably stale and my curls are a tangled bird's nest.

'We would have, but you seemed exhausted. You were snoring and everything,' Tilda says, coming to sit on the end of the twin bed. I cover my eyes and groan. 'We could barely hear Evelyn over your racket.'

'Evelyn?' I drop my hands. 'What did she say?'

'Well, she's not blown a fuse yet, but she's not happy,' Louis says.

'But that's not unusual,' Tilda pipes up. She grins, and then her smile drops as Louis perches on the bed next to her.

'She really is going out of her mind,' Louis says. 'Her parents are due back next week, and she still hasn't mentioned anything to them about Sonny's incarceration, but she's more worried about the fact that Sonny has now officially been charged with Bess's murder.'

'He's been *charged*? Oh boy.'

'Evelyn is frantic that a trial date is going to be set and we still don't seem to be getting anywhere.'

Evelyn and me, both. 'We're doing our best,' I say, 'but when it comes to Bess, no one seems to want to talk.'

'The prosecution are saying they have a strong case against Sonny and it doesn't seem as though Benjamin Fry is terribly confident about getting him off. He's spoken to Evelyn about accepting a plea and hoping they drop the death penalty.'

Yikes. Insects creep over my skin at the thought of Sonny's slimy lawyer. There was something off about him, something I didn't trust, and I don't blame Evelyn for feeling concerned.

'Has Evelyn considered hiring another lawyer for Sonny?' I ask. 'I have to agree that he doesn't seem to have the fight in him to get Sonny off.'

'Sonny is refusing.' Louis shakes his head as if he can't understand it. 'Evelyn offered to find him another lawyer and he just outright told Evelyn that Fry is the best man for the job.'

I swing my legs out of bed and head for the shower. I don't understand Sonny's conviction that Fry is the best man for the job. Standing under the water I think over our visit to the lawyer's office, the conversation we had with him. There was something Fry said that didn't sit right with me, and it wasn't just about the convention – the convention that doesn't seem to have been held in Vegas at all. I just can't put my finger on it.

Two hours later I am on the floor of the casino at the Silver Slipper, thirty minutes into my shift, when the casino manager approaches me. I think he's going to reproach me for spilling a drink on Jonny last night and I feel the flutter of nerves in my gut. *Antonia said she would deal with Jonny, but maybe he put in a complaint about me anyway?* I hope Jonny wasn't angry with Antonia because of my mistake. I hope I don't get fired before I get the chance to dig further into Bess's death.

'Follow me,' the casino manager says briskly, and I lower the tray of empty glasses I'm holding onto the bar.

'Is everything all right?' I ask as he marches across the casino floor.

'Just follow me,' he snaps. 'There's someone who wants to speak with you.' Meekly I follow him across the casino floor, my eyes on the plush carpet, still unworn as yet by the thousands of feet that will walk through this place before it is pulled down to make way for a parking lot.

At a door to the side, unmarked by any signs or emergency exit and almost invisible if you didn't know it was there, he pulls out a bunch of keys and slides one into the lock, before tucking the keys back into his jacket pocket, pushing the door open and leading me into a dimly lit corridor. Mahogany panelling lines the walls, and the carpet is thick and plush beneath my feet, a dizzying pattern of dark greens and golds. I follow Vincent (I can't not call him that) past several doors, all tightly closed, until one swings open and a woman steps out. I catch a glimpse behind her of two women sat at a table, each with a bundle of cash in her hands, a black box labelled 'CRAPS 7 SWING' in front of them.

'Counting room,' Vincent mutters, urging me on, finally stopping at the room next to the counting room. He taps on the solid oak door, a quick one-two, and then wrenches it open. I step inside, finding myself in an office, where the older gentleman from the bar at the Desert Inn when we arrived in town sits behind a vast walnut desk. Papers are spread across the surface and as we enter, he looks up and removes his spectacles. I cast a worried glance at the casino manager but he just raises an eyebrow in my direction, and then steps out, leaving me alone with the older gentleman.

'Ah, Lily, isn't it?' The man carries a regal air as he looks at me from over his steepled fingers where he rests his chin. He's in his mid-fifties, and although relatively slim his cheeks are jowly, the flesh beginning to sink around his jawline.

'Yes?' I say quizzically.

'Lily…?'

'Jones,' I say, as a knot of apprehension balls in my chest. It's hot in here, and I'm finding it hard to draw in a breath, the air is so stuffy. This guy on the other hand wears a silk cravat and suit jacket and looks as cool as a cucumber.

'Lily Jones. How are you are enjoying your new job, Miss Jones?'

Oh yikes. Maybe Jonny did make a complaint about me after all. Maybe I am about to be fired. 'Very much, sir. This is a… lovely casino.' Wincing internally, I smile to stop myself from babbling. The way he never takes his eyes off me is unnerving.

'Isn't it? I am very proud of this place.' He stands, coming around from behind the desk. 'It's mine. I own it.' He perches on the edge of the desk, his knee almost touching my thigh. Oh God. He's not going to want me to take my clothes off or anything, is he? I remember what the pool hostess said at the Desert Inn, about Hollywood folks coming to Vegas to do wild and crazy things.

'Lovely,' I say, my smile faltering as my heart claps in my chest like thunder rolling over the hills. One inappropriate move and I'll crack him right across the chops. If it was good enough for movie star Magnus Michel, it's good enough for this guy.

'So you see, that's why I'm especially interested in what goes on here.' He smiles, but it doesn't reach his eyes. 'You were at the Desert Inn. You and your… husband. You are newlyweds, aren't you?'

Fear begins to flutter in my veins and I have to make a firm effort to keep my legs from sprinting out of the small office. Instead, I meet his gaze. 'Yes. We're new in town, and we figured that was the best place to stay while we find jobs, Mr… I'm sorry. I don't know your name.'

'Of course. Zillo. Buddy Zillo.'

Mr Z. Oh blimey. My knees suddenly feel liquid, as if my kneecaps have been replaced with jelly.

'So, as I was saying, I take a keen interest in what goes on, not just here, in this casino. But in this town.' Buddy watches me carefully, and I arrange my features into a blank canvas, praying I've made a decent enough job of it and he can't tell that my heart is racing, and every fibre of my being is telling me to get out. 'It's been brought to my attention that you've been asking around about Bess Greenwood.'

'I...'

'How did you know Bess?'

Did. Clearly Buddy Zillo is well aware of what has happened to Bess. Of course he is. 'She's... she was a friend of a friend.'

'So, you didn't know her.' Zillo gets to his feet again, the space between us shrinking as panic makes my mouth go dry. 'The way I see it, you didn't actually know Bess, so therefore what happened to her is none of your business. Understand?'

'But she worked here!' The words erupt before I can stop them, fear draining away to leave me light-headed and, to be honest, a little angry. 'Aren't you concerned? Weren't you worried when she didn't show up?' A silly question, seeing as Bess was replaced within forty-eight hours. 'Does Bess really mean that little that you don't care who was responsible for her murder?'

Zillo smiles, but it doesn't reach his eyes. 'The culprit has been arrested, Miss Jones. The matter has been laid to rest, much like our dear Bess.' The words are flimsy and insincere as he steps towards me and grips my arm tightly. 'So I strongly advise you to leave things alone.' Zillo pushes me backward towards the office door, so close I can smell the whisky on his breath. He presses one hand against the closed door as my back hits it, the other hand spreading around my ribcage, uncomfortably close to the underside of my breast. 'After all, I would hate for something as dreadful as what happened to Bess to happen to you.'

My stomach lurches as he leans down to whisper the threat into my ear, the vision of Rocky pressing his gun to Tilda's head swimming in front of my eyes. 'What about Sonny?' I gasp. 'Sonny, the insurance salesman. What will happen to him?'

Zillo laughs, deep and throaty, and has the audacity to brush his hand over my breast as he pulls away. 'I have no idea who you're talking about, Miss Jones.' He opens the door, bowing chivalrously but his eyes are cold and flinty. 'Back on shift now, Lily. There's a good girl.'

Chapter Nineteen

Fuck. Fuck fuck fuck. I stand there, mute and furious, as the door slams shut in my face. Zillo's reaction tells me that we were right all along. The casino – or someone related to the casino – is connected with Bess's murder.

Not caring whether the casino manager sees me (what is his name, anyway? I can't keep calling him Vincent Price) I march on to the main floor and weave my way through the budding crowds that are beginning to fill the casino, out through the back entrance, tucking myself around the corner out of sight.

Buddy Zillo is Mr Z. He has to be. Closing my eyes, I lean against the wall, willing my heart rate to return to normal. Does Buddy Zillo really believe they have the right person behind bars for Bess's murder? Or is he covering something up? My gut tells me that Mr Zillo knows more than he's letting on and I wonder if I might have got us tangled up in something even bigger than I first thought. Cigarette smoke fills my nostrils and I open my eyes to Cassidy Clark leaning against the wall beside me.

'Hey.' She squints at me through the grey-blue smoke and then offers me the pack. I shake my head. She runs her eyes over me. 'You're working here now?'

'It's a temporary thing,' I say. 'How are you?' She looks pale and drawn, her cheekbones seeming sharper beneath her skin.

Cassidy shrugs and inhales on her cigarette. 'Have you found anything? About Bess?'

'Nothing concrete,' I say, 'but it feels as though I'm getting closer.' While this isn't entirely the truth, it isn't a complete lie either.

'Have you spoken to Daisy?' Cassidy asks, blowing out a thin stream of smoke.

'Louis did. She admitted they had a fight. She told Bess she'd find a way to get rid of her, but she was talking about getting Bess fired. I don't think she had anything to do with Bess's murder.'

Cassidy gives a slow nod, as if unsurprised. 'What about Jonny? Did anyone speak to him?'

'Jonny Valentine? Should I?' I picture the reservations book, Jonny's name alongside Bess's. Simon, Jonny's assistant, his voice low saying, '*I leaned on the girl but...*' Was Cassidy the girl he leaned on? Does he think she knows something? *Does* she know something after all? 'What about his assistant... Simon? Should I try talking to him?'

Cassidy shakes her head. 'Forget I said anything. Vegas is closed down tighter than a cat's ass. They've arrested someone and maybe it's best just to leave it at that.'

'Cassidy, if you know something you should tell me.' I swallow, not wanting to say what I am about to. 'For Bess. If it wasn't Sonny who did this, an innocent man could go to prison.'

'I can't help you; I wish I could. I did my best for Bess. I tried to tell her that whatever she was involved in was dangerous but she wouldn't listen. It's my last night here.

I'm catching the bus back home tomorrow morning. It's not the same, not without Bess. They're…' she breaks off, biting her lip, and I wait, letting the silence stretch out. 'Well, it's just not the same.'

'I'm sorry,' I say, grief suddenly snatching at my heart. It's been almost four years since I lost my mother, but sometimes it feels like yesterday. Cassidy's grief for Bess is a thick, dark cloud, raining the despair and misery that I know so well. 'For Bess, and for you. I'm sorry it turned out this way, but I am going to do everything I can to find the truth.'

Cassidy lets out a sad snort of laughter as she stubs her cigarette out on the wall behind us, flicking the butt to the floor. That's a fifty dollar fine in 2020. 'I hope you do, but I won't hold my breath, not with the way the truth seems to get swallowed up so easily in this town.' She meets my eyes, and I see her own are filled with tears. 'Be careful, Lily. Bess isn't the first dead girl in this town, and she won't be the last.'

–

I am still leaning against the wall, turning over Cassidy's words in my mind when voices filter around the corner, and then I catch a glimpse of Tilda's red hair as she and Louis approach the back door to the casino.

'Lily, what are you doing skulking out here?' Louis smiles as he sees me and my heart lifts.

'More to the point, what are you two doing slipping in the back door, and why on earth are you carrying *that*?' I point to the guitar strapped across Louis's chest. 'Where did you even get it from? And again, *why*?'

'Lou is going on stage!' Tilda announces in a dramatic whisper. 'He's going to be famous.'

'Back up guys, I have no idea what's going on.' This, following my confrontation with Buddy Zillo and Cassidy's cryptic warning, leaves my head spinning.

'Jonny Valentine's guitarist is out sick,' Louis says. 'It may or may not have something to do with the number of sidecars he drank last night, but whatever it is, he's out. I just so happened to be around when the news broke and luckily I could offer my services.'

'Convenient,' I say, dryly.

'Well, when it became clear there were no bartending positions available I had to find a way in somewhere,' Louis grins. 'I auditioned for Jonny this afternoon while you were sleeping, and I'm about to go on stage with him.' There is an undeniable current of glee running through his words. 'What are you doing out here?'

Briefly I run over what happened in the office with Buddy Zillo and recount Cassidy's words of warning. 'And now she's leaving,' I finish. 'I get the feeling she's too scared to stay here now that Bess is gone. I can't blame her.' I can still feel Buddy Zillo's fat fingers brushing over my breast.

Tilda is pensive, her nails drumming against her chin as she seems to be formulating something. 'Louis, you better hurry,' she says eventually. 'Get ready to go on stage, you can't be late. Lily, you come with me.'

We enter through the rear stage door, Louis turning to head down the corridor towards the stage. Putting a hand on his arm as he turns, I reach up and peck him on the cheek. 'Break a leg.'

Before he can reply I scurry after Tilda, through the dimly lit corridor, past the dancers' dressing room. She slows to a stop as the compère welcomes Jonny to the stage, and as the crowd claps, she pushes open the door ahead of us. We are in Jonny Valentine's dressing room.

'Bloody hell, Tilda, what are we doing in here?' I hiss as the door snicks closed behind us.

'Trust me,' she hisses back, turning her attention to the spot lit dressing table. 'You said Jonny knew Bess, right? And now Cassidy is asking whether you've spoken to him about Bess… so while he's out of the picture this is the perfect time for us to snoop and find out what he knows and whether he has any part in it. There must be a reason why he doesn't want anyone in his dressing room. If anyone comes in and finds us here, you're bringing him an after-show drink, and I'm here on Louella Parsons' instructions to interview him.' *I should have known Tilda would have something up her sleeve – she's as sharp as a tack.*

Looking over the dressing room, it's hard to know where to start. A rail lines the far wall, crammed full of suits – dark suits, pastel suits, even a sparkly jacket that I really hope never sees the light of day. A cluttered dressing table sits before a polished mirror, surrounded by spotlights – exactly the kind of thing I'd expect to find in a star's dressing room. An ashtray, crammed full of ash and butts, sits beside the mirror with a green matchbook, half the matches torn out. Alongside is a cut glass whisky tumbler that still smells faintly of booze, a tub of pomade and a bottle of Agua Lavanda cologne. The scent of the cologne fills the room, overpowering any smell of cigarettes, as if Jonny has spritzed himself with it before heading to the stage. I vaguely remember reading somewhere that this was Frank Sinatra's cologne of choice and I wonder who wore it first, whether Frank copied Jonny. A bunch of roses sits on a small side table, in the same shade of vivid pink that Jonny presented to Tilda the other night, their heads beginning to bow under the overhead lights.

'A little help?' Tilda tuts at me, as she yanks open the drawers to the dressing table. Standing beside her, I move the full ashtray to one side and open the opposing drawer. Sheafs of papers and envelopes spill out, floral fragrances rising from the papers. *Love letters from Jonny's fans.* I run my eyes over them, scanning for Bess's name or any sign that they were conducting an affair, but most of them are just signed with an X, or *your biggest fan.* Shoving them back in the drawer, I see Tilda has turned her attention to a rack of shoes in the corner, tipping them upside down and shaking them, while I leaf through the pile of papers on a small desk to the side of the dressing table. Most of that too is fan mail, gushing and soppy, and I wonder what Jonny's wife thinks of it all. I feel a wave of pity for Antonia; she seemed so gentle and sweet when I spilled that drink on Jonny, and the knowledge that he cheats on her behind her back – and may be involved in Bess's murder – is terribly unsettling.

The papers slide from the desk, a slippery stack of love letters and photographs, and as I gather them back into a pile, a battered business card slips from between two pages. Turning it over, I see the name *J. Castillo* printed in faded black ink, and a telephone number so smudged it is illegible. Something about the name tickles at the back of my mind, but ever aware that it won't be long before Jonny's set is over, I don't have time to stop and ponder, so I tuck it into my pocket for later. As I shift the mail out of the way, a newspaper slips to the floor. When I stoop to pick it up, the photograph looking back at me makes my blood freeze.

'Til,' I say, not taking my eyes off the photograph. 'Look at this.' I hold out the newspaper, folded to show the photo.

'That's…' Tilda frowns. 'Ben Fry. Sonny's lawyer.' She scans the page. It's a small article about Bess's murder, referencing Sonny's arrest, but it isn't that which makes my blood run cold. It's the fact that I know now why Ben Fry makes my skin crawl. I know where I have seen him before.

'He's a mob lawyer.' The words come out overly loud in the silent dressing room and goosebumps rise on my arms. 'Ben Fry, he works for the mob.'

'The mob?' Tilda stares at me and then down at the black and white photo in the newspaper. 'No, not Fry, Lily. He's Sonny's lawyer – isn't he meant to be the best defence lawyer in Los Angeles? It's Buddy Zillo and the goons out at the ranch who work for the mob.'

'And Ben Fry. Trust me, Tilda.' I knew there was something about the lawyer that didn't feel right.

'How do you know?'

I don't speak for a moment, not sure what to say. 'I just…'

'*Oh!*' Tilda gasps, her hand going to her mouth. 'Is it your gift? Did you see something?'

'Kind of,' I murmur. I did see something, back in 2019, but I only just realised. When Eric and I took our trip out to Las Vegas for a long weekend, we had spent a morning wandering around the Mob Museum. A former courthouse, the museum houses exhibitions on casino skimming, mob violence, the St Valentine's Day Massacre, and perhaps more critically, the second-floor courtroom is where hearings were held to expose organised crime in 1950 and 1951. The significance of the year isn't lost on me. Information panels and photographs make up the exhibitions, and that's where I've seen this photograph of Ben Fry before. On the wall of the Mob Museum, in an exhibition about the Las Vegas crime syndicate.

'I think this is something big,' I say, as Tilda waits for me to elaborate. 'If I'm right about Ben Fry, then I think Bess was involved in something really, really messy, and we need to tread even more carefully.' I think of the fear on Cassidy's face when questioned about what Bess was up to. 'If Fry works for the mob, then what if he was hired by them to make sure Sonny goes down for Bess's murder?' This would mean that potentially Sonny really is innocent… but it could also mean something else entirely, something that I think Evelyn is definitely going to have kittens about. 'We need to figure out once and for all how Sonny has found himself tangled up in this whole affair. I need to speak to Evelyn.'

Tilda reaches for the telephone on the table, but before she can lift the receiver we hear muted claps and cheering from the corridor, and then the boom of the compère's voice. 'Show's over,' she says. 'We need to get out of here.'

Chapter Twenty

Louis is positively buzzing with adrenaline as he meets us backstage, after Tilda and I make a narrow escape from Jonny's dressing room before he returns. We meet at the rear of the stage entrance, where I bumped into Cassidy, and briefly update Louis, aware that I still have a shift on the casino floor to complete, and that I am about to take the shine off Louis's evening.

'The mob? Benjamin Fry works for the *mob*?' Louis pulls back, his eyes wide. 'Are you sure?'

'Positive,' I say, glad now that Tilda had torn the photo from the newspaper before stuffing it back under the pile of fan mail. I run my eyes over the photo again, knowing 100 per cent that I am right.

'What does this mean for Sonny?' Louis reaches for the photo, pulling it gently out of my hands and running his eyes over Fry's slimy face.

'I'm not sure yet. I need to speak with Evelyn – I need to know how Ben Fry became Sonny's lawyer and exactly what Sonny's job is. Because I think we can all agree it's looking pretty doubtful that he was at an insurance convention.'

'There's a payphone,' Tilda says, 'out front by the saloon.'

Skirting the edge of the casino, I follow Tilda and Louis with my head down, hoping I don't get spotted by my new boss, pausing as we reach the payphone. It's a clunky black thing with a rotary dial in a box that only has three sides, and I shake my head.

'Not here,' I say, keeping my voice low. 'There are too many people around. I don't want to risk being overheard. We'll have to go back to the room and use the telephone there.' Briskly I lead the way, crossing the street without a backward glance. Upstairs, in the safety of our hotel room away from prying ears, Louis dials the operator and asks to be put through to Evelyn.

'Hello? Sonny?' Evelyn's voice is groggy, thick with sleep.

'It's Louis. I'm sorry to wake you.'

'Louis?' Suddenly alert, Evelyn's voice is pitchy and slightly distorted as we all huddle around the receiver. 'What is it? Did you find something? *Please* tell me you found something. They're going to set a trial date soon, and we're running out of time!'

Wincing internally, I gesture to Louis to pass me the receiver.

'Hello, Evelyn.'

'Oh,' she says, making no attempt to hide her disappointment. 'It's you.'

'Yes, it's me.' I roll my eyes at Tilda. 'Evelyn, we need a little more information. What exactly did Sonny do for work?'

Evelyn tuts. 'I already told you this, Lily. He works in insurance.'

'But what does he *do*?' I press. 'Evelyn, this is really important.'

'He…' she pauses, and I can picture her pretty face pulling into a frown, her forehead wrinkling in a way that she would never let it if she knew about Botox. 'He does collections. That's what he told me, I'm sure. He makes collections for the insurance company.'

Something sour turns in my stomach, sharp and acidic.

'And the name of the company?'

'Hold on one moment. Sonny gave me the details after I insisted on having a way to contact him while he was working away, and I wrote them down in my address book.' Evelyn hums under her breath and I hear the ruffle of pages as she flicks through the address book beside the telephone. 'Zillo Insurance, 6170 South 6th Street. Lily, what exactly is all this—?'

But I have already hung up.

'*Zillo* Insurance,' Tilda breathes, her eyes wide. 'You know what this means?'

'Yeah,' Louis says grimly, catching my eye. 'It sounds like our boy Sonny is in something right up to his neck. And it's got nothing to do with insurance.'

–

Somehow, I pull off a perfect shift for the rest of that night, leaving Louis and Tilda at the bar while I serve drinks, smiling, nodding and doing my best to keep my ears open, all the while batting away over-friendly hands and inappropriate comments, and thinking over Evelyn's revelation. First thing tomorrow we need to get over to South 6th Street and see exactly where Sonny was allegedly working. Buddy Zillo crosses the floor, raising a hand to Jonny and Frank, who sit with Ava and a subdued-looking Antonia. I keep my eyes on my drinks tray as I feel Zillo's eyes rake over me, hurrying back to the safety of the bar.

My feet are aching and my arms burn from the weight of the heavy drinks tray a couple of hours later, when I see Jonny and Antonia standing to one side, engaged in a heated conversation. Antonia shakes her head despondently as Jonny looms over her, his brow wrinkled. Curiosity piqued, I weave my way in their direction, glancing at their table as I pass by. No one else seems to have noticed their discussion, carried out beside the shadowy hallway that leads to the restrooms, as Frank laughs and winks in Ava's direction and Zillo claps him on the back. Catching sight of mean, weaselly Ralph as he stoops to speak in Buddy Zillo's ear, I shrink into a crowd of gamblers, and when I turn back to Jonny and Antonia, Jonny is pushing his way towards the table, and I see the full skirt of Antonia's hot-pink dress disappearing towards the restroom. Dumping the tray, I follow her, pushing open the restroom door.

'Mrs Valentine?' All the stalls are empty apart from one. 'It's Lily, the hostess? Are you all right?'

There is a sniffle and then the stall door opens to reveal a flushed Antonia. 'Oh gosh, Lily. Hello.' She steps out and moves to the mirror, her hands going to her hair. It looks as though she's been crying, and once again she wears a long-sleeved cardigan despite the warm weather outside.

'I just wanted to check on you.' I pause, my mouth dry. I'm pretty sure that checking on a guest isn't a sackable offence, but when the guest is married to Jonny Valentine I can't be certain. 'You seemed a little... upset.'

'Oh, you are a darling. I'm fine, honestly. Just a small domestic, that's all.' Antonia dabs at her eyes and then rummages in her expensive-looking handbag, pulling out a slim spray bottle of perfume. 'I do adore Las Vegas. I mean, who doesn't? But sometimes I'd just rather be at home with my children.'

'Well, of course,' I murmur. I can imagine it must be difficult to follow Jonny on the road and leave the children behind.

'But of course, Jonny wants me here, and Las Vegas is no place for children so... Men,' she tuts, as she spritzes herself with a mist of jasmine and rose. 'Can't live with 'em, can't live without 'em. Do you have a husband, Lily?'

'It's... errr... it's complicated,' I confess, thinking of Louis.

'Let me tell you, the longer you're married the more complicated things seem to become.' She gives me a smile, but it doesn't quite reach her eyes.

'I... guess it must be?' Is she telling me that she knows all about Jonny's affairs? My heart breaks a little for her, and I reach out and squeeze her hand. The thought of spending my life married to someone who forever cheats on me is unbearable.

'Trust me, darling, it is.' Antonia squeezes back, and then tucks her perfume back in her bag. 'It was very sweet of you to check on me, Lily, but I'll be just fine. I should get back to my husband.' With one last glance in the mirror, she turns to the door and leaves me standing there alone with the scent of her perfume on the air and a feeling of pity in my heart.

–

The following morning, the sun is barely up when Tilda shakes me awake. 'Lily. Wake up. Let's head downtown before it gets busy. We want to get to the insurance offices as soon as possible.' She bounces on her toes, yanking the blankets from me, chivvying me along until I am presentable, in an emerald-green blouse and a pair of black cigarette pants, both borrowed from Tilda.

It's barely nine a.m. as we reach South 6th Street. The roads are quiet, a few people hurrying past on their way to work, but there is a completely different vibe to Vegas in the morning compared to the evening. Evenings are bright lights, laughter, the ring of slots and the rattle of dice, heavy perfume and cigarette smoke. Mornings are the sunrise reflecting back off the mountains, rosy and warm, a slight chill in the air before the heat sets in, coffee and bagels, silence instead of a roar.

'This is the street name Evelyn gave us.' Louis pulls the car over, stepping out onto the sidewalk and looking first right then left. 'It's mostly residential.' Most of the buildings are ranch-style single-storey homes, with front yards filled with spiky desert greenery separating the porches from the sidewalk.

'This way.' Tilda points left and we walk further along the block until we are approaching 6170 South 6th Street. There is a small mini market, a beauty salon, and there, at 6170, is a laundromat.

'A laundromat?' Frowning, I turn to Louis. 'I was expecting some sort of office, weren't you? Are we sure this is the right place?' A car turns on to the street from the opposite direction, slowing as it too approaches 6170.

'*Hide*,' Tilda hisses, tugging on my arm. She ducks into the yard of a house on the block before the laundromat, dragging me and Louis with her.

'What the—?' Louis rubs at his arm where it brushes against a particularly fierce-looking cactus, the spiny needles dangerously close to his bare skin.

'Shhh.' Tilda presses her finger to her lips as the car – a sleek black Lincoln – slows to a stop outside the very property we are here to visit. The car doors open and Ralph and Rocky spill out onto the street, Ralph marching straight up to the door of the laundromat and entering without a backward glance.

'Was that…?' Louis turns to me, a frown creasing his brow.

'Yes,' Tilda says, 'our old friends Rocky and Ralph. I recognised their car as they pulled onto the street. I wonder what they're doing here? Not laundry, I bet.'

I'm wondering the same thing. The plot is certainly thickening, and I'm not sure I like where things are going. Evelyn definitely isn't going to like it.

'We need to get closer,' I say, stepping towards the sidewalk, but Tilda pulls me back.

'What are you going to do? March up there and ask them to wash your smalls? Don't you remember, they have a gun? And I for one don't want it pressed against my forehead again, thank you very much.'

'So what do we do? Just hide here in a bush of… whatever this is?' Thorns snatch at my clothes as I shift against the desert plants.

'I'll go in there.' Louis peers around the bush. 'They haven't seen my face, only yours, Tilda. They won't recognise me.'

Tilda lets out a scornful laugh. 'You? You can't go in there, Lou, you'll stick out like a sore thumb.'

'Why?' I genuinely have no idea why this is so amusing to Tilda.

'Why do you think, Lily?' Tilda waits and I stare blankly. 'How many men do you know who do laundry?' She tuts. 'Seriously, sometimes I worry about you.'

Of course Louis wouldn't be the one to do laundry. Not in 1950. He'd have a lovely housewife to do it for him.

'I could go in there. They're less likely to pop a cap in my ass than yours,' I say, anticipation making me shift on the balls of my feet.

'Pop a what in *what*?' Tilda gasps, as I bite back a laugh.

'Just a turn of phrase, Til. I mean, they're less likely to shoot me than Louis. I hope, anyway.' I shake away the image of Rocky holding a gun to Tilda's head. 'They didn't see me either that night at the ranch, and we know it's not an insurance office, so we're going to have to go in there at some point to find out why Sonny gave this address to Evelyn as his office.'

Tilda bites her bottom lip, the way she always does when she doesn't like something I've said. 'They're not nice guys, Lily.'

'I think we already figured that out.' I flash her a smirk and then step out on to the sidewalk, marching towards the laundromat before she can stop me.

–

The bell over the door tinkles as I step inside the laundromat. It really is a laundromat, at first glance anyway. A row of top-loading washing machines line one wall, with a bench running through the middle of the room for people to sit and wait, but none of the machines are running, and no one sits waiting for laundry. Behind the counter a young man with slicked-back hair and an Italian accent is talking on the telephone, and I use his distraction to peer behind him. In twenty-first century LA, the laundrette on Whitley Avenue has huge racks of dry-cleaning hanging behind the counter on some complicated pulley system, but here, behind the counter there is only a single, closed door, and no sign of Rocky or Ralph.

'May I help you, ma'am?' The man hangs up the telephone and turns an appraising eye on me.

My cheeks colour under his obvious scrutiny. I will never, ever get used to the way men in this era have a complete lack of awareness when it comes to how they make women feel. My palm itches to slap his leery face, but instead I smile, hating myself for it, and ask how much it is for a service wash.

'We don't really do that.'

'No? Well then, how much to use the machines?'

'Thirty-five cents if you have your own detergent, fifty cents if not.'

Just when I am beginning to believe that maybe this genuinely is a laundromat, and that perhaps Evelyn wrote down the wrong address for Sonny's office, the door behind the counter swings open. Laughter and cigar smoke disperse through the opening, and immediately my senses prick up.

'Gino, I'll see you later. I gotta make some collections.' Ralph swings through the open door, grasping the man behind the counter by the cheeks, kissing them loudly. Rocky follows, a grin on his big, dumb face, and I look down, pretending to fumble in my purse. Glancing up from beneath my lashes, I catch a glimpse into the room beyond. The air is thick with blue smoke, as yet more raucous laughter comes from within. A table holds a decanter of some sort, and a hand comes into view, reaching for a glass filled with something that could be whisky and I get the feeling that this is a party that started many hours ago. Rocky and Ralph head for the entrance behind me, and just when I'm not sure how much longer I can rummage in my purse, the body attached to the disembodied hand comes into view and I almost drop my bag entirely. It's Jonny Valentine. Jonny Valentine, superstar singer, darling of the music world, allegedly devoted husband and father, sitting in the back of a dodgy laundrette, with men who can only be described as goons.

'I'm so sorry.' I bat my lashes at Gino behind the counter. 'I don't seem to have the fifty cents. I'll come back later.' On legs that feel decidedly wobbly, I head for the exit, keen to be gone before the door opens again and Jonny has a chance to recognise me.

'Hey lady,' Gino calls as I pull the door open. 'You might want to bring your laundry too.'

Chapter Twenty-one

'Did they notice you?' Louis pulls me towards him as I reach the yard where he and Tilda are still hiding, both of them peering out from between leafy bushes.

'They saw me, but I don't think they *noticed* me,' I say, glancing over my shoulder. The street is empty, Ralph and Rocky's car gone, so we slip out of the yard and head back to Louis's car.

'What was happening? Were they doing laundry after all?' Tilda asks as Louis peels away from the kerb, headed back onto Highway 91.

'Definitely not laundry,' I say dryly, gesturing at Louis to pull into the diner where we met Cassidy. The parking lot is empty, and I am jonesing for a shot of caffeine. Once the same waitress as before has delivered a hot pot of coffee and I am confident we won't be overheard, I begin to talk.

'So, it's not a laundromat. I mean, it is, on the surface, but behind closed doors I think it's something else entirely.' I've watched *The Sopranos*. I know what goes on. And while the Sopranos might have used Satriale's Pork Store as a cover for mob activity, I think our guys are using something far more… fragrant.

'Like what?' Tilda screws her face up as she sips at the strong, bitter coffee. 'What did you see?'

I tell her how there was no sign of Rocky and Ralph until the door behind the counter swung open. 'But I did see someone else who might be of interest.'

'Who?'

'Jonny Valentine.'

'Jonny *Valentine*? What in the name of heck was he doing sitting in the back of a laundromat?' Louis lowers his voice, shaking his head in disbelief.

'It's the mob, isn't it?' Tilda says, licking her finger and sticking it in the grains of sugar that have spilled across the table. 'You said Ben Fry is a mob lawyer...'

There is a sour taste in my mouth than not even the burnt, bitter coffee can shift. 'Ralph said something about making "collections". Now, he could be driving around picking up high roller laundry, but can you see that happening? Because I can't. Evelyn said Sonny made "collections" for the "insurance company", working out of this office. Ben Fry is a mob lawyer. Put it all together with the ranch, Ralph dropping Mr Z into the conversation, and then Buddy Zillo warning me away from searching for the truth about Bess, and it all seems to point to the same thing.'

'Cassidy said Bess had more money and she was cagey about where she got it from, and who she was spending time with,' Louis says. 'Man, I can't believe that Jonny Valentine could be mixed up in all of this.'

'Money,' Tilda snorts. 'It all comes back to money. Sonny must have been putting the squeeze on people, collecting money for the mob.'

It does sound likely and the thought of it, of having to tell Evelyn that Sonny isn't the sweet, innocent man she thinks he is, makes my stomach drop. 'This doesn't mean Sonny is off the hook for the murder either,' I say.

'We still have this issue of the eyewitness who apparently saw Sonny running from the scene. We know that this might not be true, but how the hell do we find out for certain when the mob are involved?' *And who knows what implications this will have for Evelyn's future?* I haven't lost sight of the fact that ultimately, I am here to try and save Evelyn from a horrible fate.

'Doesn't this make it seem more likely that Sonny did have something to do with Bess's murder?' Louis leans in as a trucker enters the diner, scanning the empty booths before he makes his seat selection. 'If Bess knew something and was threatening Sonny...'

'But Ben Fry said Sonny had never been to Baker before,' Tilda says, 'that day we visited him at his office.'

'Are we believing everything Ben Fry says now?' Louis asks, shaking his head.

Tilda gives him a pointed stare. 'Just because Sonny lied about his job doesn't mean he's a murderer. And there's also Jonny Valentine to consider. He knew Bess – he must have done, he met her for lunch before she died. He's mixed up in all of this somehow – he knew the laundromat isn't just a laundromat, after all.'

'That's the thing,' I say, my heart sinking as I replay that visit to Ben Fry's office in Los Angeles. The way I had come away from there with the sensation that something he said didn't sit right with me. 'Evelyn said she had never been there before, but Fry's words were, "Sonny never went to Baker *that night.*"' I pause, waiting for the penny to drop. 'That implies that Sonny had been to Baker – and therefore the ranch – *before* that night... And it also implies that Ben Fry knows where Sonny *really* was.'

'What if...' Louis frowns, rubbing his hand over his forehead as if getting a headache. 'What if Sonny is innocent, even though he is involved with the mob, and he wants to keep Benjamin Fry as his lawyer because he thinks Fry is employed by the mob to get him off... but really,' Louis swallows, his face pained, 'what if really the mob know who actually killed Bess and they've engaged Ben Fry to make sure that Sonny is *sent down for the murder*?'

'And who knows what that might mean for us?' A stone lodges itself in my stomach, a hard rock of fear. 'Fry knows we're still poking around, even if Zillo has warned me off.' The idea that I might have placed all of us in extreme danger makes me feel a little faint.

'Oh boy,' Tilda breathes. 'You're right, Lil. This is getting messy.'

On our return to town, Louis pulls into the parking lot at the Desert Inn and I slide out of the car, heading across the street to the Silver Slipper as Tilda hurries away into the hotel.

'Lil?' Louis follows, gripping my arm as I go to step off the sidewalk. 'Where are you going? You don't have a shift today.'

'You know I'm not here to work, Lou,' I say, with a quizzical look. 'I'm here to find out what happened to Bess – to find out if Sonny really is innocent – and hope that I can save Evelyn from... well, you know what from. The fact that Ben Fry might be working against Sonny has just made it even more important that we find out the truth.' The sense of urgency has increased along with the sense of danger, and I feel as if my pulse might never return to normal.

'I know, but...' Louis looks away, pushing his hands through his hair. 'I was hoping... maybe we could talk? About... well, about us, I guess.'

'Now?' The word comes out more abruptly than I hoped, but then Louis doesn't know what I'm about to do.

'I thought while Tilda isn't around... Look, Lil, this might sound really dramatic, but this whole thing with Sonny and Evelyn... the mob, and gangsters and Jonny Valentine... it's put things in perspective for me.'

'Oh.' I pause, slowly drawing in a breath. This is it. This is the moment when Louis tells me I'm too chaotic, too flighty, too *everything* for him and it'll never work. I guess it's better that it comes now, while I am too busy to lie in my bed and cry, eating Hershey's Kisses by the handful.

Louis runs a hand through his hair, and I want to yell at him to spit it out, to get it over and done with. 'Lily, I thought everything between us was done, and then you came back, and everything is... up in the air again. I don't know what to think, or how to feel, and I don't know if you're going to just up and leave again.'

Wait. What is he actually saying? I stay silent, willing him to go on.

'This whole thing...' he waves a hand. 'We're in danger, aren't we? These people are scary, nasty people and you're willing to put yourself in this situation for Evelyn – someone you don't even *like*. And for me, that's an incredible quality. That's... that's someone I want in my life. So I know we have a lot to talk about, and I know that there's every chance you'll disappear again, but all I'm asking is that this time, when it's over, we talk. Properly.'

Swallowing hard, I reach out and press my hand to his face, feeling the faint prickle of stubble on his cheek. 'Louis, I don't know what's going to happen. You're right, of course you are, we do need to talk, and I promise that as soon as this is all over, we'll sit down together. But right now I need to focus on this one thing. On helping Evelyn.' I step closer to him, breathing in his familiar scent. I made myself forget him, the way he smells, the way he moves, the way his lips twitch right before he lets out a laugh. I wish this time I wouldn't have to forget him. 'If I don't help Evelyn now, something terrible is going to happen. I can't… I can't deal with us until I know she's safe.'

Louis nods as he brushes my hair away from my face, sending a shiver down my spine. 'Of course. I'm sorry, I'm being selfish. Evelyn needs us – needs you. Whatever happens with us, it can wait.'

It takes every fibre of my being not to throw myself into his arms and let him kiss me until my knees go weak. Yeah, I still remember that kiss at the Beverly Hills Hotel, right before I slipped back to 2019. I've thought about that one *a lot*.

'That still doesn't tell me why you're sneaking back off to the Silver Slipper.'

Pulling back, I bite on my lip to hide the grin that marches across my face. 'Isn't it obvious? I'm going to bust into Buddy Zillo's office and find out exactly what he's up to, and how Sonny and Jonny Valentine are involved.'

–

'Lily, are you sure Zillo isn't going to burst in while we're in his office?' Louis murmurs in my ear as we approach the invisible door to the dark corridor that runs behind the gaming floor.

'Not at all. That's why you're going to be my lookout.'
I offer up a prayer to the time travel gods, thanking them
for sending me back to a place that isn't bristling with
security cameras like it would be in 2020, as I pull a hair
grip from my pocket. These Fifties gals really knew that
pockets were essential. Louis stifles a groan as I wink at
him. 'Now, just a second. We need to wait here because
right about… *now*, the cashier will be leaving the counting
room.' The casino is nothing if not regular, provided you
know what to look for. I pull Louis towards the door,
asserting a no-nonsense stance so I look as if I belong here.
The moment the invisible door swings open to let the
cashier out, I walk past with a brisk nod, catching the
door before it closes and usher Louis inside.

'This is… creepy,' he says, as he takes in the panelled
walls and swirly carpet. 'Like a haunted mansion, decorated by a millionaire.'

'No accounting for taste,' I smirk, 'but there is a hell of
a lot of other counting going on in here.'

Reaching Buddy Zillo's office door I raise my hand
and knock, pressing my ear to the wood, even though his
car was missing from his designated spot in the lot.

'No one's in there,' I state, pulling back. 'Look, that
door there, that's the counting room.' I point to the heavy
oak door further along the corridor. 'And behind us is the
only door that provides access to this place. Keep an eye on
both – if anyone comes in make like you're just leaving the
counting room to deliver something to Zillo and knock
three times on this door.' I rap again on the office door,
once, then twice in quick succession. 'I'll know I have to
get out.'

'And if it's Zillo that's coming in?'

'You have an urgent phone call for him at the reception desk, but the operator system is down, and he needs to come to the front desk to take the call.'

'What if someone is coming to see Zillo in his office?'

'Then he's busy and can't be disturbed. Don't worry, it'll be fine.' Turning to the door, I jam the hair grip into the lock, my fingers slipping on the metal. My pulse is hammering in my ears and there is the faint metallic taste of fear on my tongue. *It has to be fine.* Dropping the hair grip, I swear under my breath and jam it back in place, aware of every minute ticking past. *Please God, let this work.* I don't know if this is the kind of thing that only works in movies, and once again I offer up a prayer of thanks that this is a simple key lock, and not some techy biometric thing that needs to scan an eyeball to open. Finally, my palms sweaty and my heart racing, there is a click and the door handle turns. 'Remember, three knocks.'

Louis nods and I step into Buddy Zillo's office, pulling the door closed behind me. The large walnut desk, inlaid with dark green leather, seems to take up even more of the room now Buddy isn't sat there, the Chesterfield chair in matching green leather behind it vast and empty. The desk is clear and when I try the drawer handles, they don't budge. There is a very *Godfather* feel to the room, and if you'd told me that Scorsese had based Don Corleone's office on this room I would have believed you. I blink at the thought of Marlon Brando, and the way he'd sidled up to me at Honey's premiere. It feels like years ago.

There is a solid and sturdy safe in one corner, *Victor Safe & Lock Co.* written on the front in neat gold script. There isn't an electronic keypad, but instead there is a hefty steel dial. Vaguely I think about spinning the dial and listening for the clicks — isn't that how they crack safes in old movies? Maybe I should have spent more time on safe-cracking TikTok than Taylor Swift TikTok. Drawing my hand back before I make contact with the safe, I wonder if fingerprinting is a thing yet. Bookcases line one wall, row upon row of leather-bound classics, a stepladder on a runner attached to the top of the bookcase like something out of *Beauty and the Beast*. A life-long reader, I am intrigued by the idea of a mobster settling down with a good book, and I step closer, running my eyes over the titles. *Animal Farm. For Whom the Bell Tolls. Alice in Wonderland?* I never had Buddy Zillo down as a reader. Pulling *Alice* from the shelf, I slide my finger under the cover as a voice filters into the room, making my heart leap into my throat.

'You can leave now, ma'am, thank you. Go on, off you go.' The disembodied voice is deep and oddly familiar. *Where is Louis? Why didn't he warn me?* I close my eyes and draw in a deep breath, preparing myself to turn around and confront whoever has just caught me red-handed, but before I can face the music, another voice fills the room.

'But Mr—'

'I said leave. It's fine. Here. You want me to sign this? Let me sign this for you.' Finally I turn, confusion creasing my brow as I realise the office is still empty. The book I'm holding slips to the floor as I crane my neck to look above the bookcases. It sounds as though the voice is coming from above. Pausing for a moment, I hear a door open and close, murmurs coming from the corridor outside, and when no knock comes from Louis I press my foot on to the first rung of the stepladder. It shifts slightly beneath my weight and I steadily climb the few steps to the top. *Bingo.*

Set into the wall above the bookcases is an air brick for ventilation, dotted with holes big enough to see into the counting room next door. Balancing on the top step, my stomach squashed against the polished oak of the bookcase, if I tilt my head I can just about see into the room.

'Do you really think this is a good idea, given what's happened?' It's Simon, Jonny's assistant, standing at the cash table, piles of dollar bills in front of him. Jonny stands beside him, but I can't see what he's doing. 'What about those cashiers? Won't they tell Zillo?'

Tell Zillo what? Shuffling forward, I suck in a gasp as I manage to get close enough to press my face against the air brick. Now I can see directly down into the counting room below, but I can barely breathe. *Oh. That's what.* Jonny Valentine is holding an overnight bag, stuffing it with bundles of cash. I slide down a little, gasping in oxygen. *He's skimming. Jonny Valentine is skimming the casino.*

'Like hell they will. Don't you know who I am?' Jonny snorts out a laugh. 'And anyway, I told you, this is the last time. Take this.' He zips the bag closed, shoving it in Simon's direction. 'Put it in the trunk of the Caddy – the white one. Drive it out to the usual place and leave it with the last drop.'

'Jonny, you don't need to do this. You already have houses in Florida, Los Angeles, New York... I really think—'

'I don't pay you to think.' Jonny shows his perfect white teeth, the smile of a great white. 'Simon, they trust me. *Zillo* trusts me. I am the face of this casino. I have the ear of the president, and Hoover is on my Christmas card list. Antonia buys his mother a birthday present, for Christ's sake. These boys will turn on each other before they turn on me.'

Simon shakes his head, but still takes the bag. 'I wouldn't be so sure, Jonny. Look what happened with B—'

'I dealt with it, didn't I?' Jonny's tone is ice, cold enough to burn. He moves closer to Simon, his face changing into something unrecognisable from the affable, charming man on stage every night. 'Bess is gone, and I made sure the kid got picked up for it. Who do you think made sure there was an eyewitness?'

Holy shit. I slide back towards the stepladder, fumbling for it for a moment with my foot before my shoe makes contact and I descend on shaky legs, my pulse racing. *Sonny didn't do it. He didn't murder Bess. I have to get out of here.*

Chapter Twenty-two

Sonny is innocent. I suppose this is good news for Evelyn and Sonny, but there is an undeniable flutter of fear in my stomach at the realisation that with Sonny's innocence will come the take-down of Jonny Valentine – who just so happens to be involved with the mob. The very thought of it creates ice crystals in my veins, a chill that can't be chased away by brandy or a warm blanket. Stooping to pick up the copy of *Alice in Wonderland* that I dropped, I pause as I reach down with sweaty palms. The book has fallen open on the floor and when I pick it up, it isn't Alice's familiar tale that I'm seeing. It's a list. A list of names and dates, with amounts beside them. Each amount is initialled. *It's some sort of ledger. A record.* Many of the entries are initialled JC, some RM – which could be Ralph or Rocky? – but I don't see anything initialled with an S, for Sonny. Regardless, I slide the book into the waistband of my trousers and shift the books on the shelves to hide the gap.

'Louis?' I peer into the corridor, as Louis steps into sight.

'Thank God, Lil, you were in there for ages. Jonny Valentine and some guy came in and I had to pretend I was on my way out, and then two women came out of the counting room and for a moment I thought they were going to knock on Zillo's door. I thought we were busted for sure. Are you all right? You look kinda pale.'

The spine of the book presses painfully into my hips, and I shift. 'I have *a lot* to tell you.' There is the snick of a door opening and Jonny's voice spills out into the corridor. 'Quick, we have to get out of here.' Heads down, we hurry along the corridor, out on to the gaming floor. Moments later Jonny and Simon follow, Simon glancing around anxiously as he clutches a large tan overnight bag tightly. It's a satchel-style bag, and if I didn't know what it really contained I would assume it carried important papers, or a laptop if I was in my own time. I can't believe the gall of Jonny – to walk out so brazenly with a bag full of casino money. A casino run by mobsters, at that. Jonny walks out, smiling and nodding to other patrons as Simon scurries along behind, his eyes on the floor.

'Where's Tilda?'

'Still back at the Desert Inn, I guess.' Louis follows my gaze as I watch Jonny leave. 'Did something happen in there?'

'Let's go back to the room, and I'll tell you both everything.'

–

'A novel? All the things you could have stolen from Buddy Zillo's office and you pilfered a novel?' Tilda snorts as I throw the book onto the bed.

'Open it.'

Tilda gives me an amused glance as she reaches out, the smile dropping from her face as she opens the cover. 'Oh golly, Lil. Do you know what this is? It's some sort of ledger...' She flicks the pages, a frown furrowing her brow. 'Did you find this in Zillo's office?'

I nod. 'There are more. Possibly hundreds. He has an entire bookcase lined with these fake leatherbound novels.'

'These are the proof we needed that Sonny is definitely mixed up in this somehow.' Louis points at the top of the page, at the neat black ink. 'Look here – 6170S6S. That has to be the laundromat, right? 6170 South 6th Street.'

'I can't find any initials that match Sonny's,' I say, 'but he must know something to have given that address, and to tell Evelyn that he makes "collections".' I pause. 'This is just the tip of the iceberg. There's more.'

'What?'

'Sonny didn't do it. He might be involved with Zillo somehow, but he didn't kill Bess.'

'*What?* Are you sure? How do you know?'

A wave of nausea washes over me, and I feel light-headed. 'Sit, Lil. Your face is white – are you OK?' Louis guides me to the end of the bed. 'What happened in that room?'

'I'm fine, just... I haven't eaten, and what I'm about to tell you is... explosive, to say the least.'

Fetching a glass of water, Louis comes to sit beside me and I accept the drink gratefully, droplets splashing the fabric of Tilda's borrowed blouse as I take a sip. 'Sonny didn't kill Bess. And I know who did. At least, I think I do.' I swallow, my throat dry, and wipe my damp palm over my trousers. 'I heard Jonny in the counting room, talking to his assistant. He's skimming from the casino, and he was gloating about how Buddy Zillo trusts him.'

'That's what was in the bag? Money?' Louis asks.

Nodding, I take a deep breath. 'Simon – the assistant – went to say something about Bess, and Jonny said, "I dealt with it... I made sure the kid got picked up for it."'

'So Jonny killed Bess, and set Sonny up?' Tilda presses her hand to her mouth, her eyes wide. 'This is... incredible, Lil. What a scoop!'

'Scoop? Tilda, you can't be serious.'

'Well, of course I mean after we tell Evelyn and Sonny gets released... you can't deny me a story this big. And anyway, this is perfect.'

'Perfect? How is it perfect?'

Tilda smiles, a familiar quirking of her lips that tells me she's got a plan and both Louis and I are probably not going to approve. 'Ever hear of an atomic party?'

'What the hell is an atomic party? Is this something to do with drugs?' Louis screws up his face. 'You know whisky is my limit.'

'Wait, Louis.' I hold up a hand. 'It's not drugs, it's...' The vaguest seed of a memory puffs through my mind, the mushroom cloud of an atomic bomb. 'The testing, out in the desert? They're testing atomic bombs out there.'

'Bingo.' Tilda cocks a finger gun at me. 'The hotel is holding a party tonight, upstairs in the Sky Room. There'll be drinking, and dancing, and watching bombs get detonated at two in the morning. I happened to over-hear our dear friend Ralphie talking about it at the bar.'

'What does that have to do with Jonny?'

Tilda rolls her eyes. 'Come on, Lil. Did you bang your head or something? Obviously Jonny is going to be at the party – he's the face of Las Vegas. We're going to watch Jonny's show, then afterwards I'm going flash this' – she pulls out Louella's business card – 'at the party, and get close to Jonny. I'll tell him I'm doing a piece on him for Louella, and we should probably be somewhere a little more... intimate for me to be able to interview him. If he really is a philanderer then I'm betting I can get him to invite me back to his hotel room.'

'*Tilda!* You wouldn't!' Louis looks horrified. 'What about Reg?'

'What about him?' Tilda tuts at the mention of her fiancé. 'I'm not going to do anything, Louis. Jeez. I'm going to get him so plastered that he'll fall asleep, and then I'm going to search his room to find something – anything – that will prove he was the one to kill Bess.'

'You think that'll work?' I am sceptical. But then, celebrities are still being found in compromising positions in 2020, when news can be leaked in real time. I imagine that Jonny may take the risk – after all, Tilda is a beautiful woman, and there is no Twitter, TikTok or Snapchat to out him within minutes. 'Wait. What about Antonia? How are you going to drag Jonny off to his hotel room without her seeing?' Something turns in the pit of my stomach at the idea of her seeing Tilda lead Jonny away to his hotel room. The idea of us being the cause of yet more distress to Antonia doesn't sit right with me.

'I reckon Lou can keep her distracted,' Tilda smirks, as Louis's jaw drops. 'What? You didn't think I'd be going to the party alone, did you?'

'You're going to need to be careful,' I say, picturing the way Jonny's face had changed when challenged by Simon in the counting room. 'Jonny isn't the guy he portrays himself to be on stage. He was positively threatening to Simon earlier.'

'Before we go to any party,' Louis says, getting to his feet and picking up the telephone receiver, 'don't you think we should call Evelyn and tell her we know Sonny didn't do it?'

'Hello?' Evelyn's voice is cautious, but markedly cheerier than the last time we called her.

'Evelyn? It's Lily.'

'Oh, Lily! It's lovely to hear from you.' *What? Is Evelyn having a stroke or something?* I don't think I've ever heard Evelyn pleased to hear from me. 'Do you have news?' There is an audible inhalation at Evelyn's end of the line.

'Well, yes, actually I do,' I say. 'And I think you're going to be quite pleased.'

'Oh? Well, what is it?' There she is. Abrupt, impatient Evelyn.

'Sonny didn't do it. Sonny didn't kill Bess.'

'*Oh.*' The single word is full of emotion, and I feel the bridge of my own nose begin to sting. 'Oh Lily, I knew it. I knew Sonny was innocent. Wait.' Evelyn pauses and I can picture her on the other end of the line, her blue eyes narrowing, her mouth – always ringed in her trademark red lipstick – pulling into a pout. 'When will he be let out of jail? Surely they have to let him go if you've found proof that he's innocent?'

'It's not quite that simple,' I say. 'Although I am convinced that Sonny is innocent, I don't have the proof yet.'

'Let me call Mr Fry about this. He's Sonny's lawyer, he'll know how we can use whatever information you have to get Sonny out.'

'No!' I almost shout. 'Don't call Ben Fry.' I'm certain now that Ben Fry has been sent to represent Sonny by the mob – possibly even by Jonny Valentine himself, in the hopes that Fry will be able to make sure Sonny is found guilty. No wonder he wasn't pressing Sonny's innocence

– of course Jonny will want Sonny behind bars. 'Give me a little more time to get the proof, and then we can make steps towards getting Sonny out. I just wanted to tell you that I believe you. I believe Sonny is innocent of Bess's murder… but there is one thing you should know about him. He might be mixed up with some not very pleasant people here in Las Vegas.'

'Like who?'

'Like, errr… the mob?'

'The mob?' Evelyn lets out a peal of laughter, loud enough to shatter an eardrum. Louis frowns as the noise squawks from the telephone receiver and he huddles closer to be able to hear what Evelyn says. 'Oh gosh Lily, you really are a card! I've never heard anything so ridiculous in all my life. Of course Sonny isn't involved with the mob. You watch far too many movies.'

I open my mouth to respond and Louis throws an anxious glance my way as he eases the telephone receiver into his own hand. 'Ev? Just leave things with us over here, all right? As soon as we have the proof we'll contact Fry and the Los Angeles Police Department. You just sit tight and keep Sonny's spirits up.'

'Louis! You're there, too? What about Tilda?'

'Uh, yeah. Tilda's here as well.' Tilda looks up from where she peers at the *Alice in Wonderland* ledger, running her finger down the page as if cross-checking something. Louis beckons her over and she slides off the bed with an impatient sigh.

'Wonderful. I can give all of you my news at the same time.' There is a pregnant pause as we exchange puzzled glances. Evelyn lives for the drama. 'I'm getting *married*!'

'Whaaa—' Louis wheezes, as Tilda jabs him in the ribs. 'I mean, wow, Evelyn! What… good news.'

'To Sonny?' Tilda grabs the telephone receiver.

'Yes, of course to Sonny,' Evelyn snaps. 'Who else would it be?'

'Not Paulie Brooker, that's for sure,' Tilda says, as Louis snatches the phone out of her hand.

'That's wonderful news, Evelyn,' he says, glaring at Tilda. 'Isn't it, Lily?'

My mind is working overtime and I just nod, blankly, forgetting that this isn't a FaceTime call. 'Uh… how did this happen, Evelyn? When did Sonny propose?' *Maybe I can save Evelyn. If Sonny is innocent and Evelyn marries him, then maybe I've changed things enough to save her from her wicked, murdering husband in 1953.* Sonny isn't quite out of jail yet, but I feel the burden on my shoulders lift ever so slightly. I might have done enough to save Evelyn. At that realisation, I blink, my eyes stinging.

'It wasn't the way I envisaged it,' Evelyn admits. 'In an ideal world there would have been candles and flowers, maybe a trip out to San Francisco with wine and a picnic under the bridge, but it was magical nonetheless. He asked me this morning when I visited him.'

'He asked you in *jail*?' Tilda yelps, taking her own jab to the ribs from Louis. 'At the table in the sweaty old visiting hall?'

'Scoff all you want, Tilda Jardine, I'll still be walking down the aisle before you and Reg ever get close.'

'Congratulations, Evelyn,' I say, and I mean it. Sonny might be a small-time gangster, but he's not a murderer, and if this means Evelyn doesn't die in three years' time then I'll be happy.

'Thank you, Lily,' she says graciously. 'I just can't wait to become Mrs Jackson Castillo.' And my stomach drops to the floor.

Chapter Twenty-three

Jackson Castillo. Sonny's real name is Jackson Castillo. I know
that name, I know I do, and as it dawns on me *why* I know
that name, my hand goes to my mouth and I suddenly feel
light-headed and nauseous. Louis hangs up, turning to me
with a smile, but I push past him, heading for the small
bathroom on the other side of the hotel room.

'Excuse me, I just need a second.' Closing the door
behind me, I twist the lock closed and fumble in the
pocket of my pants. Drawing out the worn business card
that I stole from Jonny's dressing room, I lay it on the sink
and thrust my hand into the other pocket, pulling out the
now crumpled newspaper article I brought with me from
2020. I smooth out the soft wrinkles and hold it up to the
light over the bathroom mirror. The ink is almost entirely
faded now, the dark curve of Evelyn's lips and the curl
of her hair as it meets her shoulder the most vivid parts.
Pressing the paper against the glass, I strain my eyes over
the faint words, my breath catching as I make out the last
lines of the article.

> Evelyn's hus...nd, 34 ye... old J...ckie
> Castillo is wan...d by ...lice for
> qu...tion...g, havi... fled the sc...ne.

My stomach swoops and dives, and there is a roaring in
my ears as if I might faint, as my eyes meet my reflection

in the mirror. *I haven't changed anything at all. In fact, I may have made things worse.* I pull out the other article, the one Tilda tore from the newspaper in Jonny's dressing room. The photograph of Ben Fry is dark and solid, every inch of his face pressed strongly onto the page. As I pull out the article, the lipstick I found under the couch at the ranch falls into the bathroom sink. I lay the articles beside the business card, my eyes going to the name *Jackie Castillo* over and over. *What have I done?*

'Lily? Are you all right?' Louis taps lightly on the bathroom door and I fold the sheets of paper with trembling hands, shoving them back into my pockets.

'Just a minute.' My voice wobbles as I turn on the tap, letting the cold water run for a moment before I splash my face with shaking hands, gasping at the icy chill. Gathering my composure, I take one last look in the mirror and smooth down my curls before opening the bathroom door and stepping back into the hotel room. Louis and Tilda both turn to me, brows knitted with concern.

'Lily? Are you all right? Why did you rush off like that? You look awful pale.' Tilda gets to her feet, peering at me closely. 'This isn't just about Evelyn's engagement, is it?'

'It is and it isn't...' On watery legs I move to the bed, plopping down onto the soft mattress with a light thump, resisting the urge to cover my face with my hands. 'When Evelyn asked us to help Sonny, I didn't realise who he was.'

'What do you mean?' Louis leans forward, from where he sits on the opposite bed. 'He's Evelyn's boyfriend – fiancé now.'

'That's the thing,' I say, slowly struggling to push the words out. 'Evelyn is going to marry Sonny... *Jackson.* Whatever I've done so far to try and change Evelyn's future has only made things worse. She's going to marry

Sonny… and he's going to be the one to kill her.' The words taste bitter on my tongue, and I have to swallow hard as nausea spirals in my stomach.

'Sonny…' Louis looks as though I have punched him in the stomach and the colour in Tilda's face drains away to leave her cheeks a bleached bone white.

'As soon as I heard his full name I realised it was him,' I say thickly. 'Why didn't she just tell us his full name? I didn't even think about it when we spoke to Ben Fry.'

'Maybe she won't marry him.' Tilda's voice is low, almost drowned out by the snort Louis lets out.

'She will, Tilda. You know she will. You saw how she was about him when we visited her – she thinks he's her perfect man. All Evelyn ever wanted was a man who would buy her expensive gifts, take her to fancy restaurants and holiday with her in Palm Springs or the South of France. That's exactly the life Sonny has promised her. Throw in a baby or two and there's absolutely no reason for Evelyn not to marry him.'

'He's connected to the mob!' Tilda screeches. 'Surely even Evelyn can't overlook that?'

'Have you *met* Evelyn?' Louis snaps, the tension in the room rising to breaking point. 'Evelyn can easily overlook something as trivial as gangsters, if it means she achieves her dream of getting married.'

'Louis…' I stare up at him, shocked by the bitterness in his voice. 'That seems… harsh.' I've never heard him sound this way before.

'All I mean is…' Louis sighs, pushing a hand through his hair, '…Evelyn is so afraid of being left on the shelf that I think she *would* overlook something like this, if she could get away with it. No matter what we tell her, there's always the chance that if Sonny goes free, Evelyn will bury her head in the sand and marry him anyway, just because he has a lot of money and spoils her rotten.'

'If only she'd told us his name before, maybe I would have realised.' I scrub my hands over my face, suddenly feeling overwhelmingly tired. 'We could have refused to help him. But now... what do we do? We know that Sonny didn't murder Bess.'

'No one else does though.' Tilda's face is serious as she looks from me to Louis.

'You can't mean...'

'No one else knows!' Tilda gets to her feet. 'If Sonny goes to jail for Bess's murder, then there's no way he'll be able to hurt Evelyn! You would be able to save her, Lily.' She turns big, wide eyes on me, and I realise that no matter how disparaging Tilda can be about Evelyn and her traditional values, Tilda does really care about her.

'Tilda, no.' Louis gets to his feet, gripping her by her upper arms. 'Look at me. You don't mean that. If Sonny goes to jail for Bess's murder, it isn't just life in prison. You know that. You'll be sending him to death row.'

'But—' Tilda throws me a desperate look and I feel the prickle of sweat on the back of my neck. The air is thick with an emotion I can't name and for a moment I can't speak.

'No, Tilda. We can't,' I say eventually. My chest feels heavy, my limbs numb. 'We can't let Sonny go down for something he didn't do.'

'But he'll just go on to murder Evelyn! And then he'll end up on death row anyway.' Tilda's voice breaks and she pulls away from Louis, snatching a tissue from the box on the table and pressing it to her eyes.

'He won't, though, that's half the problem,' I say quietly. 'He murders her and disappears. We need to find some other way to fix this.'

Tilda glares at me and heads for the bathroom, closing the door a little too firmly. Louis sighs, turning to face me. 'She's upset at the whole thing, not just you. She'll calm down and see reason in a minute, you know how fiery she is.'

I nod, feeling miserable. I've never been on the receiving end of Tilda's fury before. 'She can't honestly think we can let Sonny fry for something he didn't do? I just couldn't... I couldn't live with myself, even if he is a low-life mobster.' *Even if it is a sure-fire way to save Evelyn.* 'There has to be another way. A way to save Evelyn, and make sure that there is justice for Bess.'

The bathroom door creaks open and Tilda's face appears in the crack. Her eyes are pink and the tip of her nose shines. 'You're right,' she says after a moment. 'We can't let Sonny go to the chair for something he didn't do. Not for his sake, though. He deserves to fry for what he's going to do to Ev, but I want justice for Bess, and if Sonny is found guilty of her murder then the true culprit is going to go free.'

'I agree,' I say, relieved that Tilda has seen sense, even if she is still furious. 'We just need to figure out a way of getting Evelyn out of Sonny's clutches before it all goes horribly wrong.'

'And without letting her know that something dreadful is going to happen to her,' Louis says.

'Maybe we need to tell her more about the possibility that Sonny could be involved with the mob? Even if he isn't the one who murdered Bess, he's still connected to the people who did,' I say. 'Surely that doesn't paint the best picture to Evelyn, given how concerned she is with appearances?'

'She'll never believe us,' Tilda says, and I am relieved to see she is back to her usual self when it comes to Evelyn. Tilda reaches for her compact and begins to blot the shine from her nose, the dusty floral scent filling the room. 'She'll accuse you of being jealous, Lily, or worse she'll say I want to stop the wedding so I can marry Reg before they get married.' She pauses her blotting. 'There'll be something though. I'll think of some way that we can convince Evelyn not to—' Tilda's eyes widen as a knock comes at the door, tentative at first, and then harder, with some urgency.

'Are you expecting anyone?' Louis moves to the door as I shake my head and Tilda shoves her used tissue up her sleeve. Louis presses his eye to the peephole, raising his eyebrows at us as he opens the door to reveal Cassidy Clark.

'Cassidy?' I usher her inside, as Louis attempts to take the small suitcase she's carrying. Cassidy shakes her head and clings to the case. It's a small square Louis Vuitton, and I'm sure I saw something similar on a vintage site in my time for five thousand dollars, so I don't blame her for hanging on to it. 'I thought you left town?'

Cassidy shakes her head. She's wearing a pink and blue gingham dress with a wide collar, and dusty black low-heeled pumps. Everything looks a little ill-fitting and worn. 'I'm about to leave,' she says. 'I'm on the next bus, but I couldn't go without seeing you.' She shifts awkwardly, looking down at the patterned carpet. 'I wasn't completely honest with you the other day when we talked about Bess, but I wasn't sure… people say they want to help, or that they're not like the others, but sometimes people lie. I had to be sure I could trust you.'

'We already told you you could. What made you decide you could trust us now?' Tilda asks, her tone sharp, her nerves clearly still frayed from learning the truth about Sonny – *Jackson* – Castillo.

'I saw you,' Cassidy says. 'Coming out of Jonny's dressing room when he was on stage. I knew then that you couldn't be a part of it all. Jonny never lets anyone in his dressing room, or his hotel suite without him being there. If he was on stage, you must have snuck in.'

'Damn, girl. You're good.' I give Cassidy a smile that she shyly returns. 'If you weren't honest with us, what did you lie about?'

'It wasn't that I lied... it was more that I just didn't tell you everything.' Cassidy's cheeks flush and I catch a glimpse of the small-town girl that still lives under the fancy, tight-fitting show costumes and thick eyeliner. 'Bess told me some of what she suspected was going on.'

'Wait.' Tilda grabs her notepad and her tiny stub of a pencil and gestures for Cassidy to continue.

'She was involved with some nasty people at the casino – it's not what you think it is there. It's not just some harmless gambling at the tables and a risqué show in the evening before Jonny comes on and sings. There are some awful people involved. The casino owner, Buddy, he's a real piece of work and he has some connections to other... awful people.' Cassidy leans in as if afraid she'll be overheard. 'The mob, you know?'

Louis meets my eyes over the top of Cassidy's head at the mention of Buddy Zillo.

'Jonny Valentine isn't so innocent either,' Cassidy goes on. 'Bess was convinced that he was skimming money from the casino, but she didn't have any proof. There was a guy she was seeing, and the two of them were going to try and take Jonny down.'

'Jeez.' Tilda lets out a long breath. 'Take him down how?'

'Bess said they were going to shake him down for the skimmed money.' Cassidy swallows, blinking hard as I see my own disbelief reflected back in Louis and Tilda's faces. 'Bess said Jonny boasted about how the mob thought he was friendly with the White House, so he could get away with anything. He would skim the money and stash it out at the ranch in Baker. Because Zillo and his pals use the ranch for meetings, Jonny always thought that if the money was ever discovered there he could easily point the finger at one of the others.'

Tilda's pencil scratches furiously across the page as she jots down everything Cassidy tells us.

'Who owns the ranch?' I ask Cassidy, but she shrugs.

'I have no idea,' she says. 'Bess just told me that Buddy and his guys used it for meetings.'

'I can't believe the police haven't looked into Jonny in more detail for Bess's murder,' Louis says.

'Money talks.' There is a sharp edge to Cassidy's tone, and I get the feeling that she'll be glad to see the back of Vegas for good.

'I wouldn't be surprised at all if money exchanged hands,' Tilda says wryly. 'I know stories that would make your hair curl about Los Angeles cops.' She glances over at me and my wild corkscrew curls. 'Well, maybe not your hair, Lil.'

'So who was Bess going to out Jonny to?' Louis asks. 'Surely if she meant to tell Buddy Zillo then he would never believe her, not if he thought Jonny was loyal to him. He would have laughed her out of town. Jonny is the golden boy at the casino, he brings in a lot of money with his show. Zillo would never believe Bess; she was just a dancer. Sorry, Cassidy.'

'Bess wasn't going to tell Buddy,' Cassidy says, fumbling in her pocket for a cigarette. She lights it without asking if any of us mind, blowing a long stream of smoke into the air, and I bite back a cough as the tobacco hits the back of my throat. 'She was going to wait for Jonny at the ranch and shake him down for the skimmed money, then she and her boyfriend were going to skip town. If Jonny refused, she was going to bypass Buddy Zillo and go straight to the press. She was going to make sure that Jonny – and maybe even the casino by association – lost everything.'

'Who was he?' I ask, but even as I say it I have a horrible feeling I'm not going to like the answer. 'Who was Bess's boyfriend, the one who was involved in all of this?'

Cassidy takes one last drag and then stubs out her cigarette in the ashtray on the table. 'A tiny cog in Buddy Zillo's wheels. A collector, a man named Jackie Castillo.'

Chapter Twenty-four

'Jackie Castillo? As in *Jackson*?' Tilda's voice is almost a screech as Cassidy stoops to pick up her suitcase. 'Evelyn is going to have kittens when she finds out about this!'

'Evelyn...?' Cassidy looks confused and I shake my head, gesturing for her to ignore Tilda and continue speaking. 'Bess met Jackie at the casino one night. He works for Buddy but he's a cut above the average mob guy. Well dressed, good looking... polite, knows how to treat a lady, you know?'

'Sure,' I say, exchanging a glance with Louis. That sounds like our Sonny all right.

'I never met him, but Bess told me everything a few days before she died. Almost like she knew something bad was coming for her.' Cassidy blinks, looking down at her dusty pumps. 'I'm sorry I didn't tell you earlier, but now you know... and I'm going to miss my bus.'

'Let me see you out.' Louis takes the case from Cassidy, guiding her towards the door as I hush Tilda. 'Cassidy, can I give you a ride to the bus station?'

Cassidy nods, reluctantly relinquishing the case to Louis but never taking her eyes off it, as if she is afraid it will disappear in a puff of smoke. I guess when all your worldly possessions fit in a tiny bag, you can't afford to lose a thing.

'Where are you going to go?' Tilda asks, as Cassidy moves to the door. 'What if we need to speak to you? How will we know where you are and if you're all right?'

Cassidy shakes her head. 'I've told you all I know. And to be honest, I don't know where I'll go. Somewhere they'd never think of looking for me. Alaska, maybe. I've never minded the cold.' She follows Louis into the corridor, before turning back one last time. 'You won't say anything to anyone will you? About what I've told you? I'm glad I got it off my chest but… if they found out what I knew I don't know what would happen.'

'Of course not. Our lips are sealed.' I pull her into a hug, breathing in the cloying scent of freesias from her perfume, cut with the scent of old tobacco. 'Take care of yourself, Cassidy.'

While we wait for Louis to return from the bus station, Tilda reads over her shorthand as we try and piece things together.

'Do we tell Evelyn about Bess and Sonny?' I ask, my heart giving a stuttering lurch at the idea. She'll probably take out a hit on me if I'm the one to break the news.

'Heck, no.' Tilda clearly feels the same way, as she ruffles back through the pages of her notepad. 'That little snake. Sonny said he'd never heard of Bess when all the time they were…' Tilda breaks off, unable to vocalise it as her mouth twists. I don't know how she's going to cope when reality TV hits the screens and extra-marital affairs play out at water coolers all over the world. 'This shows you were right, Lil, when you said Fry implied Sonny had been to Baker before.'

Thinking back at the way Ben Fry had said it, I wonder now if he had been playing with me, and my stomach tightens. *There is no way I can let Evelyn marry Sonny, but how the hell am I going to stop her? And what if I can't stop her? Does that mean hanging around in the past for the next three years?*

'It's all connected,' Tilda is saying as I tune back into the conversation. 'Sonny, Bess, Jonny. They're connected and I'm going to prove it. Jonny isn't going to get away with this.'

'How are you going to prove it? Jonny seems to be Teflon-coated, and if we go to the press and expose him the way Bess wanted to, there's every chance we'll end up in trouble and then we won't be able to save Evelyn.'

'Tef-what? That sounds science-y.'

'All I'm saying is, how can we possibly prove Jonny is responsible for Bess's death?' I don't think I can break into Buddy's office again – there wasn't much to find, apart from the ledgers, and we already have one of those. I can't break the safe, not without instructions from YouTube.

'Jonny is behind it all, right?' Tilda starts to pace, tucking her hair behind her ears as she walks the ten steps from one end of the room to the other. 'We already knew he was up to something… but Cassidy said he never lets anyone in his dressing room or in his hotel suite alone. Why is that?' She continues talking before I can speak. 'Because he's hiding something, and my gut is telling me that it's something to do with what happened to Bess. I'm going to find out what it is and make sure that we get justice for that poor girl. Trust me, Lily.'

–

The well-dressed crowd, done up to the nines in their best evening wear, clap and cheer as Jonny Valentine takes the stage yet again, wearing the awful sparkly jacket from his dressing room that I hoped would never see the light of day, the bright white of the spotlight shining down on him. There is that overwhelming sensation of love in the room that you always get when people gather to see an artist they admire, but it leaves a dirty taste in my mouth, like ash. I tug at the hem of my too-short hostess uniform as the bartender loads a tray with drinks and I weave my way between busy tables towards where Tilda sits in a darkened corner.

'I brought you a drink.' I hand her a martini and she accepts gratefully, taking a large sip before nodding over my shoulder.

'See who's here?' She widens her eyes and I turn slightly to see everyone's favourite goon Ralph, sitting just one table back from Frank Sinatra.

'*Oh.*' I turn back to face her. 'Maybe he's just a fan?'

Tilda snorts. 'Oh please. He's definitely involved some-where and so is Jonny, up to his neck.' Ralph looks over and waves a hand in my direction as Tilda hurriedly looks away, tucking herself even further into the shadows. 'Go see what he wants. And keep your eyes on him... we're going to follow him into the atomic party later.'

Resisting the urge to give Tilda a salute, I head over to Ralph's table.

'Hey honey,' Ralph leans over, raking his eyes over my skimpy hostess uniform in a way that makes me want to do a tiny sick in my own mouth. 'Make sure there's a bottle of bourbon in Jonny's dressing room for after the show.' His eyes cut to the girl sitting beside him, as if making sure she is impressed.

'Of course, sir. Can I get you anything else?'

'Not for now, sugar.'

I breathe out as Ralph slides his hand on to the girl's knee and she shifts in her seat, her eyes never leaving Jonny on the stage. Louis stands to the left of Jonny, his fingers running nimbly over the guitar strings as his hair falls over one eye. If I was prone to swooning – or indeed, if I had time to be swooning – then I would just about keel over right now. Instead, I run my eyes over the table in front of Ralph's, where Frank Sinatra sits. I can make out the strong line of his profile in the dim light, his hand reaching out for the drink in front of him, but there is no sign of Ava this evening. No sign of Dean Martin, either, and I feel a pang of disappointment. There is someone else at Frank's table though… a blonde woman, her hair set into perfect, neat waves. As the stage lights swoop over the crowd I see she wears a Dior gown, the ruffled strapless bodice moulded to her body, as the skirt flows gracefully from the thin belt at her waist to the floor. The pale yellow of the gown matches her hair perfectly, and she smiles as Jonny winks in her direction, raising her glass to her lips. It's Antonia, and as I watch her sip from her martini glass I have the nagging sensation, almost like déjà vu, that I have seen her before, somewhere away from the bright lights of Las Vegas… I just don't know where. *A movie, maybe?* She has the perfectly forgettable beauty of a hundred bit-part actresses of the Forties and Fifties.

'Excuse me, miss. Another drink please.'

I turn to see Tilda, a smile dancing around her lips. 'Yes ma'am.' I lean in and lower my voice. 'What time does the party start, do you know?'

'Pretty much as soon as the show's over I guess.' Tilda shrugs. 'I'm going to watch Ralph and leave when he does.'

'Are you sure you know what you're doing? What if he recognises you?'

'Then I'm here in my capacity as a journalist, covering Jonny's show. Relax, Lil, it'll all be fine, I swear.' There is the tiniest smidge of anxiety in her eyes as she speaks. 'Head upstairs in your uniform once the crowd clears out and I'll meet you up there.'

'In my uniform?'

'Yes,' Tilda tuts. 'You need to blend in, so grab a tray and wander around looking useful. You'll be surprised how much you'll overhear.'

I guess the uniform does make me invisible. My overnight adventure in the casino restaurant proved that point. 'What about Louis?'

'The band will come up to the party, obviously, and then Lou can flirt his socks off with Antonia, Jonny's wife. Don't worry, it's all in hand.' The lights go up and Ralph gets to his feet, as Tilda runs her eyes over me. 'Go freshen up before you come, men always get indiscreet around booze and pretty girls.' She presses something into my hand, and I look down to see the lipstick I found under the sofa at the ranch. 'Something wrong? You left it in the bathroom sink.'

'No, no. All good.'

Tilda grins and then spins on her heel, leaving me looking down at the lipstick in my hand. *Boy, I hope Tilda knows what she's doing.*

—

Pressing my lips together I try not to cringe at the waxy feel of a dead girl's lipstick on my mouth as I stare at myself in the bathroom mirror. I have managed, with a lot of practice, to roll and pin my curls and with a little of Tilda's powder and mascara cake, I look mostly presentable. The uniform is a little tight, but Tilda has assured me that that's for the best, so with one final blot of my lipstick, I push open the door and head to the Sky Room. It's huge, and far beyond anything I had expected, despite the mottled blue carpet and clashing teal bucket chairs that line the edges of the room. Dated to my eyes, but presumably the epitome of chic to the folks that fill the room. A large oval bar sits in the centre of the room, lined with identical white bar stools, most of them occupied already. I spot Judy Garland at the far end of the bar, deep in conversation with Hedy Lamarr, and I vaguely remember they made a movie together in the early Forties. Slot machines line one wall – it is Las Vegas after all – but the main attraction is the windows. Despite the room having a low ceiling, the walls are dominated by huge windows that look out over the pool area, rows of empty sun loungers neatly stacked around it. In the daytime I should imagine that this room is sweltering in the desert heat, but tonight it's blissfully cool. All you can see from the windows is the thick, inky darkness outside, a smattering of stars pricked into its fabric, and the far-off lights of the testing centre. The atmosphere in here is electric, an undeniable buzz of excitement rippling through the guests. Frank arrives with Ava and he settles her into a seat by the window before moving to the bar. Dressed in a fitted black Chanel evening gown, the bust framed with a black feathery fringe that follows the line of the gown across her body and down to the floor, a sumptuous swirl of velvet and taffeta, Ava is stunning. She gazes around, her green eyes searching as if looking for someone to talk to, before her face lights up and she waves at someone over by the door.

Snatching up a tray loaded with champagne, I turn to see Antonia entering the Sky Room. Looking much happier than the last time I spoke to her, in the restroom after her 'small domestic' with Jonny, she makes a beeline for Ava, kissing her on both cheeks before sitting beside her. They are like yin and yang, Ava in her dark gown with her inky hair, and Jonny's wife in her pastel yellow dress that matches her hair.

'Ladies, can I offer you some champagne?' I hold out the tray, amazed that my hands aren't shaking. Relieved that I must look cool on the outside, I smile at the women, while on the inside part of me is shrieking at spending the evening in the company of legends like Frank Sinatra and Ava Gardner. *This will never get old.*

'Antonia, have a glass won't you?' Ava Gardner – *Ava bloody Gardner!* – takes a glass and hands it to her friend.

'Thank you.' Antonia takes a sip, her brow creasing as she runs her eyes over me. *Perhaps she's regretting being so open with me, that day in the restroom.* Aware that I am just the hired help, I back away hastily, as the clamour in the room grows louder. A commotion by the entrance reveals Jonny and his band entering the party, Louis trailing at the back, followed by Ralph and his lady friend. A crowd of high rollers follow behind, and I catch a flash of Tilda's fiery hair as they enter. I move to the door and hand out saucers of fizz, feeling flustered when Jonny Valentine deliberately brushes my fingers as he takes his glass with a wink.

Louis takes a glass, waiting until Jonny and the rest of the band have moved off before he speaks. 'Everything OK?'

I nod discreetly. 'I only just got here, and the place is heaving with celebs.' Louis frowns. 'Celebrities? Famous people.'

'You sure do have a way with words, Lil.' Louis takes a gulp of his champagne, wincing at the dry taste, as Lauren Bacall slips past us. She heads for Ava Gardner's table but Ava and Antonia huddle together whispering, and Lauren does an about-turn and heads to stand at the bar beside Frank. I'm sure I remember something about Frank and Lauren having a thing together behind Ava's back in the late Fifties. 'You think Tilda can pull this off?'

'I hope so.' Tilda is laughing at something someone has said as she stands beside Jonny, and I watch as he turns to look at her, his eyes skipping over her figure in the tight, corseted evening dress she wears. She looks beautiful, and I wonder where she got her hands on that dress at such short notice, because I'm sure she didn't pack it in the overnight case we brought. Tilda is nothing if not resourceful. Moments later, Jonny leans in, whispering something in her ear. 'It seems to be going OK so far. Your mark is over there.' I gesture with a tip of my head to where Antonia sits, her face blank as she watches Tilda and Jonny.

Louis throws back the rest of his champagne and swipes his hand over his trousers. 'Wish me luck.' I watch him weave through the crowd towards Antonia, my heart bursting. We might have had a rough ride, and he might never fully forgive me for leaving the way I did in 1949, but I have to say we make a pretty good team.

Two hours later a group of burlesque dancers from the Silver Slipper have arrived, still in their costumes, and everyone is on the jollier side of merry. Snippets of gossip reach my ears as I hand out drink after drink after drink.

'Lucy was meant to be in town… Desi did it again… another woman…'

'…Just like Ingrid… unmarried… pregnant…'

Gossip is rife and the revellers get more and more indiscreet the more they drink. My feet are aching, I smell of old booze from when an over-excited Peter Lawson jostled me with a full tray of champagne, and I am grateful for the hush that descends as the lights are dimmed in preparation for the detonation. It's as if the entire room collectively holds its breath as there is a flash, and then a mushroom cloud of smoke appears on the horizon, white against the velvet sky. Cheers erupt and I find myself being squeezed in a bear hug by a small man who I think might be Sammy Davis Jr. Extricating myself, I head for the ladies' room, hoping to catch Tilda on the way through.

Once in the ladies' room I let myself breathe, running my wrists under the cold tap, my cheeks flushed a deep pink. The Sky Room is bright and airy at first glance, but fill it with drunken playboys and tipsy starlets and the air grows thin very quickly. I dry my hands and swipe Bess's lipstick over my mouth, even though the very thought of it makes me feel like a ghoul. The door swishes open and Antonia Valentine stumbles in, considerably more worse for wear than she was earlier. *Good job, Louis.*

'Oh, hello. It's Lily, isn't it?' Antonia hiccups in my direction as she looks in the mirror. 'Are you enjoying the party?'

'Err… I'm not really here to enjoy the party. I'm just here to serve the drinks.'

'Well, that's a shame. These things are always such fun. So much gossip.' Antonia turns from her reflection, squinting as she tries to focus on my face. 'You girls must be very discreet.'

'Absolutely. What happens at the atomic party, stays at the atomic party.'

Antonia lets out another hiccup of laughter, stifling it with her palm. The bruising around her wrist has faded and when she catches me glance in that direction she lowers her hand. 'I suppose you're a fan of my husband,' she says quietly.

'I guess.' I don't think this is the right time to tell her I'd never heard of her husband until a few days ago, and what I have heard about him since would make me run for the hills.

'They're all fans of my husband,' Antonia sighs, turning back to the mirror and inspecting her hair. She pats at her immaculate waves, then starts rummaging in her purse. 'Fawning over him, making fools of themselves. Like rats, they are. Swarming a barn.' Her eyes meet mine in the mirror. 'Thank you. For the other day, in the restroom,' she says softly. 'I'm sure I don't have to ask for your discretion. It was just a silly tiff, that's all. Things get on top of me sometimes, and... well, you know. Maybe one of these days I'll be able to sleep without a stiff drink and two sleeping pills.'

'Of course, Mrs Valentine. I'd forgotten all about it.' I inch towards the door, eager to get back out on to the floor, to leave her to her tipsy ablutions. 'I should probably go. It was very nice to see you again, Mrs Valentine.' Slipping out into the corridor, I let out a shaky breath and head back into the Sky Room, bumping into Louis as I enter.

'Lou! I just saw Antonia in the bathroom. She seems...'

'Intense? Flirtatious? If you ask me she's just as bad as her husband.' Louis shakes his head.

'I was going to say tipsy. How is Tilda getting on?' I glance around, but although the crowd has thinned out a little now, I can't see either her or Jonny.

'They left.'

'What?'

'She came to find me right before the lights went out. She said Jonny had agreed to an interview, but she told him it was too noisy in here, so could they go to his hotel room? I guess he agreed, because when the lights came back up they were gone.'

Antonia appears in the doorway, her eyes slightly unfocused as she holds on to the door frame and scopes out the room.

'I think this is your cue to turn the charm back on,' I say to Louis.

'Are you kidding? I never turned it off.' He tips me a wink and then heads towards Antonia, his arms spread wide in greeting. Antonia steps towards him, tripping over the hem of her dress as she does, the contents of her bag spilling across Louis's feet before he stoops to help pick them up. I return his smile, but I can't help thinking as I pick up another tray of drinks from the bar that I have a very, very bad feeling about all of this.

Chapter Twenty-five

By three o'clock in the morning the party is beginning to wind down and when the entertainment manager tells me I can finish my shift, my mind is too fatigued to come up with a reason to stay. There is still no sign of Tilda or Jonny, and as I leave I catch Louis's eye. He sits with Antonia, Ava and Judy Garland, the same drink in his hand that he's been nursing all night. His brow crinkles imperceptibly and I give him a sly thumbs up, before Antonia shrieks with laughter, tapping him on the arm to get his attention, and I slink away unnoticed.

Back at the hotel room it is eerily quiet without Tilda's constant chatter, and I perch on the end of the bed with every intention of staying awake until the other two return. There is a small ball of anxiety knotting my insides together at the thought of Tilda, alone with Jonny in his hotel room. Even though he has a reputation of being a gentleman, the things I've learned about him over the past few days lead me to believe he is anything but, and I move to the door to peer out into the corridor more than once, hoping to catch a glimpse of her bright hair. What I wouldn't give for a working mobile phone right now – I never realised how much I take it for granted at home, the way I can keep in constant contact with Eric if I need to, and the thought that I have no way of contacting Tilda, bar marching up to Jonny's hotel room, makes me more than a little uneasy. *Should I call his room? What if he doesn't answer? What if he* does *answer, and Tilda is furious with me for wrecking her plans?* Ordering a cup of evilly strong coffee from room service, I prop myself up against the pillows on the bed, hoping the caffeine will keep my eyes open until Tilda steps back through the door.

Moments later, there is the scratching of a key in the lock and then the door opens, but it's Louis, not Tilda, who stands there.

'Lou? Have you seen Tilda?'

Louis shakes his head as he pushes his way into the room. 'She's not back yet?'

'No. Though she did say she wanted to get Jonny drunk enough to pass out, so given that he drinks every night maybe it's taking longer than she thought.' It's a valid explanation, but still I can't shake the worry that's draped over my shoulders. 'What have you got there?' Louis is pulling an envelope from the back pocket of his trousers, smoothing out the wrinkles in it.

'You're going to want to see this.' He holds it out and with a curious glance at his solemn face, I take it, sliding out a small sheet of paper.

'It's a utility bill,' I say, scanning the page. It's a type-written bill from the California Light and Power company for one dollar and seventeen cents.

'Look at the top.' Louis points, tapping the page.

'Oh. *Oh shit*, Lou.' The address at the top of the bill is for the ranch, out in Baker, and the homeowner's name sits beneath it. 'Jonny Valentine? Jonny owns the ranch?' Pressing my hand to my mouth, I sink onto the bed, my knees feeling wobbly.

'No wonder he stashed the money out there – he thinks that by letting Zillo and his goons use the place for their meetings it makes him untouchable.'

'This is proof that Jonny owns the ranch, proof that he's well and truly up to his neck in all of this.' Despite my worry for Tilda, I feel a surge of excitement. We're getting closer to blowing Jonny's lies wide open. 'Wait. Where did you get this?'

'Antonia dropped her purse,' Louis says, 'I was a gentleman and helped pick up her things. I saw the address of the ranch on the envelope so I pocketed it while she was organising her purse. She didn't even notice.'

'Good job, Lou.' Sliding the bill back inside the envelope I open the door and peer out into the corridor for what feels like the millionth time, but there is still no sign of Tilda. 'What do we do about Tilda?' I ask. 'Now we have this, maybe she doesn't need to get proof from Jonny's room. Maybe we should go and find her – it's almost four o'clock in the morning, she's been gone a long time.' I can't shake the unsettling feeling that she should have been back by now.

'I don't know…' Louis sounds doubtful. 'If we go barrelling in there and she's still with him we risk ruining everything – if Jonny tells Zillo Tilda tricked her way into his hotel room we'll be run out of Las Vegas faster than you can say Machine Gun Kelly.'

Thrown for a moment, I flounder before remembering that before the rapper Machine Gun Kelly, there was an actual gangster by that name. 'So, you think we wait it out?'

'She knows what she's doing. Tilda's a tough cookie. Let's give it a little longer.' Louis reaches for my coffee and drains the last of it, screwing up his face at the bitter taste. 'I think we're going to need more of this.'

–

I barely realise I've fallen asleep until light filters in, the sun a bright, hot disc in a sea of blue as I wake with a gasp, squinting in the daylight. The curtains in our hotel room are wide open, and I lie on top of the tangled blankets. Cautiously, I lift my head to see Louis huddled into a ball on the twin bed opposite, light snores erupting every now and again.

Flashes of the previous evening come back to me. *The raucous laughter of the atomic party guests. The white mushroom cloud of smoke. Tilda, a drink in one hand and a secret smile on her lips as Jonny leaned in, whispering in her ear.*

'Til? Are you awake?' There is no response from the cot bed on the other side of the room and I push up into a sitting position, sweeping my hair out of my eyes as the ball of anxiety returns. Pins needle my scalp and I dig my fingers into my curls to remove them. 'Tilda?' Her bed is neatly made, not even the tiniest dent in the pillow. My scalp prickles and this time it's nothing to do with the pins. I think of the way Jonny leaned towards her, a wolfish smile on his face. 'Louis? Louis, wake up!'

'Huh?' Louis rolls over as I smack his shoulder. 'Lily, jeez, what is it? Where's the fire?'

He even looks cute with mussed hair and pillow creases on his cheek. 'Tilda. Her bed hasn't been slept in.'

'Her bed…?'

'Look.' Impatiently I slide off the bed and gesture to the immaculate blankets. 'She didn't come back last night, Louis.'

'Oh gosh.' Louis sits up, rubbing his eyes. 'She hasn't…
I mean, you don't think…?'

'No, Louis, I don't think your sister – who, by the way,
is engaged – has spent the night having it off with the man
we suspect of killing Bess Greenwood.'

Louis screws his face up at my words. 'I was going to say
you don't think she's got herself in trouble, not whatever…
that is, that thing you just said. That never even crossed
my mind.'

'That's exactly what I do think,' I say, my cheeks
burning. 'That she's got herself in trouble, not that she's
been having it off. There's a reason why she hasn't come
home.' The ball of anxiety sprouts wings and flies up my
throat, strangling me with panic and worry.

'She should have been back by now. We need to go to
Jonny Valentine's suite.' Louis is already pulling his shirt on
and I turn away, not wanting to intrude. All the time the
three of us have shared a room we've all been very careful
to change in the bathroom, but this morning Louis is too
concerned about Tilda to worry about me seeing his pecs.

Moments later, we are in the elevator, heading to the
penthouse, both of us feeling jittery.

'You don't really think Jonny would have hurt her, do
you?' I whisper, as the doors open on Jonny's floor. My
mouth is dry and I have to swipe my palms over my skirt.
I am still wearing the champagne-stained uniform from
last night, my hair half-pinned, and I feel grubby and out
of sorts. 'She's been alone with him all night. People saw
them leave together.'

'I don't know,' Louis murmurs back. 'Why wouldn't
she come back to the room? Even if she found something
she would have come back and told us before haring off.'

Would she? Part of me almost hopes she has hopped off on a tip without telling us. The corridor to the penthouse is hushed and empty, and the nerves ricochet in my stomach as Louis raises a hand and hammers on the door. There is no response, so he raises a fist and knocks again, louder and longer this time. I press my ear to the door, hoping to hear movement, as the door is wrenched open and I stumble, finding myself face to face with yet another bare chest this morning.

'Well, good morning to you too, honey.' Jonny Valentine smirks down at me as I raise my eyes, a fiery heat rising to cover my cheeks and neck. 'Something I can do for you?'

'Where's my sister?' Louis's tone is hard and I watch Jonny's eyes narrow as he turns to face Louis.

'Lewis, right?' Jonny eyes Louis carefully, making no attempt to cover himself. 'You play guitar for me, don't you?'

'It's Louis, actually. I'm looking for my sister. Where is she?'

'You think I know your sister?' Jonny smirks. 'I meet a lot of girls. How am I supposed to know which one is your sister?'

I interject before Louis can speak, seeing the way one fist balls in response to Jonny's words. 'His sister is Tilda. A journalist, petite, red hair? You were talking to her at the party last night.'

Jonny makes a show of racking his brains, that same smirk on his face the entire time. 'Oh sure, I remember her. Proper little firecracker.'

'She came to your suite with you last night,' Louis says. 'She didn't come back to her room. In fact, the last time anyone saw her was with you.'

I press my foot onto Louis's, cutting him off. That isn't strictly true – that's just the last time *we* saw her. Anyone else might have seen her, we haven't asked yet.

'So,' I say, with the sweetest of smiles. 'Where is she?'

Jonny frowns. There is a faint hint of whisky about him, stale and fuggy, while the suite has that brittle stench of old tobacco about it. 'Hell, I have no idea.' He scratches a hand over his chin, the stubble rasping under his palm. 'She wanted to interview me, but I had a little too much…' he trails off. 'I fell asleep, is the long and short of it. I woke up to hear you banging on the door and…' he gestures to the suite behind him, a table full of dirty glasses, empty bottles, and overflowing ashtrays. 'Well, she's not here. You can see that. She was never here.'

'Jonny?' A woman's voice filters out from the bedroom, and then Antonia appears in the doorway. In stark contrast to Jonny, she is fully dressed in a floral day dress, her hair curled and her make-up perfect. 'Who is it? What's going on?'

'Ahh… nothing, sweetheart. Just some folks—'

'I'm sorry to disturb you, ma'am, we're looking for my sister. Petite girl, red hair, always carrying a notebook?'

'Lily?' Antonia walks towards us, a slight frown on her face as she takes in my rumpled attire, and then turns her attention to Louis. 'Hello again. You're looking for your sister? Is that the pretty journalist girl? Last I saw her she was at the party. Didn't she want to interview you, darling?' She turns to Jonny, whose face is curiously blank.

'She mentioned it,' he says. 'As you can see, your sister isn't here, so sorry we couldn't help you.'

'I do hope you find her,' Antonia says, biting her lower lip, coral-red lipstick dusting her top teeth. 'I'm sure she'll turn up somewhere, you'd be surprised how many visitors wander off in this town – they lose track of time at the tables. Even Jonny does, sometimes!' She gives a small laugh, but her smile doesn't reach her eyes. 'I'll be sure to keep an eye out for her, and if I see her I'll let her know you're looking for her. In the meantime, please do let us know if we can help in any other way.' And then she closes the door in our faces.

'Well, that was a bust,' Louis says gloomily. 'Where the heck could she be, Lil? I know she's a loose cannon sometimes, but I don't think she would just wander off without telling us, not knowing what we know.'

Something didn't sit right with me about Jonny's behaviour, but I can't place what it was that felt odd. 'Did he seem weird to you?'

'Weird? Full of himself maybe. He thinks he's a real dreamboat, but I don't get what girls see in someone like that. Do you think he was lying to us?'

'I definitely think he got a little shady once his wife appeared. I got the feeling that he didn't want her to know that he invited Tilda back to his suite.'

'And Til definitely isn't there now.'

We ride down to the first floor in silence, both of us pondering where on earth Tilda could be. We check the bar and the restaurant, the beauty salon and out at the pool, but there is no sign of her. Stepping out of the lobby, pausing by the fountain that Tilda loves so much, I look over at the Silver Slipper.

'Could she have gone to the Slipper?'

Louis follows my gaze. 'Maybe. If she saw something that led her over there.'

I hurry after him as he steps off the sidewalk, an urgency to his pace. The lobby of the Silver Slipper is quiet, and there is no sign of Tilda. Again we check the restaurant, the gaming floor and the auditorium but she is nowhere to be found. Panic begins to flutter in my stomach. Half of me had thought that Tilda would be around here somewhere, after we found she wasn't in Jonny's suite, but now the worry kicks up a gear. Tilda might be headstrong and feisty, and sometimes she might get carried away, but I don't think she would disappear on us, not intentionally.

Back in the lobby, as Louis paces and I try frantically to think of anywhere else Tilda could be, Ralph walks by, marching purposefully through the lobby and out into the street.

'Do you think—?' Louis follows my gaze and both of us quicken our step. Outside, squinting in the brilliant sunshine, Ralph gets into a Chrysler and Louis tugs me towards Christine, pulling the car key from his pocket. 'You don't think Tilda could have bumped into him last night?'

The memory of the threats Ralph made to Tilda at the ranch make me feel queasy. 'I hope not.'

'Come on,' Louis throws open the passenger door for me, before hurrying around to the driver's side. 'We could follow him. Ralph was at the party last night. If Tilda bumped into him after the interview with Jonny and he recognised her, he might have…' he breaks off, swallowing hard.

It's a stretch, but not an impossibility, and at least it means we will be *doing* something. I don't think either of us can bear the thought of sitting around in the casino, waiting to see if Tilda turns up.

Dry desert air rushes in through the open window, making my hair fly out and dust lodge in the back of my throat as we pull out of the parking lot and Louis begins to trail Ralph's car. 'If Ralph knew Tilda was interviewing Jonny and he knew Jonny had been drinking, perhaps he thought that Jonny might have let something slip. I get the impression Ralph has no problem tidying up other people's mess.' Goosebumps ripple over my arms, so hard it almost hurts, and it's nothing to do with the desert breeze.

Oh bloody hell, what a god-awful state of affairs. A pulse flutters in my throat and I can feel the beginnings of a tension headache at my temples. All I wanted to do was to stop Evelyn from marrying a murderer, and now I've blown everything up, put Tilda in danger and made everything ten times worse. *Maybe I should have just stayed in 2020.* Louis slows as the Chrysler takes a right ahead of us, pulling on to a familiar street.

'He's going to the laundrette,' I say, keeping my eyes dead ahead as Louis overtakes Ralph pulling into the small parking lot out front. 'What if he did find Tilda last night and he's brought her out here? What if he's told Buddy Zillo she's still poking around?'

Louis parks up around the corner and my feet hit the sidewalk at a jog, intent on heading straight to the laundrette.

'Wait.' Louis tugs my arm, slowing me. 'Let me handle this.' Without another word he walks away, round the corner towards the laundrette, leaving me to stroll behind at a reasonable distance. Once outside the laundrette he bypasses the front entrance, heading for the back alley that runs behind. I follow, tucking myself behind a dumpster as Louis taps on the rear entrance to the laundrette. The door opens and Ralph appears, stepping out into the alley, his moustache wiggling as he clamps a cigarette between

246

his teeth. I hardly dare breathe, and not just because of the stink of old hamburgers coming from the dumpster.

'Help ya?' Ralph's tone is abrupt and when Louis speaks I barely recognise his voice.

'Hey. I'm one of Zillo's boys.' The accent is pure, thick Brooklyn and I raise my eyebrows, before remembering that Louis and Tilda's mum is from Brooklyn; she carries just the faintest hint of an accent now. 'I'm looking for the redhead. You know the one.' Louis makes a gesture imitating Tilda's impressive chest, and I can almost feel him cringe from here.

'The redhead? What do you want with her?' Ralph takes a drag on his cigarette but his expression is full of curiosity, mixed with a hint of meanness.

'Zillo wants a word. About… what went down at the ranch.'

'The ranch, huh? With the red-headed broad?' Ralph flicks his cigarette and it lands dangerously close to where I hide behind the dumpster, fizzing as it hits the sidewalk.

'Uh, yeah.' Louis nods. 'That dame, the one shooting her mouth off.'

'Well, let me know when you see her, huh? Because I told her she'd better skip town, or else.' Ralph gives Louis a hard stare as he cracks his knuckles. 'You see her, you tell her I'm looking for her. Oh, and you can tell Zillo I'll see him later.' He turns on his heel and returns to the laundrette, slamming the door closed hard behind him.

'Louis, what were you thinking? That guy is *dangerous*, and you know this place is connected to the mob. What if Zillo had been there?' I come out from behind the dumpster, picking a shred of brown lettuce from my shoulder.

'She's not here either,' Louis says bleakly. 'I thought that maybe she'd found Ralph last night and persuaded him to bring her out here… you know what she's like when she thinks she's on to a story, she thinks she can sweet talk anybody…'

'At least we know Ralph hasn't caught up with her yet.' I slide my arm through his, leading him back towards his car, my mind working overtime. No one vanishes into thin air. Tilda must be here somewhere, but I'm starting to believe that she really has come to harm. There's only one person who would benefit from Tilda disappearing and that's—

'Jonny Valentine,' Louis says. 'He's the last one to see her. I say we go back to his suite, get him alone and interrogate him until he cracks.'

'I'm not sure it'll be as easy as that,' I muse, as Louis heads for the driver's side of the car. 'Give me the keys.'

'What?'

'I'm driving. Give me the keys. You're too upset, and I don't want to end up with broken bones when you crash into a cactus.' Visions of the horrendous car smash I witnessed on my last trip to the past flashes before my eyes as Louis reluctantly hands over his car keys.

Christine is a dream to drive and I only lurch a little way down the street, before I remember how to do things properly. I guess it's true – I haven't driven since leaving London, but it really is like riding a bike, even if Louis does keep clamping his hands over his eyes and yelping.

'You can stop crying now, we're here.' I pull wonkily into a parking space outside the Desert Inn, as Louis reluctantly takes his hands from his eyes.

'That was… interesting,' he says. 'You should be glad Tilda wasn't here to witness this, she'd never let you live it down. I'm guessing no one asked you to drive an ambulance during the war? Or maybe they did.'

I smile weakly. 'No, they didn't, unfortunately. While you were praying for your life, I did some thinking. We can't get into Jonny's suite as presumably he'll still be in there, but we can get into his dressing room. If he's saying Tilda didn't go to his hotel room, maybe he took her there?'

Louis's face takes on a hardened resolve as he opens the car door and we both slide out, crossing the street over to the Silver Slipper. 'Let's go.'

Chapter Twenty-six

Antonia is in the entrance to the dressing-room corridor as we round the corner and I yank on Louis's arm, both of us pivoting so we appear to be walking past.

'Oh, Lily! Any luck finding your friend?' Antonia smiles. She looks a little flushed, as if she's in a hurry. 'I'm so sorry Jonny wasn't any help. He had a little too much sauce last night.' She holds up the cup of coffee she's holding with a tiny shrug of her shoulders. 'He sent me down for emergency coffee, and I've already taken too long.'

'Not yet,' I say. 'But thanks for asking. I'm sure she'll turn up soon. Jonny's definitely sure she never came back to the suite with him?'

'Absolutely not.' Antonia shakes her head firmly, as she brushes something from the skirt of her dress. 'I was asleep when Jonny came back to the room, and I would have woken if he had brought someone back to our suite. It would have been highly inappropriate, don't you think? Are you sure she didn't...' Antonia pulls an apologetic face. 'Meet someone else, maybe? You know, what happens in Vegas...'

Louis opens his mouth and I kick his shin lightly before he can speak. 'We should let you get back to Jonny.'

'Please, do let us know when you find her. I'll be sure to ask around today, see if anyone saw her last night outside of the Sky Room.' Antonia gives us a concerned smile and walks away with her coffee. We wait until she's in the elevator before turning back to the corridor, and sprinting along to Jonny's dressing room, where I try the handle of the dressing-room door, turning to Louis with a frown when the door doesn't budge.

'That's odd. It's locked,' I say. 'It wasn't locked last time, when I came in here with Tilda, we just walked straight in.'

'Maybe because last time you busted in here it was the evening, and Jonny would be returning from his show?' Even as he says it, Louis looks doubtful.

'I don't know… but lock or no lock, we're getting inside.' I check over my shoulder, making sure the coast is clear before I start my breaking and entering.

'Did you hear what Antonia was insinuating?' Louis huffs, as I pull my hair grip out of my skirt pocket and jiggle it in the lock, tutting as it fails to turn.

'She was just throwing out a theory, that's all. I don't think she meant anything by it.' My fingers slip and I blow my hair out of my eyes, frustration making me clumsy. Just when I thought I was getting good at this lock-picking lark.

'Well, I don't like her "theories". Here. Let me try.' Louis takes the hair grip and wiggles it, his face screwed up in concentration. Something clicks and he turns the doorknob, the door swinging open.

'Huh. It really isn't just for the movies.' I give him an admiring glance and step inside, the room just as chaotic as it was when I broke in with Tilda. Piles of fan mail teeter on the dressing table, even higher than before if that's at all possible, pan stick foundation in Max Factor packaging lies open beside it, the lid off and exposing the make-up to the air. A small tub of black boot polish sits beside it, and I realise Jonny must use this to disguise his grey hairs. The ashtrays still overflow, and a wastepaper basket holds an empty bourbon bottle. If I hadn't already seen the state of this place before, I would have thought it had been turned over by burglars. The whole room needs a good airing to get rid of the stale scent of cigarettes and expensive aftershave, and I wonder what Jonny's fans would say if they could see how slovenly he is behind closed doors.

'I never imagined it to look like this,' Louis says. 'Where do we even start? This place is a dumpster.'

There's certainly no sign that Tilda has even been here. Not that I was hoping to find her hidden in a closet or under the suit racking, but... maybe I was, a little. What I wouldn't give for that little icon on Snap Maps, showing me her precise location. 'I think we just go through everything as quickly as we can. If she was here, would she have left us something? A clue?' If I didn't know better, I'd think *Harriet the Spy* had been based on Tilda Jardine. If she had been here and she thought something bad was going to happen, she definitely would have found a way to let us know. 'You start over there. Go through the wardrobe, Jonny's jackets. I'll take the papers and the dressing table.' Nausea sits in my stomach and I get that swaying feeling you experience when you're on a ship. If we don't find anything here, I don't know what our next option is.

The dressing table and piles of fan mail are just as they were the last time I was in here. Gushing love letters that have me rolling my eyes and probably have Jonny slapping on even more of that slightly too dark pan stick every night. The bottom drawer of the dressing table sticks when I tug it, and I realise it's locked. All the other drawers have opened smoothly, exposing a jumble of matchbooks, handkerchiefs and digestion pills, and I feel a flicker of trepidation. *Why lock one drawer? When everything else is so out on display?* Pushing the fan mail on the desk to one side I search the pots and jars for a key small enough to fit the lock on the dressing table, even shaking out an empty cigarette packet, but there's nothing. *Where would I hide a key if I was Jonny Valentine?* Hoping the answer isn't "in his jacket pocket", I move back to the unlocked drawers, pulling out the matchbooks and pills, hoping to spot a glint of silver in the tangled mess Jonny has left in there. There's nothing. Just when I am about to give up hope, a flash of inspiration strikes, and I run my hand over the underside of the first unlocked drawer.

'Yes!' I hiss under my breath as my fingers snag on something taped to the drawer base. Twisting my hand, I pick at the tape until it comes away completely and a tiny silver key drops into my palm. Sliding it into the lock, the key catches at first and then with a slight wiggle the lock gives and I am able to slide the drawer open. *Maybe I am good at this breaking and entering lark after all. Might not add it to my CV though.* A bead of sweat slips from my temple and I brush it away impatiently as the drawer glides open silently and my breath is knocked from my body.

'Lily?' Louis's voice comes from far away, as if I am underwater. 'Lily, I think you should look at this.' His voice breaks through as I reach into the drawer and pull out the item that made my heart stop dead in my chest.

'I think you're going to want to see this, too.' I turn to see Louis is standing to one side of the closet, a bundle of fabric in his hand. 'What is that?'

'A sweater,' he says, holding it up by the shoulders. 'It was balled up behind the rail of suits, as if someone wanted to hide it. Do you remember seeing it the other day when you were in here?'

I shake my head. 'Everything on the rail was hung up. That was literally the only part of the room that had any sort of order to it.'

'Look.' Louis comes closer, holding out the back of the sweater. 'See this? What does that look like to you?'

'Dust? Dirt? Louis, I have something—'

'Right! Dust – look at it properly, Lily! It's that dark orange dust that surrounds the ranch. Out here, in the town, the dust is sandier, a grey-yellow dust. The only place I've seen dirt this colour is out at the ranch. Whoever wore this sweater – Jonny, it has to be – went out to the ranch and he wanted to hide it.' He shakes the sweater at me, and I see that the cuff has started to unravel, as if caught on something. 'Maybe he just went out there to stash the money, that's what Cassidy said he did, but what if—'

'Stop.' I hold up a hand. 'I would have said maybe he only went out there to stash the money, if I hadn't overheard him telling *Simon* to drive it out to "the usual spot". Jonny wouldn't get his hands dirty on a menial job like that. And I just found this.' I hold out my hand.

'Jeez, Lily.' Louis drops the sweater. 'That's Tilda's notebook. You said she'd leave us a clue! Where was it?'

I blink, my throat suddenly closing over. 'I don't think she left it as a clue, Louis. It was locked inside the bottom drawer of the dressing table. She wouldn't have a key – and she definitely wouldn't have hidden it where there's a chance we couldn't get to it. She was here, Louis, in this dressing room, last night. She hasn't wandered off. I think...' I swallow, my chest tight, my vision growing grainy. 'I think she's been kidnapped.'

'The ranch. He must have taken her to the ranch. I don't know why we didn't think of it before. Antonia said Jonny got in after she was asleep, but he left the party with Tilda before her. What if he drove Tilda out to Baker?' Louis pulls me into a standing position from where I am crouched on the floor and presses Tilda's notepad into my hands. 'The sweater was hidden, because he doesn't want anyone to know he was there.' Louis moves to the dressing-room door, itching to leave. 'He could hardly drop this in the hotel laundry in front of Antonia, she would want to know where he'd been.' Louis stops his pacing, almost talking to himself now as he shoves his hands through his hair. 'But how would he get out to the ranch and back without Antonia knowing?'

Jonny did look tired and dishevelled this morning, something I put down to him drinking too much, but now I think about it, it could just as easily be from staying up all night driving Tilda out to the ranch.

'She takes pills,' I say, the knowledge making my blood run a little chillier in my veins. 'To help her sleep. I spoke to her in the restroom the other day – she'd had an argument with Jonny, and there was bruising around her wrist. I think she knows that he sleeps around on her but she doesn't know how to extricate herself safely from her marriage. She said something about maybe one day she'd be able to sleep without a stiff drink and two sleeping pills.'

Jonny wasn't in his suite when Antonia went to bed, despite leaving hours before. Antonia says she would have woken if Jonny brought someone back to the suite, but would she? Would she if she had taken sleeping pills? I look down at the notepad in my hand, Tilda's untidy scrawl filling the pages. 'I don't think Jonny ever took Tilda back to the suite – he's not lying about that. But I do think he brought her here, and whatever she said to him, he felt he had to—' I swallow hard, the words jagged and sharp in my throat. 'He felt he had to get her out of the way, and where better than a ranch in the middle of nowhere?'

Chapter Twenty-seven

The ranch looks different in daylight. Bigger, grander, the wood a richer mahogany, the roof a more vivid green, but still just as empty. We approach slowly, both of us searching ahead to the end of the driveway to see if anyone is at the ranch, but there are no cars, no trucks, no people. Just orange dust flying in thick clouds as Christine's tyres crunch over the gravel, enveloping the flag that still flies from the centre of the driveway.

Sliding out of the passenger seat, I lift my hair away from my neck, letting the breeze catch the damp skin there. I'm not sure if it's the afternoon heat or the idea that someone has kidnapped Tilda that makes the tiny hairs on the back of my neck stand on end and my palms grow damp. Louis approaches the house, skirting around the front of the property and heading for the rear entrance. I step up onto the porch and press my face against the stained-glass pane in the door, feeling a dizzying sense of déjà vu. *What will I say if someone is home?* The thought strikes me as I raise a fist to knock, my heart leaping into my throat. A shadow crosses the hall inside and my legs go watery, like overboiled ramen. Pulling back, my breath lodges in my throat as the door is wrenched open, and Louis stands there wearing a white vest.

'Bloody hell, you gave me a heart attack. I thought you were Buddy Zillo or one of his cronies.' Pressing my hand

257

to my racing heart, I peer over Louis's shoulder into the cool, still house. 'There's no one home? And where's your shirt?'

'Nope, nobody home. And the pane of glass I broke before is now broken again.' Louis stands to one side to let me in, holding up his fist wrapped in his shirt. Standing in the hall I glance up at the elaborate staircase that leads to the second floor. Carved from a rich dark wood, it curves up and round, leading to the wide hexagonal landing that branches off to the bedroom where Ralph pressed his gun against Tilda's head just a few days ago. Chilled by the memory, I focus on the stairs ahead of me, hurrying up them towards the bedrooms. The room Bess was staying in is clear of any evidence that she was ever here, the bed made, the curtains still fully open. Even though Bess is dead, there is something sinister and slightly eerie about it, a sense that she's gone, but not. Of course Jonny would want all trace of her being here erased. Calling out to Tilda, I close the door on the room, shutting Bess's ghost inside.

'Tilda? Are you here?' Louis echoes my words as we search the bedrooms, peering inside closets and under beds in an attempt to find any sign at all that Tilda is being held here. The idea that she might not be at the ranch at all is one that I'm not yet ready to entertain, because if Tilda isn't here, then I have no idea where she could possibly be.

'Lily, she's not up here.' Louis's face is stern, his brows pulling together with concern. 'We need to check the downstairs rooms – do you remember if there was a basement?'

'No basement. Someone *has* been here though.' I gesture towards the master bedroom, the room beside the one Bess was using. The door is wide open, revealing closet doors that swing in the breeze that drifts through the slightly open window. 'This wasn't like this last time.'

Louis brushes past me and yanks open the closet door to reveal a safe. The door to that also swings open and reveals an empty cavern set into the wall behind. 'Don't… touch it,' I say too late, as Louis peers inside, shoving his hand right to the back. 'Fingerprints,' I hiss.

'It's empty,' he says. 'Completely empty. But didn't Cassidy say that Jonny would skim the money and stash it out here? You said you heard him tell Simon to drive it out to the usual place – that has to be here, right?' He turns wide eyes on me. 'Someone has been here and cleaned this place out.'

'If someone has been here tying up loose ends, then what if Tilda is one of them? What if Tilda counts as a loose end?' Panic starts a low rumble in my gut, the unmistakable sensation that time is running out pushing my feet towards the top of the stairs, back down towards the first floor. I see it again in my mind's eye, a ribbon unspooling and slipping through my fingers.

'Wait,' Louis says as my feet hit the top step. Below me at the foot of the stairs, sunlight slants in though the stained-glass window above the front door, dappling the hardwood floors in a rainbow of colours. It's hard to imagine that a woman was murdered in this house, her broken body left crumpled in the bedroom like trash. Louis stands by the rear landing window, one hand pressed to the glass. 'Can you see that?'

'What?' I cross the landing, unable to see whatever he's looking at.

'Out here, do you see?' Louis points and I follow his finger to the edge of the lawn. At the far end of the garden, the sun reflects back from a metallic surface.

'Louis,' I grab his arm as I remember something. 'I think there are outbuildings at the far end of the property.' I remember the glint of moonlight on the tin roof of a structure that could have been a barn at the far edge of the boundary the last time we were here. 'That's what the sun is reflecting off. What if Tilda is there?'

Louis grabs me by the upper arms and for a moment I think he'll kiss me. He doesn't. 'You, Lily Jones, are a genius. Of course Jonny wouldn't keep her in the house where she could be discovered — not after having Bess's body found here just a few days ago.'

Both of us hit the staircase at a run, our feet changing colour as we hurry through the rainbow-covered hallway and out to the front of the property. As we reach the treeline and the dusty track that flanks it, Louis slows. Tyre marks run along the track, cutting deep grooves into the dry, sandy dirt. 'Someone has driven down here, along the edge of the grounds.'

'That could have happened at any time.' But I walk over to the tracks for closer inspection before raising my eyes to the treeline that protects the side of the house from the road. The driveway up to the house is long and winding, and someone could easily have driven along this track without being spotted from the road.

'It's hard to tell, but I think the tracks might be fresh,' Louis says, his eyes meeting mine. 'The wind hasn't whipped them up, the tyre marks are still pretty visible.' He begins to walk along the dusty track but I call him back.

'Stick to the edge of the track, where there are more stones than dust,' I say. 'If Tilda is here and someone drives up to the barn, we'll hear them coming but hopefully they won't see our footprints.' Louis gives a sharp nod and I follow him along the edge of the trees, feeling a prickle between my shoulder blades, as if someone is watching us, and I am struck again by just how isolated it is out here. Isolated enough for a woman to be murdered, and another woman to disappear without a trace.

The huge barn is at the very edge of the property, the worn dirt path leading to double doors at the side. Grimy windows stand either side of the barn door, and I press my face against one of them, peering into the gloom beyond.

'Can you see anything?' Louis breathes in my ear, impatiently.

'Nothing, it's too dark.'

'Stand back.' Louis gropes in the dust, his hand closing on a large rock. He raises it above his head and them smashes it down on the door, hammering it against the lock. Splinters fly as the brittle, dry wood falls apart, and I keep my eyes on the lane that leads to the driveway and back out on to the road. The last thing we need is Ralph – or worse Jonny or Buddy Zillo – turning up. It takes four good smashes with the rock before the wood gives way completely and the lock swings down.

'I've lost count of how many things we've broken into on this trip,' I say to Louis with a wobbly grin as we step into the barn, sounding braver than I feel. 'Excellent burgling skills. We make a good team.' Louis grins back, his own smile a little wobbly, and my heart turns over. *It doesn't matter that we're from different times*, I think, *we balance each other out. I've never been in sync with anyone the way I am with Louis.* The thought that my soulmate might just be from forty-five years before I was born makes me stumble as I step over the threshold. The air inside is cool and musty, but a scuffle of footprints by the door show that the barn has definitely been in use recently. Coughing, I wave a hand in front of my face as dust swirls in the air. The barn is crammed full of stuff, junk on first sight. An old tractor sits in one corner, a ploughing implement attached. The blades are rusty and the wheels of the tractor are seized with dried mud and cow shit. When Louis lifts the corner of a stained tarp, he reveals the round headlight and smooth curved hood of an old sedan.

'Wow, Lily look at this.' Louis's eyes are wide as he begins to pull the tarp back.

'No!' My voice is shockingly loud in the thick, silent air and he drops his hand. A vision of Clarice Starling breaking into the Your Self storage unit to find the severed head of one of Hannibal Lector's victims in an old motorcar swims into view and I swallow hard. 'Just... don't touch anything.'

We pick our way between more rusted farm equipment that clearly hasn't been used for years, the barn becoming gloomier the further in we go. Towards the back, hidden from view of the door of the barn, is a rack of fur coats, in varying shades from midnight black to a soft, sandy taupe. Louis turns to me with a frown.

'Here's what they're hiding,' I say softly, running a finger over a soft mink fur before swiping it on my shirt, distaste making my lip curl. 'Valuable and all stolen, I bet.' Behind the rack of furs are canvases – oil paintings, covered with a muslin sheet. 'These too. Don't touch anything, Lou, I mean it. If the police find this stuff and your fingerprints are on it...'

But it's too late. Louis is crouched beside a trunk, the lid wide open. 'Lily, look at this.' I crouch beside him, relieved to see that the hand he's using to open the trunk has been rewrapped in his shirt.

'Oh my God, Louis!'

The trunk is full of weapons. Guns – pistols and rifles – several coshes, a crowbar, and a claw hammer that has spots of either rust or blood on the metal, it's too dark to make out clearly what the stain could be.

'Zillo and his cronies – they're hiding stuff here because they think Jonny is in with the FBI, and the president. They don't think that his place would ever be searched. Let's face it,' Louis says, 'Jonny is everyone's favourite entertainer. A good husband, a wonderful father, no one would ever believe he could be involved in something like this.'

'There's still no sign of Tilda though.' Pressure builds behind my eyes and I have to blink.

'I think it's time we called in the cops,' Louis says, closing the trunk. 'This is too big for us, Lil. I know Zillo probably has the sheriff in his pocket, but surely the entire Las Vegas PD can't be corrupt? And once we show them this, well… something will have to be done, and they have the resources to look for Tilda.' He gently starts to lead me towards the barn entrance, one hand resting lightly on my back. I know what he's saying makes sense, but I can't help but feel like I've let Tilda down.

'I should never have dragged you two into this mess,' I say as we reach the creepy covered sedan, my skirt catching on a loose nail that tugs at the fabric. 'I should have never come back.'

'Don't say that. We're going to find her… if we weren't then you would have come back for that, not for Evelyn, right? The gift would have shown you Tilda instead.' Louis cups my face, forcing me to meet his gaze. 'Whatever happens, I'll always be glad you came back. Even if we can't save Evelyn. Even if Sonny doesn't get out of jail. I'll always be glad you came back.'

'But Tilda's gone. And that's not how the... *gift* works.' A muffled thump comes from somewhere close by and I freeze. 'Did you hear that?'

'A bird, maybe? Hitting the window?' We both pause, but there is only silence. Louis looks down at me. 'Lily, we will find her. We'll call the cops, and they'll break Jonny – he's not that tough. Tilda will—' The muffled thump comes again, and I pull away.

'That's not a bird,' I say and turn to the tarp, snatching at the corner. Even though that nine-year-old part of me who watched *The Silence of the Lambs* behind my mum's back is utterly terrified, I yank it off, exposing the car. The windows are thick with grime, and I cup my hands around my eyes to peer inside. The seats are all empty, but the thumping definitely came from here.

'Tilda?' There is a thud, and I realise with mounting horror where it's coming from. 'The trunk, Louis! She's in the trunk! Tilda!' I tug ineffectually at the trunk lid, the lock stubborn despite the rust that flakes away, as the pounding on the other side of the metal grows increasingly frantic.

'Wait! Tell her to wait!' Louis says, before squeezing his way past the car to the back of the barn.

'Hang on just a few more minutes,' I say as there is a break in the knocking. I can barely breathe over the hammering in my chest, and I feel sick with the knowledge that Tilda might have been in here for hours. How long does the oxygen last in a car trunk? Will it run out or is there an airflow? I feel as if this is something I should know given the number of *Dateline* episodes I've watched.

'Stand back.' Louis returns, a crowbar from the trunk in one hand. 'Tilda, lie flat. Put your arms over your head.' He shoves the crowbar under the lip of the trunk, wedging it between the trunk and the body of the car, swearing under his breath as he forces the lock. For a moment I daren't breathe as it seems as though the trunk is locked tight, before the crowbar slips and the trunk springs open. There, huddled in a ball, bound and gagged, filthy and tear-stained, is Tilda.

'Are you all right? Did he hurt you? Oh God, Tilda, are you OK?' Tilda stares blankly for a moment, then gives a small nod. 'We'll get you out, don't worry.'

Louis reaches in and she crawls towards him, as I press my hands to my mouth, my throat thick with tears.

'Oh Tilda, thank God. Thank God you're all right. We were so worried; we found your notebook...' I trail off as Louis gently pulls her free of the car, cradling her in his arms. She looks tiny, a bird with broken wings as she leans her head against his shoulder and closes her eyes. Reaching forward, I slide my finger under the gag and tug it free from her mouth.

'Thirsty,' she whispers, as she runs her tongue over her dry lips.

'Tilda?' Louis taps her cheek, but her eyes stay closed. 'Tilda, wake up!'

'I'll run back to the house and get her some water,' I say. Louis is still staring at Tilda, running his eyes over her, checking for any signs of injury. 'Louis? Can you bring her up to the house? She needs water.'

Louis looks up and I realise he is furious. His eyes darken and he presses his lips into a thin line. 'Yes, I can bring her to the house. And then I'm going to find Jonny and I'm going to kill him.'

Running back to the ranch on those wobbly ramen-noodle legs, my mind is racing. *Could Jonny be coming back here? Why didn't he kill Tilda right away like he did with Bess?* Obviously I am relieved he didn't, but there is something sour and uneasy niggling in my gut.

'Why didn't I know about Jonny Valentine?' I mutter as I hurry across the rear of the house to the kitchen entrance. 'Why have I never heard of him? If I'd even known he'd existed I might at least have had some idea of what he's capable of.' The memory of him in Buddy Zillo's office, his tone crisp and sharp enough to skin a cat, rises in my mind, so at odds with the handsome charming crooner that graces the stage every night.

In the kitchen, I find a tall tumbler and run the tap until the water loses the hint of rusty orange that it carries from the pipes and runs a cold crystal clear. As I wait, my eyes roam over the kitchen countertop. The brandy glasses that stood there the night we broke in, left by Bess and her visitor – *murderer* – are gone, and a single mug sits on the edge of the sink, coffee grains swilling around in the bottom. The smell makes my stomach roll over and I open the freezer to chip off some ice for Tilda's water, pausing as the cold air hits my face.

It's wrong. Everything we thought, it's all wrong. My eyes go to the coffee cup, to the faint lipstick stain on the rim. The same shade as the colour I wore to the atomic party. The same as the colour on the rim of the brandy glass the night Bess was murdered. The colour I found under the sofa after Sonny had been arrested. The lipstick couldn't have belonged to Bess. Whoever drank from this cup was here the night Bess died – and they've returned since. I grip the freezer, my fingers growing icy as a sour taste fills my mouth and I struggle to draw in a breath. The back door snicks open behind me, a wave of relief washing over my body.

'Louis, we got it all wrong, it wasn't Jonny, it was—'

The air goes out of me as I turn to face the open door, and it isn't Louis who stands in front of me.

Chapter Twenty-eight

'Antonia.' Pressing my back against the freezer, I wish I hadn't moved from the countertop, and I feel woefully exposed.

'Lily?' Antonia cocks her head on one side as she blinks, clearly shocked to see me standing there. Dust and cobwebs smear the skirt of her day dress.

'What are you doing here?'

'What am *I* doing here? That's a question I should be asking you, don't you think? This is my house, after all.' She unwinds the silk scarf that sits around her throat, letting it flow freely through her fingers from one hand to the other. 'Did you find your friend?' She widens her eyes, shadows dark beneath them, and I frown, as almost audibly the pieces click into place.

'It was you, wasn't it? We thought it had to have been Jonny, but it wasn't. You're the one who kidnapped Tilda last night, bound and gagged her and brought her out here. Why? What did she ever do to you?'

'That's a terrible accusation.' Antonia presses a hand to her chest in outrage, but a smile tugs at her lips. 'Whyever would you say such a thing?'

'The lipstick.' I snatch up the coffee mug and thrust it towards her. 'I found the lipstick here at the ranch and I thought it belonged to Bess. And now here we are, long after Bess is dead and buried, and the lipstick turns up on this mug.' I step closer, eyeing her mouth. 'It was never Bess's lipstick. It was yours. In fact, I'd go so far as to say you're wearing it right now.'

'Well golly, aren't you a proper little Nancy Drew?' Antonia smirks, and any hint of the sweet, gentle woman I was so concerned for this week drops away. 'Or would you rather Agatha Christie? That accent hasn't passed me by.'

'Tell me what you did to Tilda.'

Antonia slides the scarf into her purse, patting the leather as if checking she has everything. 'That little red-haired tart. Don't think I didn't spot her at his shows this week, batting her eyes and giving him those coy smiles. She's just like the rest of them. And if it had just been that, then maybe none of this would have happened.'

'What do you mean?'

'The girls who want Jonny's attention are usually pretty easy to scare away, but not this one, not your friend.' Antonia's lip curls, and I see real hatred cross her face. I grope behind me, hoping to be able to slide open a drawer and pull out something to defend myself with. 'At the party, I waited for a while after she left with Jonny and then I followed them. I had my suspicions, but even so I was hoping I was wrong. Even as I arrived back at our suite, I thought surely – *surely!* – Jonny wouldn't be careless enough to fool around while I was at the hotel.'

Antonia had said she was asleep when Jonny came back to the suite. Of course she lied, and like an idiot I believed her. I don't speak, silence filling the kitchen as Antonia sighs. 'It turns out I was wrong about her all along. She was never interested in Jonny romantically.'

'So why did you kidnap her?'

'Oh Lily, you're so dramatic. Don't you see?' Antonia steps towards me and the cloying scent of her perfume fills my nostrils. She smells like jasmine and rose, a scent too ageing for her; it's one that belongs on an old lady. 'Your friend is far more dangerous than the usual floozies. When I got to the suite, Jonny was already half cut and Tilda had her notepad poised and ready. I asked her what was going on and she very kindly explained to me that she thought Jonny might be mixed up in something scandalous.'

Sliding the kitchen drawer open behind, I press back hard against the counter to disguise the fact that I am wiggling my fingers into the gap, searching for a knife, fork, hell I'll even take a spoon if it gets me out of here without dire consequences. 'Like what?' I ask, even though I know exactly what Tilda was talking about.

'Some dreadful scandal with a showgirl.' Antonia rolls her eyes.

'And Jonny just let you do that? Just let you take Tilda? Or did he help you?' There is a metallic taste in my mouth, from fear or horror, I don't know which, as I realise I don't know where Jonny is, and whether he's about to show up too.

'Jonny?' Antonia snorts. 'Of course not. I wasn't going to involve him in her filthy lies. I poured them both a drink, but I made sure I gave Jonny a little something extra.'

'The sleeping pills.'

'Oh *brava*.' Antonia gives a slow clap. 'You really are quite the little super sleuth, aren't you? Then I took your friend down to Jonny's dressing room with the promise of exposing him for who he really is.' Her eyes fill with tears and her next words come with a gasping sob. 'He's just so, so *awful*. You have no idea what he's capable of.'

I stare at her in horror, the expression on her face so familiar to me. I'd believed her too – I'd thought that she knew about the affairs, but that Jonny had such a hold over her, emotionally and physically, that she couldn't leave.

Like magic the tears dry up and Antonia grins. 'Just like that. I could have wowed them at Paramount with a screen test like that.'

There is movement behind Antonia, at the rear door to the kitchen and I flick my gaze towards it as Louis steps inside.

'Lily?'

Antonia swings round, her hand delving into her purse. 'Oh! The brother! I should have known this would be a family affair.'

'What's going on? Lily, are you all right?' Louis asks, as he moves towards me, his gaze going from me, to Antonia, and back again. 'Where's Jonny?'

'Stay where you are,' Antonia says, her voice steady as she withdraws her hand from her purse. Only her hand isn't empty. She holds a pistol, snub-nosed and with a delicate pearl inlaid handle. I want to laugh – it looks like a gun from a film set, the kind of gun a dame would pull out of her garter in an old Western movie. Both Louis and I raise our hands.

'So, you two. As I was saying, I couldn't let Tilda get away with the things she was saying about Jonny. I gave her a drink with a little something extra in the dressing room, and then once she was out of it, I got her to the car and drove her out here.'

'What are you going to do with her?' Louis asks, his eyes never leaving the gun.

'I'm going to give her a glass of water.' Antonia snatches up the glass I poured. 'Only my glass will contain the rat poison under the sink. No one ever looks at that clapped out old motor vehicle in the barn. It could be years before she's discovered.'

Black spots dance at the corners of my vision and there is a rushing in my ears. I want to bend at the waist and tip the blood to my head, but I think Antonia will probably shoot me if I do.

'You'd really do all of this to protect Jonny?' I say quietly, hoping that she doesn't decide to shut me up with a bullet. 'He's a murderer, Antonia. You know Tilda wasn't lying – your lipstick was on the brandy glass, you were here that night. You know what Jonny did – he killed Bess Greenwood, the showgirl you showed such little regard for.'

Antonia lets out a peal of laughter, sharp and ringing in the warm early evening air, and finally her smile reaches her eyes. 'You think Jonny – my Jonny – killed Bess Greenwood? Oh honey, you've got that all wrong too. It wasn't Jonny who killed Bess. It was me.'

Chapter Twenty-nine

'You?!' Louis's mouth falls open. 'You killed Bess? But why? What did she ever do to you?'

Antonia's eyes narrow and my skin shrinks under her gaze. Now she's confessed to kidnap and murder, there's no way out of this for us. 'Before I tell you anything, tell me where the money is.'

'Money? What money?' My fingers slide back into the drawer, well hidden now by Louis standing beside me. He glances in my direction, but I keep my eyes on Antonia, not wanting to give myself away. The sharp serrated edge of a bread knife grazes my finger and I grope around, feeling for the handle.

'The money!' Antonia shrieks, stamping her foot like a petulant child. 'From the safe! I know it was in there, but now the safe is empty! I know you have it, so hand it over.'

'What money?' Louis lets his features crease into a puzzled frown. 'We don't know what you're talking about.'

'Don't lie to me, and you, Lily – get your hands above your head,' Antonia hisses, the gun wobbling unsteadily in her hand. 'No one else has been to the ranch, not since the money was brought out here. No one else even knows about it. And the safe is empty, and so is the crawl space under the house. So hand it over, or I *will* shoot you.'

Louis raises his hands higher above his head. 'We *don't know* anything about the money! I swear on Tilda's life—'

Antonia lets out a snort at that and levels the gun with two hands, pointing it directly at me. Sweat beads between my shoulder blades and I swallow, my breath coming in shallow gasps. 'Antonia, please—'

'Shut up,' Antonia growls through gritted teeth, and I don't know how I ever could have felt sorry for her, felt concern for the way Jonny treated her. Fury makes her eyes bright and her cheeks flush an unflattering shade of cerise. 'Move. Over there, to the sitting room.'

I don't want to move. I lost my grip on the bread knife when I had to put my hands over my head, but if I move now I'll lose any chance of grabbing it at all.

'Now!'

'Wait,' I say desperately, my mind whirling. 'The money. I think I know what happened to it. I know who took it. But you have to tell me what happened with Bess first. You can keep the gun on me, you can even shoot me after if you don't like what I tell you, but I want to know everything. There's an innocent man about to be sent to death row because of you.'

'Lily, no.' Louis turns an anguished face towards me and I shake my head.

Antonia tilts her head and looks at me, the gun never wavering. 'Yes, you're definitely more Nancy Drew, aren't you?'

'Just tell us,' I say, trying to inject a hint of steel into my voice, but there is a distinct wobble to my words.

'I guess it doesn't really matter anymore,' Antonia says after a long pause. 'Bess was sleeping with Jonny. Although that wasn't the problem. The problem was that she knew too much.'

'She knew about the skimming – and it was Jackson Castillo who told her, wasn't it?' I remember Cassidy telling us how Bess was his girlfriend, how they planned to scam Jonny.

Antonia nods. 'That little creep – always wanted to be a big shot, hanging around with Buddy and his friends, but he was never really part of it. He thought he was a cut above the rest, better than the other lowlifes Buddy has hanging off him. The two of them wanted Jonny out of the way so they could take his place.'

'So you decided to *murder* her?' I think of the ring of faded bruises around Antonia's wrist that day in the restroom. 'It was Bess who grabbed you, wasn't it? I thought Jonny was the one who hurt you, but Bess grabbed you, fighting for her life.' I feel sick, my mouth slick with the sourness of old lemons.

Antonia steps closer, the gun still held ahead of her. I gaze back unblinking, praying that she can't hear the galloping of my pulse as my heart races fit to burst. 'Jonny was going to stop skimming the money.'

Louis groans, pressing his hands over his eyes. 'It was never Jonny that wanted to skim, was it? It was you. You're the one who wanted the money, but you weren't important enough to get access to the parts of the casino that Jonny could enter.'

'Hands. Above. Your. Head.' Antonia waves the gun in Louis's direction and his hands go back up. I take advantage of the distraction to whip one hand into the drawer and snatch up a knife – a vegetable knife, not the sharp bread knife I was hoping for – shoving it into my waistband and raising my hands again. 'Jonny has no chutzpah, you know? When I first married him I thought he was the most wonderful man alive, but he's weak,

275

lily-livered, never quite strong enough to resist his urges. The money started rolling in, but it was never enough. It turns out I have quite expensive tastes.' She chuckles under her breath. 'I did what it took to maintain our lifestyle, that's all.'

I misread Jonny, I think. *In the counting room I took his tone as condescending towards Simon, but it was fear that made him snap. Fear that Simon wouldn't do as he was told and Antonia would find out.*

Antonia gestures to Louis with a flick of her head. 'You. Look in that cupboard behind you; there's a length of rope.' She keeps the gun on Louis as he reaches into the cupboard and pulls out a length of thick, bristly rope. 'Tie her up. Come on. Tie up your little girlfriend here.'

'Hey, now wait a min—'

'Louis. Just do it,' I say, my arms aching from being raised in the air. Antonia draws back the safety on the gun. 'Do as she says.'

Louis gives me a reproachful look but moves slowly towards me, the rope taut between his hands.

'Do it properly,' Antonia says grimly. 'No loose ends, no funny business. Wrists together and then you tie her, *tightly*.'

I wince as Louis wraps the rope around my wrists, binding my hands behind my back as he whispers an apology. His fingers brush the waistband of my skirt, faltering as he touches the outline of the vegetable knife, and then he gives my waist a brief squeeze as if acknowledging it. I can feel his breath on the back of my neck, as he adjusts my bound hands so they sit just above the knife at my waist.

'Good.' Antonia runs her eyes over his handiwork and then she steps forward, pushing me onto the floor. 'Now it's your turn.' Deftly she binds Louis's wrists in the same position as mine, before pushing him down to sit beside me, back to back.

'You were saying? About Bess. If you're going to kill me, the least you can do is tell me what happened.' I wish I had my phone. I wish it was 2020 and I had my iPhone hidden in my pocket, recording everything Antonia is saying, livestreaming on TikTok or Instagram. The light outside is beginning to dim, shadows starting to stretch bony fingers along the edge of the lawn from the treeline.

Antonia sighs, as if I am the one inconveniencing her. 'A friend called me in LA to tell me she'd seen Jonny having lunch with Bess a few days before... obviously I thought he was up to his usual tricks, but when I called him out on it, he confessed to me that Bess knew about the skimming and she was blackmailing him. So, I told him I would deal with it – he was in no fit state. It always falls to me to clean up Jonny's mess.' Antonia's mouth twists in distaste. 'Bess believed me when I called her and said I was Jonny's assistant and that Mr Valentine wanted to meet her at his ranch. She never thought for a minute it would be me waiting out here for her.'

'Clever thinking.' If I stay on her good side, maybe she won't kill me too.

Antonia scowls. 'Don't try and flatter me.' *Maybe not.* 'She was shocked when I arrived in Jonny's place, but as you've seen, I am an excellent actress.' She lets her eyes fill with tears again. 'Oh *Bess*, we have to get out of here. I've come to warn you... He's going to *kill* you, he's so angry, he hit me.' She arches an eyebrow. 'Not in a place I could have showed her, obviously. Bess very kindly gave me a glass of my own brandy for the shock.' A bitter laugh escapes her lips. 'I followed Bess as she hurried upstairs to pack the few things she'd brought with her – I guess she was hoping a roll in the hay might distract him – and then she went to the safe. She was going to take the money – she was talking about how we could team up, we could go to the press together and expose Jonny. She was going to bring him down, and I couldn't have that happen. I had no intention of ever letting Bess leave this house again.' She wraps her scarf around her shoulders with her free hand and my stomach lurches.

'The police said she was strangled with a soft ligature... that Sonny did it with his tie. But Bess was never strangled with a tie,' I say, my own voice sounding strangled and broken. 'You did it with your scarf.'

'Honestly, Lily, you could get a job with the FBI.' Antonia beams and I realise that not only is she evil, but she's also been driven mad by money and power.

'But wait a second... you were in Florida with your children.' Louis looks puzzled. 'Jonny said you arrived in town to support his show the night we arrived in Las Vegas.'

It's as if a lightbulb goes on over my head. 'No,' I say. 'You were never in Florida – you came out here, and once you were done with Bess you went back to your house in Los Angeles.' I know now where I have seen Antonia before – she's the woman I almost bumped into coming out of Googie's the morning I arrived in 1950. 'You murdered Bess and then drove straight out to LA, back to your house. Worst case scenario, if you did ever get pulled in for Bess's murder you had some sort of alibi. I saw you there at the diner the day after Bess died. I bumped into you.'

'Ralph found Bess's body early the next morning,' Antonia says. 'Obviously Jonny realised that I must have had something to do with it; after all I did tell him I would deal with Bess, and he set it up that someone – Ralph or Rocky, I presume, one of those thugs – said they saw Jackie Castillo running away from the property that night.'

'Two birds with one stone,' I say, as Louis begins to rub his wrists together behind his back, trying to loosen the ropes. I shift slightly, covering his movements and trying to lift my own hands so I can hook a finger inside my waistband to access the knife. 'You got rid of Bess, and by getting Sonny arrested for Bess's murder you took him out of the equation too.'

'You could let us go,' Louis says. 'We wouldn't tell anyone. We would go back to LA and never say a word, we swear. I don't even know Sonny – I'd be glad to let him go down.'

Antonia lets out a hoot of laughter. 'Oh golly, you are a card. No.' She sobers up, her smile vanishing. 'That's not going to happen. Everyone knows how you two and your sister have been poking around, stirring up things that don't concern you in Vegas. Once the three of you disappear there'll be some speculation as to whether you came to some grisly end at the hands of Buddy Zillo, or whether you realised you were flogging a dead horse and scuttled back to Los Angeles. Either way, I shouldn't imagine there would be too much concern over your whereabouts.' Antonia levels the gun at my head. 'You first? You seem to be the one who's had the most to say, so it seems fitting that I dispatch you first and give your boyfriend a chance to speak one last time.'

My fingers grasp the tip of the vegetable knife and I shift, managing to slide it up enough that it slips free of my waistband. Louis's fingers brush mine and I press the handle towards the rope that binds his hands, edging it slightly so it catches on the fibres of the rope. I don't have much time, but if I can weaken his ropes even slightly, enough for him to get free, then I might be able to save him. I think it's too late to save myself.

'You might want to close your eyes,' Antonia says, as she tugs her scarf up over her head, protecting her hair from my blood and brain matter, I suppose.

'Please, Antonia—'

'It's OK, Louis,' I whisper. 'Maybe this is it – maybe this was what was meant to happen. I don't know how but maybe this is the way you save Evelyn.' I close my eyes, my heart racing so hard and so fast that I almost feel Antonia's bullet won't be necessary. *This is the end. Will I really die, or will this send me back to 2020?* I have the fleeting thought that perhaps Louis and I could have been soulmates, but it was just never meant to be, and then there is a muffled thump and I feel my body tilt sideways, crashing against the oak floor.

Chapter Thirty

Am I dead? Is this what it feels like? Everything is dark, and I can't breathe properly. *Maybe the bullet hit my lung and I just haven't died yet.* Something heavy sits on my chest, crushing the air out of me. If I have died, I would have liked some angels and harps, maybe a fluffy cloud to sit on, instead of this oppressive weight.

'Lily?'

I gasp, trying to draw in a breath, when the weight is suddenly lifted.

'Lily, you can open your eyes.' A cold hand presses against my shoulder and I groan, reluctantly peeling my eyes open.

'Louis?' I blink, finally managing to inhale. I'm on my side on the kitchen floor, my hands still bound behind my back. Louis crouches over me, his hands now free. 'What happened?'

There is a cough, and then I hear the sweetest voice I've ever heard. 'I rode in on my white horse to save you losers, that's what happened. Do I have to do everything myself?'

Struggling into a sitting position, I see Antonia laid on the floor, face down and unconscious. An egg-shaped lump rises from the back of her skull, the skin slightly split and oozing a deep crimson. The gun has skittered towards the counter and Louis moves now to pick it up, holding it gingerly by the fabric of his dusty, no longer white vest. Tilda stands in the doorway, grubby, pale and despite her tough talk, looking as if she might keel over at any moment. A crowbar – the one Louis used to free her from the trunk of the car – dangles from one hand. Louis scrambles to untie my hands from behind my back and then helps pull me to my feet. I am unsteady, the blood rushing from my head.

'Careful,' Louis says as I stumble against him. 'I think I winded you when I fell on top of you just now.'

'Tilda, I can't believe… you smashed her over the head?' I step around Antonia's body, brushing her blonde hair aside to check for a pulse in her neck.

'Louis left me in the shade of the trees after you didn't come back with any water,' Tilda explains, letting the crowbar drop to the floor. 'And then when *he* didn't come back, I decided to try and make my way back into the house. I was *really* thirsty,' she says. 'That's when I saw she had a gun, so I had to find the right time before I came crashing in.' She looks down at Antonia's prone body, prodding at her with a bare toe, having lost her shoes at some point during her ordeal. 'Looks like I timed things about right.'

Louis binds Antonia's hands in case she comes to, before calling the operator to request emergency services. Stepping on to the porch outside as we wait for the police and medics to arrive, I see the car parked under the trees beside Christine. It's a dark red sedan with a slight dent in the front fender and a chill makes my scalp prickle.

'Louis, that car,' I point to the vehicle, my ankle giving a low throb as if in recognition. 'That's the car that hit me. That's definitely it. It was no accident, no kids fooling around drag racing.'

'Antonia was the one driving,' Tilda says. 'She must have heard that we were poking around asking about Bess and she thought she'd warn us off.'

Shivering, I scrub my hands over my arms. I thought I'd met some unhinged people in my time, but Antonia Valentine takes the cake.

–

Several hours later, Antonia has been driven away in an ambulance, conscious and alive but not yet talking. We have given brief statements to the police, and now we are driving back towards the Desert Inn. Tilda is curled up in a ball on the back seat, seemingly asleep, although the way she lifts her head every few minutes to peer out of the window tells me she just doesn't want to talk. Louis keeps his eyes on the road, reaching out to pat my hand every once in a while. As the bright lights of the growing town twinkle on the horizon ahead of us, I lean back and close my eyes. *The first weekend I came out to Vegas with Eric, I never would have believed the sinister undertone the town carries.* We'd laughed in the Mob Museum at the gangsters that had ruled the town, judged the little old ladies sitting at the slots as we returned to our rooms in the evening, still there when we came down for breakfast the next morning. I knew Las Vegas had a sleazy reputation, but I never bargained on any of this when I first read the article about Evelyn's death.

Evelyn. I guess we have to call and give her the good news, if the police haven't done so already. With the knowledge that Sonny really is innocent comes a sinking feeling that makes my stomach flip. I still have to find some way to figure out how to stop Evelyn from marrying Jackie – *Sonny* – Castillo, before he can murder her.

'Lily?' Louis sits up straighter in the driver's seat, his foot easing off the gas pedal. 'What is this? What's going on?' As we approach the Silver Slipper a crowd gathers on the sidewalk outside. Louis swerves off into the parking lot of the Desert Inn and we all tumble from the car, heading straight across the street to the waiting crowd.

'They know,' I say, as realisation dawns. The doors to the casino lobby open, and with a coat held over his head obscuring his features, Jonny Valentine is escorted from the building by two burly police officers. 'They know Jonny was involved in Bess's death.'

'That travelled fast,' Tilda says. 'We only left Baker a little while ago.'

Wait until social media hits, I want to say. In my time news going viral is almost instantaneous. 'I guess Jonny is hot property.'

'*Was* hot property,' Louis says, gesturing discreetly to the casino doorway. Press gather, flashbulbs lighting the night sky as they fight to get the best shot of Jonny being ducked headfirst into a cop car. 'Either that or someone was suspicious already, and they were just waiting for the chance to bring him down.'

Beside the casino entrance Buddy Zillo stands with Frank Sinatra, both with sombre expressions, as Simon, Jonny's assistant – *ex*-assistant – hands Frank his jacket. Jonny glares out from the back of the cop car, the newspaper men pressing their cameras against the window for the money shot, before he raises one hand to shield his face and the cop gives a bleep on his siren to move the crowd so he can safely pull away.

'Quiet everybody, please!' Buddy Zillo raises his arms as he calls for quiet and a hush descends, save for the sound of the odd flashbulb as the press get yet more photographs.

Jonny is going to be on the front page of every newspaper in the morning. 'I understand that the news this evening regarding Jonny Valentine is extremely shocking, but it is as yet unconfirmed. As the owner of this establishment, I would like to reassure you that while we are reluctant to speculate on what may have happened, we would like to tell you that the management here were completely unaware of events.'

Louis, Tilda and I exchange glances. Buddy Zillo might be able to fool the press and the casino goers, but he doesn't fool us. He may not have known the extent of Jonny's involvement in Bess's death, but he still didn't push for any further investigation into it, and we know that the casino is a front for his illegal mob activity.

'I know that some of our guests here have tickets for Jonny's show this week, and obviously Mr Valentine will no longer be performing here. In which case, I would like to introduce you to our new star of the stage, the incredible Mr Frank Sinatra.' Frank steps forward, his famous baby-blue eyes crinkling as he grins and waves. 'All tickets already purchased will be valid for the show, and I'm sure you'll all agree that Mr Sinatra never disappoints.' Buddy and Frank smile and wave, turning to face the cameras as they snap, snap, snap, in a frenzy of clicks.

This is how it reignites for Frank, I think as Louis and Tilda watch, Tilda patting her pockets for her pencil. *He'll leave Nancy, marry Ava and go on to rise right to the top again*. In my time, I don't know what happened to make Jonny Valentine's star dim, seeing as I wasn't here to expose Antonia. Maybe he got worried after Bess died. Maybe he convinced Antonia that life would be better out of the limelight. Either way, Frank no longer has to wait to make his debut at the Desert Inn in September of 1951 now. You'd almost think he was just waiting for Jonny to step aside so he could slip into his shoes. I watch Simon as he taps Frank on the arm and points to his watch. It's almost like he knew this was coming.

–

'We should make the call to Evelyn,' Tilda says as the crowds disperse and the familiar jangle of the slots rings out once more. 'Away from here though.' The payphones that hug the entrance to the Last Frontier Village are full of press ringing their big scoop through to their respective newspapers.

We head back to the Desert Inn and when Louis suggests a quick drink before we go up and call Evelyn, both Tilda and I jump at the chance, neither of us particularly enamoured with the idea of telling her that despite Sonny's innocence she shouldn't marry him. The bar is busy, the air alive with the chatter of gossip, and I hear Jonny's name mentioned more than once.

'Three martinis,' Louis calls to the bartender, the same guy we saw when we first arrived. It seems as if he never leaves the place.

'Ugh, not for me.' I shudder. 'I'll take a Tom Collins.'

'Sorry Lil, I forgot you don't really do martinis.'

The bartender grins as he hands over the drinks and I take a cautious sip. You never know exactly how strong your drink is going to be when you slip back into the past. 'I hear you folks have had quite an eventful evening.'

'You could say that,' Tilda says wryly as she takes a hefty slug of her martini without a wince. She still looks pale and I hope the booze will bring the colour back to her cheeks. 'News travels fast, huh?'

'Sometimes faster than you expect.' He gives her a wink and I feel a tickle of recognition.

'You're here an awful lot,' I say. 'I think you've been on shift every time I've come in here.'

'Dedicated to my job, ma'am,' he says. 'It's in my best interests – I don't like to miss a thing.' He hands me a pen so I can sign for our drinks. 'Congratulations again. You should think about joining the FBI.' He moves away with a smirk, leaving me standing there holding his pen, and a strong gin cocktail.

'Lily?' Louis frowns as I watch the bartender move to the other end of the bar, and then look down at the pen.

'Son of a gun.' A smile tugs at my lips.

'Lily, what in the heck are you doing? Are you having a stroke?' Tilda presses her hand to my forehead. 'Oh, are you having a moment? A moment connected to your... your *gift*?'

I lay the pen down on the bar where the bartender can see it and slide off my stool. 'Come on, let's get out of here. I have something to tell you.'

We ride the elevator to our floor, and once we are safely inside our room, I turn to face Louis and Tilda. 'The bartender,' I say.

'Something weird about him,' Tilda says, from where she has thrown herself down on my bed. She really does look exhausted, and I wonder whether we should get her checked over at the hospital before we head back to LA. 'He's part of the mob somehow, but I can't figure out how. He's definitely not just an eager beaver who loves his job.'

'He's undercover,' I say.

'What?' Louis balks at the idea, his eyes growing wide.

'He's with the FBI, and he's undercover. He's infilt-rating Buddy's operation by appearing to be Buddy's eyes

287

and ears in the bar. That's why he seemed so suspicious to us at first – he was reporting our questioning about Bess to Buddy. But he was telling Buddy so he could gauge his reaction. Buddy Zillo is going down and I think it'll be sooner rather than later.'

Tilda sits back, impressed. 'You could see all of that, written on his page? When? How? Was it when you touched his hand as he passed you your drink?'

'Kind of,' I say, wincing internally. It was when he passed me the pen to sign for the drinks. The pen with the laurel leaves on the side – part of the FBI logo. Everything had fallen into place. Eric had gone to the movies a few months ago to watch some mob movie he was excited about and came over to my apartment raving about it. Based on a true story, it told the story of Vito Bartelli, an undercover FBI agent who infiltrated the mob and brought them down after working his way through various jobs with them. I had been half asleep when Eric was showing me articles on his phone about the real-life agent – the only detail that stuck with me was that the guy had always used a pen with laurel leaves on it, flaunting the fact that he was undercover for the FBI right under the mobsters' noses.

'It's definitely time to go back to Los Angeles,' Louis says. 'We should get out of town before that goes down.'

'Before any of that...' Tilda hoists herself off the bed and moves to the small dressing table, lifting the telephone receiver. 'We can't put it off any longer. It's time to call Evelyn.'

Chapter Thirty-one

'Evelyn?' The telephone is answered after less than three rings, as if Evelyn has been sitting by the receiver.

'Louis? Thank goodness you called! I have the most wonderful news!' Evelyn's voice rings out tinnily from the telephone and my eyes smart at the joy in her voice. I wish more than anything that we didn't have to be the ones to rain on her parade, even though she would gladly engineer a thunderstorm over mine.

'About Sonny, right?'

'Yes, about Sonny! Oh Louis, you were right – he really didn't do it.' I raise an eyebrow at Tilda, who returns the expression. *Did a tiny part of Evelyn actually think he might have been responsible?* 'The sheriff just called. They found the person who really killed Bess, and Sonny is free to go, I'm about to leave to go and pick him up. Did you hear Jonny Valentine is involved? It's all so terribly shocking, but good news for Sonny.' Her tone turns a little smug and self-satisfied. 'I told you Benjamin Fry was a good lawyer.'

'Jeez, Evelyn.' Tilda snatches the receiver. 'Sonny might be free, but he's not a good guy. Sonny didn't get off because Fry is a good lawyer. Benjamin Fry is a mob lawyer – he didn't give two hoots if Sonny got sent down for Bess's murder.'

Louis gestures at Tilda for the phone, tutting with annoyance as she pulls away. They wrestle over the receiver for a moment, Louis snatching it free just when I think I am going to have to step in. 'Evelyn? Tilda's right. Benjamin Fry was hired by the mob – the same people that Sonny works for.'

'Don't be ridiculous,' Evelyn scoffs. 'Sonny is an insurance salesman. I went through all of this before with Lily, I don't know why you're so insistent.'

'Because it's true,' Tilda snaps, loud enough to be heard.

'Honestly, Tilda, you live in a dream world. Mobsters are... are mean, nasty men, with guns and fedoras and pinstripe suits. Sonny is sweet and kind and generous, and he's never worn a fedora in his life.'

'Ev, you don't need to wear a fedora to be in the mob. That's just what they show you in the movies,' Louis sighs.

'Tell that to Al Capone,' Evelyn says tartly. 'None of what you're saying makes any sense. Sonny works very hard as an insurance salesman, that's why he's away so much. He's the last person who would work for a horrible organisation like the mob. And if there was an ounce of any truth in what you're saying, wouldn't Benjamin want him to get off?'

'No,' Louis says. 'This was all an elaborate set-up to get Sonny out of the picture. Ben Fry was never going to defend Sonny properly, not when he was the fall guy for Jonny Valentine. Evelyn, you can't marry him.'

'Did you take a knock to the head or something? Because I'm telling you, Sonny—'

'He cheated on you, Evelyn,' Louis says, closing his eyes. 'Sonny knew Bess Greenwood, and he cheated on you with her. They were blackmailing Jonny Valentine together.'

'Cheat—' Evelyn sounds as though she's been punched in the stomach and I feel a wave of pity wash over me. She might be a lot of things, but Evelyn doesn't deserve to have her heart broken. 'Sonny would never...' There is a thick silence, and just when I think that maybe we've got through to Evelyn, and she's going to announce that she's throwing the ring back at Sonny, there is a sharp intake of breath on the other end of the line.

'I'm very sorry, Louis,' Evelyn says, that hint of self-satisfaction returning to her voice. 'But this is all utterly ridiculous. I know exactly what you're doing and I'm afraid you had your chance. It's too late for us, there's too much water under the bridge. It's time for you to move on.'

Louis looks at me, stricken, while Tilda presses her hands hard over her mouth to stifle her laughter. I take the telephone.

'Evelyn, it's Lily. I know you're on cloud nine about Sonny being released, but Louis is right, you can't marry him.'

'This is none of your business, Lily.' Evelyn sniffs, haughtily.

None of my business? I wish she'd told me that when I was haring around Las Vegas snooping in places I never should have risked being caught in. 'There was no convention in Las Vegas, Evelyn. Sonny lied to you. He was here that weekend to rip off Buddy Zillo and Jonny Valentine with Bess Greenwood.'

'Lily—'

'He was never a salesman. He collects money for the mob – specifically for Buddy Zillo, the owner of the Silver Slipper casino.'

'He's a businessman!' Evelyn shrieks. 'He has a good job and he's well respected, and Sonny would *never* cheat on me. He takes me out to dinner and to parties, and he has a beautiful apartment that we're going to live in once we're married. We'll send our children to private school and holiday in Palm Springs in the summer and ski in the winter.'

'With dirty money,' I say abruptly. 'All of that will be paid for with money stolen from other people, Evelyn. Can you live with that?'

'You're jealous, Lily.' Evelyn's voice is a low hiss. 'And I don't know why. You got what you wanted. Louis is in love with you, not me.'

I blink, pushing her words aside to process later as Tilda holds up the bound *Alice in Wonderland* ledger. 'Evelyn, Sonny is dangerous. You can't marry him. If you don't believe me, ask him about the ledgers. Ask him about the bound books on Buddy Zillo's bookcase. Ask him why his initials are in there.'

Evelyn hangs up without another word and I sink onto the bed, feeling drained.

'She's going to marry him anyway, isn't she?' I raise my eyes, scorching hot tears spilling down my cheeks as Tilda fetches me a tissue and Louis perches on the bed next to me. 'Everything we've done, nothing has changed. All of it has been for nothing.' *And once again, I am still here.* I wasn't expecting to vanish in a puff of smoke like I was last time, but I thought something might have been different.

'I'm sorry, Lily.' Tilda passes me the tissue, giving my hand a squeeze. 'I think the best thing we can do is get out of here. Head back to LA. Maybe Evelyn will be more amenable in the flesh. I'll go downstairs and grab us some snacks if you two pack up our things.' There are only a few meagre possessions lying around the room, and I realise she's trying to give us some space.

As the hotel room door slams shut behind her, Louis takes my hand. 'I'm sorry too, Lil, for what it's worth. You came back for nothing.'

'It wasn't really for nothing,' I say. 'We managed to get the right person behind bars for Bess's murder, so there is some justice. I just wish Evelyn would listen to me. It's *vital* that she listens to me, Louis. Awful things are going to happen if she doesn't — I need to find some way to make her pay attention. She doesn't even believe us about Sonny and Bess, she's so blinkered by him.'

'What about the money?' Louis asks. 'You told Antonia that you knew what had happened to the money that was missing from the safe. Were you just bluffing?'

I'd forgotten all about that. 'It was Cassidy.'

'Cassidy?'

'When she came to see us before she left town she was clutching that suitcase like her life depended on it. I thought it was just her things, but when she left I noticed orange dust on her shoes. I assumed she was wearing Bess's shoes that she'd left behind — she did say they used to wear each other's clothes — and it would stand to reason that Bess's shoes would have dust on them from the ranch. But then when we saw the safe was open and Antonia started shrieking about the money, I realised that there was at least one other person who knew the money would be stashed there.'

'Cassidy, of course. Huh.' Louis sits back, a glimmer of admiration in his eyes. 'Bess could have given her the safe code as a backup – she would never have confessed that to us.'

An awkward silence descends on the room as we both dive into our own thoughts. I don't know what to do now. Do I go back to LA and head to the Beverly Hills, ready to try and make my return to 2020? I don't like Evelyn, but the idea that I will just slip back to my own time and leave her to her fate makes something hard and cold lodge deep in my chest, an icy splinter that would never heal. And then there's the elephant in the room.

'Lily. About what Evelyn said.' Louis reaches out and takes my hand in his.

Am I ready for this conversation? I don't think I'm ready for this conversation. 'About...?' I go hot, then cold, my stomach somersaulting.

'About her mentioning my... feelings for you.' He looks down at our intertwining fingers, his palm hot against mine. 'You know I think you're special. When you were gone, I didn't date. Not a single person. Because there isn't another girl in the world who will ever measure up to you.'

Oh. Is it possible for a heart to fly and crash at the same time? 'Louis, I... I didn't date either when I went... back.'

A smile pulls at his mouth and I want to kiss him. *Badly.*

'I guess what I want to know is... what happens now?' He looks up at me and my heart turns over as I meet his eyes. I've looked into those eyes every day for the last eighteen months, every time I saw Eric, whose eyes carry that same dazzling shade of green as his great-grandfather's, but they have never had the effect on me that these eyes do.

'I don't know,' I say, honestly. 'I came back to try and save Evelyn, but it wasn't just for her. I came back for you, too. It was you I was thinking of as I… travelled.' *Am I meant to stay here? Is that why I couldn't save Evelyn? Maybe we really are soulmates. Maybe it is destiny. Maybe this time I'm meant to stay here, with Louis. Maybe this is where I am meant to be.*

'I guess what I'm asking is… are you going to leave now?' Louis looks away, gazing at the bright lights of the town outside the window. 'I know you couldn't save Evelyn, and that's… that's tough to swallow, but perhaps it'll all be OK. If you hadn't come back no one would ever have known what was going to happen, and you never know, something might happen between now and then that will change things for her. You might have already done enough…' He turns to face me. 'Are you going to go back to London, Lily?'

I open my mouth, wanting to respond but not having the faintest clue what is going to come out, when the door flies open and Tilda enters, arms full of Twinkies and packets of Mike and Ike sweets.

'You guys didn't pack yet?' She throws the snacks down on the bed and starts shoving things into the small suitcase she brought. 'I hate to say it folks, but we gotta get out of here. Buddy Zillo is on parade downstairs, and I don't know about you guys but I don't really feel like answering any questions he might have.'

Not sure if I feel relieved or annoyed by Tilda's entrance, I avoid Louis's gaze and turn reluctantly towards the pile of snacks on the bed. Tilda might have saved me from answering the most difficult question of my life just now, but I know that at some point very soon, I'm going to have to make a decision.

Chapter Thirty-two

The drive back from Las Vegas to Hollywood is mostly silent after Louis rejects my offer to drive. ('We want to get there in one piece, Lily.') We pass the sign for Baker and something dark and heavy sits on my chest. The thought of leaving without saving Evelyn weighs on my mind and I breathe on the window, tracing a finger through the condensation as the sun rises in the rear-view mirror, and we hit Sunset Boulevard.

'We should drop in on Honey,' Tilda says, sitting up straight in her seat. 'Lily didn't get to see her properly after the premiere, and she and Joe have a new place in Beverly Hills.'

'She might be busy.' My stomach knots at the thought of seeing Honey. I feel like now I have failed in my mission to save Evelyn, maybe I should hole up somewhere until I decide what to do about returning home. I don't want to be the butterfly who flapped her wings.

'Not for you she won't be,' Louis grins. 'She's missed you a lot – and you should take the opportunity to see her while you're both still in town.' His unanswered question hangs in the air between us.

'OK.' I push a smile onto my face. *Maybe if I don't touch anything?* 'We'll see if she's home.'

Honey is home, and she is overjoyed to see us, which comes as a relief. I was worried that seeing her properly would tarnish the memories I have of her as a sweet Kentucky girl who got lucky. After all, fame turned has turned many a movie star into a monster. But the woman who throws her arms around me in a familiar fog of L'Air du Temps is the Honey I know and love.

'I know y'all came back for the premiere,' Honey says, letting her Southern accent drawl in the privacy of her own – quite substantial seven-bedroom, six-bathroom – mansion. 'And I was so thrilled to see you, but tell me you ain't gonna disappear on us again, sugar.'

'Well…'

'After all, there's going to be a weddin'!' Joe appears and I reach up to hug him. His dirty blond hair is cut a little shorter and gone are the white T-shirt and dusty boots, but he still wears his Levi's.

'Your wedding?' Obviously I knew they'd got married from looking at Honey's Wikipedia page, but to actually be there? I couldn't leave now, could I? Not just yet, anyway.

'No, silly. We already did that, when we finished filming.' Honey slides her hand into Joe's with a coy smile. 'Leonard and Jean! Jean has been so very patient, but pinning Leonard down to a date is impossible when he's filming, so she threatened to make him elope to Indiana.'

'Indiana?' I say quizzically, exchanging glances with Louis and Tilda.

'Indiana! Just like Ronald Reagan and Jane Wyman did, although we all know that didn't work out. But of course, I said absolutely not,' Honey rattles on. 'I told them they could get married here. It's just going to be a simple, intimate affair. We have beautiful gardens, it's perfect. We're all set for tomorrow.' She pauses, squinting at me. 'That's why you're here, ain't it? Jean did tell you? I told her to put on the invitation that y'all could stay here.'

'Uh, yeah,' I say eventually. 'Of course we're here for the wedding.'

—

The following morning sees Tilda and me sitting in one of the bedrooms at Honey's sprawling Beverly Hills home, as her make-up girls fuss and primp at our faces. Inhaling the flowery scent of face powder I close my eyes as the brushes roam over my face, feeling oddly at home.

'Ladies, how are we this morning?' I open my eyes to Honey, grinning like an idiot in her bathrobe. 'Isn't this just so exciting? I *love* a wedding.'

It is. But I am feeling kind of bummed about what to wear. In my time, I would have ordered seventeen different outfits online, carried out a mini fashion show in my apartment by myself and then sent sixteen of them back. In 1950, Tilda had slipped back to her house last night with Louis to fetch something for the both of us to wear to the wedding. It's very kind of her to lend me something, but she's a size smaller than me and everything cuts in a little too deeply to be truly comfortable. My only other option is the dress I bought from the vintage store before I left and while it is perfect evening wear, I'm pretty sure I'll be wildly overdressed for a daytime wedding.

'So, I have something for you, Lily.' Honey grins at me and I can't help but grin back. 'I know it's not terribly exciting, but I saw the dress Tilda brought over for you and… well, I couldn't let you wear that.'

'Hey!' Tilda huffs indignantly.

'I just meant that Lily might be more comfortable in this.' Honey reaches behind her and pulls out a hanger. 'I mean, it is yours and you only wore it once.'

It's my blue dress. The one I wore to Honey's birthday party, the one I saw on the auction site before I left. 'Oh Honey, this is incredible.' She hands it to me and I run my fingers over the cool, silky fabric.

'You left all your things in your hotel room,' Honey says, with a slight frown. 'The hotel called Jean and asked what they should do with it all, and I asked them to bring it to me. It was the least I could do after... you know.'

'Thank you, Honey.' I lean over and kiss her on the cheek, before letting out a squeal as I see my sparkly rose-gold shoes in the hallway behind her. I'm not going to look out of place after all.

The wedding is a stunning affair for something that was meant to be 'simple and intimate'. The extensive grounds of Honey and Joe's home have been transformed into a winter wonderland. Huge displays of roses, rain lilies and gladioli fill the garden in icy tones of white, cream and the palest pink, creating a bower at the end of the rose-petal-sprinkled path. Tiny lights dot the trees that line the edges of the garden and despite the fact that it is still seventeen degrees outside there is a crisp, wintery feel to the day.

Gene Tierney perches on her seat at the end of the aisle, twisting round to whisper to Natalie Wood, and I spot the portly figure of Alfred Hitchcock on Leonard's side of the bridal party. Leonard himself stands at the altar, glancing over his shoulder every few seconds.

'I've never seen him so nervous,' Tilda whispers as we slide into our seats.

'I didn't even know he could feel nervous,' I whisper back as I sit down next to Louis. I feel slightly giddy, my head spinning at being back properly with the people I left behind all those months ago, believing I'd never see them again. And then I remember Evelyn, and how I failed her, and my smile drops.

'You look beautiful.' Louis's words are barely a whisper as the man at the piano begins to play Wagner's 'Bridal Chorus'. My cheeks grow heated and I give him a shy smile before turning in my seat to watch Jean walk down the aisle. She is stunning in a cream off-the-shoulder dress, fitted at her bust and waist before flaring down in a wave of silk satin to her ankles. I'm pretty sure that Elizabeth Taylor wore one very similar when she married Nicky Hilton, and I'm also pretty sure it sold in my time for over $180,000. Leonard turns to her and I swear I can see tears in his eyes.

Moments later Leonard is instructed to kiss the bride and cheers ring out, followed by the popping of champagne corks.

'I'm not crying,' Tilda says as she dabs at her eyes with Louis's handkerchief.

'It'll be your turn next,' Louis says with a wry grin.

'Or yours.'

At that I slide out of my seat, my cheeks hot, before anyone can turn the conversation to me and, more importantly, the question of whether or not I'm staying. Instead I join the receiving line and wait patiently as Leonard and Jean greet their wedding guests.

'Lily.' Leonard pulls me in for an unexpected hug. 'We're thrilled you could make it. Lucky you came back to LA, we had no idea where to send your invitation to in London.'

'Good timing, I guess,' I say, still reeling from the hug. I had expected a stiff handshake at best.

'Listen, Jean and I aren't leaving for our honeymoon until tomorrow afternoon, so stop by Googie's for brunch with us. I have an exciting new movie I'm working on and I have a proposition for you.'

'A proposition?'

'Now Jean and I are married, I'm going to need a new assistant.' Leonard smiles down at me as a wide grin splits my face.

'Are you serious?' My mind is racing at the prospect of my dream job landing in my lap like that, and I squash down the minor (major, Lily, be honest) inconvenience that this job offer is seventy years too early.

'Yes Lily, do stop by for brunch!' Jean leans in and pecks my cheek. 'And of course he's serious. When have you ever known Leonard to joke about work?' She pulls me close, her cheek warm against mine as she whispers in my ear, 'I can't tell you how thrilled we all are to have you home.' She moves on to the woman behind me and I glance over my shoulder to see Vivien Leigh, a smile gracing her features instead of a pout.

Dancing starts in the fairy-lit marquee that Honey has installed at the end of the garden, after a five-star three-course meal. Jean and Leonard take to the floor for their first dance, as the band strikes up 'I Don't Want to Set the World on Fire', and gradually people drift over to join them, Louis holding out a hand and inviting me to dance. As he whirls me around the dance floor I see Tilda on the fringes, deep in conversation with Louella Parsons. I wonder if Tilda is negotiating writing a scoop on the Jonny Valentine affair. Honey and Joe waltz past, gazing into each other's eyes, and my heart swells. After all the toxicity, secrets and lies that occurred in Las Vegas, the room is filled with love.

Not long after that, everything falls apart.

Chapter Thirty-three

'Miss Jones? Mr Jardine?' Honey's housekeeper approaches us on the dance floor where we are swaying together to Nat King Cole. 'You have a telephone call.'

'A call?' I exchange a puzzled glance with Louis. Who on earth would be calling us at Honey's house? Everyone we know is already here, at the 'small and intimate' wedding (although close to three hundred people doesn't feel that intimate to me).

'This way please.' The housekeeper leads us towards the huge, opulent hallway where the telephone sits on an intricately carved polished cedar table. 'I understand it's urgent.'

I take the telephone, my heart clattering in my chest as my mouth goes dry. 'Hello?'

'Lily? Lily, is that you?' The voice on the other end is familiar, punctuated as it is by broken sobs and gasps.

'It's me. Evelyn, what's happened? How did you know I was here?'

'I called Louis's parents' house and they said you all were at a wedding,' she sniffs. 'You need to come, right now. It's Sonny, he's… he's gone crazy.'

Louis leans in, pressing his mouth to the receiver. 'Evelyn? What do you mean he's gone crazy?'

'He's gone *crazy*.' Evelyn breaks into fresh sobs, her breath catching as she hiccups the words out. 'You have to come, please, I need you. Oh! I'm bleeding.' Her voice turns to a groan, deep and wounded. 'Oh God, Louis, there's blood… all over… me.'

Jesus. It's happening. It's still happening. Only now, because I interfered, it's happening early.

'Where are you?' Louis barks down the line. 'Evelyn, calm down. Tell us where you are, we'll be right there.'

'Out near Fort Irwin. Off Highway 91.'

'Fort Irwin? Evelyn, that's like three hours away! What the hell are you doing out there?'

'Louis, please just come.' Evelyn's voice is barely above a whisper now and a kernel of fear lodges deep in my chest. We know Sonny is mixed up with a dangerous crowd. He might not have killed Bess, but he *is* going to kill Evelyn if we don't get to her in time.

'Evelyn?' I have to fight to keep my voice steady. 'Tell us exactly where you are.'

'I'm on the road that leads to Fort Irwin, maybe a mile, a mile and a half in. You'll see Sonny's car pulled over by the side of the road.' Another sob hiccups down the line. 'Please hurry, I'm so scared.'

'We're on our way.' I hang up and turn to Louis. 'You still have that old map in your car?'

Louis nods. 'I'll go and fetch Tilda.'

'Lily? Is everything all right?' Honey appears in the hallway, looking like the movie star she is in a feathery pastel pink dress and matching heels.

'It's Evelyn,' I say. 'She's in a… spot of bother. I'm sorry, Honey, I have to leave.'

'Evelyn?' Honey frowns. 'Isn't that that sour-faced girl Louis used to date?'

'Uhhh, yeah. That's her.'

Honey quirks an eyebrow, before she steps in and pulls me into a hug. 'Well, if anyone can fix whatever it is, it'll be you. Hurry back, Lily Jones. And be careful – we've only just got you back, we don't want to lose you again.'

–

Two and a half hours later, Louis slows to a crawl as we search out the turning for Fort Irwin in the inky black desert darkness. I hold a flashlight over the map, but it isn't much good having a map when there aren't really any landmarks visible to tell you where you are in the first place. Once again, I long for the map on my iPhone, the glowing blue dot that tells me I'm on the right road.

'Anyone else get the creeps out here?' Tilda asks as we finally stumble on the dusty track that leads from the highway out to Fort Irwin. There is a closed gas station with a lone phone box on the corner before the turn, presumably the one Evelyn called from.

'I get PTSD,' I mutter, anxiety coiling in my belly at being on the same highway that led us to Las Vegas in the first place.

'PT – what?'

'Shell shock,' I say. 'Literally shell shock from heading back out this way.'

'There!' The headlights of Louis's car swoop over the back end of a car, the passenger door still flung wide open. 'That has to be Sonny's car.' He pulls over behind it and we step out into the night air.

'Evelyn?' The stars pierce the velvet sky above, and the only light is a pale watery shimmer from the moon. There is no sign of life.

'Evelyn, it's us.'

'Do you think we should have brought a weapon?' Tilda asks suddenly, making my stomach drop away.

'What?' I turn to frown at her, unable to make out her features properly as clouds gather and cover the moon. 'You don't think… do you think Sonny might have a gun?'

'Shhh.' Louis presses his fingers to his lips. 'Did you hear that?' A slight rustling comes from behind a pile of rocks. 'Evelyn?' he whispers, his voice carrying on the slight breeze. 'Is that you?' There is a heart-stopping pause as the rustling comes again, and I don't know if I'm more afraid of it being Sonny and a pistol, or a coyote. And then Evelyn steps out.

She is dishevelled and covered in dust; the hem of her once neat pencil skirt is torn and trailing in the dirt. She squints as Louis shines the flashlight over her, raising a hand to shield her eyes. 'You came.' Evelyn steps forward, stumbling over the small rocks that litter the dusty track, the heel of one shoe snapped clean off. Tilda holds out a hand to steady her.

'Of course we came,' Louis says. 'Are you all right? You said you were bleeding.'

'Oh.' Evelyn looks down at her hands, at the rusty stain that scars her palms. There is an oozing smear on her bottom lip that looks black in the darkness. 'Oh.'

I realise she's in shock and I turn back to the trunk of Louis's car and pull out a blanket, wrapping it around her shoulders. 'What happened, Evelyn? How did you end up out here?'

Evelyn draws in a deep, juddering breath. 'I went to the jail to pick Sonny up and I was just *so happy* to see him.' A tear slides over her bottom lashes, and when Louis tracks the flashlight beam over her face, I see her lip is cut and swollen, and the skin around her eye is puffy and already turning an alarming shade of purple.

'We went back to his apartment and then this evening he told me to pack a small bag, that we were going to take a trip. He was taking me to Las Vegas,' she turns her gaze on me. 'Once I realised that's where we were headed I remembered what you had told me, Lily, so I asked him why we were going to Vegas. At first I thought…' Evelyn swallows, wincing as she does so and I think I can make out the faint mark of fingerprints around her throat. 'I thought it was perhaps a small vacation… that he might say we were going to get married, that he couldn't wait for me to be his wife. I so wanted you to be wrong, Lily.'

'Oh Evelyn.' She might be saltier than soy sauce on sushi, but my heart aches for her. 'What did he say?'

'He said he had a little bit of business to attend to and then we'd go somewhere lovely and hot for a vacation.' She shakes her head. 'I hadn't packed a swimsuit.'

Oh *Evelyn*.

Evelyn raises her eyes to mine as she tugs the blanket more firmly around her shoulders. 'I said to him, I said, "Are you going to see those mobsters you're involved with?"' Her voice takes on a sharp tone. 'And he flat-out denied it. "Evelyn, baby," he said, "I don't know what you're talking about." But I knew he was lying, Lily. I could tell by his eyes.'

'I'm so sorry.'

'I didn't even notice when we pulled off the highway onto the road to Fort Irwin.' Evelyn gazes past us to where the car sits haphazardly on the side of the road, the passenger door still swinging open. 'That's when I asked him about the ledger.'

My throat constricts and for a moment I can't breathe. *This is all my fault. I never should have told her to ask him about the ledger.*

'He flipped out.' Evelyn begins to cry properly now, fat salty tears that splash onto the dusty ground. 'He started yelling at me, then he pulled the car over and dragged me out into the dirt. I tried to say I was sorry, but it was no good, he just kept hitting me. I felt the blood running down my face.'

While she has been talking, Tilda has been making a futile attempt to clean Evelyn up, using a stash of napkins and a canister of water from the trunk of Louis's car, and now she pauses in her work, her brow furrowing.

'Tilda, what is it?' Louis swings the flashlight down on to her face from where he has been scanning the horizon, looking for Sonny, or coyotes, or maybe even Buddy Zillo and his mobsters.

Tilda straightens, her face oddly blank. 'Evelyn?'

'Yes?'

'This blood… the blood all over your hands. It isn't yours.'

Glancing down at the crimson that stains Evelyn's skirt and her now semi-clean hands, I slowly raise my gaze to meet Louis's eye. I see my own horror reflected back at me on his face as he gently presses a hand to Evelyn's shoulder.

'Ev?' Louis says quietly, even though there are only the bare branches of scrubby desert bushes and the stars overhead to hear us. 'Where is he? Where is Sonny?'

Chapter Thirty-four

'Evelyn?' Louis asks, a little more strongly this time. 'Sonny. Where is he?'

Evelyn raises her hands to cover her face, wincing as she meets her split lip and black eye. 'He's over there.' She gestures behind the huge rock that she emerged from when we arrived.

Tilda throws me a worried glance as she takes a single step forward. 'Is he... all right?' But Evelyn doesn't reply; instead she sobs into her hands, her shoulders heaving. Following Louis, we step cautiously towards the rock, Tilda picking up a smaller one as we approach. I give her a quizzical look. 'He might come at us,' she says with a shrug, and then as one we step around the edge of the granite.

'Oh jeez,' Louis looks away, pressing a hand against his mouth.

Sonny lies on the ground, blood and dirt and something else that might possibly be his brains splattering the area around him.

'Bloody hell,' I breathe, as a fly buzzes perilously close to my ear before swooping down and landing on Sonny's nose. Or, where his nose used to be.

'Is he... all right?' Evelyn's voice is wavery and thin.

'Uhhh... no, Evelyn, to be honest I think it's the end of the road for Sonny,' I say. 'What did you *do*?'

'He was yelling at me as we pulled off the highway, and I knew he kept a gun in the glove compartment so when he got out of the car I took it.' Evelyn keeps her eyes averted from Sonny's figure as her entire body begins to tremble. 'He dragged me out of the car and behind this rock, and he was yelling and hitting me, and I felt like my face was just *exploding* with the pain and then… and then I shot him.'

'Oh my gosh.' Tilda's face is a weird shade of green in the light of the moon. 'Evelyn, you killed him.'

'It was an *accident*,' Evelyn shrieks. 'I never meant to kill him. Louis, you have to help me.' She snatches desperately at his sleeve, and his nose wrinkles a little as I watch him resist the urge to pull away. I'm not sure how accidental a shooting is when you have explicitly taken the gun.

'I never meant to kill him.' Evelyn turns her tear-stained face to me now. 'I just wanted him to *stop*. He would have killed me, Lily. He would have beaten me until he killed me.'

A vision of Evelyn's face peering out in blotchy black and white from the newspaper article I found swims in front of my eyes, and I know she's right. Sonny would have killed her.

'You need to calm down, Evelyn. We'll figure out a way to sort this out. Louis?'

Louis is staring at the space where Sonny lies, the gun a few feet from his body where Evelyn flung it away after it went off.

'Tilda, take Evelyn to my car.' He doesn't look at her, instead raising the flashlight and swinging it out, so that the flat, scrubby desert is illuminated. 'I'll take care of this.'

'No, Louis,' Tilda says in a low voice, her arm around Evelyn's shoulders. 'We should call the police. Sonny was going to kill Evelyn, she acted in self-defence. The police will understand.'

'No!' Evelyn cries, her voice hoarse and scratchy. 'Please, Louis. Don't call the police. I couldn't bear it… the shame of it, it'll kill my mother to have our name dragged through the newspapers.'

'Louis, we have to—'

'We can't call the police,' Louis says. 'Sonny would have killed her, you're right, but we can't tell anyone this has happened. Right now, the mob don't know Evelyn exists – if this gets out, the press will drag her name through the mud, and if the wrong people think that Evelyn knows more than she does… we could put her in even more danger.' Louis turns to me. 'Lil, drive Tilda and Evelyn back to Evelyn's house in Christine. I'll take care of things here, and then I'll drive Evelyn's car back to her house.'

'Are you sure this is—'

'I'm sure. Trust me. I'll see you back at Evelyn's in a few hours.'

–

The drive back to Evelyn's house is long and arduous. My eyes are gritty and tired, as I try my best to concentrate on driving an unfamiliar car along unfamiliar roads, the vehicle thick and heavy with a suffocating silence. The darkness is absolute, the absence of any streetlights meaning that the thin beam of the headlights is the only guide I have to see by, but that doesn't make me any less relieved that the roads are so deserted. What felt creepy on the way out here now feels like a miracle when we don't come across anyone who might question why three women – one of whom is covered in blood – are out driving a deserted highway in the middle of the night. Tilda sits up front beside me, twisting strands of her red hair around her finger as she gazes out of the window, while Evelyn lies on the back seat. I think she's sleeping and I feel a tickle of incredulousness. Only Evelyn could shoot a guy dead and then sleep all the way home.

She rouses when I park on her street, right outside her perfect picket-fence house, allowing Tilda to guide her inside.

'When are your parents home?' I ask as Evelyn pauses at the foot of the stairs.

'Tomorrow afternoon.' Her make-up has worn off and her blonde curls are limp and straggly as she looks down at me. She looks like a five-year-old at the tail end of a tantrum. 'Thank you, Lily. For everything. I know I haven't been the most—'

'It's cool, Evelyn, don't worry about it.' I flap a hand, too tired to listen. 'Go up and take a bath and give Tilda your clothes. Then go to bed, and in the morning wake up and behave as if none of this ever happened. If anyone asks you, you picked up Sonny from the jail and when you got home he confessed to having an affair with Bess Greenwood.' Evelyn's eyes widen, but I don't let her speak. 'You threw him out and said you never wanted to see him again. You think he might have gone to Vegas.'

'What about the bruising?' Tilda asks, nodding at Evelyn's face. 'Look at her, Lil. People are going to ask questions.'

Evelyn could tell the truth and say that Sonny beat her, but I know how proud she is and that's the last thing she'll want people to know – plus, when Sonny doesn't surface again we don't want any questions asked. 'After the fight, you were so upset, you had too much to drink.'

'Lily, I would never—'

'Just this once, Evelyn, OK? You drank too much and fell down the stairs, hitting your face on the telephone table. But only if anyone asks, and make sure you use as much pan stick as necessary to cover it, until the bruising fades.'

Evelyn nods and gives me a watery smile before she turns and heads up the stairs, Tilda close on her heels.

Later, Evelyn is sleeping soundly and Tilda and I have built a small fire in the grate in the sitting room. We sip Evelyn's father's expensive whisky as Tilda pokes the last remains of Evelyn's blood-soaked skirt into the flames, prodding them deep into the orange glow and then sitting back with a satisfied exhale.

'Do you think she really loved him?' I ask, watching as the flames lick over the fabric, and it shrivels away to ash.

'Hard to say,' Tilda shrugs, her words on the edge of slurred. 'I think she loved the *idea* of him – the parties, the fancy apartment, and the good tables in the best restaurants. But the reality is, he wasn't a good guy.'

'She killed him, Til.' Part of me still can't believe it and my eyes go to the wall clock, wondering for the hundredth time where Louis is.

'He would have killed her.' Tilda leans forward and puts her empty glass on the coffee table. 'That's why you came back, isn't it?' She reaches out and squeezes my hand. 'You did it, Lil. Again. Two for two.'

The front door creaks open and we both freeze. That would be just our luck, for Evelyn's parents to walk in now, but it is Louis who stands in the doorway, exhausted and filthy.

'Lou!' Tilda flies to his side, holding his upper arms and scrutinising his face. 'Are you all right?'

'Just tired.' He gives a wan smile and I pour him a hefty shot of whisky that he accepts gratefully.

'Is it all… is everything sorted?' I ask.

Louis drains his glass and then gives a brisk nod. 'All taken care of.'

'How did you—?' Tilda begins but Louis holds up a hand, cutting her off.

'Is Evelyn sleeping?' he says.

I nod. 'She's out for the count, and she knows what to say if anyone asks her anything. Her clothes have been… disposed of.' My eyes go to the fire, the flames beginning to die down.

'Good.' Louis gives me a weary nod. 'I took care of… everything back there. I know you wanted to call the police but… well, the more we keep Evelyn out of this, the better. It's the only way we can keep her safe.'

'If Evelyn is asleep, I think it's best we get out of here before the neighbours notice she has company,' Tilda suggests, and I have never been more relieved to leave Evelyn in my life.

–

I have a creeping sense of déjà vu as I swim up into consciousness a few hours later, back at Louis's parents' house. I didn't think I would sleep, and I kept seeing Sonny's bloody features every time I closed my eyes, but I must have done because now I am awake and I don't want to open my eyes, because I don't know if I am still here.

Slowly, I creak my eyelids open to see Tilda on the bed opposite mine, sunlight beginning to inch its way through the thin drapes. *I am still here in 1950.* I did it. I stopped Evelyn from being murdered. My heart should be singing, but something heavy sits on my chest. I wasn't sure if I should try and get back to 2020 when we first got back from Las Vegas, because I hadn't solved the problem of Evelyn and her murderous husband, but now… Sonny is gone, Evelyn is safe, and I have no reason to still be here.

Carefully I swing my legs out of bed and pull on the dress I picked up in the vintage store and slide my feet into my Converse, avoiding the crumpled, stained blue silk of my party dress on the floor. I wonder how they'll get the stains out? Maybe I should leave Honey a note telling her to burn it. Tilda rolls over, mumbling under her breath, and I freeze until she settles, one bare foot on the floor. Then I move to the door, pausing to look down at the red-haired figure swamped in blankets one last time.

'Goodbye, Til,' I whisper, my throat thick. 'I'm going to search all of your by-lines when I get home.'

Sneaking down the stairs before I can start to cry properly, I pause once more before I slip out of the front door. The top of Louis's ruffled dark hair is just visible over the arm of the couch, where he sleeps soundly. I wonder why he didn't sleep in his old room, and then realise that maybe he thought Buddy Zillo might know where to find us, and my heart clenches. How I wish everything could have been so different.

Tiptoeing across the room I bend down and kiss him lightly on the forehead, and then sneak out into the morning sunshine, to catch the bus that will drop me on the corner of Sunset and N Crescent Drive, right beside the Beverly Hills Hotel.

–

The skeleton key I brought with me still works. I slide it into the lock of the Paul Williams Suite and turn. I had half expected a sleepy response when I did the standard housekeeper's knock, but the room is empty and I let out a breath at the familiar surroundings. The piano, the chaise, the bucket armchairs. I walk through to the bathroom, and eye the marble bath.

All I need to do is fill the tub and step in. Think of home. Of LA. Of Eric. And I'll be back there. It'll work, it has to. It did last time. But what if it doesn't? I hope I don't have to risk another concussion before I can get back this time. I reach out, but my hand hovers over the tap. Is this really what I want? Last time I was here, I thought I had no option but to go back, to cleaning toilets and my crappy apartment. To Eric. I turn the tap on half a turn and cold water begins to trickle into the tub. *What if I stayed this time?* The thought tickles the back of my brain and I chase it away. I can't stay here in 1950. I could change too much. What if I changed things so that Eric was never born? I couldn't live with myself. *But can you live with being miserable?* a voice asks. That same voice I heard before – my mum's voice. She has a point. What do I have to go back to? Cleaning toilets and waiting tables. Eric is going to move in with Saffron and I'll be back to spending every evening alone, watching old movies and crying into my Ben and Jerry's.

I can't stay. I don't belong in Hollywood in 2020, but I don't belong here either. Biting back a sob, I turn the tap on fully, watching as it thunders into the tub, steam rising. I reach behind to unhook the clasp at the neck of my dress, tears rolling down my cheeks.

'What are you *doing*?'

A yelp escapes my throat and I turn to see Louis standing at the door to the bathroom, squinting at me through the steam.

'Did you really have a room here the whole time?' On seeing that I am still fully dressed Louis steps into the bathroom. 'Wait.' He looks me over, seeing me standing there in the vintage evening gown. 'You were going to leave, weren't you?'

I stand to one side as he reaches over and turns off the taps, and the silence that follows is deafening. 'Louis, what are you doing here?'

'I knew it.' He pushes his hands through his hair, making it stick up in sexy little rumpled spikes. 'I followed you this morning.'

'You followed me? You were asleep.'

'No, I wasn't. I had a feeling that you wouldn't stick around, so when I heard you creeping out I followed you. I thought you would be going to the bus station. Not… here.' He looks around as if expecting something to happen. When nothing does happen, he carries on. 'What is this? One last look around for old times' sake before you vanish back to London without a word?'

'Louis, you don't understand.'

'No, Lily. I don't understand. I get that you came back for Evelyn, but why can't you stay for me?'

'I don't belong here.' Somewhere, deep inside my chest, something breaks and I think it might be my heart.

Louis steps forward, so close our bodies are almost touching, and he reaches out and wraps my hands in his. 'How can you say that?' he murmurs, his eyes never leaving mine. 'How can you say that when if you leave, you'll break everyone's hearts, not just mine.'

'I—' *can't because I'm scared of the butterfly effect, and I'm worried that by staying I'll mess everything up for everyone?* No matter how hard I think, I can't find the right words.

'Lily, Evelyn was right.' And then, with his next words, everything changes. 'I am in love with you, Lily. Probably since the first time I clapped eyes on you in the hotel lounge six months ago. So how can you say you don't belong here? You belong with me, and I belong with you. I know you're not like other girls, Lil. But I'm not like other guys. You want to go to work, you go to work. You want to stay home and have babies? Well, that's fine too.'

I let out a splutter.

'What I'm trying to say, Lily, is that wherever your home is, is where you belong.'

I think of LA in 2020, of the ache in my calves at the end of a shift at the Saddle Ranch. Of the way the skin on my knuckles gets sore after cleaning hotel rooms at the Beverly Hills. Of the homeless guy on the corner of Vine who spits on your feet if you don't have anything for his change cup. Of Eric, who loves me but has finally found his own little piece of home with Saffron.

'Home isn't a place, Lil.' Louis moves closer and I feel his breath on my cheeks, can smell the warm, sunshiny lime scent of him. A scent that makes me feel at home. 'Home is people who love you and care about you, and want to be with you more than anything.'

My heart soars, and something clicks into place. Jean, telling me, '*I can't tell you how thrilled we all are to have you home.*' Honey, her arms around my neck as the scent of her hair fills my nostrils, telling me, '*We've only just got you back, we don't want to lose you again.*'

Louis is right. I don't want to go back to my own time and be alone and lonely, in a place that doesn't feel like home. *I could stay. I could try it.* 'Maybe it could work. Maybe I could stay,' I whisper as his arms go around my waist, pulling me towards him, and he kisses me properly, and even though it's the third time, the fourth time, I don't even know which kisses count, it still feels like the first time.

'Promise? I'm not going to wake up and find you gone?'

I grin, pressing my face against his, finally feeling that it's OK. Everything will all work out. I'll make sure it does. 'Promise.'

Louis quirks an eyebrow and grins back. 'In that case, Lily Jones, let's get you home.'

'Wait!' I say, a moment later as we hit Sunset Boulevard. 'I can't go home with you, Louis.'

Louis pales as he tightens his grip on my hand. 'What? No. Don't do this—'

'I'm not *leaving*,' I say, secretly loving the way his hand grips mine. 'I have to go to Googie's. I have to go and see a man about a job. Leonard wants to see me, remember?'

And I let him lead me towards the diner.

Article in the LA Times, dated 8 December 2021

DESERT BONES BELIEVED TO BE MISSING GANGSTER

Bones discovered off I-15 six weeks ago are believed to belong to missing gangster, Jackson Castillo. The bones were discovered a mile and a half from the Fort Irwin turnoff off I-15 six months ago, after geocachers moved cairn stones in a treasure hunt. Sheriff Peacock of the local police department said that the revelation had been discovered after DNA testing was carried out on the bones.

Castillo – known as Jackie – was twenty-nine years old when he disappeared, following his release from prison after being falsely accused of murdering Las Vegas show-girl Bess Greenwood. Castillo was believed to have been heavily involved in the mob, with strong connections to the Zillo crime family who operated out of various casinos in Las Vegas.

Sheriff Peacock said, 'We strongly believe that the Zillo crime family had something to do with Castillo's murder, and we can confirm that a gun believed to be owned by the Zillos was also found at the burial site.'

Buddy Zillo's operation was brought to a crashing halt in early 1951 when he was exposed by undercover FBI agent Vito Bartelli. Bartelli infiltrated the family by working in the lounge bar of the casino owned by Zillo, and his findings brought Zillo in front of judges where he was sentenced to life in prison.

Evelyn King, Castillo's girlfriend at the time of his disappearance and potentially one of the last people to see him alive, passed away in 2009, but her daughter, Iris Brooker, commented when contacted, saying, 'My mother always said that Mr Castillo would come to a sticky end. She never really recovered from his disappearance, telling us that she knew in her heart he was dead.'

Mr Castillo has no surviving family members and the bones will now be buried in an unmarked grave.

A Letter from Lisa

I loved working on *The Mysterious Double Death of Honey Black* so much that I couldn't have been happier when Hera Books said they wanted another book, and after a trip to Las Vegas it seemed there really was only place the gang could go. I walked around the Mob Museum (it's a real place!) and I knew that whatever happened with Lily and Louis, Vegas was going to be their next adventure. There is such a rich history in that town, and for someone like me who loves all things mob-related, it seemed like a no-brainer to send my characters to uncover something even seedier than anything they'd encountered before.

It's difficult not to include real life events and people when you're writing about a time that so many people are fascinated by, but as usual I have used my poetic licence to rearrange dates and times slightly to suit my narrative. The Desert Inn didn't open until 24 April 1950, and the Silver Slipper opened its doors in September 1950, but I have them both open in January 1950 to suit the story. The scene in Ciro's between Franchot Tone and Florabel Muir did allegedly take place, but I have had it happen slightly earlier than it really did. The same with Frank Sinatra – it's common knowledge that Frank's career took a dip in the late Forties/early Fifties, but I have had him make his Las Vegas debut in 1950 as opposed to 1951. Who knows, maybe if Jonny Valentine had been a real person that might have been the case.

If you'd like to know more about Las Vegas as it was, *Las Vegas Then and Now* by Su Kim Chung is an absolutely brilliant book that shows Vegas in all its glory. It was invaluable to me, and even though this book is finished I still find myself going back to Chung's, just to relive the glorious moments captured between its pages.

Writing this book was the perfect excuse for me to lose myself once again in the movies. I have to say that watching *The Godfather* trilogy (for the hundredth time) is quite possibly the best way to spend a Sunday, especially when it's followed up by *Goodfellas* and *Casino*. And of course, I rewatched *Ocean's Eleven* (the original and still the best).

If you do enjoy reading *The Case of the Singer and the Showgirl* I would love it if you would consider leaving a review – it helps to spread the word and us authors are eternally grateful!

If you'd like to keep up to date with news, you can follow Lisa here:

X: @lisahallauthor
Instagram: @lisahallauthor
Facebook: https://www.facebook.com/lisahallauthor

Acknowledgements

I think anyone who has followed my career in any way knows that there would never be any books without my incredible agent, Lisa Moylett – thank you once again for all your brilliant support and insight. I dread to think what these ideas of mine would look like without you to rein me in.

Thank you to the brilliant team at Hera and Canelo, but especially to Keshini Naidoo – dreams do come true, haha! – Jennie Ayres, Iain Miller, Thanhmai Bui-Van, Kate Shepherd and the brilliant Dan.

I don't usually send my work in progress to anyone other than my editor and agent (and my mum), but this time I needed a fresh pair of eyes to make sure that what I thought made sense, actually did make sense... thank you Mark Fearn for being that fresh pair of eyes and giving me the most enthusiastic feedback I've ever received. And thanks to my mum, who once again had to read fifteen different versions of the same book.

To the usual suspects – Darren, Annabel and Diane. Thank you for all the voice notes, the lunches, the wine and the support.

Thank you to all the bloggers and readers, especially those who took part in the incredible blog tour for *The Mysterious Double Death of Honey Black*. I read every single one of your reviews, and it made all the hard work worthwhile to see so many people loving Lily's story. Here's hoping you all love this one just as much.

Finally, thanks to the best team of all – Team Hall. Even though half of you have left home I am grateful for the FaceTime calls, the middle of the night texts, and for the cups of tea, obviously.